Suzannah heard Valentine shouting at her, but she ignored him. There was nothing her brother could say that would make any difference. She would not leave the mill in his hands. She would fight him with everything she had. . . .

Returning to her room, she hurried to the dormer window. Many years before, she had discovered a secret panel that opened to reveal a little chamber just large enough to hold a jewelry box. Now she touched the wood lightly and the panel rose. The box was still there! She snatched it up and opened the lid. Only then, seeing the huge diamond in all its splendor for the first time in years, did Suzannah dare to believe in its reality. She lifted the stone from its velvet bed and held it in the palm of her hand. After years in darkness, the intricately faceted gem caught the flickering candle flame and leapt into radiance.

"What's that?"

She whirled. Valentine was standing in the doorway.

"Give it to me."

He lurched toward her, sneering.

"No, Valentine!" Suzannah screamed and twisted her body wildly. "You can't. . . ." She staggered backwards, the diamond still locked in her fist. Valentine was behind her, heading for her like a huge, hungry bear. . . .

THE HOPEWELL SAGA

Ask your bookseller for these other titles:

BROKEN PROMISES

SILENT DREAMS

Stolen Passions

Drusilla Campbell

A Dell/Banbury Book

Published by
Banbury Books, Inc.
37 West Avenue
Wayne, Pennsylvania 19087

Dell ® TM 681510, Dell Publishing Co., Inc.

ISBN: 0-440-08130-0

Printed in the United States of America

First printing—August 1982

For Rocky, who is also brave

PART I

Chapter 1

He was a born showman, an entertainer throughout every inch of his body.

Mickey Quick looked at the three children sitting cross-legged before him in the front parlor of the Hopewell mansion. He grinned, and with an extravagant flourish, produced from his top hat a stream of color, a seemingly endless silken rainbow of scarves. None of the children had ever seen a magician before. They gasped and laughed and held their breaths, wondering if the chain of color would ever end. And when it did . . . ?

"Aha!" cried Mickey as the last of the scarves swirled to the floor and a cluster of miniature American flags popped out of his hat. With a flick of his wrist, he set the flags spinning. The children were delighted, and from the back of the room Mickey heard that sweet sound of adult applause.

Mickey knew who was watching the show from the shadows. He was particularly conscious of Suzannah Hopewell Paine, the mistress of the house. To be invited to perform for her son's birthday was a splendid opportunity for him, the kind of great good luck that might assure his career and forever keep Mickey Quick out of the mills.

He had known how to charm an audience since childhood, that dimly recalled time in Ireland when he had lived on hopes and dreams because there was little else to nourish him. A child of Dublin's streets and alleys, he had been a scavenger without home or family. Whoever had spawned him was lost somewhere beyond the reaches of his memory in a time he remembered only for its pain and despair, a blanket of troubles that had covered and almost smothered Mickey Quick. Almost.

His real surname was not Quick. That name had been given him by the carousers in Dublin's taverns where he had earned a pittance doing tricks and juggling. Having forgotten his own name, he stayed with Quick, and it was the pubs that had enabled him to survive. But the work had been hard, for often the friendless boy had been the brunt of taunts from drunken men and women trying to escape their own troubles. And then there had been the gangs of other homeless boys who had resented Mickey's independence and the talent that kept him better fed. Twice the hoodlums had beaten him up, robbing him of his clothes and the coins he had managed to tuck away in a bag that hung from a piece of string that circled his waist inside his trousers. After that Mickey had resolved to leave Dublin as soon as he could save the price of passage to America. He found a better place to hide his savings and learned to use a knife.

In America, everyone said, opportunities were unlimited. Every day Mickey had counted his coins, knowing his future was waiting for him. Now, in the doorway of the Hopewell parlor, he caught a glimpse of Mercy, the nurse to Patrick Paine. This was Patrick's sixth birthday. When Suzannah had been planning the celebration, Mercy had told her that Mickey Quick had a real talent for entertaining. Mercy also

had told Suzannah that he charged a dollar and a half
for each show, a great deal more than Mickey would
have dared demand.

"She'll pay it, sure," Mercy had assured him.
"Suzannah Paine is as rich as God Himself."

Incredibly, although all of New England was in
the grip of economic depression, what Mercy had
promised had come true. Even now, as Mickey's deft
hands fished paper flowers out of the air, and a cup
and saucer too, he could feel the dollar and a half
jingling in the pocket of his shiny black suit. His good
luck had inspired him and his moves were particularly dexterous, his manner unusually entertaining.

If he could prove himself before these important
Yankees, Mickey knew he would receive other invita-
tions to entertain. In time he might even be able to
leave Amoset, a crowded, noisy mill town on the
Amoset River in Massachusetts, to seek his fortune in
Boston and New York. For a young man of nineteen,
whose hands and wits and ready humor were made to
entertain, there was no limit to what prizes might be
won in the cities of America.

He reached out to Patrick Paine, who was sitting
front and center with his sea-green eyes wide and his
mouth rounded in surprise, and from behind the boy's
ear Mickey withdrew a coil of glossy satin ribbon that
was the color of Ireland's lush hills. The coil unwound
until yards of it lay on the carpet in front of the
amazed child. Before Patrick could find his voice,
Mickey reached behind his other ear and drew out
more and more and more.

"Mother, did you see?" Patrick cried, turning
toward Suzannah, who was standing beside her sister-in-law Margaret Duffy. "He made ribbon come
out of my ears!" Patrick tugged on his cousin Louisa's
sleeve. "Did you see?" he demanded. "He made all

that come out of my ears." Patrick had a clear, strong
voice and spoke well for a six-year-old.

Mickey could scarcely control his own glee. The
show was going perfectly. The new trick, which had
put him in debt to the general storekeeper in the Irish
immigrant community called the Gully, was worth every penny he had paid for the price of the ribbon. He
heard the adults' applause and his heart was thumping
so hard he thought they must be able to hear. His show
was a success!

One worry buzzed around in his head, however,
and it was far from trivial. When Mickey first had arrived in the Gully, he had run with a gang of Irish
youths. Restless from unemployment and chafing under the insults they met everywhere in Amoset, they
amused themselves by fighting with the privileged
Yankee boys who worked in the mills as doffers and
bobbin boys at a time when all employment notices
stated "Irish need not apply." In recent years Mickey
had tried to break his ties to this wild group, for
though he was tough and as quick with his fists as
might be expected of a boy with his name and history, he was smart as well and could guess what the
future would hold if fighting became his way of life.
His old pals resented his defection and jeered his aspirations. Just that morning they had threatened to
break in on the party. If they dared do that, Mickey
knew his reputation would be ruined with the influential Yankees in Amoset.

"Careful now," he whispered to Patrick as he
slipped his hand inside the lapel of the boy's grey suit
jacket. "Keep still, Master Paine," he cautioned in a
tone of breathless excitement that made Louisa and
Alexander Duffy draw close and peer forward.
Mickey withdrew not one, but four bright apples.

"How could they . . . ?" Patrick stopped his

words and stared. Mickey was juggling the apples; they were bouncing in the air like balls and then. . . . Patrick and his cousins gasped. The apples were disappearing, one by one! Soon all but one were gone, and it was rising higher and higher in the air, about to touch the parlor's twelve-foot ceiling. But just then there came a sharp rattling of stones thrown at the window. Mickey caught the apple and like the others it disappeared, but his audience was not watching this grand finale. The adults, with the children pressing against their skirts and trousers, stood at the window, staring out.

A large stone had cracked the glass.

"It's those damned guttersnipes from the Gully," snarled Valentine Hopewell, Suzannah's older brother.

Mickey Quick sighed. He wanted so little from life, really: a stage to stand on, a scattering of applause, a few coins for food and lodging. And now he knew he'd come as close as he ever would.

"I told you not to pay good money to a bog fly!" Valentine, a tall man of thirty who was built big and bearish like his invalid father, more and more lately had been showing the marks of the dissipated life he led. Despite his insults against the Irish, both Margaret and Suzannah knew he spent the better part of most days in the Gully, gambling and drinking up his share of the Hopewell fortune. He turned on Mickey now and his face, slightly bloated about the eyes and jowlish as an old man's, was florid.

Margaret Duffy laid her plump hand on his arm. "It's not this boy's fault, Valentine."

He shook her off.

"Leave him be, Valentine," she told him.

From the window Suzannah cried, "Who's that one?"

One of the Gully boys had not fled with his comrades. He stood a short distance from the house, staring at the building as if he could see inside and fix his hatred on the occupants themselves.

"Mickey," Suzannah asked, "who is that boy?" Though she was sure she hadn't seen him before, he was strangely familiar to her.

Reluctantly Mickey Quick walked over and stared through the glass. He didn't want to tell. He was no snitch.

Valentine wrenched Mickey's arm behind him. "Who is it?" he hissed. "You Irish all know each other."

The children, as curious as the adults, now ducked around them so they could see.

"I know him!" cried Alexander Duffy. "That's Simon McMahon."

The boy still had not moved from where he stood on the dead grass.

"McMahon? You mean the overseer's boy?" Suzannah squinted slightly. She was only twenty-eight, but her vision was no longer perfect and the white winter light glared through the overcast sky.

In spite of himself, Mickey groaned as Valentine twisted his arm higher up his back.

"Is that Foster McMahon's brat?" Valentine insisted.

Mickey knew it was, but he was determined not to speak. In the space of a few moments, the good will he had felt toward Suzannah Hopewell Paine and her family had disappeared and in its place he felt only the leaden distrust and hatred he had felt for Yankees ever since he had come to Amoset.

"Is it?"

"You're hurting him, Valentine. There's no call . . ."

"It *is* Simon McMahon!" declared Alexander. "He

was a little ahead of me in school and I know perfectly well who he is."

"Let him go, Valentine," demanded Suzannah. "Mickey had nothing to do with this." She stared into the young man's dark, angry eyes. "Are you all right?"

Mickey nodded. He heard the kindly tone in Suzannah's voice, but he didn't believe it, not for a moment. She was Valentine Hopewell's sister, after all, and as he was known for his callous nature, the same might be expected from her and from all her kind.

"There go Bosley and the dogs!" exclaimed Patrick, jumping up and down at the window. "They'll catch him, that's for sure!" The children cheered the Hopewell caretaker as if the chase were part of the day's entertainment.

Valentine was still holding Mickey, but now he relaxed his grip enough that the boy was no longer afraid his arm would be broken.

"I said to let him go, Valentine." Suzannah spoke with authority. For the past six years she had conducted the business of Hopewell Mills and by now was accustomed to giving orders and having them followed without delay.

Valentine obeyed, but without good grace. "Forgive me, my dear sister, for bothering myself to assist you. I had forgotten how well trousers become you." He bowed mockingly to Suzannah and then to Margaret, including her in his insult because she was Suzannah's friend. "Ladies, you will excuse me?"

"Valentine, stay for the rest of the party. There is no call to leave." The children, having lost interest in the chase, fixed their attention on the arguing adults. "Patrick will be disappointed."

Valentine laughed. "I doubt that, Suzannah. You are more than sufficient for a fatherless child, I assure you."

Suzannah stared at him in exasperation as he left the room. After six years she should have been accustomed to her brother's sarcastic gibes, but they still wounded her. For the thousandth time she wished she could make him understand that what she did was for the good of all of them. Years before, when their father had disappeared, Suzannah had been forced to take over the management of Hopewell Mills. If she had not done so, the family fortunes would have suffered a fatal turn, for Valentine had neither the will nor the understanding to do the job and Eben, the elder of her two brothers, was in Savannah handling the family business there. Again and again she had struggled to make Val understand that she had acted out of necessity, but he was adamantly against her. After all those years, Valentine's taunts should have lost their power to hurt her, but as she stared after him, her eyes were glassy with tears.

Margaret Duffy put her arm around Suzannah comfortingly. "Come along, dear. The children are anxious for cake and sweets. Think of Patrick. It's his party." Turning to Mickey Quick, she said, "Mickey, you provided us with a wonderful show this afternoon. I wish the finale could have been more pleasant, but we live in troubled times."

Suzannah tried to be gracious. "Will you go into the kitchen with Mercy? There's cake and chocolate pie and lemon cordial . . ."

Mickey shook his head, his look unforgiving.

"Please excuse my brother. He doesn't always understand."

Margaret patted the lad on the shoulder as if he were no older than her ten-year-old Alexander. "Now don't let silly pride deprive your stomach of what it craves. Think of the lovely treats Mercy will give you. And you deserve them. After all, you put on a fine show. And talent like yours, I know, is perfected only through hours of diligent practice. Isn't that true? Well, of course it is. Come along with me, Mickey Quick. You've been wrongly treated, but it's over now. Be done with it."

Suzannah watched them go, followed by the chattering children. When she was alone she returned to the broken window. For a long time she stared out at the yellowed winter grass, the leafless trees stark as skeletons against the white sky. Winter was upon them. There would surely be snow before nightfall. She thought of the Gully boys in their tarpaper shacks, their faces pinched with hunger and envy. Years ago Suzannah had visited one such hovel and had sipped tea from an old chipped cup that was a poor woman's treasure. That memory was still vivid. She remembered the woman's sweet, shy pride and the way the children had gathered about, gazing with awe at their fine guest, their eyes round and shining with want.

How long can it go on? Suzannah wondered. The Yankees in Amoset, the Irish in the Gully. Two cultures living side by side, separated by a gentle rise of wooded hill and a mountain of hate. How long would it be before boys like Mickey Quick and Simon McMahon rose up and demanded the bounty they once dreamed America could guarantee them?

Chapter 2

Later that day, while the children in their fancy hats feasted at a table decorated with paper ribbons, Suzannah and Margaret rested in the sitting room adjoining Suzannah's office and across from Martin Hopewell's study. A servant knocked softly and entered, pushing a tea wagon laden with sweets that neither woman could stomach after the day's excitement.

"Take it away, Dolly," sighed Suzannah, sinking deeper into the cushioned sofa. "I'll have some sherry. Will you join me, Margaret?"

"Indeed I will. Bigelow abhors spirits, but even he agrees that there are some days when a taste of wine is absolutely called for."

Bigelow Duffy was Margaret's husband and the vicar of St. Thomas' Episcopal Church in Marivale, about ten miles downriver from Amoset. He was a good-natured man, a lover of books and lofty ideas, who so adored his pretty, plump wife that in his eyes she could do no wrong. Though Margaret frequently mentioned Bigelow's preferences, it was clear to Suzannah that in the Duffy household, Margaret reigned supreme in all but religious matters.

Now, as she sipped her wine and rested her head against the cushions, Suzannah thought about Margaret's loyalty to her through so much. Time and trials had made them as close as blood sisters.

"What would I do without you, Margaret?"

"You always say that, Suzannah, and I always tell you the same thing. You would do just fine. You are definitely a survivor." Margaret held her glass to the light and seemed to study the amber liquid, her expression thoughtful. "Do you ever . . . wonder? About Travis, I mean?" Travis Paine, Suzannah's husband, was Margaret's brother. He had fled Amoset more than six years before and had been entirely out of their lives.

"Of course I do, Margaret. I ask myself what he's doing, if he's healthy, if he's found peace." Suzannah closed her eyes. Intimate as she was with Margaret, there were some things her sister-in-law must never know. Margaret had an accepting nature. But if she ever learned that Suzannah's infidelity with James Shawn had driven Travis to beat his wife mercilessly and then abandon her in shame for his own cruelty, she would never forgive Suzannah.

"Bigelow has kept Travis in his prayer cycle all these years, so there can be no doubt the Lord is well aware that my brother needs His help. But, sometimes I wonder . . . do you suppose he might be dead?"

Suzannah shook her head. Somehow she did not think so.

"If he were . . . dead, would you marry again, Suzannah?"

Just hearing the question spoken aloud made Suzannah uneasy. She stood up and restlessly began to pace the pretty chintz room, idly fingering the china ornaments her mother had brought from England on the occasion of her marriage to Martin Hopewell. "Hopewells should never marry. We aren't fit for it," she said, thinking of her mother and father, who lived in the same house yet never spoke or acknowledged one another's existence. "My parents haven't laid eyes on one another for six years. And if they did, nothing would be gained. She would see a crippled madman and he wouldn't recognize her or even care that she's almost as mad as he." Sometimes it seemed to Suzannah that her home had become a kind of asylum. For herself, she had learned a kind of wry acceptance of her demented parents, and even Valentine's peculiarities were so much a part of her life that she rarely questioned them now.

But what of Patrick? There were nights when Suzannah couldn't sleep and lay awake staring at the ceiling, thinking of her fatherless son. Skeptical of religion, her only prayers were for Patrick, that he might grow up strong and vigorous despite the influence of his uncle and his strange grandparents. And she prayed, too, that he would be good and wise like his father, James Shawn.

"You've endured so much these last years, Suzannah."

Suzannah did not seem to hear Margaret, but murmured, "Perhaps Valentine's only wise decision was not to marry. He has but to look at the experiences of his brother and sister to know the worst."

"How is Eben?"

Suzannah shrugged. "Letters tell so little and it's been years since I visited him in Savannah."

"But you think he's unhappy in his marriage?"

"Yes." Suzannah went to the window. The clouds were pillowy and white and so low that she imagined the elm at the edge of the yard could already feel the touch of snow on its uppermost branches. "He and Amanda have been married for five years. There are no children and I know that grieves my brother."

"A strange man."

Suzannah tilted her head at Margaret quizzically. "That comment is unlike you, Margaret. Why do you say he's strange?"

"I meant no unkindness, Suzannah, but it has always struck me . . . well, I shouldn't say." Margaret fiddled with the fringe of navy blue that decorated the shoulder capes of her dark green dress.

Despite her moodiness, Suzannah laughed. "After all these years, Margaret, can't you speak your mind with me? I want to know what you think. Please tell me."

Margaret sighed. "Well, I know it must sound silly. Bigelow would scold me for being illogical and you may, too, but I have always thought there was a brooding, almost a secretive quality in your brother. It's as if Eben holds within him some truth he dares not speak about. Actually, it's hard for me to imagine him happy, no matter who his wife might be."

"I know what you mean, Margaret. I sense it in him too. And of all people to be married to such a man, Amanda seems the worst possible choice. She's twenty-two now, but in her letters she seems as childish as she was when I first met her. It's almost as if she's been unable to mature beyond twelve or thirteen."

Margaret clicked her tongue in sympathy. "Bigelow says that of all God's gifts to man, an understanding wife is the greatest. My heart goes out to your brother. But why did he marry a child? Somehow I can't imagine Eben Hopewell . . ."

"Business."

"Of course," said Margaret softly. "I didn't think. I often forget that matches made from love are a rarity."

"You are so fortunate, Margaret. Hardly a day

goes by that I don't envy you your happy home and
your lovely children."

"Did you love my brother?"

Suzannah sighed. "I don't know. I've forgotten.
Once I must have, I suppose." The distant mountains
were lost in white clouds now; the snow was almost
upon them. Another winter had arrived and with it
had come a familiar uncertainty that was edged with
fear, the dread of long, cold nights, dark days and
dampness that chilled the marrow and froze the
heart. "I've been alone so long I scarcely remember
any other life." Suzannah was twenty-eight now, and
stretching out before her, she saw the rest of her life
in terms of winter and loneliness.

"You have Patrick. A handsome boy and bright,
too. With him, you will never be truly alone, Suzannah."

"I know that. But there are times. . . ." She let
her words fade away, not bothering to explain that
sometimes she wished Patrick had never been born
because with each passing day he looked more like
his father. When he had been an infant and a toddler,
Suzannah had been able to look at him without being
reminded of James Shawn, the man she loved. Now it
was impossible.

In six years' time, James had risen to prominence
in the Amoset valley and now he was the area's representative in the General Court in Boston. His career
had been such that Suzannah could not ignore his existence. From time to time, they ran into each other
at social events in Amoset. On such occasions they
were polite and cool, and if James felt in his heart the
smallest yearning for the passion that had once lit up
their moments together, he gave no sign. Nor did she.

"In some ways, I can't help feeling angry toward
my brother," Margaret was saying. "A woman needs a

husband and by disappearing as he has, Travis has made it impossible for you to have any kind of normal life. How will you ever know whether he's alive or dead?" Margaret made the sign of the Cross on her breast. "The Lord forgive me if I speak unkindly, but the truth is the truth, as Bigelow says. Nothing can change that."

"No matter what happens, I'm never going to marry again. The warm parts of me have all gone cold now. I couldn't give myself to another man." Of course, Margaret would assume she was speaking of Travis, just as she assumed that Patrick was Travis' son. It was what Suzannah wanted her to think, but it was not the truth of the matter.

Six years before, Suzannah had parted forever from James Shawn, only to be reunited a few hours later when he had carried her emaciated father home in his arms. James had found Martin Hopewell babbling and screaming and imprisoned in a cave, not far from the dead body of his captor, Crazy Edythe Whittington. In men and women less conscious of right and wrong, honor and discipline, this second meeting might have been enough to destroy their good intentions, but Suzannah and James were hardly ordinary. In their determination to do right, they knew their painful good-bye must be unalterable and for all time, and James had returned to his wife, Helen, and their farm on Cooper's Mountain.

Suzannah, carrying the child of their love in her womb, had done her best to care for her father, who had been driven mad by months of inhuman treatment. She had tucked him in bed like a child, soothing his brow and spoon-feeding him bowls of steaming broth. She also had sent for the India Man of Cartland House, the same man who had cared for Eben years before when he had returned from his grandfather's funeral in Savannah full of inexplicable madness.

For the last few years, Suzannah's life had centered around her son and the management of the mill. With every year she had become more successful at denying her warm heart and her passionate nature. On the night of her son's birth, she had held the infant Patrick in her arms and had whispered his true father's name. But from that moment onward, she had vowed never to speak or think of love again.

"I am through with love, Margaret," she declared now, as the first snowflakes floated down to the lawn on this night of Patrick's sixth birthday. Soon all beyond the side yard was obliterated by the swirling white flakes. Suzannah was cold throughout, as if the season had invaded her very soul.

Margaret came to her side and gently touched her arm. "God is love, Suzannah, and God is everywhere. You cannot say you're done with it."

"But I am," she whispered, beginning to tremble. "And if God is love, then I am done with Him as well."

Chapter 3

Before the snow had begun to fall in the Amoset valley that evening, Valentine Hopewell had reached the crest of the hill dividing Amoset from the Gully. He rested his horse there for a moment and surveyed the scene, his mood uncharacteristically thoughtful. Turning in the saddle, he looked back on the town with Cooper's Mountain rising behind it and his own home nested on the mountain's lower flanks. He watched as one by one the dark windows glowed golden, imagining the Irish servant girl called Peggy moving from room to room as she lit the lamps. Seeing the house shining like an ornament against the dark mountain, for an instant Valentine thought his home looked warm and hospitable. Then he laughed aloud and called himself a fool. Built of grey stone from a quarry a mile or two beyond Amoset, the Hopewell mansion, for all its thick carpets and warm fires in every hearth, always seemed cold to Valentine. He could not remember a time in his life when he had not dreamed of escape.

A house of the dead, he thought, a house without laughter or merriment of any kind.

Though Valentine was too self-centered to care much for others, he was genuinely fond of his nephew Patrick Paine. It was a feeling strong enough to make him sorry for the lad, who had to grow up in such a frozen atmosphere. And with such a mother!

Valentine no longer remembered the time when he had loved Suzannah. As he sat on his horse, staring back at the house and town, he tried to summon up some memory, some shard of bright recollection concerning his sister. But there was nothing.

He tucked his brown scarf more securely into the collar of his worsted overcoat against the sharp edge of the wind. Below the house he could see the outline of Hopewell Mills, the most modern and progressive factory in the Amoset valley. It rose like a monolith constructed in honor of industry. Inside its walls, for five and a half days a week, more than four hundred men and women toiled at weaving, spinning, carding and dressing the cotton that arrived from Savannah. Its fame rivaled that of the Lowell Mills and each year the mill was visited by dignitaries not only from America, but from all over the world. This should have made Valentine proud, but he felt nothing for the mill or for his prominent family except mild disgust. And even this was so diluted an emotion that it scarcely moved him.

Now he turned back to the view immediately before him. The Gully and its inhabitants sometimes made him angry, oftentimes hilarious and always entertained. If anyone in his family had ever bothered to ask him why he spent so much time in the Irish community, he would have told them that there he felt himself to be a part of life at last.

The Gully was a shantytown, yet he, a man from wealth and influence, found his only happiness there. The irony did not escape him. Valentine's contradictory nature never was more apparent than in his feelings for the Irish. He both admired them and was disgusted by them. Boys like Mickey Quick were

nothing more than hooligans who had no place in
Yankee society. But in their own environment, Valentine was often amused and even charmed by their
wit, their clever and devious minds, their capacity for
laughter and tears. From where he sat astride his
horse, the whole of the Gully was spread before him
as if frozen, awaiting the snow. Frozen, yet full of life
and joy.

The Gully was a crisscross of lanes and muddy
alleyways that divided the barnyards and vegetable
gardens and cabins. The cabins, built seven to ten
feet high of slabs and rough boards, were turfed to
the eaves. There was usually a window at one end
and small holes high up along the sides through
which the smoke of the cooking fires drifted. Inside,
the cabins were dark and stank of smoke and cooking,
of unwashed bodies and livestock. On one lane between two such cabins, a frame church with a high,
narrow steeple had been built the year before, and
named for Saint Anne. The church and the pub one
block or so away called the Lavender and Lily were
the most substantial buildings in the Gully. Valentine
supposed that by the next spring and summer more
such buildings would be erected. In time the shantytown might become a little city.

At this thought of what the world called
progress, he kicked his horse irritably and proceeded
down the track into the town. He sensed that as the
Gully grew in respectability, his affection for the
place would disappear. Where, then, would he go to
find himself?

The Lavender and Lily was crowded that early
evening. Sensing the coming snow that heralded the
onset of winter with its hardships and sorrows, people
seemed to want to fortify themselves against it at this,

the last moment. Valentine tied his horse to the hitching post and shouldered his way through the heavy door.

He was greeted by a chorus from the bar and tables.

The barmaid, Coo Magee, handed him a cup of warm grog and grinned at him toothlessly. "By my *sowkins*, Master Val, you must be mad to leave a goodly fire on a night like this."

"Aye," agreed another woman, raising her cup in salutation, "we'll be havin' snow before the day's gone round the other side. You'll sleep in the Gully tonight, Master Val, or freeze your whatsit on the way home."

Her loud comments drew ribald laughter from the twenty or so occupants of the Lavender and Lily. Valentine joined in heartily as he hugged Coo Magee close and pinched her ample bottom.

"I know a bed that's warm enough for any wintertime!" he cried. Downing his drink quickly, he then pounded the tankard on the bar. "Another and another quickly after that, my friend! The day's been long and cold!"

From a rough plank table in the corner by the wood stove came another greeting. "But the dice are hot, Master Val, and your coins are good here, winter or no. Will you have a try?" The speaker was a wizened man of indeterminable age whose narrow blue eyes habitually flicked from side to side as if he expected an attack at any moment. His name was Jamie Teig, and if he dressed a little better than his friends in the pub, it was chiefly due to the money he had won from Valentine Hopewell. Now he raised his eyebrows and shook his fist, as if about to roll the dice. "Well? Will you be havin' a game with me, Master Val?"

Valentine shook his head. He thought to make

some explanation for his refusal, but instead he
turned away. On the last occasion when he had been
forced to ask Suzannah for money to pay his gambling debts, he had resolved that he would not again
let himself be lured into a game of chance. He didn't
know whether Jamie Teig cheated or whether his luck
was just exceptionally good. Whichever the reason,
Valentine rarely won when he gamed in the Gully
and he swore to himself that he would refuse all invi-
tations rather than face the humiliation of begging
from his sister.

But Jamie was not so easily put off. He sidled up
to Valentine, and as soon as his tankard was empty,
handed Val a full one. "Be my guest, Master Val. 'Tis
only hospitable, eh?"

Valentine hesitated.

"Go on, drink up, my friend. You'll not be poi-
soned by it." Jamie put his hand on Valentine's elbow
and steered him to a quieter corner of the pub.

Valentine protested. "I'm here to socialize, Teig. I
came to. . . ."

"I know, I know. But I've got a bit of news I'm
thinkin' you'll want to know. A moment of your time,
sir, that's all I ask."

"News?" A chill of apprehension raced through
Valentine. "Say what it is, man!"

"Don't rush me, lad. After all, I'm a poor old man
and far from me homeland. If I move a mite slow,
you'd do well to understand."

"You want money for this information?"

"Master Val, the way you say it makes it sound
right shameful."

Valentine sighed and fished in his pocket for a
silver coin large enough to satisfy Teig. The old character pocketed it quickly. "There's a woman come to
the Gully askin' after you. It's Valentine this and Val-

entine that wherever she goes. I thought you'd like to know about it."

"A woman? What kind of woman? I mean, what did she look like?"

Jamie Teig shrugged and made a face. "They're all the same, ain't they?" He wiped his mouth hard. "And I'm fearful parched."

"Coo!" called Valentine. "Bring Jamie here another drink!" He turned back to Teig. "Well? Can you remember now what she looked like?"

Jamie rolled his eyes. "It's comin' back to me, now as you mention it. Comely she was, with a fanciful name like a queen might have."

"A queen?" Valentine stared at the sawdust-covered floor. "She's Irish?"

"Aye," replied Jamie, gulping down his drink. "A servant girl, she said she used to be."

Valentine had to laugh. Since becoming a man he'd known dozens of servant girls and most of them had been Irish. To think of which one Jamie Teig was talking about was like searching for a treasure without a map. And by this time Valentine had drunk four tankards of warm grog, so his mind just wouldn't concentrate. He laughed again and thumped Teig on the shoulder. "Whoever she is, God bless her, I doubt if I'll know her name."

Teig joined in laughter. "'Tis the way of men, eh, Master Val?"

"Aye, the way of men it is, Jamie Teig." Valentine picked up the lilting cadence of the Irish brogue when he was drinking. Coo Magee once gossiped to a friend that she knew when Valentine Hopewell was well-and-truly drunk because then he sounded more like a Dubliner than she did.

"Come along back to the table," urged Jamie. He heard the lilt in Valentine's voice and past experience had taught him that now was the time when the Yankee liked to gamble on a throw of the dice. "The game don't hardly seem like fun without you, lad."

For a moment Valentine was tempted. Gaming was a gentleman's pastime. Why shouldn't he risk a few coins on a throw of the dice? He was a rich man's son, the heir to a manufacturing fortune. Didn't he deserve a little fun?

In the past, such rationalizations had worked well for him. Like his mother, Sarah, who had traded an addiction to nerve tonic for a love of brandy, Valentine could almost always convince himself that what he wanted to do was what he should do. But this time was different. Suzannah's disapproval and the threat she had handed him a few days ago were still ringing in his ears.

He had gone to her in the mill office during working hours, seeking the money to pay his gambling debts. With her mouth set in a straight line, she had heard him out.

"This is the second time this month," she replied, eyeing him coldly from behind the big oak desk that had been their father's. "Last time you owed fifty dollars; now it's thirty and you want another twenty for what you call miscellaneous expenses. I suppose by that you mean your bar bill."

During the previous year Suzannah had taken to wearing steel-framed spectacles for the close work required in the mill office. She stared at him over the rims and Val was reminded of a crochety schoolteacher. It made him feel as awkward and embarrassed as a little boy caught misbehaving behind the woodshed.

"Well? Have you anything to say?"

"I have as much right to the family money as you do. I remind you I am a male. My father's heir."

She laughed curtly. "You have no right to what you cannot take the time to earn."

Good God, he thought, not this again. Suzannah always lectured him on the virtues of labor as if she had invented the code herself.

"I've heard all this before, Suzannah. Just tell me—do I get the money or not?" He didn't look at her. He couldn't. Instead he fixed his gaze on the desk, on the swirls and eddies of the wood grain.

"What happens if you don't pay?"

He looked up, afraid.

"Well?" she persisted when he didn't say anything.

"I am a gentleman, Suzannah. I must pay."

"But suppose you don't? Would your Irish friends come after you? Would they beat you up?"

He gritted his teeth and leaned forward, his hands on the edge of the desk. "I have to pay, Suzannah."

"I see." She sighed and pursed her lips. "They would hurt you." She flipped open a book of vouchers and wrote quickly, signing her name with a flourish. Tearing out the voucher, she handed it to him. "Take this to the counting room. I won't have you hurt and I won't permit the family name to be dishonored."

He turned to go, already breathing more easily.

"Before you go I want you to understand one thing, Valentine." She was talking to his back. "Turn around and look at me, please. If you are so concerned about being a gentleman, then you at least can have the decency to face me when I speak to you."

He turned slowly. "You are not speaking to young Patrick, Suzannah."

"And pray God I never feel toward him as I do

toward you at this moment. I'm warning you—this is the last time, Valentine. I will not rob from this company to pay your debts, not even once more. If you lose beyond your limit, you will have to face the penalty. I will not help again."

Valentine met her eyes and he saw that she meant it.

"I've lost my taste for gambling, Jamie," he said now.

"If you're short of *siller*, I'd be happy . . . ."

Valentine shook his head. His debts were paid and his pockets were just full enough that he could pay cash for his drinks that night. "You can't tempt me, my friend. I've reformed."

Coo Magee heard this and hooted in disbelief. "The man's reformed!" she cried out.

"And the world is as flat as a pancake!" someone yelled.

There was much laughter all around, and though the bantering was good-natured, it made Valentine uncomfortable. Might he throw the dice just once to silence them? He put his hand in his pocket and felt the coins and paper money there. When he balled it up in his fist it felt like a great deal to him, more than he possibly could spend or gamble away in a single evening. He might as well risk a few pennies with Jamie Teig.

All at once the front door of the Lavender and Lily opened, letting in a rush of damp, cold air.

"It's begun!" cried Coo, pointing outside. A woman stood in the open doorway and behind her the air whirled in white. "Winter is come!" Coo cried again.

"Close the door," yelled the barkeep.

The woman in the doorway stood still. Silhouet-

ted against the falling snow, she appeared a dark
shadow.

"Is Valentine Hopewell here?" she called out in a
clear voice.

"Damn you, woman, close the door before you
freeze the fires of hell!"

"Aye, Hopewell's here," answered Jamie Teig,
pointing at Valentine. "Step forward, Master Val. 'Tis
the woman I told you about."

Valentine peered through the barroom smoke.
The figure blurred and wavered, became double. He
blinked.

"I've come back, Valentine," said a voice that was
distantly familiar. " 'Tis I, Victorine."

Chapter 4

Valentine followed Victorine out of the Lavender and Lily and up the street to a lean-to built against a larger cabin. Already the snow had begun to bank against the turf wall facing north.

"Come inside," she said. "I'll build a fire and warm some grog for you." She didn't look at him. She seemed to have no doubt that he would do as she suggested.

Valentine staggered slightly and she held his arm to support him. "Duck your head," she told him as they entered the low door of the one-room cabin.

Inside it was black and the air was close. Victorine lit an acrid-smelling oil lamp that illuminated a space not more than six or seven feet square. Valentine rubbed his eyes. They were red and stinging, and nothing he saw with them was clear. Indicating a pallet on the floor, Victorine said, "You can lie down if you want. But don't be sleepin'."

Mutely obedient, he sank onto the mat that was laid on a space of ground which had been covered by a thick layer of reeds and bark to protect it from the damp. The dirt floor of the cabin was covered with several inches of straw, but Valentine knew that when the ground froze the cold would reach its fingers up through the straw and into every corner of the dank, cramped room.

"You live here?" he asked, holding his throbbing head between his hands.

"Aye. It isn't hardly the Hopewell mansion, eh?" She was grinning down at him, the same old Victorine with her laughing brown eyes, broad, expressive features and ample, warm body. She knelt before a little stove, rubbing her flint against a stone. After a moment a tiny flame appeared and caught in the dry grass and sticks in the grate. "There," she said, "we'll be warm in no time."

Valentine stared at her. He hadn't thought of Victorine since he went away to Boston for his ill-fated try at divinity school. Her sudden appearance in the Gully after so much time should have made him uneasy, but he was too drunk to worry. Instead he found himself recalling the boisterous times they'd rolled and sported in his bed in the big house while his mother walked the hall outside his door and other servants prepared his clothes for his move to Boston.

"So you never finished divinity school, eh?" Victorine poured a dark liquid from a crock into a pewter tankard and handed it to him. "I never thought you had the callin'. But then you never asked me, did you?" she laughed.

"I didn't last long," he admitted as the warm drink mellowed his spirits and made him forget the cold. He knew if he tried to stand, he would be unsteady and the bleariness of vision would no doubt return. But as he reclined on Victorine's narrow bed, he felt quite content. "At least it was an excuse to leave Amoset."

He had never spoken to anyone else about his failure at Harvard. For obvious reasons he had preferred to have his family believe he'd lost the calling for God's work. "I tried, but the work was tedious, with no fun in it. And the professors had a righteous attitude that nearly drove me mad." Actually, he had begun spending more and more time in Boston's disreputable waterfront pubs where the Irish he met made him laugh at the seriousness of university life. "The last few months, I didn't bother to attend the lectures. And once," he chuckled, "I hid beneath the stairs amidst the cobwebs when a tutor inquired after my health at the boarding house."

"I never did know why you hated it so in Amoset. After all, you're Mr. Hopewell's son and whatever you want, you have only to clap your hands and it's yours."

Now Valentine laughed. "Ah me, Vicki, you were always a dreamer of fine dreams."

She looked at him archly. "And you were always a liar, Valentine, my darlin' boy."

She dropped down beside him on the pallet and took the tankard from his hands. After a long drink she said, "Aren't you curious about me? About where I've been and all I've seen?"

Before Valentine could admit that, frankly, he had forgotten her the moment she was out of his sight, Victorine began the story of her life since then. "I left your family in '33 and went to stay with a cousin in Waterford. After a bit I got a position with a family there. They worked me hard, but the wages were fair and there were other Irish about so I was never lonely. 'Twas a fair enough life if I had cared to stay a servant."

"Why did you come back?" Valentine was rather glad to see her, but in the recesses of his mind a nagging suspicion had begun that Victorine had something planned, that her return to the Gully and their meeting at the Lavender and Lily was anything but accidental.

She didn't answer.

He finished his drink and set the tankard down with a metallic ring on the edge of the iron stove. He tried to get up.

" 'Tis early yet. Where would you be goin'?"

"Home. Before my poor horse freezes to death." He heaved himself to his feet with great effort.

Victorine stood up beside him and slipped her hands inside his worsted coat. "You feel the same, Valentine Hopewell. Strong and manly." She pulled herself close against him and nuzzled the long hair behind his ears. "And you smell good, too. Like that sweet water you kept on your dresser. What did you call it? Violet water."

Valentine teetered slightly, holding on to Victorine to keep his balance.

"Stay a while, Valentine," she whispered in his ear, her tongue making wet circles at the opening. She took his hand and pressed it hard against her breast. "Feel how my heart still beats for you?"

A combination of factors was making Valentine quite sick to his stomach. Apart from all he had drunk that evening on an empty stomach, the cabin smelled of cabbage, and beneath the layers of heavy clothing she wore, Victorine smelled of sweat.

"Got to go," he mumbled, pushing past her roughly.

She followed him out into the snowy night, grabbing his arm as he strode toward the pub where his horse was still tied. "Before you go I have somethin' to show you."

He shrugged her off. "I don't have time."

She laughed, a tinny sound. "I think you do, my darlin' boy." Seizing his wrist again, she pulled him back. When he resisted she told him, "This will take but a moment. After all these years, surely you have a moment for Victorine."

It was easier to give in than to argue. He went with her, but instead of going back to her tiny lean-to, she opened the door of the cabin next door without knocking.

"Hush," she cautioned, putting a finger to her lips. "I want to show you somethin'."

They stood in the shadows of the doorway without making a sound. The family in the cabin took no notice of them. Wrapped in tattered blankets, they were gathered near the stove, sipping tea and eating biscuits spread with melted grease that Valentine could smell from the doorway.

"What do you see, Valentine?" Victorine whispered very softly.

A woman dressed in ancient rags, her head completely covered by a wool scarf, an old man noisily sucking a stale biscuit between toothless gums, a boy of nine or ten.

Valentine was tired and in no mood for puzzles. "What . . . ?" he started to ask.

"The boy, Valentine. What do you think of him?"

Valentine squinted to see in the smoky room. The boy was standing near the stove with his back to the door. His head seemed too large and he had long, fair hair that fell shaggily almost to his rounded shoulders. Even in the gloom of the cabin it was clear that his body was misshapen somehow, as if a mighty hand had twisted it at the moment of birth. One arm seemed short, and as he turned, he did so with an awkward limp that showed one hip to be several inches higher than the other.

"A freak," muttered Valentine, looking away in disgust.

Still holding his arm, Victorine laughed softly. "Look again, Valentine."

The boy was facing the doorway now. Instantly

it was clear to Valentine why Victorine had brought him here. Despite his disfigured body, the boy's face was perfect and the image of Valentine's. The family likeness was so alarming that Valentine gasped and stepped back against the door, banging his head painfully against the low frame. From beside the stove the woman and old man stared at him.

"Who's that with you, Victorine?" the woman asked. "I told you not to bring your business here. The child. . . ."

Valentine shoved Victorine to one side and staggered out the door, but she followed, pulling at his coat.

"Get away from me!" he cried, lashing out with his arm and hitting her across the shoulder. She fell back, but in a moment she was beside him again.

"You know who that is, don't you?"

"I know nothing."

"You can't deny him, Valentine. It's there in that beautiful face."

"I don't know what you mean. The boy's a miserable freak. Why doesn't somebody put him out of his misery?"

"You saw his face, Valentine. You know. You know."

"I know nothing but that you are a curse to me, woman, and I wish you gone from here."

"The blond hair, the pretty blue eyes, the shape of the chin and cheeks, the moody Hopewell brows. . . ."

"Shut up!" he cried. But when he tried to hit her again, this time she was too quick and easily evaded his blow. He had reached his horse. Clutching the reins, he heaved himself into the saddle.

"You know who he is. You may not deny him."

Victorine stood in the snow beside the horse, holding on to the stirrup.

Valentine tried to kick her away. "I deny everything. The boy is a monster."

Suddenly Victorine laughed. "But he is your monster, Valentine. I swear by God he is your child!"

"No!" Valentine jerked the horse around, kicked him hard and galloped out of the Gully. But behind him, in a ringing voice so clear that it almost seemed she was riding in the saddle behind him, he could hear Victorine. He could hear her screaming into the icy night.

"The freak is your son, Valentine! And his name is Hart!"

Chapter 5

You have to go in, Suzannah told herself. Do it now.
She reached for the brass knob on the oak-paneled
door to her father's study.

A voice stopped her.

"I may speak with you please, Mrs. Paine? On a
matter of some importance?" It was the India Man,
Mr. Harahsi.

She turned to him with a pleasant smile that
completely disguised her dislike. "Of course, Mr.
Harahsi. I have a moment now, if that is convenient?"
She never knew how to treat this male nurse from the
other side of the world. Whatever had brought him so
far from home? And what was he, anyway? A servant,
a nurse or a witch doctor? "Shall we go into my office?" she suggested.

It was a pretty and decidedly feminine little
room, but it was functional as well. When Suzannah
had realized that mill affairs required that she work
at night, she had determined to make her work environment as much a reflection of her personality as
possible. It was this that the India Man had first noticed about Mrs. Paine's office. Like her, it was both
beautiful and practical. The furnishings, a chair, a
desk and a table, were in the Shaker tradition. The
austerity of the finely crafted items pleased his eyes.
Suzannah pleased him, too. Although he was not at-

tracted to fair-skinned women, he could see that she
was beautiful by the standards of any nation. She was
tall and slender and dark-haired, and her sea-green
eyes never failed to astonish Harahsi with the intensity of their inward gaze. He found such introspection
most unusual in a Yankee. And her work in the mill
had given her a sense of self-confidence that was rare
in the women he had met in this strange country of
America. He thought her confidence might be the reason that she had retained the spark and fire that were
characteristic of women much younger.

"Does this have to do with my father, Mr.
Harahsi? Sit down. Please."

He knew he made her nervous. It was a shame,
but there was nothing he could do to change the fact
that she had taken an instant dislike to him. She was
always fair and pleasant with him and never had
made the smallest complaint concerning his work as
Martin Hopewell's companion. Still, there was no
doubt in Mr. Harahsi's mind that Suzannah Paine disliked him.

"It's the matter of your father's legs, Mrs. Paine."

"You've got to make him exercise. I've seen you
work wonders before, Mr. Harahsi."

"Soon the atrophy will be such that he can never
hope to walk again."

"He has to walk!"

"May I ask why, Mrs. Paine?" Harahsi had trouble understanding her compulsion concerning her father. Why should the man want to walk after all he
had been through? Was it any wonder that he wanted
only to sit or lie down in that frigid, dimly lit room,
the reverse image of his wife, Sarah, who was swelter-
ing upstairs in her pool of brandy, the fireplace in her
room blazing.

When she didn't answer immediately, Harahsi

went on. "Your father suffered terribly in the hands of that madwoman. He was caged in a cold, dark cave for months and he'll never even know why. Now he must rest."

Suzannah stood up, irritated. "For six years! The doctors say there is nothing wrong with his legs. Therefore, he should be able to walk." She leaned forward, her hands gripping the edge of the desk. "Isn't that logical?"

"Life is not always logical, Mrs. Paine."

She laughed abruptly and sat back down. "Well, you needn't tell me that, Mr. Harahsi."

"No, Mrs. Paine."

As far as Harahsi could tell, Suzannah Hopewell Paine did not like to hear the truth spoken. She claimed to know that life was not always logical, yet she clearly was angered by his having mentioned it.

Harahsi's dark eyes and sensuous mouth never changed their expression when he spoke to her. It was this, among other things, that drove Suzannah wild with frustration. She would have liked to see him laugh, cry, dance, rage, bellow—anything! Instead, he acted more or less the same from minute to minute and hour to hour. On any day, at any time, Mr. Harahsi greeted her with the same benign look. She had no idea what it could mean to be so placid, except that it was completely contrary to what she knew about behavior and therefore seemed suspicious.

But whatever he was, Harahsi knew his business. Without him, the care of Martin Hopewell would have been an intolerable and perhaps even impossible burden on the family. When James Shawn had found him in the cave on Cooper's Mountain, her father was almost unrecognizable. He had shrunk from his

former height of more than six feet and his body was
covered with foul sores that oozed and itched.

It had been her brother Eben's idea to call the
India Man from Cartland House. Years before
Harahsi had cared for Eben after he and Martin had
returned from a business trip to Savannah. Something
had happened on that trip, something more than his
grandfather's death, and whatever it was had driven
Eben mad. But Harahsi was capable of miracles;
Eben had more than recovered.

For this reason, Suzannah covered her aggrava-
tion. "Perhaps you are right. For now, let's not worry
about making him walk. Concentrate on . . . well, the
other things you do."

Harahsi stood up and bowed his white-turbaned
head.

"Before you go, can you tell me how my father
is, Mr. Harahsi? Besides his legs, I mean. He doesn't
seem to change from day to day and it's difficult to be
encouraged."

"I am neither encouraged nor discouraged, Mrs.
Paine. Your father will do what he will do."

Damn the man! she thought, but what she said
was, "Thank you, Mr. Harahsi."

When she was alone, Suzannah turned her chair
around and opened the drapes of a window overlooking the rose garden. The storm had passed and now
the sky was navy blue and sparkling with stars. A
fat-faced moon stared down on the rose garden and
the rolling lawn beyond it. White on white, the night
was as brilliant as day. Without the protection of the
heavy drapes the room turned chilly, but Suzannah
didn't notice. Her thoughts were in other places.

"I'm a hypocrite," she said aloud after a long
time, and was surprised when her breath made a

cloud. She closed the drapes and, going to the fireplace, added a new log to the embers. It caught
quickly and she knelt at the hearth, warming her
hands.

Yes, she was a hypocrite and she suspected that
Mr. Harahsi knew it as well as she. She mouthed
hopes and dreams for her father's recovery, but the
words were bitter in her mouth. The truth was more
like this: she was happy as manager of Hopewell
Mills; it gave purpose and challenge to her life. She
never wanted her father to recover because it would
mean she would have to return to the sheltered life
she had known before.

Despite what she might say publicly, Suzannah
had an inner honesty that could be ruthlessly to the
point. She acknowledged to herself that she was an
unloving daughter, but then what had Martin
Hopewell ever done to deserve love from his offspring? He had beaten her and locked her in a closet
when she was young, he'd cruelly rejected one son
and shown nothing but indifference toward the other.
The truth of the matter was that none of his children
cared if their father recovered, and if he died they
would only pretend to weep for him.

She returned to the window, and drawing aside
an edge of the drape with her hand, looked out again
on the cold landscape. She hated to think of Valentine
down in the Gully, drunk and God-knows-what-else
on a freezing night like this. Nevertheless, her patience had worn thin after years of such escapades.
He had tried to reform a time or two and as much as
six months might pass without incident, but he always
reverted to his old habits sooner or later. Suzannah
was well acquainted with his pattern by now and she
was sick of it. She had given up hoping that her

brother would change. He was a wastrel, a ne'er-do-well, another one of Martin Hopewell's victims.

She turned from the window and, gathering a handful of papers from her desk, left her office and crossed the hall to her father's study.

You have to go in, she told herself again. Do it now. She reached for the knob.

Inside, the grates were clear of ashes. The room had been without heat since last winter and smelled like a cave. Suzannah took a shawl from a hook by the door and wrapped it about her shoulders.

"Father? It's Suzannah. I've come to visit for a little while. Do you have time for me today?" As her eyes gradually accustomed themselves to the semidarkness, Martin Hopewell seemed to emerge from the shadows.

He was immensely fat from inactivity and a compulsive desire to eat. It was as if he were afraid that each meal might be his last, that at any time the madwoman might rise from her grave and capture him again. Despite the cold, he lay propped up on a day bed with only a thin blanket across his lap. His chest was bare and the folds of white flesh that roped his torso seemed to spill out over the flimsy cloth blanket, embarrassing Suzannah as much as if he had been completely naked.

She looked down at the papers in her hand. "Shall we talk about the mill tonight? I have some news that isn't very good, I'm afraid."

"What?" Once Martin Hopewell's voice had possessed the power to shake walls and terrify the masses, but now it was nothing more than a hoarse whisper.

"It's the depression, Father."

"What depression?"

"The one we've been suffering since '37, Father." From one day to the next she couldn't be sure what her father remembered. She dared not underestimate him, however, for he had a way of snapping into sanity for several moments or sometimes hours at a time. When he did, it was as if the old Martin, the man of hard strength and implacable will, lived again. That Martin frightened Suzannah, and she knew she must never risk making him angry.

"I'm going to have to lower wages again. That makes twice in just eighteen months." It was either that or fire Yankees and hire Irish. She was not prepared to do that, for Suzannah felt an unspoken, but nonetheless binding agreement with the Yankee women who made up the largest percentage of her female employees. While times were hard, she would keep them on and not hire from the vast immigrant force that clamored to be let into the mills. But in order for her to do this, the operatives had to see Suzannah's point of view as well as their own and accept a lower price per piece of work or take on extra looms and frames.

She went on talking. As she began to run out of things to say her words tumbled forth faster and faster, as if she hoped to outrun the final moments of her interview with Martin. Finally even this effort failed her and she sat quite still, her hands, almost numb with the chill, folded in her lap.

"Is that all?" he wanted to know.

"I believe so, Father."

"Very well."

She stood up.

"You may kiss your papa good night," he said, leaning forward slightly to receive his due.

She cleared her throat. "I have a little cold, Papa."

"Never mind. Come close."

In the instant when her lips brushed Martin's cheek, Suzannah was almost overcome with revulsion. Though she knew Harahsi kept him as clean as a pampered infant, to her his skin retained the aroma of the pustules that once had covered his body and face. His skin was cold against her lips.

"Good night, Suzannah."

"Good night, Father."

Chapter 6

She left her father and went upstairs, dimming the banister lamps one by one until the broad carpeted treads and polished rail were washed in saffron shadows. From the first-floor landing, she stared back down the stairs and decided there was enough light for Valentine to see by if he came home that night. She certainly didn't want him to break his neck!

Patrick's room—part nursery, part battlefield littered with legions of perfect metal soldiers, cannon and horses—was across the hall from her own. She nudged open the door a crack and listened. He was breathing noisily in a deep slumber after his wonderful, exhausting birthday.

Smiling, Suzannah stepped in softly and knelt at her son's bedside. As she bent down to kiss his cheek, she thought of her father's cheek, which was like a mound of bread dough. Her father's skin was cold, but Patrick's had warmth and vigor and sweetness, like a taut-skinned little apple.

I wonder if Father ever loved me the way I love Patrick? Did Martin Hopewell ever feel his insides melt with love for me?

Not likely!

She felt so about Patrick a lot of the time. His beauty and innocence were combined with youthful virility. The lean broad back, the strong legs and already doubting brow stirred her in a way that she recognized as sexual. Perplexing as this feeling was, Suzannah had learned to accept it as she had most things about herself.

Six years old! Was it possible?

When Patrick was born, no one had questioned his paternity. Although Travis had, many months earlier, deserted his wife of less than a year, Patrick was naturally assumed to be his son. But Suzannah knew that if anyone cared to do some close figuring, there was a small discrepancy of time that proved otherwise. Six years had elapsed without a whisper of gossip, however, and she had ceased to worry that anyone would guess that Patrick was James Shawn's son.

"James Shawn." That name, spoken aloud in the dark, had once had the power to break her. When that had still been so, she had felt compelled to say it, as if the almost ritualistic suffering was required of her. At last, however, his memory had lost its power to destroy her and now she could hear his name and hardly care at all.

But with every year, Patrick's likeness to his father became more pronounced. The boy had Suzannah's green eyes that could change from an almost transparent greenish-gold to a darker shade that was like pools in a slow river. And Patrick had the Hopewell brows, thick and melancholy. Apart from these two characteristics, however, Patrick was very like his father. Sometimes recently, Suzannah had seen James Shawn looking out at her, but from eyes that might have been her own.

The sleeping boy made a gentle noise, yawned, turned and scratched himself. Suzannah wondered if James Shawn slept in the same fitful way. She never had watched her lover sleep, for their encounters had been too brief and passionate for that quiet kind of intimacy. They had been together no more than a dozen times, but in a way it had been enough. For all time, James and Suzannah would belong to each other in their hearts.

When James had ceased to be a part of her life, she had given herself over to the work at the mill and let herself be swallowed up by it. Only Patrick was more important than the mill. And increasingly, she saw them as one and the same, for Patrick was the only heir to the Hopewell empire. Eben and Amanda might yet have a child, but it seemed unlikely. Theirs was not a happy marriage. As for Valentine, he probably had a dozen bastard offspring between Amoset and Boston, but none of them had any legal right to anything. Therefore, there was every likelihood that Patrick would someday inherit the major portion of the Hopewell fortune. And so, when Suzannah worked, she worked for him.

Lost in these thoughts, she lingered at her son's bedside. It was time to go to bed, she realized. In recent years it had become her habit to breakfast early, between five and six, so that she could be at her desk in the mill just after six. A servant always brought her midday meal down from the house, and around three she had a cup of tea and a little cake. Sometimes in the winter months she didn't see daylight from Sunday to Saturday. But far from exhausting Suzannah, it exhilarated her to be so totally involved that the hours could pass unnoted. Work was a joy to Suzannah, who had spent her girlhood bored by the safe female pleasures like needlework and kite-flying. Was it any wonder she prayed that her father would not recover? If she were to be driven out of the mill and back into the house, it would be a kind of death for her.

She tucked the bed linens up about Patrick's chin, straightened the goose down comforter and brushed his sandy hair away from his eyes.

"Good night, Patrick Shawn," she whispered.

The next day was Sunday. Suzannah awoke early, then, remembering that she didn't have to go to the mill that day, she treated herself to some extra sleep. Later, after attending services at Reverend Strickland's Unitarian Church and sharing a meal with Patrick, Suzannah felt restless without mill affairs to occupy her mind while the boy rested. Margaret and her children, who were visiting for a week or two, had driven off to Marivale early that morning to attend the services at St. Thomas' Episcopal Church. They wouldn't be back until late afternoon and, until that time, Suzannah knew from past experience that she would chafe with idleness. She tried some needlepoint, but the thread kept slipping and, anyway, she didn't want to wear her spectacles. She managed to write half a letter to her sister-in-law, Amanda, before the effort became too tedious. She paced around the parlor restlessly, then, on an impulse, went out to the foyer.

Grabbing a coat and scarf from the clothes tree, she dragged the heavy door open and walked out on the verandah. The marble tiles were slippery and the boots she was wearing were not really suitable for outdoor winter wear. Suzannah clutched a pillar for support. The air was so dry it pinched her face with its mean little fingers, and when she breathed, it hurt the back of her throat. Moving gingerly from pillar to pillar, she reached the edge of the verandah where the view of the Amoset valley was vast and breathtaking. It made Suzannah's eyes ache to see such an expanse of whiteness beneath the sharp blue sky.

She was about to turn away and go inside when a moving dot of black caught her attention. It was a carriage, quite a large vehicle, and it was headed up Cooper's Mountain.

That's strange, she thought. There's only one house up that way. Who's going up to the Shawns at this time of year?

She found out several days later.

"The whole Shawn family is together for a reunion. I'm told they'll all be here until after Christmas." Margaret put down her knitting. "I must say I hope it's a happy occasion for that poor family. I don't hear a word about James Shawn without remembering that boy of his. . . ."

"Talleyrand."

"He was killed in the gears of a loom!"

"I was there, Margaret."

The older woman's face blanched. "Oh Lord, forgive me. Of course you were! I had simply forgotten the details. Oh, Suzannah, how frightful of me to remind you." Tears filled her eyes.

Suzannah reassured her with a smile. Margaret didn't always listen to herself when she talked and this sometimes made her say untactful things for which she was always afterwards extremely contrite.

"You must think me the most insensitive soul that ever lived. I only meant to say that one cannot help sympathizing with a family that has suffered so. And to rejoice with them in their happiness, too. The Shawns' daughter Lucy and her husband, Thomas, have a daughter. Delphia, I think her name is. But the most wonderful news is that the Shawns' younger daughter, the asthmatic one, has finally been pronounced cured and has come home from Virginia.

She's been away for such a long time! She's seventeen now."

"I know. I received a letter from Ingrid Shawn a few months ago."

Margaret's eyes opened wide with surprise and she looked a little hurt. "You didn't tell me."

"I've hired her to teach at the mill school."

"But it's closed. The depression. . . ."

"I intend to reopen it in the new year."

"Who will pay for it, Suzannah? The poor operatives are already extended to the limit and you've said yourself that the cost of maintaining the boarding houses is. . . ."

"I will pay for the school until times improve." Seeing a particular look on Margaret's face, Suzannah turned away and began leafing through a book of drawings.

"You are a wonder, Suzannah Hopewell Paine. The smartest thing my brother ever did was get you into our family." Margaret put her work aside and crossed the room to where Suzannah was sitting. She knelt beside her chair and grasped her friend's hands. "I mean it, Suzannah. There's not a soul in the world who can say it's your place to pay for a schoolteacher when the agreement makes it very clear that you provide the room, but the operatives must pay for the teacher. You're doing this because you're a good person. Good and generous."

"It's only good business, Margaret. I'm going to have to lower the price per piece in the spring. I have no alternative. I only hope that providing a teacher for the children can somehow soften the blow to my operatives." She made a little face at her sister-in-law and smiled. "Well, what do you think of me now, eh? Not quite so good and generous, I'll wager!"

Margaret was still gazing at her in admiration,

however. "Let me add the word pragmatic to the list of your attributes, Suzannah." She laughed a little and shook her head. "More and more, my dear, I am in awe of you."

They were interrupted by a curt knock on the door. It was Valentine.

"I understand you want to see me in the holy of holies."

Suzannah frowned. "Excuse me, Margaret. I must go and serve the cause of pragmatism a little more to-day."

When they had gone into her study, Valentine slammed the door. "What the hell was that supposed to mean?"

"What?"

He mimicked her voice and posture. "I must go and serve the cause of pragmatism a little more to-day."

"It means I am offering you a job."

"Forgive me if I am less than thrilled."

Suzannah cocked her head a little and her eyes darkened as they often did when she was puzzled. "Tell me something, Valentine. Do you intend to go through life without so much as raising a finger for your own support?"

"I'm not going to let you shove me into a slot and leave me there, if that's what you mean. When I work it's going to be the kind of job I can do well." He turned to go.

"I think that's what I'm offering you."

He stopped and faced her again, a cautious look on his face. "Oh?"

"According to the almanac and various other prognosticators, this will be a stormy winter in New England. Even during a moderate winter, it becomes difficult to move about town. Business slows down."

She went to her desk and, from a leather folder embossed with her initials, she withdrew a sheet of paper. "Ten other mill owners and I have formed an association to pay for keeping the roads and paths passable this winter. We want you to hire the Irish for us." She held out the paper to him and gave it a little shake. "Read what it says."

Valentine ignored her outstretched hand. "They won't be able to do it. They don't have the clothes for winter work. They'd freeze to death and then we'd have to spend all our time burying them."

"Read the agreement, Valentine! In it the association agrees to provide boots and woolen piece goods as part of the laborers' pay. It's a good bargain."

Reluctantly, Valentine took it and read the simple explanation. Suzannah, watching his eyes, could tell that he had scanned the words a second time before he said, "I'll do it."

"Thank you, Valentine."

"How much are my wages?"

"A percentage based on the number of men you reliably produce every day during the winter. There may be work for as many as fifty men five days a week."

Valentine nodded absently and Suzannah knew he was making calculations in his head. "It won't be much," he finally said.

"But it's fair. You can't deny that." Before he could change his mind, Suzannah dropped her businesslike manner and touched her brother's arm gently, hesitantly, for contact between them was rare. "Please take the job, Valentine. You need to work, to occupy your days. And you would be doing me, the association and the whole town a service by acting as our liaison with the Irish." Valentine started to interrupt, but she wouldn't let him speak until every argument was before him. "I assume that some of those people are your friends. Well, think of this as a service to them. There is terrible poverty in the Gully. This project means food and clothing and perhaps even coal in the stove. Valentine, you're always saying I don't try to include you in the mill business. Now I'm offering you something you'll be good at. Take it, Valentine. Take it."

Chapter 7

Valentine accepted, of course. But not without some
reservations. Victorine and her alarming son, Hart,
were in the Gully and he would be seeing them again
if he intended to frequent the Lavender and Lily.
Since it was the principal meeting place for the men
of the Gully, just as St. Anne's belonged to the
women, much of the business of Valentine's new job
could be carried out in no other place. Valentine wondered if Suzannah was aware that she was sending
him back into the seeps of temptation. Thinking of
this and the responsibilities of his new job, he was beginning to feel boxed in again, cornered, as he had in
divinity school.

Valentine accepted the offer despite these appre-
hensions, however, because he knew it was a job he
could be good at. He liked the Irish when they were
on their own ground and they liked him in their
shifty way. Valentine couldn't always tell when they
were playing with him, so he wasn't sure whether he
actually had friends in the Gully or merely prompters
and stooges. But even with this uncertainty, he liked
the men and women at the Lavender and Lily better
than any lot he'd met before and he knew they would
jump at the chance to work for him.

The promise of boots and woolen piece goods
was indeed a powerful inducement to labor. The day

the jobs were announced on the gate of Hopewell
Mills, Valentine was down at the Lavender and Lily,
signing up laborers and handing out clothes like a
haberdasher. Through three feet of snow and a knife-
edged wind, men came from as far south as Marivale.
One by one they strode out of the wild western
mountains to stand ankle deep in slush, waiting for a
job that promised warm woolens and dry feet.

Valentine stood on a table so that he could be
seen and heard by everybody. "I can use only fifty to
start, but by the middle of the month, just before
Christmas, I can guarantee I'll have jobs for seventy-
five to one hundred strong men every day." He held
up his hand to silence the loud cheers of approval.
"Now don't go thinking, my friends, that the work
will be easy. On the contrary, I guarantee you'll earn
your shillings and pence. Most of you are new to
these shores from a temperate island. Let me warn
you, in case this is the first you've heard of it—Massachusetts Bay State is the mother of all storms, the father of all cold. If you have gloves, wear them.
Without them your hands may freeze. And cover your
ears, but be careful with scarves or other clothing
that can trip you up. You'll be expected to work
fast."

The crowd listened and groaned, but in the end
there were more men than jobs and many went away
disappointed. Most hung around the Lavender and
Lily for a while before heading home to a turf hut for
"a spot o' tea."

The pub was almost empty when Victorine appeared.

"Sorry. We're not hiring women." Valentine was
stone-cold sober, but looking at Victorine in her
bright blue bonnet, her skin flushed from the cold,

was enough to make him feel half-gone with liquor. Why was that?

"You hurt me bad, Val. What you did was wrong." She was pouting and he remembered all at once what it was that he had liked about Victorine when they had first met. Her mouth was irresistible, the lower lip heart-shaped and as glossy as a ripe plum. The juicy little fruit demanded kissing.

"I want no part of that boy, Victorine, but you . . . ah, you're a different matter." He pulled her by the hand into a dark corner of the pub that was partitioned off and used as a storeroom. "Say anything you like. Do what you like. I will not own that . . . that monster, even if his life depends on it."

She didn't reply. Her face was only inches from his and her lower lip trembled exquisitely.

Valentine's hand darted out and into the folds of her skirt. She squirmed and backed up until she was leaning against the wall. It was damp and cold.

"You stay away from me, Valentine Hopewell." She gave him a weak shove. "You've had me before, true enough, but that don't guarantee the world. Why should I be nice to you? You've shown me no kindness since you learned of Hart." Valentine had separated Victorine's several petticoats and, at last, his hand touched her warm skin.

She shook her finger in his face. "You have to promise something first. I'm a working girl, Valentine. Don't forget that. I used to be a respectable servant, but because of you I couldn't work with decent folks and had to sell myself to feed Hart." He stroked her and she moaned against his shoulder. "Promise, Valentine, or I swear I'll haunt thee after death."

He answered quickly, his mouth a fraction of an inch from that luxurious lower lip that seemed to cry out for him to suck and bite on it. "I'll see the boy again. One more time," he whispered, pulling her down and lifting himself onto her.

She grinned obligingly. "In that case, may I give thee some encouragement, Valentine, m'dear?"

Hart lay in the straw with his back against the stove. Though the fire had gone out some time before, it was still warm there. Holding an edge of ragged blanket in his fist, he sucked his thumb noisily. After a while, his blue eyes glazed over and he stared without blinking at a dark corner of the shack. He was almost asleep when his stomach started growling. He squirmed harder against the stove.

His mother had been gone since before nightfall. She had left him with a dying fire and the heel of a loaf of stale bread. She often left him alone this way and it seemed to make no difference to Hart for, like a dog or cat, he had little comprehension of time. In his life there had always been stretches of time when he was alone or cold or hungry. Waiting, his eyes fixed on nothing in a kind of self-induced hypnosis, the hours passed. His mother would come home and bring him something to eat. She would hold him then, and stroke his silken hair.

When he heard the latch lift on the door to the shack, he uttered an excited squeal and rolled awkwardly to his feet. "Mama!" he cried, his body trembling all over in anticipation.

But this time she had someone with her. Hart shrank back into the shadows as if someone had kicked him. When his mother brought men to the room, it was always bad. Sometimes the men drank too much and laughed at Hart, and though the boy could not understand the gibes, he felt keenly their intent to wound and hurt. When his mother had a man with her, Hart slept in the corner and covered his ears with his hands.

He looked up cautiously. His mother and the man were staring at him.

"Come over here, Hart. There's naught to fear." Victorine removed her shawl and knelt before the little stove. She tried to coax a fire from the embers. "Show yourself to Mr. Hopewell. Smile so he can see how pretty you are."

The contrast between the boy's perfect face and deformed body held Valentine in fascinated horror. There was no mistaking the Hopewell family likeness; it was remarkable, almost as unnerving as meeting one's double on the street. But Hart's wrecked and useless body was an insult to that exquisite face, the joke of a mad creator with a cosmic grudge against the Hopewells.

Valentine reconsidered this thought and almost laughed aloud. He was beginning to think like the bloody Irish!

The fire caught and Victorine quickly shored it up with sticks from a basket next to the stove. She handed a wooden bucket to Hart. "Fetch water for tea," she told him, "and be careful how you step. It's slick outside tonight."

Valentine sprawled on Victorine's pallet and stared at the light flickering amidst the shadows on the low ceiling of the shack. The place was primitive, but somehow he didn't much mind. In fact, he admitted to himself with grim humor, he was as happy in Victorine's hovel as he would have been in his own luxurious home.

He held out a packet of fresh buns he had bought for them at the Lavender and Lily.

"I'll make a nice tea and you can see how Hart is," she said as she took them.

"I'm not interested in how he is."

"He's sweet, Valentine. Really, he is. And have you ever seen a more beautiful face? When he was born, the midwife cried. She said he was half angel and half monster."

"The monster is what I noticed." Valentine shifted his weight on the pallet. He was rapidly losing the feeling of contentment that he had felt after his and Victorine's hasty coupling. Restless now, he was critical of everything. And he was hungry, too. "I thought you said the kid would be back in a hurry. What's taking him so long?"

"He'll be along presently, Valentine. I can't leave to check on him for fear these buns will burn." With a long-handled fork, Victorine deftly turned the rolls on top of the stove.

"How long does it take to get water around here, anyway?" Valentine's throat was dry and the smoky air in the shack made it sting. "Where's the well?"

"It's a spring a few houses down." Victorine had begun to worry. "There's always standing water down there. I suppose it may have frozen over. . . ."

"Holy creation! I might as well go back to the Lily as wait all night here."

"You go look for him, Valentine. Please?" She kissed the air between them, her lower lip still wet from his mouth.

With a curse, Valentine lunged out through the low doorway and into the deserted street. By moonlight, the scene was like a memory of war where everything of beauty had been destroyed. Winter moonlight revealed the Gully at its most miserable. In warmer seasons, oaks and maples gentled the shame of the Gully's ramshackle shanties and cast generous shadows to hide the dirt. Now the trees were bare, and in the white light, their silhouettes were a parade of scrawny refugees.

Valentine saw Hart coming up the street at last, the bucket he held on his short side giving an odd balance to his body. As he walked through the mud and ice with a rolling side to side motion, Valentine was even able to see something graceful in the boy and was fascinated by the way he compensated for his deformity.

Suddenly he went down. Valentine heard him cry out, a sound more of exasperation than pain. He hurried up the street toward the boy, stopping several feet away. His instinct to help disappeared as he watched Hart slowly and patiently lift his torso out of the mud, using only the strength of his arms. From where he stood, Valentine could see the boy's expression of total concentration. It elevated him in his father's eyes and made him no longer simply a monster, but now a monstrous creature of formidable will and hidden strength. From his knees, Hart looked around for support and saw Valentine.

They stared at each other. Valentine imagined in that moment that Hart had recognized him as his father, and he had to fight the desire to turn and run before the trap snapped shut on him.

"Help?" The boy managed to say the word quite clearly and Valentine could not ignore it. "Help?" he asked again, and raised his hand.

Valentine stepped back. He wanted no part of the pitiful child. He wanted to be anywhere but on this moonlit street, chained by a stare to a child who was half monster, half angel.

"Help?" repeated Hart, his voice small and feeble in the silent street, his eyes beseeching.

A moment passed. Another. Then . . . Valentine held out his hand.

PART II

Chapter 8

"Amen." Helen Shawn looked up from her folded hands and smiled as she began to serve her family breakfast. The kitchen was the oldest part of the Shawn farm. When the young Helen and James had left her parents' sprawling homestead on the northern side of Cooper's Mountain, they had moved into this one room, built many generations before by no one knew whom, and it had served as their house for that first winter. Over the years Helen and James had worked side by side, building a generous loft for the children and then a room for themselves. Most recently a parlor had been added on and filled with furnishings suited to the home of a legislator in the government of Massachusetts. But it was rarely used. James had to spend much of his time in Boston, the children were gone, and even when the family was together, the kitchen was warmer and more congenial.

One wall was taken up by a large fireplace and two arched brick ovens. Above, hanging from a massive lintel of solid oak, was an assortment of iron pans, skewers, porringers, toasters and the like. And standing sentinel on either side of the hearth were two ladder-backed chairs with cane seats. Against a wall of whitewashed brick was the ancient Hildebrand dresser Helen had brought to the marriage as part of her dowry. Its three long shelves held an assortment of family pewter and crockery and some carved wooden plates. The center of the large room was dominated by a trestle table and benches long enough to seat the entire Shawn family.

Helen seems younger, James thought as he watched his wife's quick, efficient movements. It's having the children about her that makes the difference. Without her family, she's a strange woman.

"Ingrid, pass the fritters to your papa. And the syrup." They were having apple fritters made from the last of the orchard apples and drenched with home-tapped syrup as sticky as treacle. "Delphia, see, I made a special one just for you." Helen dropped a fat golden morsel on her granddaughter's plate and did not protest when the four-year-old picked it up in one tubby fist and crammed it into her mouth. It was easier being a grandparent than a mother.

"Delphia!" Lucy admonished her child in a tone of voice James recognized well.

"You sound like your own mother," he observed, smiling at his elder daughter.

Lucy didn't smile. "I don't know about that. What I do know, however, is that Delphia wouldn't be so cheeky in her own home. It's the farm that does it. She's behaving like a hoyden."

"It doesn't matter, Lucy," said her husband, Thomas Kilmaine, putting his hand on her arm.

She shook him off and roughly wiped Delphia's face with a napkin. The child endured the cleaning for only an instant before she began to squirm.

"Hold still!" her mother demanded.

"Let me do it," said Helen. "Please."

"Oh, very well!" Lucy threw down the napkin and got up from the table. As Delphia submitted angelically to her doting grandmother's ministrations, Lucy stared at the fire, her back to the table.

"Are you all right, Lucy?" asked James, troubled.

She nodded, but her head was turned and he couldn't see her expression. James always had been able to read his Lucy. Her girlhood fibs and fabrications never had fooled him, for in her bright blue eyes he could always find the truth.

He looked away from her now and thought, I don't want to know, I don't want to know.

Lucy and Thomas Kilmaine had been married since 1837, and in the five years since that event, James had seen a good deal of both of them. The business of the state legislature forced him to spend many months of every year in Boston, which was where the couple lived. During those months James was comfortable at his club, but also happy to be near his daughter's home, where he was always welcome. Though Thomas and Lucy both did all they could to make his visits a pleasure, and though he truly was smitten with four-year-old Delphia, James was aware of an undercurrent between Lucy and Thomas. More precisely, he sensed an empty space between them where something should have been.

I don't want to know, he insisted to himself, but he remained unconvinced. He *did* want to know what was troubling his star-child, the fair-haired Lucy of his childhood.

James Shawn had been hardly more than a boy when his daughter was born. Although he had carried the responsibilities of adulthood with apparent ease, for he was a hard worker, a considerate man and honorable by reputation, still he had been little more than an overgrown adolescent with an even younger adolescent for a wife. When Lucy came into the world, she was a wonderment to him. He had doted

on her as she grew, and in the pictures he held
framed in his mind, there was one that touched him
most. Lucy was standing in the barn loft, a tot of four
up to her waist in hay, with sticks of straw pointing
out from her head like antennae. There was dirt on
her face, but her hair and her eyes gave her identity
away: she was an angel come to earth with too sudden a thump.

"Catch me, Dada," she had cried, and with no
further warning, she had leapt into glorious motion
—arms outspread like Icarus, her seraphlike face suf-
fused in sunlight from the open barn door. For that
brief instant, James had been a pagan, worshipping a
tiny goddess.

Then he had dived to catch her. They had
landed painfully, but not seriously, in each other's
arms on the floor of the barn, halfway inside a horse
stall.

The incident had terrified James the more he'd
thought of it, and from then on he'd been hard on
Lucy in an effort to inhibit her exuberant courage.
Now, as the irritable give-and-take of dinner table
conversation went on around him, he wondered if
he'd been too harsh. Perhaps, he now considered,
Lucy had been born to take chances. Thwarting that
might have altered the original course of her life.

Certainly James knew that Lucy should never
have been as she was now—thin-lipped, a little prim
and more or less constantly cross. He watched her
poke at the fire with an iron and wondered at her
rigid back, her white knuckles. What had become of
his angel of light? She was twenty-six now, a mother
and the wife of a prominent journalist. Only twenty-
six, yet her silver-blonde hair seemed to have dulled.
Could she possibly be greying? The thought saddened James profoundly.

"Well, will we, Dada?" His baby, seventeen-year-old Ingrid, still called him by the old pet name.

"Will we what?"

"Go to the social?" Though her face was plain, Ingrid was pretty enough when her expression was animated by excitement.

"What social?"

"Really, James Shawn. You might at least get your mind off politics and give us your loving attention for a few hours. Is it too much to ask?" Helen's tone was bantering, but as always he detected a slight edge of hostility in her teasing. Perhaps Thomas Kilmaine had heard it too, for he looked oddly at his mother-in-law.

Ingrid told her father that a messenger from town had come to the farm a week earlier with a special invitation for the whole family from Reverend Strickland to attend an open house on New Year's Day celebrating completion of the Unitarian Church's new parish hall.

"Reverend Strickland continues to prosper, I gather," James commented.

"And he's taken a wife," gossiped Ingrid. "Her name is Beatrice." She giggled and covered her mouth.

Even Helen could not suppress a smile. "Mrs. Strickland is a lady from New York and quite impressive, we are told."

"Well, in that case, I shall look forward to meeting her on New Year's Day."

Almost knocking Thomas over, Ingrid jumped up from her place and ran around the table to kiss James noisily on the head. "Thank you, Dada!" She whirled on her mother. "May I wear the blue dress with the white ribbons?"

Helen compressed her lips. "You won't go at all

unless you can control your frivolity." She dabbed at some crumbs on the tablecloth with her index finger. "Anyway, I don't know why we all have to go running into Amoset when this is the first chance we've had to have the whole family together since . . . Talley's death. God rest my baby's soul."

"But it's so quiet up here," Ingrid complained.

Helen turned on her. "Don't *you* begin with that! I've heard it from everyone else in my family and I don't want it from you." Delphia began to cry and Thomas tried to comfort her in low tones.

"I don't understand . . ." Ingrid looked at her father for some explanation.

Before James could speak, Helen went on. "I know you've been a bit out of touch with life down in Harpers Ferry, Ingrid. And I know that now that your lungs are better, you really want to. . . ."

"Live, Mama. I want to live."

Helen was going to say something more, but this from Ingrid stopped her. She looked at everyone. Delphia was squalling, but otherwise the room seemed awkwardly silent.

"I'm going for a walk." Lucy opened the door, letting in a cold draft. While the rest of the family had been arguing, she had strapped on snowshoes.

"You shouldn't go into the woods alone," cautioned James, getting up from the table. Thomas stood up too. "Stay where you are, Tom. I've been wanting to talk with Lucy."

"Can I go too?" Ingrid asked, reaching for her coat on the rack near the door.

"Stay with your mother, Ingrid."

"Please?"

Helen touched Ingrid's arm and asked her to help clear the table.

* * *

Lucy was already some distance from the house by the time James caught up to her. The broad paddled-shaped shoes had made her easy to follow.

"Where are you going?" he asked.

"I need to be alone, Papa." The cold air had put roses in her cheeks.

James shook his head. "For once I am not going to honor your wishes, Lucy."

She smiled at him wryly. "Don't you know I'm a grown woman? When will you stop riding herd on me?"

He smiled back. "Never."

They walked single file through the black and white woods. It had snowed the night before, and with its burden of winter, the forest possessed a purer beauty than summer's ripe cascade. James thought he could see the outline of trees and shrubs more clearly than he ever had before. Some were fan-shaped, others tall and angular. There were a thousand different configurations. Black on white. It was all so simple and yet far more complicated than he ever had realized.

"You are quiet this morning, Papa."

"I want to honor your need to be alone with your thoughts."

"What were you thinking of? Your expression was . . . peaceful. Not politics, I'll wager."

"I was thinking of how much I love this farm, this mountain. And especially in winter."

"I feel the same, Papa."

They went on to the lookout in silence. It was a wide, rocky outcropping that afforded a panoramic view of the mountains to the west of Amoset. Today, however, there was nothing to see, for the mountains were obscured by low, wet clouds of sleet and snow.

"I think we're in for a hard winter," James observed as he surveyed the threatening scene. "It'll be rough on those in the Gully."

"Why do you worry about them, Papa? They can't vote. They're not your constituents."

In the Massachusetts State Legislature, James had made quite a reputation for himself when it came to what many called the "Irish Problem." To James' mind there was no problem. He was in favor of hiring the Irish because he felt that only by working side by side with Yankees would they be assimilated into the population. And when that happened, when the Irish were given the chance they deserved at America's dream, James told his fellow legislators there was no end to what they would accomplish in time. "They're a smart lot, Lucy. Don't make the mistake of underestimating our Irish brothers and sisters. Not only are they smart, they also are shrewd. They'll be able to vote one day and when they do, they'll vote for someone who's been a friend in the past."

Lucy tilted her head. "Are you always so conniving, Papa?"

"I like my work, Lucy. I'm good at what I do. I hope to stay in the government as long as I'm useful."

"Thomas has heard rumors . . ."

"That there is talk of the governorship." James shook his head. "I don't want it. I think I can do more good where I am."

James leaned against a vertical sheet of rock that was protected from the wind. Lucy was a little distance away, leaning against the same rock. He watched her profile silhouetted against the white sky for a long time before he asked, "What's troubling you, Lucy?"

She turned her head and stared at him, not answering. He moved toward her, but she stopped him with her outstretched hand. "I'd like to talk, Papa. I need to talk. But not too near, please. I don't want you to look at me too closely." She closed her eyes and sighed. "It is so difficult to pretend when you're in someone else's home. All the familiar hiding places are gone. It's like being exposed to the sun for too long."

"I don't know what you mean, Lucy."

"When I'm at home, in Boston, I do quite well. You know that, Papa. You see Tom and me a good part of the year. You know we seem . . . well, like any other married couple when we're in our own home. But up here everything is out of the ordinary. Even Delphia senses it. She's never so difficult when she's in her own home." Lucy pulled up the fox collar of her cape so that it covered her ears, as if she wanted the garment to engulf her completely. "I feel so guilty, Papa."

"But why, Lucy?"

"Tom is a good man and brilliant in many ways. He deserves better than he's got."

This aggravated James. Though he was fond of his son-in-law, he thought the man was rather humorless and stiff. "You and Delphia are a treasure. He's a damned lucky man!"

She thanked him with a grateful little smile. "I don't love him, Papa. I can't make myself. Inside," her voice dropped to a hoarse whisper, "I am like this world. Cold. Cold."

"Lucy . . ."

"Please stay away." James heard tears in her voice.

"Don't cry, Lucy. It's too cold."

She covered her face with her muffler and for a moment James was reminded again of his seraph. By the flat white light of the winter morning, Lucy's hair was bright again. In her smart plum-colored coat and hat, with her silvery gold hair caught up at the nape of her neck with only a ribbon, she was, although troubled, still a beautiful woman. His heart ached as he thought of her confined in a loveless marriage. It was a fate James Shawn could wish upon no one.

"Is there someone . . . ?" He stopped himself.

"I'm an honorable woman, Papa."

"Of course. I wouldn't even imagine otherwise. But I have often wondered why you married Kilmaine when it seemed quite clear to me that you were in love with Eben Hopewell." He was a blunt-speaking man who said what he thought. "You should have married Hopewell, Lucy."

This appeared to amuse her. "He didn't ask me, Papa." She put a silencing finger to her lips. "Let me tell you how it was with us. It's been over six years now since I saw him and I've never told this story to a living soul except Delphia. When she was an infant, I used to stand over her bed and tell her about Eben and me until finally I realized I was making myself more miserable. So I stopped right away. It's been a long time since I spoke of him."

"Come here to me, Lucy. I'll keep you warm." James could see that she was shivering, but she shook her head firmly, ignoring his outstretched arms.

"I don't want to cry, Papa, and if you comfort me, I know I will." She stared at the snow-covered mountains. "I didn't like him at first. He was Suzannah's brother and a Hopewell. You know how I despised them all. I thought he was like the old man, Martin, all gold-grubbing dirty fingernails, a man who thought he could buy anything. I found out differently. Eben just kept coming back to me no matter how horrid I was, until finally I started listening to my heart instead of my hate. Then I knew he was different and not like the rest of his family. But by then it was too late. He was betrothed to a girl in Savannah. She was only fourteen when their match was set and Eben never was consulted on the matter. He felt he had to marry her. I felt I had to marry Tom."

"But you didn't have to!"

"Have you forgotten how hard times were for us just then, Papa? Talley'd been dead only a few months. Ingrid was still terribly ill. You had no job and I . . . I had been involved in the labor troubles. I'd had my fill of factory life. Marriage to Tom gave you and Mama enough to help with Ingrid's care and refurbish the farm while you looked for work along the river."

James did recall what those days had been like. He had been nearly driven crazy trying to hide that he was torn in half from the loss of Talley and the sacrifice of Suzannah. For weeks he had thought only of holding himself together and the effort had taken all his emotional energy, leaving him drained and exhausted. He had lost weight and become churlishly silent. He had chopped a dozen cords of wood. Finally, one day as he raised his axe, he had heard an anguished cry. His own. He saw that the axe had slipped from his hand and he fell to his knees, letting his head drop forward until his forehead touched the earth. He had sobbed without restraint there in the forest's kind silence, bidding farewell to his lover and child. When the outburst had come to an end, he wiped his face with the back of his dusty hands, knowing at last that he would survive.

"You were so strange then, Papa. In another world, for some reason."

"So you married Thomas."

"I'm fond of Thomas, Papa. And I respect him greatly. It's just that I feel nothing. I'm so cold."

"What of Eben, I wonder? I've heard nothing about him these last few years."

Lucy laughed. "Now we come to the strangest part of this story." She looked at James. "Two years ago, you might remember, Thomas wrote a series of articles that were sharply critical of the Yankee businessmen who were making fortunes off the South and slavery. Somehow Eben got hold of those articles and wrote my husband to present another point of view. Thomas said the letters were highly persuasive and made him curious to meet the author. The next time Eben was in Boston, they had dinner together and since then they have been fast friends. They write regularly and occasionally meet for dinner when Eben comes north."

"You've followed his history then?"

"I don't know too much about him. I'm afraid to ask too many questions, not wanting Thomas to misjudge my interest. He knows that Eben and I were friends in childhood, but nothing more, of course." Lucy breathed into her mittened hands. "Sooner or later I'll have to see him. I've begged off twice now and I don't think Thomas will tolerate another excuse."

James absorbed this news in silence, rubbing his forehead. Then he shook his head. "When I asked you to confide in me, I think I expected some problem like a skinned knee or a lost shoe. I see now. . . ." He stopped and looked at her. "I must begin treating you like a grown woman, Lucy."

She ran to him and buried her face in the collar of his greatcoat. Feeling her silent sobs against his chest, he held her more tightly. Give them to me, he wanted to say. Give your tears to me, little girl, my darling. Papa will care for everything.

But, of course, he couldn't.

Chapter 9

Because her children had teased her unmercifully about never stepping foot off Cooper's Mountain, Helen Shawn finally relented and agreed to attend the social at the Unitarian Church in Amoset on New Year's Day.

"I declare, Mama, you're getting to be a hermit!" Ingrid shook her finger playfully at Helen. "Watch out or you'll soon be as crazy as old Crazy Edythe!"

"Ingrid! For shame!"

"I only meant . . ."

"I don't care what you meant." Helen Shawn, up to her elbows in a tub of hot sudsy water, didn't stop to look at Ingrid while scolding her, but kept on scrubbing clothes. "I said I would go to the social, so that's the end of it."

"I never meant to upset you, Mama. I only meant. . . ."

"Again, let me say that I do not care what you meant. Edythe Whittington was my friend and she was wise in many ways. I will not hear her maligned."

Thomas, who was standing by the sunny window nearby, leafing through a book, looked over at her with some surprise. "She locked up Martin Hopewell in a cave for almost half a year, Helen. An old friend she might have been, but a saint she was not!"

Helen glared at her son-in-law. Since they were

almost the same age, she could hardly scold him as she did the girls. Still, she thought him disrespectful and would have said as much except that he intimidated her with his city clothes and educated talk. She glanced over at Lucy, who was wringing the clothes for Ingrid to drape across the big wooden drying rack that hung from the kitchen ceiling all winter long.

"What's the matter with you, Lucy?" Helen asked crossly. "You're scowling."

"You have to admit, Mama, this mountain can have a strange effect on a person who stays up here alone too long. You need to see more of the town and be with other folks. You used to be fond of socials, Mama. Remember when we were kids and the whole family would traipse down the hill to Reverend Pike's church? It was fun, wasn't it?"

"Those were the old days."

"You still need some fun, Mama. Laughter and conversation with friends is what you need."

"Lucy's right," declared Ingrid, her voice muffled by a mouthful of wooden clothespins.

Helen didn't answer. She kept her eyes on her work and scrubbed all the harder, leaning her back into the push against the board. Gradually the heavy blue work shirt James had been wearing the night before when he stoked the fire came clean. The water burned her hands and she could feel her pulse throbbing in them as well as in her temple. A hank of greyish-blonde hair fell across her eyes and she blew it back absent-mindedly. She was thinking of what Lucy had said.

This mountain can have a strange effect on you.

It was true. Living for almost forty years on Cooper's Mountain had shaped Helen Shawn into the woman she was as surely as if she had been an artist's creation. She was quiet and stoical and careful and frugal and suspicious because of lessons the mountain had taught her. She resisted change because, like the mountain, she had become solid and fixed in her place.

But she had agreed to leave Cooper's Mountain for a few hours in order to be sociable with Reverend Strickland and his Beatrice. She knew that if she stayed at home the gossips would chew the air and spit out poison at her expense. As it was, she thought they'd have enough to keep them occupied just by making fun of her old-fashioned dress and country manners.

Alone, Helen never thought about how rustic she was. But surrounded by bubbling and self-confident Ingrid, a girl with Talley's bright, risky courage, and the newly elegant Lucy, grown into a Boston lady, Helen was beginning to realize to what extent she was a bumpkin in the modern world of 1842.

I suppose, she thought, that if I moved off the mountain and lived in Amoset or went to Boston with James, I would change as my daughters have.

But she didn't want to change; that was the whole point. It was what made Helen so different from the rest of her family. She never had wanted to change her life. Not for one moment did the charms of the manufacturing city tempt her, nor the social life of a legislator's wife, the Boston parties and bright talk. Not only did she not feel tempted, the very thought of herself in such an environment horrified Helen. She was a country woman, a mountain woman, and she would stay that way until she died.

Though in the early years Helen had fought her children's departure for the mill town, time and a mountain-bred fatalism had quieted her objections. But she couldn't forgive James for abandoning her.

Was the word too harsh? Abandonment meant that he had left her to her own devices and had given up caring for her and for his family. That was certainly not the case. But Helen felt abandoned anyway, for James had succumbed to the lure of the city as if it were another woman he preferred to her.

If they could have been lovers she might not have felt so rejected, but for many years lovemaking had been physically painful for Helen and so they slept apart and almost never touched. With the passage of time and the many separations caused by his work as a legislator, the relationship between Helen and James Shawn had changed from one of intense intimacy to a cool neutrality.

He loves me like a sister now, or one of his daughters. The thought made Helen's eyes sting with sudden tears she could barely force back. All at once she was exhausted. "Finish your father's shirt, Ingrid," she said, wiping her hands on her apron. Her head was throbbing and all she could think of was bed. "I have to rest for a few moments." Ignoring her children's stares, she hurried to the bedroom. As the door slammed behind her, the noise zigzagged through her brain like lightning. She staggered to the narrow bed and fell down on it.

The door opened. It was Lucy. "May I help you, Mama?"

"Leave me alone for a while, that's all."

"Shall I go get Papa from the barn?"

"No. I'll be all right in a while, Lucy." Helen closed her eyes and the sense of mad spinning finally stopped. "Leave me alone, child. Leave me alone."

Beatrice Strickland, late of Boston and New York, was like a large mourning dove: all velvet breast and haughty tail feathers. The coos came out of her in honeyed rushes.

"I'm delighted to meet you, Mistress Shawn. My husband speaks so highly of your family." The women moved a few steps away from the door where James had been trapped, immediately upon entering the hall, by Selectman Stoat. "I hope Senator Shawn is in a talking frame of mind because everyone I know is eager to speak with him." Beatrice Strickland looked at Helen directly. "Your husband is a most important man, Mistress Shawn."

Helen smiled. The expression came easily enough, for despite everything, she was proud of James' work in the General Court. But beyond the smile, which was beginning to be a strain, she could think of nothing to say to Beatrice Strickland.

"The Sunday school children and I spent all afternoon decorating the new hall. Didn't they do a fine job?" Beatrice's cooing was fast becoming the chatter of sparrows. As she and Helen did a slow promenade of the hall that was quickly crowding with guests, a number of these greeted Helen, calling her by name. She had been out of touch for so long a time, however, that none of the faces were very familiar and the names Beatrice supplied were strange.

At one end of the rectangular room a table had been laid with heavy white cloth and decorated with ferns and wild berries. On it were several dozen dishes of food of all kinds. Maple cookies and chocolate fudge and pumpkin cake and apple pandowdy were placed side by side with savory concoctions such as porkpie and turkey sausage.

"Quite a feast, I must say!" Helen admired the plates of carefully prepared and presented food. When her house had been filled with children, she had enjoyed cooking. But now, with only herself to worry about most of the time, she lived on eggs and bread and milk. Anything else, a Sunday chicken, perhaps, or some pork side, was usually too much trouble.

Beatrice preened. "Everyone was most helpful when I told them Senator Shawn would be here. He is truly admired." She pointed at a particularly elegant pie near the center of the table. "Mistress Hathaway even agreed to bring her French cream pie."

Helen blinked. "The mill owner's wife made that?"

Beatrice tittered with laughter until she realized her rudeness. "I beg your pardon, Mistress Shawn, but you are so amusing! Can you imagine anything more unlikely than Mistress Hathaway in the kitchen?" She laughed again and they continued to walk.

After her blunder, Helen was more tongue-tied than ever. She had shown just the countrified ignorance she expected from herself. Now she was glad for Beatrice Strickland's serenade of inconsequentials, because at least they decorated the space left by Helen's total lack of anything to say. When she wasn't chattering, Beatrice had a pleasant, soothing voice that finally calmed Helen, who looked around the room for her children.

Ingrid was beside Lucy near a row of wooden benches set along the church wall side of the hall. For an instant, Helen felt detached enough from both girls to be almost objective. Lucy seemed tired and the somber voile dress she had chosen, of blood-black maroon such as a widowed matron might wear, made her appear gaunt. Her magnificent hair, which could have brightened her face, was entirely hidden beneath a matching turban. The costume was beautifully tailored and at the height of fashion, but Helen felt it didn't suit Lucy to be so stylish. Beside her in a simple new dress of blue wool, even plain little Ingrid looked radiant. And what was she whispering to her sister about anyway? Helen shook her head a little and her lips formed a narrow, critical line.

Had she known what Ingrid was talking about, she would have been a good deal more disturbed than she already was.

"When do you suppose she will arrive, Lucy? Is it fashionable to come early as we did, or later? Later, I think. Am I right? I believe I read it somewhere. Next time, we are going to come late!"

Lucy couldn't help smiling at her sister. She looked around the room, finding Thomas at last. He was where he always stood at parties, in a knot of men discussing politics or emancipation.

"Do you think she'll speak to me?" asked Ingrid, tugging on Lucy's sleeve.

"Suzannah Hopewell Paine is hardly the Queen of England, Ingrid. I'm quite sure she'll speak to you."

"You used to be best friends. Tell me what she's like."

Lucy sighed. Her back hurt and she wanted to be home with Delphia, who was being looked after by one of the girls from the next farm over. Normally Lucy wouldn't have been so concerned, but that morning the child had developed a cough that would have been worrisome at any season. Instinct had told her to stay at home, but another instinct that was perhaps more basic to Lucy's personality had overridden it. Though she would never have let on, Lucy was as excited at the prospect of seeing Suzannah as Ingrid was.

It had been more than five years since they had

seen each other and that had been facing one another
on opposite sides of a labor negotiating table. Years
before then they had been, as Ingrid had said, best
friends. Lucy could no longer remember the childhood argument that had driven a wedge between the
two girls who had loved and valued one another. But
after that there was a long period she did remember
clearly. A time when Lucy hated Suzannah. Lucy had
been a mill operative in those days and a leader in an
organization called the Spindle Sisters. The young
women had fought for better working conditions for
the operatives. The dislike Lucy had felt for Suzannah in those distant times had seemed necessary, but
after many years away from Amoset and the mill environment, there was no longer any point to it. Lately
she had begun to wonder about her old friend. Was
she happy? Did motherhood appeal to her? What was
it like to be a woman and have charge of the mill?

"There she is!" whispered Ingrid, clutching her
sister's arm.

"Just watch yourself, Ingrid. If Mama finds
out. . . ."

"She has to know soon enough, Lucy. I mean to
do it."

Suzannah stood in the arch between the cloak-
room and the hall as Reverend Strickland slipped a
fur-lined cape off her shoulders.

"She's beautiful," whispered Ingrid, clutching her
sister again. "I thought she was old."

"She's only twenty-eight."

Suzannah wore a costume of velvet and wool in a
sandy color that suited her well. A snugly tailored
brocade waistcoat covered the bodice. Her dark
brown hair was swept back and worn high, without
the distracting little cascades of temple curls that
fashionable women were affecting, and the finely

chiseled bones of her face were subtly prominent. Her most striking feature, eyes as luminous as green moons, seemed larger and brighter than Lucy had remembered.

Beside her stood a boy whom Lucy took to be Patrick, Travis Paine's son, but the boy didn't look at all like his father. What took Lucy's breath away for a moment was his resemblance to Suzannah's side of the family, Eben particularly. The coloring was wrong, the body was wrong, but the eyes and the brooding line of the brow were the same and were enough to make Lucy's heart pound foolishly. Since her conversation a few days earlier with her father at the lookout, she had been thinking of Eben more and more. He was so much with her now that she had grown increasingly irritated with Thomas. Every distraction only reminded her the more painfully that Eben was far away and no one to her, while Thomas was real, her husband and the father of Delphia.

Chapter 10

"Lucy, how good to see you!" Suzannah's smile was genuine as she came toward her friend with her arms outstretched. "I believe our last meeting was in the old common room where this hall now stands." She touched Patrick's shoulder. "Patrick, I would like you to meet an old friend of mine. We played together as children. Mrs. Kilmaine is her name and her family comes from Cooper's Mountain. Senator Shawn is her father."

As the six-year-old lad bowed stiffly from the waist with perfect good manners, he grinned at Lucy and his eyes crinkled at the corners. Something undefinable in his expression surprised and alarmed her. Patrick Paine had the appearance of an ordinary Yankee boy and there was nothing in his looks to move or disturb her, yet her feeling was real and she couldn't shake it. Her discomfort went unnoticed, however, as Ingrid was chattering gaily for both of them.

"I got your letter just the day before I left Harpers Ferry, Mrs. Paine. I'm so glad I didn't miss it." Ingrid twisted one long, light brown ringlet around and around her index finger.

"I'm glad, too, Ingrid. And you look wonderfully well."

"Oh, indeed, ma'am. My lungs are completely healed." Her cheeks shone with excitement.

"Teaching school won't be easy."

"I know that, ma'am."

"Many of the children are like your own sweet brother, Talley. They have no real desire to learn, but their parents force them to attend. Can you manage, Ingrid?"

"Oh, yes, ma'am. I think I'll make a good schoolteacher."

"She has talked of nothing but teaching at the mill school since I arrived home."

"Your mother is agreeable then?" Suzannah glanced about the room as she spoke.

Ingrid twisted her ringlet tighter and chewed the inside of her lip.

"My mother is as yet uninformed of Ingrid's plans," said Lucy after a moment's silence.

"But I'm planning to tell her soon. Tonight, I hope. I've just been waiting for the right time."

"Do you think she'll disapprove, Lucy?" asked Suzannah.

Lucy raised her brows and smiled a little. "It seems likely."

"But I'll convince her, Mrs. Paine. I really will. When she knows how much I want to teach, she'll give her permission. She has to. For Talley's sake."

At this second mention of Talleyrand, Lucy realized what it was about Patrick Paine that troubled her. Though clearly a Hopewell, he was rather like Talley had been at the same age.

"Is there something the matter, Lucy?" Suzannah asked.

Lucy blushed and ruffled Patrick's shaggy blond hair. "A silly thought. It's just that your son reminds me of Talley for some reason." Before Suzannah could reply, she went on, "Did you know that Thomas and I have a daughter? Her name is Delphia."

"What a beautiful name. And is she very pretty?"

"We think so." Lucy smiled. "But then, we are noted for our bias."

"So much has happened, Lucy. I want you to know," Suzannah paused a moment, looking for words that would honestly express her complicated feelings, "I regret the ways our lives have grown apart. We had such a thrilling childhood. We were so brave!"

Lucy smiled. "It was all so simple then."

"Had we but known it."

The two women nodded, smiled, then looked away from one another, embarrassed by their sudden intimacy after so long a time.

The new parish hall was crowded and noisy with the sound of many voices laughing and talking. In the corner, a fiddler had struck up a tune and several young couples were making lines for a reel. Standing near the punch bowl with his son-in-law and some of the local gentlemen, James Shawn pretended to listen to their talk of Abolition while his eyes roamed the room. He watched Helen in a corner with Beatrice Strickland and some other women he did not recognize. The smile he saw painted on his wife's face was intended to conceal an almost immobilizing social awkwardness. He watched as she dipped her head up and down repeatedly in response to a question and saw her hands twisting together like snakes in her lap. James sympathized with Helen in her discomfort, but the shyness that characterized her visits off the mountain he took to be a kind of stubborn unwillingness to admit into her life any form of change, any challenge.

The men's conversation recaptured his attention.

"You know I think well of Suzannah Paine. She's

taken a man's hard job and done it well. I'll give her credit for that," said mill owner Hathaway.

"But she's a mite of trouble to us all," complained Mr. Stoat, one of the selectmen who administered the affairs of Amoset.

"How is that?" James' tone was neutral and his eyes scanned the room again.

"She's too damned independent, that's how." Selectman Stoat was a rotund little man with thick, curling mutton chop sideburns and heavy eyebrows that bobbed up and down as he spoke. "And she refuses to hire the Irish."

"Which makes all the rest of us look bad. If the Yankee girls would work for as little as the Irish, I'd be more than happy to hire them back." Hathaway twirled the ends of his mustache. "Not all of us have a steady flow of raw cotton coming up from the South every week."

"Slave-picked cotton," commented another gentleman disgustedly.

"But surely this recession has hurt Mrs. Paine as much as anyone," observed Thomas.

Stoat shook his head. "How could it? I'm not Hopewell's banker, but it stands to reason their family has plenty of money, what with manufacturing up here and cotton and rice and railroads down in Georgia."

"Railroads?" James didn't know there were Hopewell railroads.

"Haven't you heard? In a few months' time, a year at the most, Eben Hopewell will toss the first shovel of coal into an engine set to travel two hundred miles into Cherokee country. He and his partner financed the line."

"Georgia is a boom state now that the Indians are

gone," remarked Thomas. "Their lands have been opened up for farming."

Hathaway went on. "Anyway, the rest of us are just manufacturers. How can we compete with men like Eben Hopewell and women like her unless we hire Irish?"

"Well, I don't like it," insisted Mr. Sharkey, the owner of a wool mill on the Amoset River. "Suzannah Paine makes us all look bad for hiring immigrant labor at cheap rates, yet the high salaries she pays her Yankee women come from the sweat of Negro slaves." Sharkey spat into the brass cuspidor to the left of him. "Disgusts me, it does. I'd like to see a boycott on Southern cotton."

"That would hurt all of us, Sharkey," Hathaway pointed out. "After all, I get a fifth to a quarter of my raw materials out of New Orleans twice a year."

"You're more honest than most, Mr. Hathaway," commented Thomas. "Most Northern manufacturers don't care to admit the extent to which they are dependent on the institution of slavery."

The conversation continued along this line and James let his attention drift away yet again. The room was now so crowded that it was impossible to see everyone. From time to time, through the milling guests, he caught sight of Lucy and Ingrid and beside them. . . .

As an overcast day may become suddenly bright from the random movement of clouds, all at once the room cleared and James saw Suzannah standing directly across from him, her dark head bent toward Lucy. In that instant he ceased to hear the talk of slaves and mills, the scrawing of the fiddles, the laughing, gossiping guests. It was as if the room suddenly had emptied and there were only the two of them, enclosed in a field of intense white light. From across the room, Suzannah turned and caught his glance. They stared at one another and in the room, in Amoset, in all the world and across the stars, only the two of them existed.

"Excuse me," James interrupted, without so much as glancing at Thomas, Hathaway or the others. His heart pounded; his palms were moist. He had an absurd desire to weep, so glad was he to discover that in the years they had been apart Suzannah had become more beautiful and the chemistry between them more volatile. He strode through the crowd to where she stood with Lucy and Ingrid and. . . . He stopped in the middle of the room. Other guests greeted him and shook his hand, but he was unaware of them. His eyes darted from Suzannah, who was smiling at him faintly, to the boy at her side. The boy who must be his son.

"Father," called Lucy, seizing his hand and drawing him into the group, "here is Suzannah Hopewell. Suzannah Paine, I should say."

He bowed carefully, his eyes never leaving Suzannah's face.

"It has been many years, Mr. Shawn," she said, extending her hand. "I have followed your career with admiration."

"Then I am assured of your vote, Mrs. Paine?"

"Forever."

Ingrid laughed. "I hope Dada doesn't stay in politics for that long. Mama couldn't bear it."

Suzannah ignored the girlish interruption. "I want you to meet Patrick, my son."

The boy stared up at the big man introduced to him as Senator Shawn and seemed to take the measure of him. He held himself erect as he had been told a proper young man must, and in perfect imitation of his elders, he held out his hand.

"Good day, sir," he said. The two shook hands solemnly.

"Isn't that cute?" cried Ingrid. Impulsively she leaned down and swooped Patrick into her arms. "Remember, Lucy, how Talley used to try to be so manly? Even when he was little like Patrick." She squeezed him tightly. "Will you come to my school and learn your letters, Patrick Paine?"

The boy looked uncomfortable, but he was too well bred to protest Ingrid's embrace.

"School?" James looked closely at Ingrid. "What are you hatching, my girl?"

"Ingrid has been hired to teach at the mill school," Suzannah explained quickly. "I've told her she may begin as soon as she wishes."

"Does your mother know this, Ingrid?"

"Don't tell her, Dada, please. I will. I promise I can make her understand." Ingrid put Patrick down and smoothed the front of her dress. "You don't mind if I do it?"

James couldn't answer so quickly. On the one hand, he perfectly understood and sympathized with Ingrid's desire to become part of the world away from Cooper's Mountain, nevertheless he couldn't suppress an angry disappointment as he imagined Helen's reaction to the news. He had hoped Ingrid would stay on the farm and be the home-child her mother craved. All at once and for a dozen different reasons, life seemed unfairly harsh to James Shawn.

"Girls," he said, "I would like to speak with Mrs. Paine alone for a moment. Ingrid, will you take Patrick to get some refreshments?"

The girl looked stricken. "You won't make her take my job away? Please, Dada, I couldn't bear it."

Seeing her sister almost in tears, Lucy added anxiously, "You wouldn't, would you, Papa?"

"I don't want to hear any more about the job or about what I may or may not do. Is that clear, Ingrid?"

"Yes, Dada," she replied, turning to go. At the last minute, she suddenly pirouetted. "But it wouldn't be fair. You let Lucy go and then Talley. . . ."

"That will do, Ingrid," interrupted Lucy, glancing warily at her father's darkening face. She took Patrick's hand. "Come along, Patrick. We'll find some of Mrs. Hathaway's cream pie for you."

When they were gone, Suzannah and James, with unspoken understanding, moved to a more secluded corner of the church hall where they could talk with less chance of interruption. Even so, neither of them could forget the crowded room, and to avoid calling attention to themselves, they made a point of standing far apart and in casual postures.

"You won't make her give up the job, will you, James?"

"Of course not. But she'll have to fight her mother for it. I won't intervene on her behalf."

"That seems harsh to me."

He laughed a little. "What seems harsh is that Helen must once again be alone and just at a time when she is hopeful of a little company."

At the mention of Helen Shawn's name, Suzannah's expression hardened. "How is Mrs. Shawn?"

"As ever. She is here tonight."

James wanted to say so much to Suzannah, but in that public place with all the noise about them it was impossible. He wanted her to know that despite the years of separation between them and the hopelessness of their future, he still loved her as he had loved no woman since his life began and expected to die loving her. He wanted to say to her that to have known her in secret, in the darkness of his Marivale cabin, was not enough, but more than most men dared dream of. Instead he said, "Patrick is a fine boy."

Suzannah's face brightened. "And sweet and smart, too."

"He has the Hopewell brow. A touch of melancholy."

"But in so many ways, James, I see you in him," she said softly. "Sometimes you are there in his expression and I wonder that the whole world doesn't comment on the similarity." She swallowed hard and looked away.

"I want us to be friends, Suzannah."

"What do you mean?"

"I mean that there never can be anything else between us. I am a married man and you . . . ?"

"I am sure Travis is still alive. I believe I will know in my heart if anything should happen to him."

"We can only be friends, Suzannah. That's all there is for us. But it can be a great deal. We've been apart too long and now I want to see you and know Patrick."

"Is it only Patrick that draws you back to me?"

"Suzannah. . . ."

"I forgive you if it is," she cut in quickly. "I'm older now, I know, and less attractive to you."

"You are beautiful and I will always love you and want you. But it's impossible. You understand that, don't you?" James forgot himself and as he spoke, he leaned forward. They were so close he could feel the strands of Suzannah's hair touch his cheek and the perfume of her skin filled his nostrils.

"Be careful, James," she whispered. It would have been wise to step away from him, but she couldn't bear to break the moment.

"Say you understand, Suzannah. Say we can be friends."

She sighed, staring at her hands. "I've done well without you. I've made the pain go away; I've forced it back. Now all of a sudden I hurt again."

"If ever I can help you, Suzannah, you must swear that you will come to me. Do you understand? Swear it." He gripped her arm.

"Don't touch me, James." His hand dropped. "I can't bear it."

"Swear."

She nodded, still staring at her hands. When she lifted her eyes they were full of tears. "I couldn't have survived these years without Patrick and my work at the mill. During the day my hours are full. Even in the beginning, I scarcely thought of you when I was tending the business. And having Patrick has been like having a part of you that belongs to me alone and cannot be taken away by anyone. Not even Helen Shawn."

"My God, I am such a villain." It was James' turn to look away.

"You are no more that than I am bad. I only tell you this to let you know that I am . . . in a way . . . content now without you. Of course I'll be your friend. But if I seem cool to your suggestion, it's because I have fought for what peace of mind I have and I mean to keep it. I was a girl when we loved and parted. The hearts of girls mend easily enough where there's a will. But I'm not a girl now and another test of our love would destroy me, James." She looked at him and her green eyes had a hard, metallic brightness. "I won't be destroyed by love, James. Before I let that happen, I'll turn my back on you forever."

Chapter 11

Riding home at dusk in the sleigh, Ingrid wrapped herself in a woolen blanket against the cold and ignored the conversation of her family. Muffled up to her ears in warmth, she alternately daydreamed about being a teacher and dreaded the time when she would have to tell her mother of her plans. She expected tears and accusations, but the fear of these was not enough to dissuade her from the course of work she had been planning for many years. Ingrid wanted to be a teacher more than anything else in the world. It was this dream that had made her years as an invalid in Harpers Ferry tolerable.

She was eight when she was sent away from her family to live with the Davis clan in West Virginia. All her short life she had suffered from weak lungs and it was the opinion of the doctors that she would not survive her childhood if she stayed in Amoset, where the humid summers and long, damp winters aggravated her condition.

The Davis family had been recommended by Reverend Strickland as upstanding and trustworthy. A few years earlier, Malcolm Davis had left Marivale, the village downriver from Amoset, moving his family to Harpers Ferry, West Virginia, to begin a lumber business. The forest around Harpers Ferry was noted for its stands of magnificent timber. With all the cash he could borrow as well as the family's savings, Malcolm Davis purchased a monstrous, unpathed acreage of black walnut, maple, oak and cedar.

The first years were slow, demanding hard work from everyone in the family. Malcolm and his wife Janet were glad for their six strong sons who worked in the forest and mill from dawn until moonrise during clement weather, but Janet was lonely. She missed her Marivale friends and longed for a daughter to work in the cabin beside her. She became pregnant and produced a seventh son. A year later, the day before her fortieth birthday, she was delivered of son number eight and was told what she already knew—she could bear no more children.

It was at about this time, early in the 1830s, that the Davis lumber concern began to flourish and finally the family could afford to send Janet back to Marivale for a visit. Since the birth of her eighth son, she had been weepy and distracted. Her menfolk, returning from a long day's work, would find the hearth cold and Janet asleep or, what was worse, lying open-eyed on her bed, staring at the ceiling. So Malcolm sent her back to Marivale, hoping the trip would enliven her.

While she was staying with her sister, she had occasion to attend Reverend Strickland's church, where she heard of the plight of young Ingrid Shawn. She volunteered to take the child home with her, for a small remuneration, of course. And so it was that Janet Davis returned to Harpers Ferry, smiling and enthusiastic, with the little girl she had longed for.

Though Ingrid had tried to be helpful and companionable, Janet was a difficult woman to please. When Ingrid, as frequently happened, would suffer a relapse, the woman blamed her and didn't bother to conceal her resentment at having to care for a sick child as well as nine men and boys.

Now, as Ingrid rode home from the social in the long winter twilight, even the voices of her family could not distract her from her memories. She loved her parents too much to tell them how she had suffered in the Davis home. They had sent her to strangers in the belief that it was the only way she could be saved and she had paid the high price of loneliness.

Janet Davis had devised two ways of dealing with Ingrid. When the girl was well and able to help in the house, Janet treated her kindly, even affectionately. When she was ill, however, Janet ignored her except to bring in her food, and this she did grudgingly. Ingrid's clothes were rarely washed unless she had the energy to do it herself and her bedclothes went unchanged for weeks when she lay feverish.

If it had not been for the books Lucy sent to her sister once or twice a month, the years would have been intolerable and surely Ingrid would have pined away and died. But Ingrid discovered early on that there were worlds of escape between the covers of books. She would read the volumes her sister sent her over and over until, in some cases, she had memorized whole pages.

It was when her brother Talleyrand was killed in a mill accident that Ingrid decided she wanted to be a teacher. She thought that she could do some good by passing on her love of learning to boys and girls who might otherwise be condemned to spend their lives in the gloom of mills and factories. This ambition assuaged her grief and she set about learning all she could. The big, loudmouthed Davis boys teased her for being a bookworm, but one by one she taught them to read and to write their names. She knew that since she had success with them, she could teach anything to anyone.

When the doctor in Harpers Ferry pronounced her lungs completely strong, Ingrid wrote to Suzannah Hopewell Paine and boldly asked for work at the mill school that had been established after Talley's death. Though she had no formal education, Ingrid knew her letter was well written and composed. She described herself, her life and her aspirations and then prayed every night that her dream of being a teacher would come true.

And now it had. But there remained one obstacle before Ingrid could rest easily; she must win her mother's blessing. Beside this formidable task, all the other challenges in her life seemed insignificant. She knew that her mother would be desperately hurt when she learned of her intention. Ingrid also knew that, in trying to conceal her hurt, Helen would be cruel. But the girl was determined to have her own way in this matter despite the problems involved. Not once had she seriously considered sacrificing her dream and settling into life beside her mother on Cooper's Mountain.

On the morning following the social, Lucy and Thomas went into the barn with James to help him finish winterizing the old structure. At breakfast there had been some talk of a new barn, but that would have to wait until the spring; meanwhile the hay was getting wet and the chickens wouldn't roost in the damp hencoop. While her parents worked out of doors, Delphia stayed in the farmhouse with Helen and Ingrid. As the women made bread on the long oak table, she toddled after a toy made from a spool and gabbed happily to herself in amusing baby talk.

Twice Ingrid tried to tell her mother about her job, but twice she lost heart. It was painfully clear that Helen enjoyed having her around the house and Ingrid was a kindly girl who could not knowingly give pain to anyone, least of all her mother.

Nevertheless, she ventured into the subject a third time.

"You have something on your mind, girl," her mother said, looking up from the mound of dough she was kneading. "You've been stammering like Delphia for the last half-hour. What is it?"

"I saw Suzannah Paine last night."

"So did we all. Very much the grand lady, I must say." Helen said this with a supercilious curl to her upper lip that, for a moment at least, effectively silenced Ingrid.

"I like her, Mama," she offered finally. "And her little boy is very sweet. He reminds me a bit of Talley."

Helen pounded her fists into the dough, flipped it and pounded again.

"You know, they haven't had a teacher for the children at the mill for quite a while. The girl who was teaching there got diphtheria and had to leave Amoset, and because times were so hard, they didn't replace her."

Helen glanced at her daughter. "Why are you telling me all this? You know I don't care a fig for the affairs of Amoset. That place has brought only grief to me and mine." Placing the dough in a large bowl, she covered it with a damp cloth and set the bowl on a shelf to the right of the fireplace. "Is yours ready?" she asked, turning back.

"I'll hurry, Mama," Ingrid answered, tackling the dough with more energy. But Helen suddenly felt impatient with Ingrid's methods and nudged her aside to work the dough herself.

"I don't know what that Davis woman was thinking of when she taught you how to bake bread. It's a wonder your loaves don't float, they're so full of air." Her face set in grim determination, Helen did the work she thought her daughter couldn't do.

Tears sprang to Ingrid's eyes as she looked on. She felt like a dolt. No matter how she steeled herself, Helen's gruff and opinionated manner hurt. Ingrid realized all of a sudden that if she stayed with her mother on the mountain, it would always be like this. Unless she asserted herself now, she would be forced into a child's inferior role forever.

"I have a job at the mill school," Ingrid blurted out.

Helen stopped moving.

"Suzannah Paine is reopening the school and I will be the teacher." Ingrid held her breath.

"You?" First Helen looked incredulous and then she began to laugh. "What do you know?"

Ingrid flushed. "A lot, Mama. I've taught myself numbers and geometry and . . ."

"Whatever that is."

"And I can read and write as well as anyone. Better, perhaps."

"Well, you can't go. I don't care if you've been down to Harvard and Yale, I won't let you leave this mountain. And there's the end to it." Helen slammed the dough on the floured table top.

"I've given my word, Mama."

"I don't care. You will just have to un-give it."

"But they are counting on me at the mill. There are students waiting to learn. You have to let me go!"

"I don't have to do anything." Helen put the dough into a second bowl, covered it and placed it beside the other on the high shelf.

"Please, Mama. . . ."

Wheeling on her daughter, Helen grabbed her

shoulders. "I've heard enough of this, Ingrid. It seems I've been arguing with my family about Amoset for my whole life and I am determined not to do it again. I've lost one baby to that place and I will not let you go down there and be destroyed!"

"I know you hurt from Talley, Mama. We all do. But believe me, the mill school is completely safe. And teaching is an honorable profession. I'll make you proud, Mama."

"I don't care about pride! I only want you healthy and here at home with me!"

"But there's nothing up here!" Ingrid wailed, pulling out of her mother's grasp. She saw her life before her and it was miserable, lonely, decrepit. "I want to meet people and have adventures. I've spent my whole life locked up in the Davis house. Please understand me, Mama. I must go. I must!"

"If you leave Cooper's Mountain, there is no need for you to come back. Ever. Is that clear?" Helen did not look at her daughter. As she delivered this ultimatum, she busied herself about the kitchen.

"That's not fair! You didn't say that to Lucy when she went down to the mill. Or to Talley. Or to Dada."

"You are my baby. The only one I have left. If you go, I don't want to hear about you or know what terrible things will happen to you."

"Nothing horrible will happen. I'll live in a boarding house and teach school. Nothing more."

"I don't care what you say. If you leave Cooper's Mountain. . . ."

Ingrid's voice was louder, higher. "I must go there, Mama! I made a promise."

Helen threw down her dishcloth and faced Ingrid squarely, her expression fixed in rigid lines that aged and disfigured her. "You've decided then. Go pack your box."

"I don't have to go yet, Mama."

"I want you out."

"But . . ."

"Out!" The woman screamed and, rushing at Ingrid, she struck out at her with her flour-covered hands.

At that moment the door opened and James stepped into the farmhouse. Slamming the door behind him, he hurried over and pulled his wife and daughter apart. "What's going on here?" he cried. "Why are you fighting in front of Delphia? Look. You've made her cry."

Neither woman had noticed that during their argument Delphia had been growing increasingly upset.

"Don't blame me!" Helen cried. "Blame Amoset! Blame Suzannah Hopewell Paine!" She ran to the bedroom, but the door had no sooner banged shut than it opened again.

James stood in the doorway. "Explain your meaning, woman."

"Leave me alone. Go help your baby daughter pack. She's leaving. But then, I suppose you knew that. I suppose I'm the only one who was kept in ignorance."

For a long moment Helen and James stared at one another. He wanted to touch her, caress her into easiness, but they had long ago lost the habit of touching one another so he stayed in the doorway and she stayed where she was, facing him, her expression fierce and unyielding.

"She's seventeen," he said at last. "And too smart to waste on either the farm or the factory." His voice softened. "Let her go. Let her go, Helen."

"Why do you want to give all my children to that woman?"

"You're speaking nonsense, Helen."

"I'm not and you know it. First Lucy and then Talley and now Ingrid. What is it about Suzannah Hopewell that my children all want to leave me for her?"

"It's naught to do with her. Our children want work. They want to be part of the new order, progress. You can't blame them, Helen."

She sneered. "I don't blame them. I blame you." Before he could respond, she went on. "You could have made them stay. When Lucy decided she was going down to be an operative, you could have stopped her."

"I tried, Helen. But I can't stop change. No one can." He took a step forward.

"Lucy was always your favorite. She wanted to leave the farm and you let her because you've never been able to say no to her."

"That's not true, Helen."

"It is. You know it is. You used to call her your silver-haired angel, and if she had wanted a king's fortune, you would have found a way to get it. You did anything for her. I always was second in your life."

James was stunned. "You turned your back on me, Helen. Remember? You wouldn't see a doctor. You rejected me. You preferred . . ."

"You had finished with me long before that, James Shawn," she cut in. "The truth is, I never really had you to myself since we were married. I took a while learning to be a wife and by the time I'd stopped being a scared little girl, Lucy had come along. How could I compete with a silver-haired angel?"

"I loved you, Helen," James whispered.

She spat on the floor between them. "I care nothing for your love."

"You don't mean that."

Her laugh bordered on hysteria. "Oh, don't I?"

"Helen. . . ." The light in her eyes, the thin screech of her voice, the hysterical laughter—he wondered if his wife had become a bit mad. As Lucy had said, the mountain did strange things to people.

"You can get out too," she yelled at him. "Go back to Boston and the work you love. Take your baby daughter down and give her away to Suzannah Hopewell Paine. Do whatever you like. I don't want or need any of you."

Chapter 12

When Lucy Shawn had gone down to Amoset in
1832, the boarding house owned and operated by
Hannah Quinn had been recommended to her. There
she had made her home for the years she worked as
an operative in Hopewell Mills. It was at this same
residence that Ingrid sought and found a room. Like
her sister's had been, it was on the top floor and
crowded with the beds and packing boxes of five
other girls. Ten years earlier, the walls had been
freshly painted and the carpet on the stairs less
threadbare. There had been crisp gingham curtains at
the dormer windows and the bedding was kept fresh
and sweet by a handful of servant girls who also
swept the landings daily, cleaned the grates and polished the woodwork, all under Hannah Quinn's stern
command.

By the winter of 1843, however, many changes
had taken place at Hannah Quinn's. The effects of
several years of depression were as visible in her
boarding house as in all the others. As the cost of
providing decent room and board for working women
had increased, owners like Hannah Quinn had begun
to economize. Often three girls were made to sleep in
beds where two were already uncomfortably crowded.
At meals the fare was now simple and starchy, with
meat on the table only three or four times a week.

Fruit was a treat the hard-working women rarely enjoyed.

Though Mrs. Quinn still owned the boarding house, she had given her job of housekeeper to Julia Dewitt, a woman who had lived there since before Lucy Shawn's time. It was Julia who showed Ingrid to her drab room and told her where to put her personal items.

"Meals are served promptly," she said, looking down her long nose at Ingrid. "Breakfast is at four-thirty, midday dinner is from noon to twelve-thirty and supper is at eight. If you're late . . ."

"I won't be." Ingrid spoke quickly, her eyes glowing with an excitement that could not be dulled by the unsmiling Julia.

". . . you'll go without," Julia continued, not to be cheated out of the pleasure of being bossy. "Food is never permitted in the bedrooms. The front door closes and locks at ten and no one is let in after that under any circumstances. There is no foul language permitted here, and no spirits, card-playing or dancing. We keep our voices low. You are expected to attend church every Sunday unless you obtain an excuse from me. If you have any problem with these rules, I suggest you find another place to live now, before you've gone to the trouble of unpacking."

Though once an operative, Julia played her role as housekeeper perfectly. She wore her hair, now streaked with grey, pulled tightly behind her ears. And with access to the kitchen, she had grown stout and lumpy.

"Oh, but I want to live here! My sister stayed here for years. Perhaps you know her." Ingrid was proud. "Lucy Shawn?"

"Of course," Julia replied with a smile that scarcely turned the corners of her mouth. She had supposed this to be so from the moment Ingrid had introduced herself. "I knew her well. Where is she now?"

"Married to the newspaperman, Thomas Kilmaine. They live in Boston and have a little girl."

"And she is happy?"

"Oh yes! She has everything she wants. And Delphia is the dearest little angel in the world. Her hair is just like Lucy's, too, all silver and gold."

"How nice for her. I often have wondered what became of Miss Shawn."

"Were you a good friend?"

Julia waited a moment and then said, "Not quite. We each had our own circle of acquaintances. But I knew her. I knew Lucy Shawn."

Ingrid, off on the subject of her adored sister, heard nothing unusual in Julia's answer. It never had occurred to her that anyone might dislike Lucy. "She was one of the leaders of the Spindle Sisters when they organized the big turnout back in '36. Were you a Spindle Sister?"

"No." Julia pursed her lips. "And I would advise you to stay away from workers' organizations, too. Such activity is forbidden in this house." She turned and left the room.

Ingrid laughed and called after her, "Oh, I won't become involved. After all, I'm a schoolteacher." She stood up straighter when she named her profession.

But Julia, already halfway down the flight of stairs, was not impressed. Over her shoulder she said, "You may be a teacher, but you are also Lucy Shawn's sister."

Leaving Ingrid puzzled by this remark, Julia hurried all the way downstairs and through the hall to the rear sitting room where she found Hannah Quinn, her stocking feet propped up before the coal fire. The years had done little to change her austere appearance, but a crippling arthritis had made walking difficult and painful and she had trouble hearing without an ear trumpet.

"Lucy Shawn's sister has arrived. I put her in the top room with Jerusha and the others."

"Who's come?"

"Lucy Shawn's sister," yelled Julia crossly. "Ingrid Shawn is now a boarder here."

Hannah looked outraged. "I won't have her!" she declared, snapping her toothless gums together like a tortoise.

"We need the money, Mrs. Quinn. We're not at liberty to turn anyone away." Julia poked at the fire, then rang the bell pull for a servant to bring tea.

"Those Shawns are all troublemakers!"

Julia shook her head. "This one is a mouse, I think. She's a teacher at Hopewell's mill school."

"No good comes of pampering those children," muttered the old woman. "That's what's wrong with this country. Young people don't know the meaning of work anymore." She sniffled and scratched herself, rearranging her bony hips on the chair with a sigh as she launched into a lengthy opinion on the causes and cures of the depression that had gripped the economy of New England for several years.

As she droned on, Julia Dewitt stared at the fire, not paying much attention. When Ingrid Shawn had appeared at the door that morning, it had called up recollections of the time when she had known Lucy Shawn and hated her. Had she been asked to explain her hatred, Julia would have said that Lucy was a rule-breaker, a troublesome girl who did what she wanted and spoke her mind too freely. But the true cause for the animosity between them was subtler than that. At a time when Julia had held sway in

Quinn's boarding house, Lucy had appeared. Almost immediately Julia's influence was diminished. She had tried to regain her position by using weapons that had served her well in the past. But Lucy had been unimpressed and unafraid of Julia's sharp, malicious tongue and domineering manner, and the other girls in the boarding house were drawn to her courage. In a matter of a few short months Julia had entirely lost her influential position in the house, despite her obvious seniority.

Now, hearing that Lucy had married an important man and was rearing a daughter, the old and nearly forgotten jealousy rose to the fore once again. As she stared at the fire, Julia recalled the insults, the slights, the times she had been overlooked for fair-haired Lucy. These memories, strengthened by years of lurking in the back of her mind, had the power of fire to burn her anew with envy.

"I don't like it," Hannah Quinn was muttering. "I don't like Shawns."

"Never mind, never mind," Julia responded automatically, reaching out to pat the old woman's arm. "She'll behave herself. I'll see to that."

Or else.

Jerusha Billings was delighted to make Ingrid's acquaintance.

"I knew your sister well!" she cried. "And I loved her, too. I was a very young girl when we met, but, oh, she taught me the looms and how to keep an eye on everything at once. When I began I could hardly manage one and now I supervise five all alone."

"Five looms?" Ingrid was incredulous.

"It's got to be done or there's no money to be made at Hopewell's." Jerusha sighed. "It isn't like it used to be here in Amoset. You can tell your sister that." She grinned and Ingrid realized with surprise that Jerusha was, despite her many years' seniority at Hopewell Mills, still a very young woman.

"How old were you when you came to work here?" she asked.

Jerusha laughed. "I told McMahon—he was the overseer in the early days—that I was fifteen, but really I had just passed my fourteenth birthday when I went into the weaving room."

So, thought Ingrid, this assured young woman is only twenty years old. Was it possible that in three years' time in the city she would be as poised and confident? Ingrid doubted it, for she was at an age, neither adult nor child, when youth seemed an eternal burden.

Jerusha continued to chatter as she helped Ingrid unpack her small box of possessions. There were a pair of workaday dresses, a meeting dress, a scooter bonnet, a coat, an extra pair of shoes, pairs of hose and some books and writing implements. "When I first came to Amoset, the town was famous all around the world. We had lending libraries and self-improvement circles, a literary magazine, a lecture forum, discussion groups. It was wonderful back then!"

"You don't like it now?"

"I wouldn't say that I dislike it, but all the mill towns are changing since the owners began to hire Irish. There're only two lending libraries left on this side of town and my friend Meredith, she knew Lucy too, says the literary magazine won't last another season. The mill operatives aren't as keen on learning as they used to be. Many can't read or write. Some can scarcely speak the language!"

Ingrid held up two books, *Pierpont's National Reader* and *Colburn's Arithmetic*. "I intend to change all that," she grinned.

Jerusha looked doubtful. "You'd make more money in the mill. Right now I can count on almost two dollars a week over room and board. What does Suzannah Paine promise you?"

Ingrid wasn't to be discouraged. "Thirty cents a week plus my room here and meals. But money isn't the thing, you see. I want to teach so that boys and girls who come to the mill when they are eight or nine will have a chance to better themselves."

"I wish you well. 'Tis true, the mill can be a trap for little ones. As for me," Jerusha danced away to look at herself in a small oak-framed mirror near the door, "I intend to marry. Perhaps this year."

"You are promised?" The very words thrilled Ingrid. To have a friend who was engaged to be married was certainly a sign that she was entering an exciting new world.

"Promised? Well, not exactly." Jerusha smiled. "But I know the man I want."

"Tell me, please!" cried Ingrid. "I would love to hear about him."

"If you are very nice to me, I may even introduce you."

"He lives in Amoset?"

"No, but he comes here. I look for him in the early spring. 'Twas then I met him last year." Jerusha wet the tip of her index finger and stroked the line of her eyebrows as she admired herself. "He's a preacher."

"A preacher?" Ingrid could not be sure if this was exciting or not.

"But not a stuffy parson like old Strickland, you may be sure. He goes from town to town and everywhere he preaches there are crowds and crowds that turn out to meet him. His name is Thaddeus Temple."

"What a grand name," sighed Ingrid. "And does he love you?"

"Well, not yet, perhaps. But I have no doubt he will. He came perilously close last year. He told me I was like one of the ancient heroines of the Bible, born to beget the children of God." Jerusha hugged herself and did a little pirouette. "And, Ingrid, you should hear his voice. 'Tis like the thunder and the rain combined. And when he sings, I can hear the angels."

"Oh, Jerusha," sighed Ingrid. She sank onto the bed and closed her eyes, imagining Thaddeus Temple in all his glory. Surely and at last the mysteries of life were opening before her.

The next day, Jerusha and Meredith escorted Ingrid to the mill before the ringing of the five a.m. bell. She was taken directly to the counting room where Suzannah had her office and was already at work. In the austere little work space, her dress covered completely by a dark muslin smock, Suzannah was very different in appearance from the grand lady Ingrid had met at Reverend Strickland's social. Ingrid found this businesslike woman more intimidating than that other Suzannah. She held her hands behind her back to conceal their trembling.

"Are you ready to begin today?" Suzannah asked. Without waiting for an answer, she went on. "I will announce that classes can begin tomorrow for those who want them. That will give you all of today to arrange the room and plan your lessons." She handed Ingrid a sheet of paper. "Here are the names of your students. As you see, they vary in ages and few of them have any abilities. A formidable job lies ahead of you, Ingrid."

"I know, ma'am."

But did she? Later, when Ingrid was alone in the schoolroom, a section of a storehouse in the mill yard that had been partitioned off for the purpose, she was assailed by doubts. Her confidence evaporated as she looked about the room at the tables and benches and slates that were her equipment. In less than twenty-four hours, seven boys and girls would be seated opposite the big old teacher's desk that Suzannah had provided, and they would expect her to teach them. Ingrid Shawn, who had never attended a day of school in her life!

She sat at the desk and burst into tears. Before she had even begun, Ingrid feared the task was hopeless. She would make a fool of herself and be forced to return to the farm on Cooper's Mountain, bearing the burden of failure. She would bring ridicule to her family and herself. Worst of all, the boys and girls who looked to her for help would be gravely disappointed. The more she thought of the job to be done, the more terrible she felt.

However it was too frigid in the storeroom to sit still and cry for long. Very shortly Ingrid's hands and feet were so cold that she had to get up and stoke the fire in the iron stove. When she had warmed herself for a few moments and watched the glowing flames, she felt more confident. As she drew water and scrubbed the table tops and benches, she hummed a little tune, and by the time she got to the sweeping, she was singing aloud in a way she did only when she was at her most happy and confident.

Once the room was cleaned thoroughly and most of the old storeroom smell was gone, Ingrid sat at the desk and, with her hands in gloves, her shoulders covered by a shawl and a woolen scarf looped around her ankles, began to plan her lessons by lamplight.

Ingrid was a great success as a teacher at the mill school. The children liked her immediately and she returned their affection. In every little face she saw her brother, and this inspired her to the patience her job required. The long hours did not trouble her and as the weeks passed, she made many friends among the mill operatives who lived at Quinn's boarding house, so that at work or leisure her hours were filled with stimulating activity. She thought often of her mother living alone on Cooper's Mountain and wanted to use her few free hours for a visit. But that year's heavy winter snow made the excursion impossible unless she were to hire a sleigh. For a woman earning thirty cents a week over room and board, this expense was unthinkable, so she concentrated all her thoughts and energies on her challenging new life.

It was, after all, what Ingrid had dreamed of.

Chapter 13

Amoset had a record snowfall in January of 1843. That month Valentine Hopewell and his crew of Irish laborers were kept busy most days of the week, plowing and shoveling the streets of the town. Then, near the end of January, there was a false spring. Suddenly streets with any slope to them became rivers of melted snow. There was mud everywhere, but at night, when the temperature dipped below freezing, there was ice.

For the Irish in the Gully, that winter was a time of suffering and hardship equal to any they had suffered in Ireland. The weight of the snow caused roofs to collapse on sleeping children and flimsy walls caved in beneath snow banks ten feet deep, burying whole families. Icicles hung from the eaves like dragons' teeth and even the homes that survived intact suffered through a freezing wind that blew for days on end. There was no escape from the winter. Children and livestock, the old and the ailing died in unheard-of numbers, so that by mid-February scarcely a shanty did not show a black ribbon on the door.

During this time the Lavender and Lily did a thriving business. Feargus Muldoon opened his doors just after dawn and rarely did he close before midnight. His profits were enormous and he gave generously to St. Anne's so that Father Snee kept himself warm on those icy nights with dreams of a parish hall as fine as Reverend Strickland's in the town. Muldoon's old wife, Peggy, set up a serving counter in the tavern. While a father drank to warm his innards, his wife and children took their fill of hot soup and thick slabs of coarse bread that was filling and nutritious.

Hearing of the suffering in the Gully, Suzannah Paine contributed to Muldoon's soup kitchen, and through an anonymous gift to Father Snee, coats and blankets were provided for the most needy. Word of this kindness spread throughout the Gully community, so that when Valentine appeared at the Lavender and Lily as he did several times a week, he was assured an enthusiastic greeting.

Since the night when he had helped Hart up from the rutted road and had carried him home, Valentine had been more and more drawn to the boy. Not so much from affection—he insisted to himself and Victorine that he felt nothing for the boy except disgust—as from a nagging fascination. The boy whose face was so beautifully angelic was made up of contrasts that made him seem as much a miracle as a freak. It was remarkable to Valentine that Hart, crippled and deformed in a dozen ways, was able to survive the winter at all. But the lad was healthy, and while other children perished from pneumonia and other cold-related ailments, Hart thrived. He was energetic and robust despite his crooked leg and arm, his twisted back and shoulder.

Victorine and her luscious lower lip continued to tempt Valentine, although he told himself he was a fool for it. To make her hovel more appealing, he brought wooden planks and laid them down to form a thick, uneven floor and he gave her skins from the tanner's to cover her narrow bed. Some nights, lying beside Victorine after they made love, he stared up at the roof of the shack and wondered at his unwillingness to return to his warm and comfortable home. Victorine was no beauty and she couldn't bathe often enough, but he liked her anyway. Her laugh was loud and uninhibited as were her temper and her sexuality. He admired this lusty vitality and sometimes felt that compared to her, he was less than fully alive.

Though no one in the Lavender and Lily would have dared to speak aloud of the resemblance between Valentine and Hart, their relationship was clear to all who cared to use their eyes. Gradually the attitude of the Irish toward Valentine Hopewell changed. As he cared for Victorine and the boy, improved their little lean-to shanty and provided them with warm clothing and shoes, the Irish treated him more gently. There was less goading and teasing in their banter with him. After all, he organized work parties, jobs that kept families from starving, and he acted the boss in a way that was fair to every man and offended no one's dignity. He had turned out to be more than a slumming, dissolute Yankee aristocrat. That winter Valentine had stayed sober and had given up gambling. And he had proved himself to be a just man, an honorable man worthy of respect.

Victorine herself was surprised to discover all this. In the beginning, she had intended to use Hart as a kind of blackmail that would bring her a few dollars. But she discarded this plan as soon as she realized that there was goodness in Valentine that could be of even greater benefit. She was an opportunist to the core of her being; life had taught her that she could not afford to be otherwise. Still, she liked Valentine more and more that winter and it warmed and touched her to see the way Hart followed after him

like a pup, trying awkwardly to shift his rolling gait
to match his father's. If Valentine was delayed or for
some reason did not visit the Gully for several days,
both Victorine and Hart missed him. The boy would
stand in the doorway, sucking on an icicle and staring
wistfully up the snow-packed road toward Amoset.

In the Lavender and Lily one wintry evening in
late March, Victorine introduced Valentine to a friend
of hers.

"Her name is May. May, meet Mr. Hopewell."

May was a little raisin-eyed woman with masses
of dark wiry hair that she tried unsuccessfully to
cover with a frilly cap. She smiled at Valentine and
dipped her head respectfully.

"And this here's her boy, Simon."

"You!" exclaimed Valentine. "You're the lad who
dared to interrupt my nephew's birthday party last
year. You mend your ways, boy, or you'll find yourself
in trouble. Your poor mama here deserves better."

Simon, a scrawny chicken-necked adolescent with
small eyes and mouth, leaned against the long bar
and picked his teeth with his fingernail.

"He's not a bad boy, Mr. Hopewell," whined
May, shying as if she expected to be hit. She reached
out and stroked Simon's dark hair. "It's just sometimes . . . well, he was used to better things."

"Her man is Foster McMahon, who was foreman
up at your mill," put in Muldoon from behind the
bar. "He's no good, that one."

Simon McMahon leapt for Muldoon, but Valentine caught him and held him back.

Muldoon shook his fist. "I've told you before,
boy—you cause trouble in my place and I'll see you
don't set foot in here again! I mean that, missus!"

May clutched her son. "I know. I know." Looking
at Valentine, she added apologetically, "He's not a

bad boy. But he misses his father. You can't blame a boy for that, can you?"

"What happened to McMahon? He was supposed to go south with my brother Eben and then he disappeared. Where's he gone to and why did he leave you behind?"

"He didn't want that job. He said it was pure and simple unfair what was done to him after he served your family all those years." May shied again. "Beggin' your pardon, sir, but that's what he said."

"Where is he then?"

May didn't answer.

"If he's abandoned you, how do you and the boy live?"

"She's a working girl like me, Val. Like I was," Victorine added quickly. She put her arm around May. "It's all right, love. You can tell my Valentine. He's a fair man."

"Tell me what?"

May still would not speak. Muldoon, keeping a wary eye on Simon, who stood sullen-faced beside his mother, answered for her. "McMahon's been in and out of town a dozen times since way back then. When he comes he's got money in his pockets and he spends it all on drink."

"Then he beats up on May." Victorine gave her friend a little shake. "That's true, ain't it, dearie?"

May nodded. She was crimson with shame.

"No need to look guilty about it," cried Victorine. "It's not you as is doin' the beatin'. He's a beast, that man of yours. Admit it."

"Shut up, you stupid whore!" Simon made a move toward Victorine and once again Valentine had to stop him.

He held him by the shirt collar so that the boy

unwillingly stood on tiptoe. "Watch what you say to this lady."

Simon spat in Valentine's face. Furious, Val shoved him against the bar. He would have hit him, but May intervened.

"He can't help it, Mr. Hopewell. Don't blame him for what he can't help." She took the boy in her arms and comforted him while he glared at Valentine with hate.

Valentine wiped the spittle off his face with his shirt sleeve and ordered another drink. When it was gone, he said, "Where's McMahon now?"

May and Victorine looked at each other.

"For God's sake, someone answer me!" Valentine was furious with everyone in the room except possibly Muldoon. For the first time in many weeks, he'd drunk too much. His voice was so loud it stopped all the conversation in the Lavender and Lily.

"He's coming here," May answered finally in a small, dismal voice. "I heard that he was in Marivale on Saturday. He could be here anytime."

"Well, when he comes you tell him from me that he'd better beat some sense into this boy or. . . ."

As if on cue, the door of the Lavender and Lily opened.

"Close the door, damn ye!" cried Muldoon, as a rush of winter air invaded the little tavern.

Simon broke away from May and ran to the man whose large, bulky frame filled the dark doorway.

"Da!" he cried. Full of gloat and victory, he yelled at Valentine, Muldoon and the others, "Now you'll get it! Me da's come home. Like Mama said, me da's come home."

May began whimpering. Stepping back, she

leaned against Victorine and clutched her friend's hand.

"What're you doin', woman?" McMahon stepped into the light. Big and barrel-chested, he moved with a threatening gait directly to the bar. Muldoon poured a drink in silence as McMahon's small beetle-black eyes scanned the room and stopped at Valentine. He glared at him. "You're a Hopewell."

"You've come just in time, McMahon. Your son here wants a good firm father's hand else he'll get himself in trouble."

"Oh, yeah?" McMahon had very little chin, but what he had he stuck out belligerently. "Since when do Hopewells count for anything here in the Gully?" He reached out and grabbed May's arm. "Well, my fine lady! Aren't you happy to see your husband after these many long months?"

"O' course I am, Foster."

"Then how about showin' it?" He jerked her toward him, twisting her arm as he did so. She gasped and uttered a little cry as he kissed her noisily. Laughing, he pushed her away. "I'll have another grog, Muldoon," he ordered, banging his fist on the bar. It was apparent that McMahon already was quite drunk, but he had put his coin on the counter. As Muldoon was fond of saying that a drunk's money is as good as anyone's, he poured another and shoved it toward him. McMahon finished it off in a long swallow, then turned to Simon. "Well, boy, what's your complaint?"

Simon squirmed against his father. "That one there, he said he'd hit me."

"Hopewell?"

"Your brat's out of control, McMahon."

McMahon squinted. "Say that again."

It was very quiet in the Lavender and Lily. Muldoon stopped wiping the counter and stared from one man to the other. "I don't want no trouble, McMahon," he muttered.

"I said," and Valentine pronounced each syllable precisely, "your boy's a brat and he's out of control. He's got a filthy, wagging tongue and he's been snooping around my place. If I ever see him near my property again, I'll beat him black-and-blue."

"That true, boy? You been up at Hopewells'?"

"Only once, Da. Me and my pals went up 'cause Mickey Quick was up there doin' a show."

"It's one time too many, McMahon." Valentine was not a fighter, but he had taken an instant dislike to McMahon. With several strong drinks in his system, he was prepared to take on the man if necessary.

McMahon smirked. "The high and mighty Hopewells never change. Always thinkin' they're too good for the rest of us."

"You've no call to bear us any grudge, McMahon. You were given a second job when my sister fired you. You could have gone south with my brother and made good money in Savannah. It was you who chose to. . . ."

McMahon spat on the floor between them. "I don't care *that* for your Savannah. I wasn't going to work with a gang of black devils. I worked hard for Hopewell Mills and I deserved to keep my job. That slutty sister of yours. . . ."

Valentine lunged for McMahon and threw him to the floor before the bigger man could protect himself. His hands were on McMahon's throat. But it was only a temporary advantage, for McMahon, with his superior weight and strength, quickly gained the upper hand. There was a furious scramble as Valentine tried to escape, but McMahon was on top of him, his knee pressed into his chest, his fists like clubs that slammed

again and again into Valentine's face as Simon
danced about them, clapping his hands and crowing
in delight.

"That's my da!" he cried, over and over and over
again.

"Stop them!" Victorine screamed, running up behind McMahon and dragging at his coat. She tried to
pull him off, shouting for help as she wrenched at his
hair and dug her fingernails into his neck.

Muldoon leapt over the bar. With the help of
three other men, he was able to break up the fight,
but not before Valentine had been badly bloodied.

"Get out!" cried Muldoon. "You and your stinking
son. Now! Out!"

McMahon hesitated. He pulled the boy close to
him.

Valentine lay with his head cradled in Victorine's
lap while she bathed his cuts with a cloth wet with
snow that someone had given her.

"You heard me, McMahon! Out!"

"I've got as much right. . . ."

"Out!" the owner bellowed.

"All right," he finally agreed, his eyes cold and
menacing. "But I won't forget this. I won't forget any
of this." McMahon turned to Valentine. "So help me,
if I hear you've been abusing my boy again, I'll kill
you, Hopewell. I'll kill you and be glad for the excuse."

Valentine tried to get to his feet, but Victorine
held him close.

"Hush, love. Stay still. You can't. . . ."

"And you can tell your stinking sister that if I
had my way, Hopewell Mills and all your kinfolk
would be dead along with you."

"How dare you!"

"I'm not fooling, Hopewell." McMahon strode to

the door, his son close behind and beaming proudly. "I don't say things I don't mean. I'd as soon see all of you dead and left to rot."

The door slammed behind him.

Outside the Lavender and Lily, McMahon stopped a moment to pull on a ragged wool stocking cap, a type commonly worn by Irish workmen. Glancing up, he saw that the last of the recent snowstorm had passed entirely and the starlit sky was glassy. Even the wind had died for a while, but the temperature was so low that the snow on the track squeaked like cornstarch. Shoving his hands into the deep pockets of his coat, McMahon trudged away from the inn toward Amoset, unmindful of Simon's scurrying after him.

Uncertain of his welcome with the father he both adored and feared, Simon kept to the shadows and was silent. He thought there was the smallest chance that McMahon would turn and discover him and invite him to walk as his companion. Such a simple invitation would have seemed an act of monumental love to a boy starved for paternal affection. But there was a better chance that McMahon would see his son and fly into a fury of suspicion. Simon knew this and with blind love forgave his father. Rather than risk it, however, the youth moved stealthily in the dark, content to watch and admire from a safe distance.

Simon was fourteen, and in all those years he had spent scant time with Foster McMahon. As a tyke he had been May's responsibility alone and later, when McMahon became Martin Hopewell's chief overseer at the mill, Simon was sent to St. Andrew's boarding school. On his infrequent visits home, his father was always too busy with overseeing the work at the mill to give his son the attention he craved. When McMahon lost his job, there was no money to keep Simon in school. He had come home then to his abandoned mother, who had possessed neither the will nor the wisdom to raise a spirited boy. From the big house on the river, they had moved to a shanty in the Gully, where May sold her body for their support. Simon despised her for it.

At fourteen, Simon was old enough to compare the way things had been when the family was prosperous with the way they were now. And in that comparison he was bitterly conscious of his own weakened state. Once he was a boy with important connections and a future that promised great things. Now. . . .

A worm of hate had worked itself deep in Simon McMahon's young heart. He blamed his mother, the Hopewells, everyone but his father for the family's loss of status.

McMahon crossed the rise that separated the Gully from Amoset and headed toward the river and the mill pond where operatives and their friends congregated in the wintertime for skating. But he didn't join the others at the shore. Instead, he stood on the slope of Cooper's Mountain where he had an unobstructed view of the pond and the crowd of merry young women and their escorts.

A bonfire had been built near the edge and around it were gathered more than a dozen skaters, muffled in coats and scarves and colorful knitted caps. Foster McMahon could hear the sound of singing, but the words were frozen somewhere in the air between the fire and where he stood. The ice was crowded with skaters and, reluctantly, he admired their grace. But this admiration lasted only a moment. In the next instant, he was recalling that he never had had the time to learn to skate. Looking back on his life, all he saw was labor and struggle. And what had he received for this? Insult, only insult.

He remembered a time many years earlier when he had stood in almost the same spot and had watched Lucy Shawn skate in the arms of Eben Hopewell, the bright moonlight flashing in her silver-blonde hair. Even now, years later, his fingertips tingled with the longing to touch the treasure of her hair. Like a warm wave, the memory of Lucy grew and then engulfed him and his body pounded with the old familiar need. The compulsion. The demand that could not be ignored.

He turned away from the mill pond and strode back into town.

It was almost nine in the evening, but the streets of Amoset were still crowded with operatives. Though many of the cultural features that had made Amoset famous throughout the world had disappeared in the tough depression times, there remained much to entertain the workers on their off hours. McMahon roamed the streets and, like his son behind him, he sought the shadows. On Front Street he stood for a long time, stamping his feet to keep them warm and watching the half-dozen women gathered near the steps of a boarding house. Their heads were bent close and they were giggling merrily over some secret. One of them had hair that was as yellow as the sun.

"We'll meet again tomorrow," the blonde girl called out gaily, waving the fringed end of her blue muffler in farewell as she turned away from the group and hurried up the street, still laughing to herself.

McMahon fell into step behind her, an anonymous pedestrian in workingman's clothes and an Irish cap, following her as she turned the corner onto Lester Street. The shops were closed and dark at that time of night. There were deep snowdrifts in some places, making it difficult to walk. The young woman sank to her knees in snow and McMahon heard her mutter to herself. She turned to walk back to Front Street and saw him in her path.

"Excuse me," she said, about to pass him. "The snow is deep here. You'll have trouble walking."

"Aye," he replied. Then his arm shot out, blocking her way.

"What . . . ?"

They looked at each other and in that moment she seemed to realize her fate. She opened her mouth to scream, but McMahon clamped his meaty palm over the noise, smothering it completely. With his other arm, he grabbed her around the waist and dragged her back into the dark, narrow space between two buildings. The area was free of snow, but it was slick with ice and McMahon couldn't keep his footing. He slipped and fell against the stones.

"Mother of God!" he muttered as the girl pulled away. He lunged for her, his fingers grasping and then losing the hem of her wide wool skirt.

"Help!" she screamed in a voice like a siren. She stumbled out of the alley and onto Lester Street again. A boy stood gaping at her. She pushed him out of her way as she ran, still screaming.

McMahon heard the sound of windows and doors opening and suddenly he was hot and sweating with terror. He scrambled to his feet.

"Who's down there?" a voice called from a window high above. "Stop where you are!"

Slipping again, he careened into a wall and then bounded out onto Lester Street. In passing, he shoved against the watching boy and knocked him over into a drift without noticing that it was his own son. Then he darted out of Lester Street and onto the road that fronted the river. All around and above him, windows and doors were open. As McMahon ran, the faces were a blur and the accusing voices were a threat without words.

Gagging for breath, he raced away from the noise and his pursuers. Where Front Street left the town he felt safer, but he didn't dare stop running, though the night air seared his lungs and throat and his muscles burned with exertion. A mile beyond the town, he reached McGill's Tavern, a shoddy inn where questions never were asked. He fell against the door and pounded on it with his fists.

It opened. "Well?" A brutish heavyset man stared at him.

"A room," gasped McMahon.

McGill gestured with a move of his head and McMahon staggered in and collapsed on the floor.

He was safe.

PART III

Chapter 14

From the little window of the breakfast room, Lucy
Shawn Kilmaine could look through the white or-
ganza curtains at a patch of front garden and the narrow residential street on which she and Thomas had
lived since their wedding in 1837. The street had
changed considerably since then and their Boston
friends insisted it was time for them to move off
Moon Street. Thomas and Lucy, however, were reluctant to leave their comfortable little house with its
neat three stories and compact back garden, where
every summer Lucy was able to grow vegetables that
were the pride of her dinner table. Furthermore, their
mutual egalitarianism told them it was wrong to leave
a pretty house on a pleasant street simply because the
neighbors on one side and across were immigrants.

Squeezing a wedge of lemon into her tea, Lucy
turned her head a little to watch Mrs. Flynn next
door sweeping the steps. Lucy liked the easy back
and forth motion of her arms. It wasn't hard to imagine that she often sang as she worked. Her round face
was lined, but in some peculiar way of which Lucy
was vaguely envious, the bloom had not left Mrs.
Flynn's face. Despite the lines and what Lucy knew
to be a rough life, Mrs. Flynn had the appearance of
a young woman. The Flynns had been the only Irish
on Moon Street until the Greens, their cousins, came.

"That's the way a neighborhood begins to deteriorate, my dear," Mrs. Dewey, the wife of Thomas' editor, had told her months before. "Best you find a home more suitable to Thomas' position and prospects."

But the Kilmaines were reluctant. The little brick house on Moon Street had two dogwood trees in the side yard and every year they bloomed as if they didn't know they were city trees, born to soot and shallow soil. Lucy didn't want to leave those trees or the forsythia hedge she had planted in front of the house, where most of the houses on Moon Street had low iron fences. She had put it in during the first year of her marriage, when she still had hopes that she could grow to love Thomas and be a good wife to him. Its joyous yellow flowers heralded every spring and, though Lucy could never again be as happy and hopeful as she was that first year, those blossoms never failed to lift her spirits for a while.

The Kilmaines were far from rich, but they were comfortably set in life, thanks to Thomas' excellent position and growing reputation as a journalist. The house on Moon Street was large enough to require the services of a maid, an Irish girl named Maureen, and a cook and a nurse for Delphia, all of whom came in every day before breakfast. It was still difficult for Lucy to believe that she had gone from a life of near poverty on Cooper's Mountain to the luxury of three servants. Sometimes whole days went by when she had nothing specific to do with her time, none of what she thought of as "chores." The idleness chafed her Yankee spirit a bit. Since she was not quite comfortable with what she had, she didn't want to leave Moon Street for even greater affluence.

"Here's the post come, madam." Maureen produced a half-dozen envelopes from the commodious pocket of her apron. "When shall I serve breakfast, madam? Mrs. Tippits has done wondrous scones this morning. Like shortbread they are."

Lucy smiled. "Mrs. Tippits will have to put us all on sailors' rations after this. But you may serve breakfast as soon as Mr. Kilmaine comes downstairs. Only a few more moments."

Maureen bobbed her dark head. "Yes, madam."

From the corner of her eye, Lucy caught sight of Mrs. Flynn greeting her husband. He was just coming up the street with his coat slung over his shoulder and a hat knocked back on his head. When he grinned, Lucy saw that he had no more than a pair of teeth in front.

I think she is really glad to see him, thought Lucy. She didn't know what Mr. Flynn did for a living, but it was night work and on many a day she had observed this same reunion. Mrs. Flynn always seemed happy to see her husband. The thought saddened Lucy and she looked away, surprised by tears.

One of the letters on the dish before her was from Ingrid. Lucy slit the envelope with a pearl-handled opener and quickly read the news of her sister's work and social life. A paragraph near the end took her attention completely.

> There has been another dreadful attack on a young woman here in town. Another blonde. She works in Swenson's lace factory and her name is Annabella. Somehow she was able to escape from the villain and there were bystanders who can give at least a bit of a description of him. It is said that he is from the Gully, for he wore the typical Irish hat and the girl believes he spoke to her in an Irish brogue. All about the town there is

outrage and the selectmen are threatening to
go into the Gully and roust out the miserable
fellow, wherever he is.

Lucy put down the letter and stared at it for a
long time. Her head reeled with memories and faint
recollections she longed to have forgotten. By now
there had been . . . how many murders in Amoset?
Lucy had lost count, but she remembered one thing
about all the young victims. They were all of them
blonde as she was herself. It was the killer's fondness
for fair hair that haunted Lucy. Since leaving Amoset
almost seven years before, she had been troubled by a
recurrent dream in which she was the killer's victim.
In this dream, the criminal's face and name were always known to her, but in the morning she could
never remember.

For a long time Lucy thought it was McMahon,
the man who had been the general overseer at
Hopewell Mills when she had worked there. During
the hellish time when she had been forced to submit
to him so that she and some of the other Spindle Sisters wouldn't lose their jobs, he had been obsessed
with her hair. He would fondle it and stroke it and
hold the thick curls in his mouth as he penetrated her.
Once, he had made her kneel before him, her head of
lavish silver-gold curls bent as if in worship. He had
pleasured himself with his hands that time and his or-
gasm. . . . Though Lucy had washed her hair in the
river, scouring her scalp with fine sand, for months afterward she could feel and see and smell him on her.
Memories of those vile encounters sickened Lucy. A
woman of less firm will would have gone mad. but
Lucy had determined long before that she would not
let McMahon destroy her. There was but one victory
she could hope for over him and that was to survive.

The murdered women in Amoset had been discovered beaten and half-dressed, their faces rigid with terror. Because of what had happened to her, it was not difficult for Lucy to imagine McMahon sneaking through the night streets of Amoset in search of innocence. But as the years passed, Lucy had stopped suspecting him of the crimes. Though the overseer had left Amoset and had, in fact, disappeared, the dreadful crimes had continued to occur.

I wish it were McMahon, she thought. I would like to see him hanged.

She was startled by something touching her. Thomas had just kissed her hair.

"Sorry to disturb you, my dear. A penny for your thoughts." Maureen put a plate of scones before Thomas and he dug into the butter and jam immediately.

Thomas Kilmaine was a man in his early forties with a boyish face that was pleasant and open. He smiled a lot, as a boy might, but Lucy knew her husband well and had learned to disregard this apparent lightheartedness. In reality, he was a man almost totally without a sense of humor. Oh, he told jokes from time to time, but he did so mechanically. Joviality went against his nature. Instead, he regarded the world and everyone in it as serious business. In the smallest event, he could find ramifications of a practically cosmic nature.

Looking out the breakfast room window, he commented, "You know something, Lucy? I like the Flynns. I would say that family represents the power and strength of tomorrow." He popped the last of a second scone into his mouth and chewed it thoughtfully. "How is our Delphia this morning?" he asked presently, touching his mouth with a napkin. "Did she sleep the night through?"

"Brownie says she did. But when I looked in a little while ago, she seemed flushed. I think perhaps Dr. Fish should be called."

Thomas shook his head. "Give her another day. Tell Brownie to watch her closely. You know I don't like this dependence on doctors, Lucy. I shouldn't have to speak about it more than once."

Lucy bit her lip and stared into the street. Among much that she found unlovable in Thomas, his paternal manner was the most destructive to their relationship. Although he told her repeatedly that he respected her and thought her wise and clever, his everyday manner clearly proved the opposite. Thomas treated Lucy like a little girl, and in many years of marriage, she had not been able to break him of the habit. By now she felt certain she never would.

She glanced at her husband. Completely oblivious to the fact that she was seething inside, he had begun to read his mail. The word insensitive came into her mind and stayed there. No doubt Thomas was a caring man. Lucy would be the first to praise his honor and fidelity. But for all of this, he was an insensitive man who never would understand his young wife.

She couldn't stop her mind from opening, as if the word insensitive had been the key. She stared out the window, recalling the scene that had taken place between them the night before.

"You're hurting me," she had whispered. "Be gentle, Thomas. Try." But the poor man did not know how to be. His hands on her breasts were always too rough, and when he fondled her nipples they flattened and became satiny to avoid his hard fingers. She had closed her eyes tightly and tried to think of something other than his grasping, pulling, demanding hands. In the beginning of her marriage, the mere thought of Eben Hopewell's name had aroused her shamefully. But in her guilt Lucy had learned to close him out in time. She would squeeze her eyes shut and think only of enduring, enduring, enduring.

In all her parts, she was as dry as an old woman and she would cry in pain as Thomas penetrated her. Fully erect, he was the stallion men dream of being and, to keep from screaming, Lucy would dig her teeth into a corner of the bedclothes. The blessing was that it never lasted long. When Thomas had spent himself, he would slip out of her like an eel and fall asleep instantly. It was always the same. Remembering the night before, she might have been thinking of dozens and dozens of nights.

Though she had a tendency to be critical of Thomas for much of their incompatability, Lucy was honest enough with herself to acknowledge that her clumsy husband was not wholly to blame. Sometimes she believed their marriage had been doomed from the start because of Foster McMahon. Since her experience with him, she had been uneasy with all men. Despite the passage of time and the security of her present life, she had never entirely lost the fear that one day McMahon would reappear and claim her again.

"Hello!" cried Thomas, indicating the letter in his hand. "Here's a bit of good news. Eben Hopewell is in Boston on business. He suggests we have lunch together at the Yale Club. Well, I most certainly will take him up on his offer. When Eben is in town, it's a rare treat." He glanced at Lucy. "Did you hear me, my dear?"

"You are glad that Eben has invited you to lunch," Lucy answered, not looking at Thomas as she rolled her napkin and placed it in a sterling silver ring. "It is, you say, a rare treat."

"Now, Lucy, why do you take that tone? What have you got against Eben Hopewell?"

"I have nothing against him, Thomas. We've talked about this before."

"Now, don't think you can fool me so easily, Lucy. I know you pretty well by this time."

Lucy wanted to tell him he didn't know her at all, that there was only one man who could tell from her face what she was thinking and he was her father. You know nothing, she wanted to yell at Thomas. Nothing!

"Isn't this a good time for Eben to have supper with us?" Thomas persisted.

"I don't want to have him in the house, Thomas."

"But why? Surely you've gotten over all that foolish prejudice against the mill owners."

"I don't like him. I don't have to like him, do I?"

"No one is forcing you . . ."

"I don't want him in my house." She hesitated, then touched his hand. "Please, Thomas."

"Lucy. . . ." He stared at her, at her hand on his, then sighed. "Very well. What have you planned for today?"

"I'll see to Delphia . . ."

"Remember, I don't want her coddled. Is that clear, Lucy?"

She stood up, brushing the skirt of her pastel gingham morning dress. "It is clear, Thomas."

"Off so early? Won't you take another cup of tea with me?"

"You'll excuse me if I don't this time, Thomas? The first daffodils have come up and I want to pick them early. That way they last longer in the house. And I must sort some mending for Brownie or she'll spend the day dreaming of the grocer's boy."

Thomas laughed. "You are an extraordinary

woman, Lucy. I cannot tell you how I admire your ability to manage this house as smoothly as you do. And you're still pretty, Lucy, as pretty as a girl."

When she had gone upstairs, Thomas refilled his teacup and, resting his elbows on the chintz tablecloth, stared out the window at his neighbors, the Flynns.

Mr. Flynn was standing on the top step of his house, looking extremely comfortable as he enjoyed the first blush of spring. In one hand he held a teacup and in the other a pipe from which he took long, savoring draws. Several steps below him in the tiny yard, Mrs. Flynn was planting seeds in a narrow strip of flower bed. Thomas enjoyed watching her body as she worked. She moved with determination, which he always admired in anyone, but also with grace and a certain sensuality. Thomas could easily imagine that Mrs. Flynn liked the way her body felt when she worked it hard.

He had long ago ceased to censor such thoughts from his mind, although he knew they were what Christians called sinful. He had given up churchgoing and organized religion around the same time he became a reporter, but he had been raised to be devout and so the old words like sin could not help but occur to him when his mind wandered into ancient taboos.

Lusting after Mrs. Flynn, if Thomas' pale thoughts could be called that, was not the worst of his sins. Thomas dreamed of a new life, and this he knew to be unfaithful to Lucy and Delphia. But the daydream, the fantasy of a new life in a new place, was nothing he could shove to the periphery of his mind and will himself to forget. It was necessary, he had come to believe, to maintain his control. If he had not been able to escape Lucy, Moon Street and the newspaper and lose himself in wishful thinking, there was no telling what he might do in his frustration.

Faintly, the sound of the Flynns' laughter reached him, reminding him of when he had first begun to dream of leaving. The Flynns had just moved to Moon Street and Thomas, meeting the Irishman early one morning as he returned from work, engaged him in conversation. Flynn was garrulous and had a lot to say in their next several encounters. Thomas had learned that this was Flynn's second wife. The first had died, leaving him a widower with three young ones. With what was left of a small inheritance, he had brought his family to Boston ten years earlier. He had begun a new life in a new world. The new wife and her five children, who had been orphaned the year before, came not long after.

It would be impossible to exaggerate the effect this story had on Thomas. The envy that rose in him when he heard it was immense and strangling. For days and days he went about in a rage because of it and no one could please him. For weeks he despised his wife, a cold, uncaring woman. His child seemed to him a burden so great that his shoulders were bent from it. Then, out of his imagination, the fantasy had begun to emerge. He imagined a new life for himself in the West, one in which he was the owner, editor and chief reporter of a frontier paper. There was no one to depend on him. He took a new name, let his hair grow long and cultivated a mustache. He began a new life as Flynn had.

Kilmaine thought, in time, he might take a new wife, though life on the frontier was apt to be dangerous and the kind of place he envisioned would likely seem unhealthy to most women. But he dreamed of a special breed of woman. Thomas closed his eyes and saw her, heard her voice. Her willing kisses touched

his lips and when he caressed her she did not push
him away or call him rough.

The dream clicked off when Thomas realized he
was becoming excited. It was all very well to have a
fantasy or two, but when they became so vivid. . . .
He shook himself. What was the matter with him
anyway? Didn't he know that Lucy was an adorable,
sweet-hearted girl? Didn't he know he was the luck-
iest man in Boston? He had no business blaming Lucy
for being unresponsive in the marriage bed. After all,
she was a lady. And, more practically, she was a
small woman while he was a very large man. Such
physical differences could not be helped.

Besides, for Thomas' dream to come true, Lucy
would have to die. After all, the substance of it was
built on her nonexistence. Then there would still be
Delphia to worry about. He couldn't imagine taking a
little girl into the wilderness. So his dream was constructed on her death as well. Thomas groaned and
put his head in his hands.

He was a monster. He didn't bother to deny it.
Only a monster could find joy in imagining his wife
and child were dead.

Chapter 15

"Feeling better, darling?" Lucy asked, squeezing Delphia's hand. "Are you warm enough?"

Delphia nodded and burrowed deeper under the covers so that only her blonde curls showed.

"I'll just close the window, I think. A nasty draft came into this room and made you ill. We don't want any more of them, do we?" A moment later Lucy returned to the bed. "Now, if you need anything, you just call Brownie. And if you don't feel well, be sure you tell her. Promise?"

"Where are you going, Mama?"

"I have some errands, sweetheart. Just a few."

"Will you bring me something?"

Lucy laughed. "A hug and a kiss." She went to the door. "Sleep now, baby. Sleep will make you better." She closed the door softly behind her.

For a few moments she stood outside Delphia's door and stared at the patterned hall carpet. There was nothing left to do in the house. Lucy had sorted the laundry, arranged flowers and planned the evening meal with Mrs. Tippits. Now there was nothing left to do but the errands she had spoken of to Delphia. Why was she reluctant to leave the security of home?

She went downstairs and put on a warm, double-breasted coat with a cloth collar and a pair of sturdy walking boots. The boots were easy to walk in and would protect her from the muddy streets. Then, though the sky was clear, she hooked an umbrella over her arm. Boston weather was changeable in the springtime. On her head, she wore a hat of olive drab felt that matched the color of her coat. Lucy was just opening the front door when she thought better of the hat. Not stopping to ask herself why, she withdrew from a milliner's box on the top shelf of the closet a hat she had never worn. Like the other, it was olive green, but for decoration it had three splendid pheasant feathers and a wide velvet band of dull blue embroidered in gold and green.

"Oh, madam, it do look splendid!" From the sitting room double doors, Maureen admired her mistress, her dusting forgotten. "Are you having luncheon out, madam?"

Embarrassed, Lucy replied with a question. "Why do you ask?"

"You do look nice, madam. That new hat . . ."

"I have nothing special planned. Only errands." Lucy shut the front door sharply a moment later. She was flushed, certain that Maureen had seen through her to the truth, a truth she was barely able to admit to herself. She did have errands to run, that much was true, but she had chosen to do them in a part of town that was far removed from the unfashionable Moon Street shops.

The Yale Club was located on a circle on the low side of Beacon Hill in a neighborhood that was largely made up of the stylish clubs for the gentlemen who lived in the area. Handsome and substantial, the building, like those on either side, gave the impression that its red bricks and polished brass ornamentation, and even its unusual lavender glass, had existed from the Boston dawn and would continue to do so for centuries to come. In the landscaped square

across the street from the club, Lucy sat down on an
iron bench, next to a complacent tabby cat who
stretched and then curled up again when she saw her.
Overhead, a sugar maple was valiantly in new bloom.
Despite the fine sky, Lucy was chilly, and the new
leaves danced frantically in a grey wet wind that was
blowing in from the sea.

She glanced at her pocket watch. It was almost
lunchtime. Wearing a timepiece had been Thomas'
idea. It was a scandal, he had said, the way women
used time. At his insistence, she had been wearing her
great-grandfather Hildebrand's clock on a gold chain
for several years. The seventeenth-century engraving
of a fabulous bird, a kind of peacock, made the lid
not only beautiful but, by Boston standards, defiantly
exotic as well. Inside, the face was neatly done in Ro-
man numerals and easy to read. Five minutes before
twelve. She sighed and rubbed her gloved hands together. She had just begun to wish for a fur muff
when a maroon two-seater drawn by an arrogant
chestnut horse clattered around the cobbled circle
and came to a halt in front of the club. It pulled
away in time for her to see two men, one of them her
husband, entering the Yale Club.

Damn, why hadn't she planned more carefully?
She should have realized that to see anything more of
Eben, she would have to wait until after lunch when
he would come down the stairs and call for his gig.
Now she would have to wait. Damn!

Lucy had taken up mental cursing a year or so
before. It was one of her more satisfying secret rebel-
lions against Thomas' pomposity. Thinking this, she
laughed aloud. The sound alarmed her as well as the
cat, who got up and walked away. Lucy looked nervously from side to side, expecting to be recognized.

Lucy Shawn Kilmaine. She was the wife of a

fine, honest man and the mother of an innocent child. Yet here she was, immoral as a pagan, spying on the man she loved and the man she had married. She chafed her hands in the cold to help the moments pass. Endure, she thought, endure.

Thomas and Eben emerged from the Yale Club about an hour later. They stood side by side on the porch for a moment or two, shaking hands. Thomas actually seemed to be laughing. Lucy had a perfect view of Eben. He was, of course, as tall as ever and he seemed to have grown in substance. Slender-hipped and broad-shouldered, he had added muscle and actually appeared rather formidable to Lucy. His dark hair was worn long and tied back like a young Thomas Jefferson. Though he stood at too great a distance for his features to be clear, she knew his melancholy brows, the eyes like troubled seas, and her heart quickened. The gig appeared. A moment later it pulled away, leaving Eben on the sidewalk.

He began walking toward Chestnut Street. Without stopping to think, Lucy followed him. Like a man of property, a man with land of his own, Eben took long strides that bit the earth with their assurance. Lucy was grateful for the sturdy boots and mountain upbringing that enabled her to keep him just a block ahead. In this manner, they hurried down Chestnut Street and Mt. Vernon, along Pinkney, and into a neighborhood where many of the old brick homes contained offices. In front of one of these, Eben stopped. As Lucy kept to the part of the side path that was shaded by chestnuts, she saw his face clearly for a moment and knew that he was suffering.

When Eben had gone inside, Lucy approached the house and read the brass sign beside the step: Wayne Wilkinson, Physician and Surgeon.

He is ill!

She stepped back, away from the brass plate, as if by doing this she could erase the little segment of her life that had brought her to this thought.

He must not be ill!

In a moment's passing she envisioned a dozen morbid possibilities. Her eyes filled with tears and, when she tried to brush them away, her hand trembled. Across the street and down a block from Dr. Wilkinson's, she leaned against a chestnut tree and, facing away from the doctor's office, wept without inhibition.

Lucy was a sensible young woman, not normally given to public demonstrations. She knew when she was letting maudlin fantasy take hold of her, but it felt good to cry for Eben freely. She had never done that before, and so, in a sense, her tears were a necessity and long overdue. Or was she crying for herself? For all she had lost? She was confused, heartbroken, weeping for a past that was inadequate, a future without hope. Long ago Eben had told her one Bonfire Night that he loved her and she had spurned him. By the time she realized that she could reciprocate his love, it was too late. By then each had made promises to others that could not be broken; it was as simple as that.

In her reticule Lucy found a handkerchief and wiped her eyes. She looked up at the shallow bow windows lining the street. As if they were eyes, she expected their lids to open, blinds to fly up, and a dozen accusers to be revealed. Pulling down at the brim of her smart hat, she tossed her head a little, as if to say she didn't care who saw her, and hurried down the street. But some distance beyond, where she found a little corner garden with a bench, she sat down.

It was getting late and she hadn't done her shopping, but she had to wait for Eben to leave the doctor's office. She must see his face and know that he was healthy before she could think of moving on. When a vendor appeared on the corner, she bought some hot tea and a sausage roll. While she sat, an old couple came into the corner park and walked up and down before her, leaving no doubt in Lucy's mind that they wanted her to move. But she refused to budge. When the sun disappeared behind the city's chimneyed roof tops, the park became colder and the old couple finally went away. Still Lucy stayed where she was. Her feet were so cold that they hurt when she stood up, suddenly alert, and looked at her watch. It was almost five!

Lucy hurried away from Dr. Wilkinson's office toward Moon Street. With a shock she remembered Delphia's illness and was overcome with guilt, imagining her daughter's suffering. She ran a good deal of the way back to North Boston, jarring her ankle and twice almost slipping on the cobbles. Passing the Church of the Mathers', she was reminded of "sinners in the hand of an angry God" and knew that in all of earth and hell there could be no greater sinner than a mother who neglects her child. As she had earlier with Eben, Lucy imagined monstrous events that might have befallen her daughter in the space of an afternoon. But this time, instead of dissolving her energy in tears, the frightful imaginings gave spurs to her flight.

At the door she was greeted by Maureen.

"Holy Mary, I'm glad you've come, madam." Her round Irish face was white and strained so that the freckles stood out like yellow blotches.

"It's Delphia! What's wrong with her?"

Maureen began to weep. "I don't know, madam. I swear I don't."

"What happened?" She shook Maureen roughly. "Stop crying, damnit!"

The girl blinked. "Yes, madam."

At this moment, Brownie Tompkins, Delphia's nurse, hurried into the foyer. She too was crying. "I swear I was gone only for a couple of minutes, madam. Truly and to God. I never meant . . ."

"You left Delphia alone?" Lucy threw her hat and coat at Maureen. "Do I pay you to abandon . . . ?"

"Maureen said she'd look in on her and then she went and forgot."

The coat and hat slipped from Maureen's hands. "I was that busy, madam. Mrs. Tippits made me. . . ."

Lucy took the stairs two at a time, rushing breathlessly into her daughter's room and throwing herself down beside the bed.

Her worst fears were realized, for Delphia lay shuddering with chills.

"Cold, Mama. Cold," she whimpered through dry, cracked lips.

Lucy touched her cheek. "My God, she's burning!"

"Cold, Mama."

"I know, darling. I know, my baby," Lucy murmured, tucking the comforter and blankets more closely around the child. "Go for Dr. Fish, Maureen," she ordered without taking her eyes off Delphia. "And, Brownie, fetch more blankets and a fresh nighty. The flannel one. We have to keep her warm." When Brownie did not move, but stood mewling to herself, Lucy turned on her. "Stop that sniveling at once, or I will put you out and forget your wages. Is that clear?"

"Yes, madam," bawled the frightened girl.

"And bring some brandy."

"What, madam?"

"Brandy! For the ague, damnit!"

When Dr. Fish arrived a short time later, he said, "I see you have the situation well in hand, Mrs. Kilmaine. You are doing just what I would do myself." He took the brandy glass from Lucy and put it to the child's lips. "How long has she been like this?" he asked, shoving his spectacles up on his molelike nose.

"I don't know. I came home . . . from running errands, you see, and discovered her this way."

"Let us hope and pray the fever doesn't last too long."

"What do you mean, Doctor?"

"Well, it has been my experience that when these childish agues are severe and of long duration, the patient is rarely the same afterward. Little ones tend to lose the sparkle in their eyes, as if the ordeal robs them of their youth." But, seeing Lucy's stricken look, he reassured her. "You did the right thing, Mrs. Kilmaine. You did the right thing."

The doctor had a laconic, fatalistic manner and Lucy couldn't keep the irritation from sounding in her voice when she asked, "But when will we know if she is all right?"

He shrugged. "Hard to say in cases like these. I think the best thing for you to do now would be to sponge the little lady all over, across her back and on her chest and limbs, to try to bring down the fever. Meanwhile, I'll go down and wait in Mrs. Tippits' kitchen."

"You're going downstairs?" Lucy asked. "Isn't there something more you can do?" She looked at Delphia. The child was still shaking with cold, though her flesh was hot to the touch. "This seems so little . . ."

"You're doing fine, Mrs. Kilmaine. Just fine."

A period of time passed. Lucy didn't look at her pocket watch, but if she had, she would have been surprised by how small an interval of time it was. As she tried to comfort Delphia, the moments seemed endless and tormented. She knew she was the worst of all human beings—a bad mother, a neglectful mother, a careless mother. The labels were accusations she repeated again and again in her mind. And as the time passed and Delphia's fever did not break, Lucy knew that she had risked her daughter's vitality, maybe even her life, just so that she could see Eben Hopewell and weep. The shameful truth of this thought was more than she could bear. In a breathless, inaudible whisper, she prayed. "Save her, Lord, and I swear I will give up all thought of Eben. Save her, Lord. Save her."

The little nursery was silent but for the sound of Lucy's murmured prayers and Delphia's agonized breathing. Outside the wind rose and complained among the eaves of the little house on Moon Street. Thunder grumbled distantly, and when the rain came, it beat against the windows angrily. But Lucy heard nothing of this. For her, all the universe consisted of no more than a guilty mother and a suffering child. Lucy was roused from her prayers when the child thrashed away her bedclothes. Delphia's fever had broken at last. In a moment her nightdress and sheets were wet with perspiration.

"Brownie! Maureen!" Lucy called from the bedroom door. "It's broken. Bring fresh bedclothes. Hurry! And tell Dr. Fish her fever has broken."

Delphia was whimpering for her mother.

"I'm here, darling. Everything will be all right now. You're going to get better. You're going to be well, Delphia. I promise. I promise." There were no words to describe the gratitude that rose in Lucy at that moment. Kneeling at the bedside, she offered up prayers of thanksgiving that were eloquent in their sincerity. Tears poured from her eyes as they had for Eben that afternoon in what now seemed another lifetime.

When Dr. Fish relieved her of her nursing duties, Lucy was reluctant to go, but the doctor insisted. He could see that she was exhausted and so emotionally unstrung that she was in danger of becoming ill herself. Finally, against her will, she left the room. In the hall mirror outside the nursery, she caught sight of herself and recoiled in shock. It had been close and hot in the nursery. Lucy had unbuttoned the front closure of her heavy street dress so that the lace-edged top of her camisole showed. Beads of perspiration stood out on her skin as it had on Delphia's, and the bodice of her dress was stained from it. Her hair had come out of its pins and had fallen about her shoulders. The vision of herself in such disarray recalled the agony of the last few hours in fresh detail. Leaning against the wall, Lucy gasped for breath to keep from sobbing in uncontrolled relief.

When she felt a little better, she glanced at her timepiece and realized that Thomas would be home at any minute. She would have some explaining to do. Nevertheless, she stopped halfway to her bedroom, realizing more than anything, more than a bath, clean linen or a fresh dress, she wanted a cup of Mrs. Tippits' strong tea. With Brownie engaged with Dr. Fish and Maureen probably still in hysterics, Lucy decided that it would be more practical if she got the drink herself. She was on her way down the stairs when the door opened.

"Lucy, I'm home!" From the foyer where he was

closing his umbrella, Thomas called out, "I've brought someone with me." He turned to the man behind him.

Eben Hopewell was standing in the foyer.

"Hello, Lucy," he greeted.

Chapter 16

It was a moment Eben knew he would never forget. In all his thoughts of Lucy during the long years of their separation, he had always envisioned her as the girl he had loved on Bonfire Night. Now, suddenly, here she was before him, a woman drawn and exhausted. The sight of her at the top of the stairs so surprised him that he took a step back.

"Perhaps another night, Tom."

"Not at all. I won't hear of it." Kilmaine turned to Lucy with barely concealed anger. "I sent word home to Mrs. Tippits and you were out somewhere. Why aren't you prepared to meet your guest?" Thomas put his foot on the first stair, and as he did so he appeared to realize his young wife's suffering for the first time. "What in heaven . . . ? What happened, Lucy?" He hurried up the stairs to her, his anger forgotten.

When he tried to embrace her, she shrugged him away. "I'm a mess, Thomas. I've been with Delphia for hours. Mrs. Tippits must have forgotten to tell me about. . . ." Her voice trailed off and she stared at Eben for a long moment before she turned back to go to her room.

Thomas hurried after her. "But my dear, what's happened? Is Delphia all right?"

Eben couldn't hear her reply, but he saw her nod

her head slowly in the affirmative. Then he heard the sound of a door opening and closing. When Thomas didn't return immediately, Eben was left alone in the foyer, his hat in his hand. He wondered if it might be best for him to write Thomas a note and then leave for his club. After deciding to do this, he did nothing. He had seen Lucy and didn't want to leave.

For the past several days, ever since he and Marianna St. Clair, his quadroon mistress, had arrived on the packet from Savannah, Eben had been in a state of troublesome anxiety. He was a man of ordered country habits, unused to the noisy scramble of the northern cities, and he disliked the racket Boston made. There were too many voices, the accents many and unfamiliar. Heavy wagon, horse and cart travel made the cobbled streets a noisy push and shove and hurry place. In some ways, he was eager to get back to gentle, elegant Savannah.

But he needed to be in Boston now. Dr. Wilkinson was the only man in the country who might be able to help Marianna. She suffered from a painful ailment, the same she said her mother had had. Though Marianna claimed to know and accept that there could never be a cure, she was the one who showed Eben the piece about Dr. Wilkinson in a New York periodical he had once carried into her home and then had forgotten. It hadn't been easy for Eben to arrange a trip to Boston with his mistress, but he had managed. He'd left his wife at home with her adored slaves, Biddy and Dora, preparing Georgia Day banners. When Amanda had waved him off as he left in the packet, she hadn't known that Marianna was aboard as well. Dimpling beneath her yellow silk parasol, Amanda had called out, "You get all your business taken care of now, y'hear? And don't come back till you've done every little thing so's for once you can pay some attention to me. You hearing me, Eben Hopewell?"

For Eben, business meant seeing Lucy Shawn . . . Kilmaine. Somehow, before that moment in the foyer, he had never really thought of her as being married. Not truly married. Yet it was clear from overhearing the short exchange between Lucy and Thomas that they were familiar with one another as only those who live together for long periods in the intimacy of marriage can be. And they had a child. Parenthood had a way of changing people. It had changed Eben.

Amanda was childless and petulant about it. She took it as a direct affront that fate had dealt her barrenness, but Eben saw it as a blessing. She was too lightheaded to be a mother. She would rather be off picking apples with her playmates, Dora and Biddy. But four years earlier, Marianna had given birth to a son whom she called Christian. Eben was joyous, but never had the illicit nature of their relationship been more difficult to tolerate than when he wanted to bellow his joy from the roof tops. Christian was darker than his mother and his features were less fine, and for a while after his ebullience had subsided, Eben could scarcely believe that this could be his son. But when Christian was about a year old and his features began to take permanent shape, the Hopewell in the boy began to appear. Like his father, he had the stormy Hopewell brows, and Eben could tell by looking at him as he took his first steps that he would be tall like his father and grandfather.

Christian's birth had changed Eben slowly, subtly, inexorably. More than love, more than need, Christian bound Eben to Marianna. He supposed that Lucy must feel somewhat the same about Thomas. But in their relationship there were legalities, formal

vows meant to last through life and into eternity. No
man who cared for his soul would step between a
wife and husband.

But still Eben knew he must see Lucy. Beside
this imperative, his soul was nothing. Though he had
not seen her in many years, not since the day she had
made him close his eyes while she walked away,
Lucy had often been in Eben's mind. Despite pain
and frustrated longing, he had come to accept her
presence there and to be glad for it. By now he knew
he would always love her. It was one of the givens of
his life.

When Eben and Thomas had begun their corre-
spondence, Eben did not realize that the newspaperman was Lucy's husband. What had gotten their
relationship started was a series of blazing abolitionist
articles Thomas had written for the *Boston Globe*.
Though the articles contained much that was true,
they also perpetuated grave distortions of the Southern lifestyle. Eben wrote a strongly worded correction
or two back to Thomas. The older man rebutted, and
so began a friendship by mail that had, by the time
Eben realized who Thomas was, come to mean a lot
to both men. Undoubtedly Kilmaine was a humorless
and pedantic fellow, but he also was widely read and
interested in a great many things besides Abolition.
Eben had few friends who shared his varied interests
and so he valued Thomas' friendship highly.

But there were times when Eben wondered what
part Lucy might play in his fondness for Kilmaine.
Was it possible that he cultivated him solely to be
near Lucy again after so many years? Eben despised
the thought of such cupboard love and dismissed it
easily. He liked Kilmaine immensely. That Lucy was
his wife was . . . chance.

Later that same evening, Lucy, Thomas and

Eben sat down to a meal served by a red-eyed
Maureen. Lucy, too, showed signs of having suffered.
Although she had bathed and changed for dinner, her
wide blue eyes were shadowed with grey and she
seemed older to Eben than twenty-six. Her manner as
a hostess, particularly under these trying circumstances, also impressed him as mature beyond her
years. Though Thomas dominated the mealtime conversation, she participated as well. When Eben talked
about the railroad line that he and his partner Gregory
White would soon open into what had once been
Cherokee country, Lucy listened intently and she
asked the kinds of questions that reminded him of
why he loved her. Her wit was as sharp as ever and
she did not mince her words.

"The railroad is wonderful, of course," she commented. Her eyes met Eben's for a fraction of a second, but before they could lock, she glanced away.
While she talked she didn't look at his face, but at the
space above his head. "I believe in railroads, but it
seems a crime that you Georgians are free to drive a
whole nation of people off their homeland with
scarcely a second thought."

Thomas laughed. "My Lucy is a woman of strong
opinions, Hopewell."

"I remember her that way."

Again their glances touched and this time she did
not look away quickly enough. There was an instant
of communication before she reddened and, looking
at Thomas, changed the subject.

They were alone only once and for fewer than
five minutes. Thomas had gone into his study to find a
volume of essays by a man named Emerson of whom
he thought highly.

As soon as he was gone, Lucy leaned across the
table and asked, "Are you well, Eben? Is everything

well with you?" She almost asked him about Dr. Wilkinson, but dared not reveal where she had been that afternoon.

"I am well. Never better, thank you, Lucy. But you . . . ?"

"I'm strong. Today has been difficult, but there's nothing wrong with me. I'm only tired." She pushed back a silver-blonde ringlet and seemed about to ask a question, but something stopped her. All at once, she smiled as he remembered her smiling when she was a little girl and something particularly pleased her. Her eyes crinkled at the corners, her nose wrinkled slightly and her pretty teeth flashed. She exuded happiness with that smile. "I am very glad to see you, Eben."

"I've missed you, Lucy." He stared at her hand with its plain gold ring.

"I know. I should say, I . . ."

Thomas burst into the room. "Well that didn't take too long, did it? Haven't I said, Lucy, that nothing beats an organized library?" He tossed the book down before Eben. Lucy's hand disappeared from the table. The moment was lost.

An hour later, Eben's carriage left Moon Street for his hotel, but instead of going directly, he told the cabby to drive him along the river for a time. He would have to see Marianna when he got in and he couldn't face her yet, not so soon after being with Lucy. No matter what, he couldn't hurt Marianna. He had sworn this to her long ago and Eben was a man of his word where she was concerned.

Even as he thought this, he knew it wasn't true. It was simply one of several—or was it many?—lies he told himself from day to day, lies that were like threads in a garment that held him together and gave order to his life where otherwise he feared there would be chaos. For two hours he had sat across the table from Lucy and now he could think of nothing so much as the effort he knew it would take to continue without her for the rest of his life. He stared at the moon-spangled Charles River and tried to believe that Amanda wouldn't drive him mad in time with her girlish stupidity and that Marianna's need for him wouldn't eventually shove a wedge between them that would make loving her as much a burden as marriage to Amanda. He stared into the quiet moonlit night and tried to make himself believe that he could give up Lucy Shawn Kilmaine. Thirty minutes passed and he was not successful.

Marianna was staying in a room on the second floor of the Lester Hotel. Eben had a suite on the top floor with a view of Boston's droll, chimneyed roof tops. After glancing up and down the second-floor hall, he rapped on her door. She opened it quickly.

He had been away since midmorning, but Marianna didn't scold him for leaving her alone or even question. It wasn't her way. Sometimes Eben wished it were so that he wouldn't find it so easy to take advantage of her.

She looked up at him, her amber eyes luminous. "May I get you something, *chéri*? It's late. You must be tired."

He was.

"A brandy, perhaps?"

He nodded and, sinking into a deep, comfortable chair, closed his eyes and squeezed the bridge of his nose. Seeing this, Marianna removed the lamp from the table beside him and dimmed its light. Then she poured some brandy into a snifter and brought it to him.

"What have you been doing all day . . . and night?" he asked when he had taken a sip of brandy.

"I was reading when you came. Before that I worked on Mrs. Delacourte's table napkins. She expects them to be ready by the time we get home and I would hate to disappoint her." Marianna was one of Savannah's finest seamstresses and she was proud of the fact that she could have supported herself and Christian on what she earned. "I wrote a letter to Christian, but then I realized old Bess won't know how to read it to him."

"He's getting along fine without you, Marianna. Don't upset yourself with worry. We've only been in Boston a few days."

"I know. You're right, Eben." She sat down on the cushioned hassock beside his chair and gazed at him expectantly. When he didn't speak after some time, she ventured a question. "Did you see that Dr. Wilkinson today, Eben?"

"Who?" He looked at her. "Oh, yes. Dr. Wilkinson. I saw him this afternoon."

"And what did he say?" Marianna's small, delicate face was hopeful.

"He says you'll have to go into the hospital. He has to study your case."

She looked away, shaking her head emphatically. "I can't, Eben. You know that. I told you."

He was instantly irritated and his voice showed it. "And I told you that if it is necessary for you to go into the hospital to make you well, then you simply will have to do it."

Marianna got up and began to pace the room. "I can't. I just can't. I can't."

"Good Lord, you're as bad as Christian!"

With her hands on her hips she stood before him, as close to outrage as Eben had ever seen her. "Hospitals are where people go to die. If you take me to the hospital, I know I will never come out. I know it, Eben. Believe me when I say I know it."

"But Dr. Wilkinson has to study your disease. You don't expect him to diagnose and cure you in an afternoon, do you?"

"I don't expect him to cure me at all."

Now Eben was furious. He jumped up and grabbed her thin shoulders. "You listen to me, Marianna. I didn't bring you all the way up here for nothing. There *is* hope. You must believe it!"

She shook her head. "This is the way my mother died, Eben. The headaches, the sores . . . the rest. She died this way and so did half the people on the St. Clair plantation."

Eben shoved her into the chair and leaned over her, resting his hands on the upholstered arms. "If you tell me that again, so help me I'll. . . ."

Almost engulfed by the soft cushions, Marianna had never seemed so small and frail. He saw how her collarbones protruded at the neckline of her nightdress and her hands were so thin they made him think of claws. The anger drained out of him instantly. Dropping to his knees, he wrapped his arms about her legs and rested his head in her lap.

"I don't want to hear about dying, Marianna. You mustn't say it. If I lose you, I'd lose myself."

"Those are only words. There's no truth in them."

"I love you, Marianna. I love you."

"I know that, Eben, but you would learn to live without me. You would find someone else to make you happy. It's the way of things, *chéri*."

"You have to see Wilkinson. He told me today it isn't hopeless."

She touched his thick hair and smiled tolerantly. "How can he know when he hasn't seen me?"

"You *must* see him! I'll drag you there if I have to!"

She laughed, as if the image amused her. "But not to the hospital, *mon amour*. Promise me that upon your honor. I'll go to this doctor's office, but never to the hospital. Never."

Chapter 17

It was several days before Dr. Wilkinson was able to see Marianna for the length of time necessary to observe her disease. In the meantime, Eben went about the city on matters of business. He was well received by the "Millionists" of Boston society, for although he was a Georgian by residence, Eben was known to be every inch a Yankee when it came to business affairs. With Brahmins like Harrison Otis and Ebenezer Francis, the Dwights, the Sears and the Appletons, he talked about the thousands of farmers and their families who would move to Georgia and how all their goods might be shipped aboard trains of the Cherokee and West Georgia Line.

Not one of these eminent gentlemen thought to comment on the homeless Indians as Lucy had a few nights earlier. Every man of business knew that, where property was concerned, the strong would always dominate the weak. Because of this knowledge, Eben sensed that the rich and powerful of Boston did not really admire him and accept him as an equal, despite their respect for his business acumen. They regarded him as they did all Southerners, as a man of the past. They had to remind themselves and each other that Eben Hopewell also owned one of Massachusetts' most flourishing mills and half a city, as well.

One man, a banker named Owen Barnaby, was curious about Amoset. "What sort of place is that, Hopewell? One hears such contradictory reports. First that it's a haven for the rural intellectual, the birth-place—we are led to believe—of industry. Then there is news of yet another attack on a young woman. Aren't your streets safe? Must you hire constables? Don't you worry about your sister, Hopewell?"

Another man, Joseph Appleton, was amused. "From what I hear, Mrs. Paine can take care of her-self."

Eben spun around. It was an insult to hear his sister's name brought up in gentlemen's conversation. Appleton was quick to apologize. "See here, Hope-well, you've been south too long. You should have known I meant no disrespect to your sister. On the contrary, she is a fine businesswoman. Shrewd in her own way."

"But from what I hear, she yields too quickly to employee demands. No matter how well a woman might work in business, a man can always do better." The speaker was a venerable old gentleman named Conrad. He spoke through a thick beard and mustache that were snowy white. Eben was half-in-clined to respond angrily, but Conrad's great age was intimidating and, furthermore, he realized that the old fellow had meant only to discuss Suzannah's skill at business as he would any man's.

So instead of an angry retort, Eben said some-what dryly, "Thank you, sir, for that advice."

During those few days, Marianna was often alone at the Lester Hotel. Sometimes she went for a morn-ing walk. The streets of Boston frightened her, but she found her outings highly exhilarating and it was usually hard to settle down to Mrs. Delacourte's table napkins when she returned. She was becoming in-

creasingly eager to visit Dr. Wilkinson. In a serious-
minded city like Boston, wasn't it possible that a
doctor had found a way to ease her pain or even ban-
ish it from her forever? Who was she, she wondered,
staring down on the busy street below her hotel window, to contradict Eben in these matters? He had
been to a university and throughout the South he was
known for his clever ways. Who was she to doubt
him?

Whatever was wrong with Marianna, there were
some days when she felt quite herself and could move
her limbs without pain, but a lot of the time she suffered. Even sewing had become difficult. The day before her visit to Dr. Wilkinson, her hands hurt so
much she couldn't hold a needle. When the pain in
her bones was particularly acute, she could only believe that she was dying, slowly and painfully, as
her mother had died.

Marianna was with Dr. Wilkinson for more than
an hour before he returned to speak to Eben, who
was pacing the sitting room of the doctor's home. Mrs.
Wilkinson had come in from time to time with offers
of tea, but he had refused her politely. If he said yes,
he had reasoned, he might have to make conversation
with the woman and talk was unthinkable with his
mind and heart so utterly involved in what was happening behind the door to Wilkinson's surgery.

But now the doctor would not go into details
with him. He even seemed evasive. "I am examining
her with the greatest care and delicacy, Mr. Hopewell, and that's all I can tell you at the moment. I came
out here only to say that I've given the young lady
something to help her sleep. She is uncommonly agitated."

"She thinks she's going to die."

Wilkinson nodded as if he understood. "May I ask what relation this woman bears to you?"

Eben cleared his throat. "As I told you when I first spoke to you, she is my . . . sister."

The doctor raised his eyebrows. "You are people of color, Mr. Hopewell?"

"What?"

"Though extremely light-skinned, Mrs. St. Clair . . . your sister . . . is of Negroid blood, Mr. Hopewell."

"Well, she's not my full sister. . . ." Eben looked at Dr. Wilkinson, then shrugged and smiled lopsidedly. "Mrs. St. Clair is a friend, Doctor. Only that. I trust you will honor this knowledge."

The doctor was unperturbed. "I am not an arbiter of morals and behavior, Mr. Hopewell, I'm a doctor. Now," he suggested with an understanding look, "I have other patients to see while Mrs. St. Clair rests. It probably would be best if you could find something to occupy you this afternoon. Come back this evening. By then I should have something to tell you."

Following the doctor's advice, Eben walked through Quincy Market. After he had spent considerable time in the bountiful confusion of the place amidst festoons of sausages, monuments of beef, rabbit and poultry and precarious pyramids of fruit and vegetables, his spirits lifted and he became more hopeful. Before he knew it, he had crossed Blackstone Street in North Boston and wasn't far from Lucy's house.

When he knocked at the substantial oak door of the house on Moon Street, it was opened quickly by Maureen. She greeted Eben with an enthusiastic, "Oh, and good day to you, Mr. Hopewell, sir." He was shown into a little sitting room at the side of the house. While he waited, he stared out the window at two vigorous white dogwoods that reminded him of the forest on Cooper's Mountain.

Presently Lucy entered, leaving the hall door open. "Hello, Eben. This is a nice surprise."

Rested and carefully groomed, Lucy was more like the girl Eben remembered. Her wonderful hair was braided and twisted near the base of her neck, but it refused to be contained completely. Wispy tendrils framed her face with gold and she resembled nothing so much as an icon. Eben could not take his eyes off her.

She blushed. "Would you like tea, Eben? Mrs. Tippits enjoys showing off for guests. I can assure you that her Lady Baltimore cake is perfection."

"Tea, cake . . . yes, anything."

Her blush deepened. "Please sit down, Eben. And you mustn't stare at me that way. It isn't proper."

"I don't care." All thoughts of Marianna had temporarily left him. He was so enchanted by Lucy that he didn't even wonder why he had come. When she asked the purpose of his visit, he could only shake his head. "I don't know, Lucy. I just know I couldn't stay away."

"But you must, Eben."

"Why? Who is being hurt by this visit? No one. The door is wide open, Lucy. What could be more respectable than for two old friends to meet in this way?"

"I've made a vow, Eben." She wouldn't look at him.

"And so have I!" he cried, thinking she meant her marriage to Thomas. "Does that mean we can't be friends?"

"For me, yes. It does mean that." She went to the door and pulled the servant's bell. When she had asked Maureen to bring the tea and they were alone again, she said, "I made a vow to God on the night Delphia had the fever. I swore that if He would save her, I would never . . . think of you. Never."

If Eben hadn't been so horrified, he would have laughed aloud at such a vow. "Is this reasonable Lucy speaking? As I recall, you were frequently in trouble at Mrs. Quinn's boarding house for your failure to attend church. Have you suddenly converted?" He peered at her playfully.

She refused to smile. "I made a vow, Eben."

"And so I must suffer the lack of your company for a few days? Lucy, I'll be in Boston only a little while longer. If I were your neighbor, there might be some merit to such a vow, but that is hardly the case, is it?"

"How much longer will you be in Boston?" she inquired, almost timidly.

"A week at the most."

"Then you're going back to Savannah? Forever?"

He couldn't help smiling. "Hardly that. But I *will* be gone, Lucy. Gone. And then you can keep your vow and never so much as speak my name for fear of hellfire and damnation."

She made a little face at him. For an instant they were children again. "You think I'm foolish, but you don't know. You don't have children, Eben. When your only child is suffering and you can do nothing, then perhaps you'll know why people bargain with God."

He wished he could tell her that he did have a child and that he sympathized with all his heart, but he didn't think Lucy would take the news of Marianna and Christian happily.

"Please, Lucy," he begged, coming close behind her where she stood staring at him in the mantel mirror. "Forget about me when I'm gone, but while I'm in Boston. . . ."

They spent a pleasant hour together, talking of shared acquaintances and childhood times. Lucy asked about Suzannah and Eben told her some of what he had said to his business friends earlier in the week. But he added, "I think she's lonely, Lucy. She has her sister-in-law Margaret Duffy and they are very close, but I don't believe she is happy living in that big old house with my mother and father. They aren't fit company for anyone. You and she were friends once; I wish you could be again."

Lucy nodded. "And so do I. But it's not easy, Eben, when the argument between us has stretched on so long without resolution. I don't even remember what it was about, but I know we said some hateful things to one another. The scars remain and sometimes hurt despite all the time that has passed."

She went on to share her news of Ingrid and her job at the mill school and Eben told her more about the railroad. In whatever they were saying, however, there was always an undercurrent that tugged Eben's mind away from the subject and there were awkward pauses in their conversation, as if both of them had drifted for a while on this tide of forbidden emotions and words unsaid. When he left at last, it was almost with a sense of relief. To be in the same room with Lucy, unable to express all that his heart contained for her, was an exhausting exercise in restraint.

At the door he said, "I return you to your vow, Lucy. For a day or so, at any rate."

A look of panic crossed her face. "I mustn't . . ."

"One more time. Have you forgotten that Thomas invited me to dine with you and your father so that I can meet Miss Dorothea Dix, the champion of the insane?" He smiled bitterly. "Perhaps I should ask her if she has any advice for someone in my sad state." He stared at Lucy from beneath his scowling brows.

"Eben, there is no cure for this." Leaning disconsolately against the doorjamb, she added, "Except perhaps time. Time."

"When I leave Boston, I'll have nothing left to me but time. Until then, I cannot stay away, Lucy." He put his hand gently beneath her chin and tilted her head so he could see into her eyes. "Do you understand that it is useless for me even to try?"

"I know, Eben. I know."

When Eben returned to Dr. Wilkinson's surgery, it was late in the afternoon. He was shown into the cubbyhole office that adjoined the large surgery, which occupied half the first floor of the brick residence. The office was untidy. Every horizontal surface, a desk and table, a bookcase and the windowsill, was piled with assorted papers. There were journals, letters and reams and reams of notes. Dr. Wilkinson motioned for Eben to sit down.

"Well, I have examined Mrs. St. Clair thoroughly," he said, a deep crease forming between his eyes. He rubbed it thoughtfully. "It's a perplexing case."

"Can you cure her, Doctor?"

"That is hard to say, of course." Wayne Wilkinson gazed at the ceiling a moment. "How long have you known Mrs. St. Clair?"

Eben thought a moment. "Just over ten years."

"And has she always suffered?"

"I don't know. I only learned of her pain in the last year." One day he had found Marianna in her chair at a sunny window, her head buried in her hands. She was weeping. "She's a fine needlewoman, but lately it has been more and more difficult for her."

Wilkinson nodded. "And does she complain of other pain?"

"No." It was not in Marianna's character to complain. She was a stoical woman, sometimes irritatingly so. "But. . . ." He hesitated.

"Anything you can tell me might be of help, Mr. Hopewell."

"I think she suffers more than she lets on to me. It's there in her face sometimes." Eben sighed. "I wish I could be of more help to you."

"Mrs. St. Clair tells me that her mother died of an ailment that began with a simple stiffness and discomfort in the bones. Did you know Mrs. St. Clair's mother?"

"No." He thought a moment and then added, "She was a slave, Doctor. On the island of Martinique."

"Mrs. St. Clair is a slave?" Wilkinson looked horrified.

"She's a free woman now, Doctor."

Though Dr. Wilkinson looked as if he would like to know more about this, he continued, "I have read a little in a French journal concerning an ailment that seems to affect people of color. However if Mrs. St. Clair is only disturbed by painful joints, I don't think this disease can be the cause of her discomfort. Instead I suspect the pain is caused simply by a slightly premature aging of the joints. Not at all uncommon."

"Then there is no cure?"

The physician shook his head. "She must learn to endure it. If you could help her get rid of the idea that she is going to die as her mother did, it would probably do much to alleviate the pain. And hot compresses will help when the discomfort is acute."

Eben felt himself growing inexplicably short-tempered with Dr. Wilkinson. He was an expert, one of the most learned doctors in America, yet he was telling Eben nothing more than to apply heat. Old Bessie, an ignorant black woman, had told Marianna the same thing months earlier. Eben felt cheated by Wilkinson.

"You can tell me nothing more than this?"

"You came to Boston for my opinion, Mr. Hopewell, and I have given it."

"This other disease, the one you read about in the French journal, is it fatal?"

Wilkinson rolled his eyes and nodded his head emphatically. "A dreadful thing. The pain is excruciating and death is a long time coming."

"And you can guarantee that this is not what Mrs. St. Clair has?" Eben leaned forward, his elbows on Dr. Wilkinson's cluttered desk.

"I can guarantee nothing, Mr. Hopewell." Wilkinson shifted nervously in his chair.

"You are saying, then, that the problem might be premature aging of the joints or that it also might be this . . . other?"

"It's possible."

"Then she might be dying." Eben's voice was quiet and hard. When the doctor did not speak immediately, Eben asked, "Might she be dying?"

"It's possible. It's possible."

Chapter 18

James Shawn stood on the steps of the Common-
wealth Club in Boston and looked up at the sky. Tendrils of cloud were streaking in from the sea and it
looked as if there might be rain within the hour. Still
time enough to walk to Lucy's home on Moon Street,
he thought. He had spent the better part of the afternoon hunched over a pile of letters and reports relat-
ing to the ten-hour workday. Perhaps because of his
intimate knowledge of mill work, James favored this
legislation, though many of his colleagues in the General Court believed this would infringe upon the
workers' rights to work when and where and for as
long as they wished. James had been thinking about
this matter for weeks now and today's marathon reading session had been only the most recent of many.
He was stiff and cranky and thinking longingly of the
woods on Cooper's Mountain as he set off at a brisk
stride toward North Boston.

Tonight he was to meet Miss Dorothea Dix. As a
state senator, James was in a position to help the phil-
anthropist in her efforts to create refuges for the men-
tally ill. It was work James believed in, but with all
that was on his mind, he could not regard it as cruci-
al. Still, he looked forward to meeting the woman and
doing what he could to assist her. Eben Hopewell
also would be dining at the Kilmaine home and this

both troubled and enticed James. Though he anticipated with some eagerness this reunion with Suzannah's brother, it disturbed him to know that Eben and
Lucy had been spending time together.

James knew more than he cared to admit about
the pangs of forbidden love. Despite his assertions to
Suzannah at the New Year's social in Amoset that
they must remain friends, he sensed that for true lovers this must be impossible. He wanted to be Suzannah's friend, but he didn't want to be drawn into her
company very often. A passionless relationship would
be, he knew, too painful to endure. Could the same
situation exist for Lucy and Eben? As James hurried
along the crowded cobbled streets amidst horsemen
and wagons and pedestrians, he wondered and worried over this.

Though born and reared in the wilds of Cooper's
Mountain, the Yankee James Shawn, as he was known
to his constituents, enjoyed the bustle and confusion
of the great city of Boston. The city was dynamic,
changing, pulsing with vitality. As he strode along the
streets past buildings that were already considered
landmarks of historic importance, symbols of freedom
in a democracy that was not even a hundred years
old, he saw himself as part of a noble experiment.
Years before, when asked to run for office, James had
been reluctant, thinking himself too ordinary a man
for such a task. But he had quickly discovered, as had
his political opponents and friends, that he possessed
a natural ability for lawmaking. This was based in
part on his intense belief in self-government coupled
with a willingness to consider all points of view in
any argument. Nevertheless, no one had been more
surprised than James when his name was tossed about
as a possible candidate for either the United States
Senate or the governorship of Massachusetts. At first

he had discouraged the talk. In time, however, he had become more comfortable with the idea. He recognized the signals of trouble rising like Indian smoke on the country's horizon and he knew he would be shirking his duty if he turned from challenge to the pastoral life on Cooper's Mountain.

He wanted to talk seriously with Eben about disturbing trends he had noted in Southern politics. In everything James read and the talk he heard about the South, he sensed a gradual drawing away from the Union. It was his fear, and that of many of his fellow legislators, that catastrophe lay ahead for the United States unless the questions of tariffs and States' rights could be settled to the satisfaction of both North and South. There was open talk of plans for a Caribbean nation that would include the Southern states and have an economy based on agriculture and slave labor. Thinking of his ancestors who had fought and died for freedom, James knew that if called he would do the same to defend the Union.

Passing the Union Oyster House, he caught a glimpse of Daniel Webster, now serving as Secretary of State to President Tyler. The Union Oyster House was a favorite haunt of the orator's when he was in Boston. Webster liked to sit for hours near the bar and hold forth on whatever subject warmed his heart at that particular moment. Just now, James supposed he would be defending his president who, though a Whig, had managed to alienate himself from that party and almost everyone else. James crossed the street, thankful that the garrulous and opinionated Webster had not seen him.

James shook his head a little as he walked, thinking it no wonder that the ship of state was sailing in troubled waters. Not only was the South belligerent, but the economy of the whole country was suffering.

And was it any surprise? Since seven years ago when Andrew Jackson had left the presidency, there had been three men in that office and not one of them was what James Shawn would call a statesman. First there was that super politician, Van Buren, the one some called the "little magician." He was followed by poor William Henry Harrison who, in James' opinion, had had no business trying to be a national leader. Harrison hadn't even had the good sense to come in out of the cold on Inauguration Day and, consequently, had died of pneumonia, leaving the country in the hands of the Virginian, John Tyler, who was reportedly sympathetic to secessionist views. During all these changes, the tired nations of Europe, particularly England, had looked on with undisguised glee. Nothing would please them more, James knew, than to see the upstart United States brought low. But he and others in the North were determined that the Union should not crumble or the economy collapse. Democracy was the most enlightened political system devised by men, representing as it did the triumph of idealism over venality, and it was worth any sacrifice.

James would tell Eben Hopewell as much and more that evening!

Thinking of Eben, James recalled Suzannah again. Closing his eyes, he could summon up her image in his mind, recalling each detail of her face and form as if he had been with her only the day before. He had not seen her that winter, had not, in fact, been back to Amoset to see anyone, including Helen. The harsh weather had made travel difficult. And now that spring had arrived, his desk was burdened with paperwork he couldn't ignore. From time to time, when James was being particularly honest with himself, he knew that had he wished to see his wife he might have done so. But since the confrontation in their room at the close of the Christmas holidays, he had felt no motivation to make the effort. He always insisted to himself that if he no longer loved Helen, he did at least care for her well-being. But lately even that seemed doubtful, for days and days would pass without a thought of her entering his mind.

Now, striding through the dusky Boston streets, passing the lamplighters on their rounds, he hid from the truth by concentrating on Lucy. She was his angel child, the daughter of his delight. The essence of the love he no longer felt for Helen and must never feel for Suzannah he transferred to Lucy.

The little house on Moon Street was brightly lighted and festive that evening. Mrs. Tippits had outdone herself with a feast fit for a royal visitation. There was a subtly flavored lobster bisque, a sausage pudding and a masked fish and then a roast of lamb with assorted fresh vegetables which Maureen had picked out at the Quincy Market just that morning. Thomas had been to a wine merchant's near Beacon Hill and had brought home several bottles of wine and sherry and a mellow, nutty brandy the color of caramel. Such lavish entertainments were not usual in the Kilmaine household, but Miss Dix's presence at their table was an event of major importance to both Thomas and Lucy, who admired the woman greatly for her unselfish philanthropic work.

"Of course, there are a great many people who think I am mad myself," Miss Dix laughed. "They cannot imagine why anyone would bother with those poor men and women—even children!—who live in the darkness of insanity. But no Christian heart can be untouched by their suffering. By setting up homes where these unfortunates are safe from mistreatment and ridicule, I hope to prove that some of them are capable of leading productive lives." Dinner had been over for some time. The gentlemen had enjoyed cigars and brandy alone while the women freshened themselves and now the men and women were together again in the Kilmaine drawing room.

"But, Miss Dix, I know you understand that the draw upon public monies is already so great as to make each new expenditure. . . ." James had no chance to continue. A woman of strong beliefs, Dorothea Dix was not about to be intimidated.

"Senator, I propose to you that we are either a Christian nation or we are not. If we are, then what I have seen in the poorhouses and asylums of this state, this heartland of democracy, is a sin and a shame before God."

Miss Dix patted a dark attaché case on the settee beside her. "Read these, Senator. Read my notebooks, my journals, my reports and you will be appalled. I have found men and women and children living like animals, chained to the floor or enclosed in lidded cribs in which they can neither stand nor even sit comfortably. I have seen Americans like you and me with iron collars about their necks, their clothing no more than filth and vermin-ridden rags. More than once I have seen and wept and felt righteous anger on behalf of children, boys and girls, chained, naked and lashed with cruel rods." Her plain face was grim and thin-lipped. "All I ask is that you read what I have written. If your heart is not moved. . . ."

Lucy listened with only partial concentration. What Dorothea Dix described was deplorable in the extreme, but it wasn't much of a surprise to her. She had known Foster McMahon and this knowledge had prepared her for the worst life had to offer. Are men monsters? she wondered to herself as she poured coffee for her guests. Glancing up, she intercepted a look from Eben and quickly turned away.

What was she to do about Eben? She had made a solemn oath to God that if He would save her daughter, she would give up all thoughts of Eben. Ever since then, such thoughts had challenged her devotion at every moment of the day. It was all very well for Eben to say that he would be gone soon, but even then, she knew that he would still dominate her thoughts. A sense of painful helplessness led her into an uncharacteristic fancy in which she imagined that good and evil, God and the Devil, were warring within her body for ascendancy. She began to feel she had no more to say about the outcome of this war than does the field on which armies rage against one another or the black sea on which armadas battle.

This is madness, she told herself. To abdicate responsibility in the matter would mean that she was no better than the poor lunatic creatures Miss Dix was describing. This thought was wryly amusing. Perhaps love is a kind of madness, Lucy thought. Looking up again, she saw that Eben was still watching her. She wanted to cry out to him to stop, to go away from her with all speed and never return. But an even stronger urge was to bid him stay and come to her and love her, despite all the laws of God and man that forbade it. These contradictory thoughts made her feel flushed and uncomfortable. As she poured the last cup of coffee, her hand shook so badly that the cup clattered in its saucer.

Noticing this, Miss Dix spoke to her. "I am disturbing you with all these nightmare tales, Mrs. Kilmaine. You must forgive me. But I fear that unless I speak out. . . ."

"No one will know." Lucy smiled as she stood up. "Your work is so important, Miss Dix, that I would not for a moment inhibit your conversation with my father. But to tell the truth, what you are saying *is* disturbing and I feel warm. Would you excuse me if I went outside for a moment for some air?"

"Are you all right, Lucy? You were with Delphia when she was ill. Have you contracted her sickness?" Thomas got up and hurried to his wife's side.

Embarrassed by the attention, Lucy stepped back toward the door. "No, really, I'm fine. And Delphia only suffered from one of the innumerable fevers that plague every childhood. You mustn't worry about me."

Eben stood up. "Let me go with her, Thomas. You have guests."

"No, really, it's not necessary."

"Nonsense," said Thomas. "Lucy, you shouldn't be alone if you don't feel well." He spoke in the paternalistic tone that so infuriated Lucy. If he had taken any other tack with her, she would have discouraged Eben's companionship. But when Thomas treated her as a child with only a partial grasp of reality, it had a way of angering her and making her say and do what she would otherwise forbid herself.

"Very well," she responded, her tone cool and contained, a perfect counterpoint disguise for her true state of mind. She turned to Eben. "Let me show you our garden, Mr. Hopewell."

The rain had stopped, but the garden was too damp to walk through, so they sat on the iron bench in the summerhouse Thomas had built the year before. It was a delicate little wooden structure with a pretty scalloped roof and a graceful railing running all around, a favorite place of Lucy's. She liked to sit there in the warm weather, a book of poems in her lap, admiring the bountiful garden she cultivated each year.

"There's nothing much to see now," she said to Eben, talking quickly. "But in a month or two I'll have roses and petunias and marigolds the size of hot cross buns. And I grow vegetables, too, you know. I seem to have a gift for gardening." The statement sounded idiotic to her ears and she stopped talking, embarrassed.

"I love you, Lucy."

"I don't want you to say that."

"But I must." He took her hand and she didn't try to pull away. "I want you more than anything in the world."

"Oh, Eben, you don't know what you're saying. We are both married; I belong to Thomas and you to Amanda."

He laughed, a brief, sharp sound. "No. I belong to myself and you belong to you."

"Thomas is my husband, Eben. I honor him." A tear slipped down her cheek and before she could brush it away another came.

"Do you love him, Lucy?"

She didn't answer.

"Do you love him?" he insisted.

"It's not a matter of love. There is honor and fidelity and. . . ." True, she had made a pact with God on her child's life, but as the tears glistened on her cheeks, God no longer existed and she cared for nothing she had ever said or done before. It was too cruel that she must always be denying herself, always disguising or stifling her true emotions. In that moment Lucy forgot about God, forgot about Thomas, forgot about Delphia in her room at the top of the house. Even Foster McMahon's eyes and mouth and touch were blotted out by a storm of emotion. In a rush, she flung her arms about Eben's neck and pulled him close to her. The smell of his skin was intoxicating and her body responded almost drunkenly with a wantonness that Lucy had never dreamed existed in herself.

Eben groaned and, grabbing her warm face between his hands, pressed his mouth against hers in a fierce, demanding kiss that left her breathless and terrified of the heat rising in her. Gasping for air, half-sobbing, Lucy returned his kisses hungrily, her mouth open and wet with desire. It was as if a kind of madness had taken hold of her and she was both its mistress and its victim. He kissed her mouth again and again, then her cheeks, her neck, the soft rise of her breasts in the low-cut gown she wore.

A stray sound from the house stopped them. Suddenly they were aware again of where they were and what they were doing. They stared at each other, transfixed by a wonder that was also terror.

Pulling away she whispered, "Tomorrow. Maureen will be gone in the afternoon."

From the moment he closed and locked the sliding doors of the drawing room behind him, Lucy knew that whatever else happened in her life, she would be happy for having loved Eben Hopewell. He stood before her, tall and wonderfully built in his grey cutaway coat, snug trousers and knee-high riding boots of moroccan leather. His expression was darkly handsome, brooding and, in its way, frighteningly intense. He meant to have her. She saw that clearly and, for some reason, it made her think of Foster McMahon, who had found joy in hurting and abusing her spirit. The memory of him was so vivid that she stepped back, suddenly alarmed that Eben might yet prove to be the villain she long ago had thought him.

But before her fear could reach her body and tell it to flee, Lucy experienced a flash of prescience that killed the fear forever. Looking at Eben's hands and lips and eyes, feeling his magnetism, she knew that Eben in this totality was the only force in the world that could bring her body back to life after McMahon and the years with Thomas Kilmaine. In that soaring moment, her love became more than a matter of choice. It was a necessity.

He strode directly toward her, taking the length of the drawing room in a few long paces, to where she stood by the window in a pale peach gown.

"Close the curtain," he commanded. And she did.

She had only a few more moments to think before he kissed her, and she saw in those moments the guilt she would suffer when this sweet inevitability was over. When Eben was in Savannah, she would beg God to forgive, knowing in her deepest heart that He never would. When Eben was in Savannah, her thoughts and dreams would teem with guilt, but it would be worth it.

"I've wanted you all my life," Eben murmured, his mouth against her ear as he opened the sash that held the front of her gown and reached inside, letting the palm of his hand brush against her breasts in their silken chemise. Her nipples were hard and exquisitely sensitive and this filled Lucy with wonder. Once, hurt and disappointed, Thomas had spoken without thinking, calling her a woman of ice, a woman with winter in her blood. She had believed him and in time had come to accept the blame for the anger or disgust or, worse by far, the resigned boredom brought on by her husband's touch.

Now, in Eben's arms, it was glorious to discover the truth, that she was warm and womanly and capable of desire. It made her tremble through all her being, as if she had never known a man before. As Eben slipped his hands between her thighs and stroked her, Lucy surrendered to him completely. "Go slowly, Eben," she begged. "I want to feel it all."

PART IV

Chapter 19

In Amoset there was snow on the ground until April. On the first of February, January's false spring had veered back to winter overnight as the river valley was subjected to the worst ice storm in anyone's memory. Even those who had lived in the shadow of Cooper's Mountain since before Martin Hopewell and his mill, old-timers from the days when Amoset was a trading village on the river, the last outpost before the wild western mountains, could not remember such a sudden, almost vicious, turn of weather.

It had begun with rain on a windy afternoon and by dusk, the temperature had begun to drop. Operatives lighting their petticoat lamps in Hopewell Mills looked up when they heard the mellow drum of rain become the icy whisper of sleet as it scraped against the windows. Going home at quitting time, their heads and shoulders bundled in woolen scarves, they didn't talk or laugh, and the crowded streets were strangely silent. By eight, the low sections of Front Street had been made perilous by wide stretches of sheet ice and all the streets were empty, their lamps unlit. Though shuttered down both inside and out, the outlines of the boarding house windows, row upon row of them, glowed faintly like distant beacons of a warmer land. When the town awoke next morn-

ing at four o'clock to the sound of the mill bells, the
storm had passed.

In her own room overlooking the town, Suzannah
heard the bells and she awoke as unwillingly as any
operative in Amoset. But she was more fortunate, for
a maid had slipped in while she was still sleeping and
lit the fire. It was warm and comfortable to sit up in
bed and sip hot chocolate while she thought about
the day ahead. Later, when Suzannah was dressed
and about to go downstairs for breakfast, she opened
her shutters and saw that in the night her world had
been transformed. Washed in frigid moonlight, the
town, the river and the mountains were white and
glistening. Ice covered every surface, each angle and
curve and slope. It laced the trees and decorated the
bushes like a mantle of diamonds. Through this chaste
scene, Suzannah watched the operatives slowly making their way to work by lantern light, a procession of
fireflies.

In the cavernous mill, the workers lit the petticoat lamps that hung from every loom, casting a sul-
furous glow about the workrooms as they filled the air
with burning whale oil fumes. When the looms
clanged into operation, the brown air was clouded
with cotton lint. This part of the year was lighting up
time, a time of stinging eyes, punishing headaches,
aching chests and hacking coughs that lasted for
months. It was a filthy time when most of the operatives gave up caring for their appearances and
dragged to work in the warmest clothes they owned,
no matter how grimy they were with smoke and mud
and slush.

This was the year when a group of female operatives at Hathaway's Mill refused to work by candle-
light and complained that winter mill work was

injurious to their health. When this information was
conveyed to him, Mr. Hathaway himself came down
and locked the mill yard gate. The operatives spent
the night in the old mill and the next morning, hungry and trembling with cold, they capitulated to the
owner. There wasn't an operative in Amoset who did
not sympathize with the girls from Hathaway's, but
jobs were hard to come by in the winter of 1843, so
they had to stand alone.

After the attack on the operative named Annabella
that had taken place when the last snow of the year
was on the ground, women had stayed cooped up inside their mills or boarding houses, reluctant to go
outdoors in the evening, even when the weather improved. In every boarding house, as they gathered in
close circles about the fireplace or stove, busy with
their tatting, they dreamed up theories to explain the
murders that had plagued Amoset for more than a dec-
ade. The more the girls talked, the more certain they
were that the man had been an Irishman from the
Gully. And as the operatives reached this conclusion
in their sitting rooms, the gentlemen of Amoset, the
manufacturers and selectmen, reached the same in
theirs. There were several angry discussions, most of
them led by Selectman Stoat, but in the end all they
had were suspicions. There was no solid evidence
with which to indict anyone, so the men knew they
would simply have to wait and be watchful. The men
cautioned the operatives against going around town
alone, but the admonition was hardly necessary. Every woman in Amoset was frightened.

Except, perhaps, Ingrid. Terrible as the attack
had been, Ingrid felt so far removed from it that she
couldn't be afraid. Jerusha and Meredith told her over
and over that there had been many murders in
Amoset and clearly the most recent attack had been

made by the same man who had ravaged and then
murdered the other young women. But they never
managed to frighten her, although she did go along
with their precautions and never walked about alone.

For Ingrid, life was just beginning and into its
steady, stormless skies she would not admit even a
hint of winter or the merest touch of death's cold.
Through ice storms and blizzards, Ingrid Shawn's
little mill school stayed open. Because the mill with
which it shared a common wall stood in the way of
the north wind, the area of the school was protected
from the worst of the weather. But to keep her school
open, Ingrid worked harder than she ever had
dreamed would be necessary. Not only was she the
teacher, she was the handyman as well. She scav-
enged wood and, with a borrowed hammer and three
cents' worth of nails, she shingled the cracks in the
window shutters and around the door. Across the icy
cobbles, she carted bundles of fuel and kindling on
her back. Before the children came to school at seven,
she would build a fire in the iron stove that squatted
near the center of the one-room shed, sweep the floor
and scrub the benches. When this work was done,
Ingrid would clean off her own desk and sit down to
plan her lessons for the day, the fumes from the desk
lamp burning her eyes.

She had only seven students that first year. The
oldest was a thirteen-year-old boy, but the rest were
girls between the ages of seven and twelve. These
were the fortunate children whose parents, despite
the hard times, considered an education worth a few
months' leave from the mill. Most of the children employed by Suzannah Paine, bobbin boys and sweepers
and runners, stayed on the job.

The school operated with the barest minimum of

equipment. There were half a dozen benches about five feet long, a dozen slates that could be held in the hand and one large one that Ingrid used for lessons, a teacher's desk and two other roughly built tables that could be used for anything. No textbooks were provided. Ingrid was expected to teach from her own books, *Pierpont's National Reader* and *Colburn's Arithmetic*. She taught reading, writing and arithmetic, with occasional digressions into history and geography. Ingrid never had attended school herself, therefore she had no model to go by, save the one she had devised in her imagination. Consequently, the classroom atmosphere quickly took on the shadings of Ingrid's personality. The children learned that they could laugh a lot in her school and ask as many questions as they pleased, so long as they balanced this with silent diligence when necessary and politeness at all times. She rewarded their successes with lavish praise and her criticisms most often ended on an encouraging note.

"I hear only good things about you, Ingrid," Suzannah said one morning when she paid the school a visit before classes began. She stamped her cold feet a time or two and peered at the wood stove. "Don't tell me you're burning wood, Ingrid! On a morning like this?"

Ingrid didn't say anything. She hadn't known she had a choice.

"How careless of me not to think! You need coal, Ingrid. I shall see that you have some this very morning." Before Ingrid could thank her, Suzannah went on. "I have had inquiries about your school from several children. It seems that word of your skill has invaded even the secret haunts of the bobbin boys and runners. Shall I send you half a dozen more children in the spring?"

"Well, I have seven students now and slates for twelve, Mrs. Paine."

"I'll see you get more if you need them." Before leaving, Suzannah turned and surveyed the little school. She looked satisfied. "Ingrid, your sister would be proud of you."

Several other times that winter, Suzannah ventured into Ingrid's schoolroom to observe the teacher and her students. Ingrid's admiration for the woman was without bounds, though Jerusha and Meredith did their best to discourage it.

"Don't think she does it out of the goodness of her heart," Meredith cautioned. "Owners don't do anything unless it suits their business."

The three friends were seated side by side on the stairs outside the bedroom they shared with three other operatives. One blanket was spread across their laps and tucked about their knees. They were sucking on hard lumps of brown-sugar candy bought from a vendor who had knocked on the boarding house door after dinner. The house was silent now, but for sleeping sounds, and they spoke in whispers to keep from waking anyone. If they were to cause any disturbance, they would be brought before Mrs. Quinn and humiliated.

"Don't forget, Ingrid, 'twas your sister got that school for you. Before Lucy organized our turn-out, there was no school and no thought of one. Suzannah Paine only agreed because. . . ." Meredith stopped and listened a moment. Someone was moving about in a room below them. They heard the clank of a chamber pot being set on the floor. Meredith grinned and held her nose, causing Ingrid and Jerusha to dissolve into stifled, red-faced giggles.

"Hush!" They were instantly silent, although

Ingrid had to clamp down hard on her mouth to keep the laughter from bubbling out of her. Meredith shook a warning finger. "We can't be brought before Mrs. Quinn again, Ingrid Shawn. The next time she'll report us all to the mill. You know that! How sweet will your friend Suzannah Paine be then, I wonder?"

Women who disobeyed the strict rules of boarding house life were subject to dismissal from their jobs at the mill. It was a hard rule and more and more operatives were finding it difficult to live with. Many of them were women in their late twenties and thirties who felt they had a right to order their own lives. They complained against the regimenting bells, the early curfew, the mandatory church attendance and the lights-out cutoff, but because they were law-abiding and afraid of losing their positions, most of the operatives followed every rule regardless of how petty. Jerusha, Meredith and Ingrid were remarkable among the women at Mrs. Quinn's in their steadfast refusal to obey without questioning. Half of the boarders envied them and the other half thought they were unspeakably bad for daring to challenge authority.

Julia had told them that the next time they were caught eating on the stairs after lights out or otherwise breaking the rules, Mrs. Quinn would report them for termination. But Ingrid wasn't much afraid of Julia's threats, for she simply couldn't believe that Suzannah would terminate her for the crime of talking late at night.

"She would never sacrifice the school," declared Ingrid, tucking the blanket more tightly about her knees. "She cares about learning. I even think she cares about me."

Jerusha and Meredith looked at one another as if

to ask what hope there was for a dunderhead like Ingrid. But there was affection in their glance, for both of them believed it was their place to guide and protect Lucy Shawn's little sister. Jerusha and Meredith had worked in Amoset for a good many years and there was very little they didn't know by now about the town and its mills. Though each of them had been drawn to mill life because it promised good wages and cultural pleasures, they had long since been disillusioned. And with that disillusionment had come a bitter determination not to be fooled again. No matter that Suzannah's treatment of the operatives had always been fair and honest, they still eyed everything she did with suspicion and assumed the worst.

Such cynicism was typical of Meredith's personality, but Jerusha was still a decided romantic about most other matters. Her dreamy, hopeful nature seemed to have been created in her as a kind of shield against the discouragements of a difficult life. The eldest of ten children of a Pennsylvania miner, the wages she earned for her family made the difference that enabled them to keep their home rather than live in shabby, overcrowded lodgings. Therefore, despite the tarnished reality of mill work, she had no choice but to continue in it.

"I'll show her one of these days," Jerusha declared, sucking hard on her candy. "One of these days I'm going to tell Mrs. Paine that I don't give a fig for her job."

Meredith laughed. "Oh yes, I would like to see that! When will you do it, Jerusha? I want to be there."

"You can make all the fun you like, but when I get married . . ."

Meredith hooted again and mimicked her friend. ". . . and Mr. Thaddeus Temple calls for me on his white charger . . . !"

Jerusha was cross. "You can make fun all you like, Meredith, but you just wait and see."

Meredith continued to laugh softly. She was a small red-haired woman with round blue eyes and a patchwork of orange freckles spread across her nose. Though she was slight and always spoke in a low voice, the impression Meredith gave of vulnerability was a false one. Actually, she was a young woman of determination who had suffered and survived more in twenty years than most do in a lifetime. She had never known her father, and her mother had died before she was five, leaving her in the hands of three loving but careless older brothers. They had all died in a cholera epidemic in New York City so, at an age when most girls are still beside their mother's skirts, Meredith had struggled to support herself. It was an existence that had left her with few illusions, yet something of sweetness had been saved in her despite all this. When her heart was touched, as it often was by Ingrid's innocence and naiveté, she could be gentle and caring.

To Ingrid, the value of these two friends was incalculable. Because she had spent half her life as an invalid, friends were still the stuff of dreams to her. Later that night, from her place in the middle of the creaking bed she shared with Jerusha and Meredith, Ingrid stared at the ceiling long after the curfew bell had rung. She was reviewing the lucky fortune that had brought her to this thrilling time of life. It didn't matter about the cold or being terminated or anything at all except her two friends and the work she did. She had the exhilarating sense of living on the edge of life, of looking out on endless possibilities. She had work that was important and challenging. She had stalwart and amusing friends. And every dawn she awakened to the bells, eager and wondering what surprises the day would hold.

Chapter 20

By mid-May there were wildflowers in the high meadow above Amoset on Cooper's Mountain. One Saturday afternoon when the weather was particularly balmy, the three friends climbed up there for a picnic. As they came over a rise, they beheld the spectacle of dozens of varieties of wildflowers, a profusion of color. They ate their meal of bread and cold meat beside a sparkling brook whose banks were carpeted with blossoms and over whose stones the moss fell like water. Afterward they lay back in the new grass, chewing on stalks of sassafras and wondering aloud about the shape of clouds, the movement of the earth and the meaning of it all.

In the midst of this, Jerusha blurted, "I've got something wonderful to tell you both!"

After a moment of surprised silence, Meredith asked in a gently mocking way, "Well, tell, Jerusha. Don't keep us waiting."

"Thaddeus has come." It was a statement spoken in round portentous tones, deserving of a drum roll or a trumpet fanfare.

Meredith laughed. "And who is he? God Almighty?"

"Meredith, don't blaspheme!" cried Ingrid.

"But the way she says it! 'Thaddeus has come.' It

puts me in mind of some noble personage and not a gypsy preacher with a painted cart."

"You're only jealous because he didn't like you!"

Meredith tossed her head and raised her eyebrows. "And should I care what a penniless nomad thinks of me?"

"Stop arguing, you two," said Ingrid crossly. "I want to hear about this Thaddeus Temple."

Thrilled to find an audience, Jerusha turned her back on Meredith. "And you will do better than hear *about* him, Ingrid. You will actually hear him speak."

"Spring is preaching season. For them that don't have churches."

Jerusha whirled, face flushed and eyes red. "What do you know about it, Meredith? If Mrs. Quinn didn't make you, you wouldn't go to church from Christmas to Christmas. You're practically a heathen!" Then she explained to Ingrid, "Thaddeus has no church because the world is his church, his cathedral. He has nothing against churches or meeting houses like the one at Reverend Strickland's Unitarian, but he just doesn't think they're necessary. Thaddeus says . . ."

Meredith groaned.

". . . that when God created the earth, He meant it to be His church. The whole world."

"Even down in the mines with your daddy?" Meredith wondered carelessly, making herself even more comfortable in the sweet green grass.

Jerusha stared at her, finding it hard to believe that her friend could be so flippant.

"Well?"

"I know it's hard for you to understand, but yes, even a mine can become a church. Thaddeus has been down to Pennsylvania and has gone into the

mines to preach to the men working there. He's not
afraid to go anywhere because he believes. . . ."

"Tell me how you met him." Ingrid's eyes were
shining. "Have you walked out together?"

Meredith snorted.

"Well, not exactly." Jerusha cast Meredith a
wounding look. "But after last year, I have every reason to believe we will."

Ingrid grabbed her hands. "Tell me, then. Everything!"

"Well, last spring I went to hear him preach and
he talked about the mines then, so afterward I went
up to him and told him that my father and brothers
are in the mines. He asked me where and though he
hadn't been to my home town, he knew of it. We
talked a little about the countryside and the folks that
live thereabouts." She grinned at Ingrid. "It was easy
talking to him. Right off I felt like he was kin to me."

"A kissing cousin."

"He kissed you?" Ingrid cried. She was loving every moment of this.

"Meredith, you promised!" Jerusha flung herself
on her friend and shook her hard. "You promised on
your oath you wouldn't tell!"

"It's all right." Ingrid tried to pull Jerusha off.
"You can tell me. I won't think you're horrid if you let
him kiss you."

Meredith, though much abused, began giggling
and, catching the distracted Jerusha off guard, she
gave her a hard push and jumped up. Laughing now,
her pale red hair a wildly tangled mess about her
face, she shook her finger at Jerusha. "Tell her. Go on!
You know you want to. When you came home two
minutes before curfew that night last summer, your
face was as red as a beet and you were so full of
yourself that you were actually spluttering. You

couldn't wait to tell me how you prayed together, how he walked you to the bridge, how. . . ."

"It was wonderful, Ingrid," Jerusha cut in, wanting to tell the story herself. "Truly it was. There was just a little tiny bit of a moon, but the stars were brilliant. I'd never seen the heavens look like that before. Thaddeus says the skies are part of the wilderness God has created for us to come through to Him, and that the stars are like welcoming bonfires so we won't ever feel lonely along the way."

"How beautiful!"

"How beautiful!" mimicked Meredith, flopping down on the grass again. She groaned. "A bit too beautiful, if you ask me."

"When he talks, his voice sounds like music. Sometimes it's light and happy and sometimes it's like thunder. It wraps all around you and almost seems to get inside you. When we were standing beside the bridge, looking up at the stars and talking about God and heaven and all, I thought I'd swoon. When you hear his voice, Ingrid, you'll understand."

"But when did he kiss you?"

"That's good, Ingrid! Keep her to the point."

Jerusha tossed a handful of grass at her taunting friend. "Well, I was getting there. After a bit he stopped talking about the stars and we just stood there. I don't know why I didn't say good night like I normally would when it's close to lockup, but I didn't want to go in. It was so nice standing there with him, not saying anything." She blushed. "Then . . . well, he put his hand under my chin and tilted up my face so I was looking right at him. I couldn't turn my eyes away."

Ingrid sighed.

"Then he slowly brought his face down close to mine and . . . kissed me."

"What did you do then?"

Meredith rolled over on her stomach. "I'll tell you what she did. The silly dumpling ran home! She hasn't seen her precious Thaddeus Temple since."

"Is that true?" Ingrid was clearly disappointed.

"He'll be here tomorrow. I heard some people talking about a sign they'd seen in town that said he'd be in the little bowl off Cooper's Mountain on Sunday at two. That gives us plenty of time to get there after dinner." She looked back and forth at both her friends. They looked a little doubtful. Jerusha's confidence began to wither.

Meredith sighed and, reaching out, she gently patted her friend's knee. When she spoke, her voice was kindly and not at all teasing as it had been. "Try not to be such a silly dumpling, Jeru. Do you think that life is fairy tales like Cinderella?"

"You're trying to hurt me. You're cruel."

"If I sound unkind, forgive me. Don't misunderstand my teasing. I only meant to make you laugh a little, to help you take yourself less seriously when it comes to Thaddeus Temple. You see, Jerusha, to some men a kiss beside a bridge is nothing. Scarcely more than a handshake, I'm afraid."

"You're just jealous because. . . ." Her shoulders slumped and she stared at the ground.

"I'm telling you the truth. You know I am." Jerusha began to cry and Meredith put her arms around her comfortingly. "It can't be such a shock, Jeru," she said with compassion. "You've known it all along. You know you have."

Ingrid watched the scene with fascination, first taking the part of one girl and then the other. In the end, she was left somewhat confused about Thaddeus Temple and the kiss beside the bridge. Was it a very terrible thing to let a man kiss you that way? Or was it, as Meredith had said, scarcely more than a handshake? She wondered whether Thaddeus Temple was the wonder Jerusha portrayed him as, or whether he was something of a cad, however musical his voice. And in that case, was he truly a man of God?

Regardless of what he was, Thaddeus Temple had begun to live in her imagination, a large man and brighter than light.

The meeting was held in a shallow bowl of meadowland behind the old churchyard at the top of a hollow where Talleyrand Shawn had been buried with his Hildebrand and Shawn ancestors. In spring and early summer, a little stream cut through the hollow and beside it grew several shimmery birches close together, like people talking. Jerusha led her friends to a spot on the gently sloping hillside where they could look down toward the trees and stream. They spread out blankets to sit on and opened their parasols for protection from the sun.

They were early. Jerusha had rushed Meredith and Ingrid through their midday meal and then, as they climbed the steep hill up Cooper's Mountain, she had maintained an almost steady trot that kept the other two huffing and puffing to keep up. Now Ingrid was glad for a chance to catch her breath and look around as the bowl began to fill with men and women, coming in groups of two and three.

She was not a deeply religious girl, although it never had occurred to her to disbelieve in God and Jesus Christ. When she had lived with the Davis family in Harpers Ferry, her churchgoing had been regular but uninspired, for she found nothing uplifting in the cramped chill of the Lutheran church. She had learned to appear devout while actually thinking of what she would do when the service was over, and in this way had passed many years of Sundays. Now, as she glanced at the serious faces around her, she saw men and women she remembered dimly from her early childhood, from the time before she had left the mountain and had gone to stay in Harpers Ferry. That couple over there. . . . She thought a moment and remembered that somehow, distantly, they were kin to her. The men and women from the mountain were easy to distinguish from those who lived in Amoset or other towns along the river. These country folk wore drab clothes and, sitting side by side on the grass, they didn't laugh or talk to one another. By contrast, the young women from town with their gaily printed dirndls spread about them, the sunlight filtering through their parasols and casting a flickering, jewellike glow, kept up a merry conversation and bubbled like springs in their eagerness.

Ingrid's thoughts were interrupted when a scene took place before her, entirely capturing her attention and filling her with pleasure. A wagon painted canary yellow, drawn by a grey mule in an old felt hat, was coming up the hollow to the bowl. Alongside ran a threesome of yapping spotted dogs and at the rear there was a cow, attached to the wagon by a length of rope, and behind the cow a silver-white horse of great size and wonderful proportions.

"There he is!" whispered Jerusha, jabbing Ingrid in the ribs.

From the front of the wagon jumped a man in his midtwenties with a thick head of curly reddish-gold hair. When he glanced around at the thirty or so people who had come to hear him speak, he smiled boyishly, wrinkling his bright blue eyes.

"I thank you all for being here. This is the third year I've visited Amoset and it's good to be welcomed back by friends." Thaddeus Temple turned to unhitch his mule, but he moved aside when a pair of men in high-crowned, wide-brimmed hats stepped out of the congregation to do it for him. He looked around at the people in the crowd. "Brother Bradshaw," he said, recognizing one man. " 'Tis good to see you. And Sister Irma." He grinned beguilingly. "Have you brought me another of your fine berry pies this year, or have I come too early?"

Ingrid watched this exchange, and when Thaddeus then moved to another part of the congregation and spoke to some mill operatives who had never come to hear him speak before, she began to hope that he would come this way and speak to her. Or at least to Jerusha, who was quivering with excitement beside her. She could hear her friend's squeaky, gasping breaths.

"Thank you for coming, sisters," he said when he got to the three of them.

Jerusha was right; his voice was marvelous. Ingrid had never heard tones so deep and rich in subtlety.

"I was here last year," ventured Jerusha timidly. "Do you remember . . . Jerusha Billings?" Her voice quavered.

Ever afterward, Ingrid would not be sure if Thaddeus Temple's eyes had shown a flicker of doubt before he said, "It's good to see you, Miss Billings. And thank you for bringing your friends." He looked directly into Ingrid's eyes and her mouth went dry. "May the Spirit move in you today, sister."

When he was gone, Ingrid could not look at Jerusha beside her, for she was afraid her friend would see right into her disloyal heart and know. She was feeling guilty about something, though she had no idea of what specifically. She was squirmy, however, and suddenly out of sorts. The day seemed to have lost its freshness. But if Jerusha noticed anything out of the ordinary in Ingrid, she gave no sign. She was entirely consumed with herself.

"He didn't remember me," Ingrid heard her whisper incredulously. "He didn't remember that he'd kissed me. I was like a stranger to him."

Meredith murmured something in an attempt to comfort her.

"Do you want to leave?" Ingrid asked almost hopefully.

Jerusha shook her head and her expression settled into the stern lines of a country woman. "I came to hear him preach. It doesn't make any difference whether or not he remembers me. After all, it's what he has to teach us of God that's important." Though she tried to look proud and cold, Jerusha was clearly miserable.

As Thaddeus settled himself on the back of his wagon, the congregation moved closer. The three spotted dogs wandered about, nosing hampers and bundles for bits of a picnic meal or a square of sugar and settled down at last in the shade under the yellow wagon. Thaddeus Temple began to speak.

At first he spoke so softly that everyone had to lean forward a little to hear his words, but his voice commanded their attention. "Beauty is the handmaiden of love," he said. His voice rose. "Beauty is the handmaiden of love. Wherever there is love there is beauty. Wherever beauty exists, there is also love." He jumped from the back of the wagon and began to walk about the clearing before his listeners, using his voice to alert them as thunder can announce a storm when the sky is hardly clouded. The men and women sat up straighter. Though Thaddeus spoke loudly and clearly now, still they strained forward, as if they could hear God Himself speaking through a mortal man.

"God created us and the earth and the heavens above out of the immensity of His love. Because of His love we are beautiful. The lowest, the most infirm, is still magnificent in the Creator's eye, for He loves every one of us and everything around us." Thaddeus opened his arms wide. The sunlight glinted in his copper curls and it appeared to Ingrid that he was lit by some inner fire, for his handsome, boyish face was radiant.

"Look about you," he demanded. "See this meadowland. It is not beautiful by accident. God made it so. Love made it so. Think what can be more magnificent, more touchingly beautiful than an infant at the warmth of its mother's breast. Love made it so, for when we love one another we do God's bidding. As He loves us, He would have us love one another. As He made heaven and earth beautiful with His love, He bids us love one another and strive always for that which is beautiful and true. In this way, by loving one another, we are all made more beautiful and more like God Himself. This is His message to us . . . love one another. In the beauty of love lies the meaning of life."

Chapter 21

When the preaching was over and the people were
gathering up their things to go, Ingrid took leave of
her friends to visit Talley's grave. She climbed the
hillside to the neglected churchyard, which was overgrown in some places with wild red raspberry and
trumpet creeper. Here and there, graves like Talley
Shawn's were cleared and manicured. Once a little
church had stood in the middle of the plot, but long
before Ingrid's birth, in the days when Martin
Hopewell had first come to the Amoset valley, the
church had fallen into disuse and had been abandoned. Only the foundation rubble remained, surrounded by the grave sites and enclosed by a
crumbling stone wall over which hung the limbs of a
chestnut tree. Families on Cooper's Mountain still
used the area as a graveyard, however, and Ingrid
could walk from plot to plot and never see a name
that didn't carry with it some intimate association.

At the time of Talley's death, Helen Shawn had
planted a dogwood sapling near his grave. With in-
finite care she also had transplanted a wild azalea that
was covered in spring with masses of pink frilly
edged blossoms. The bush had by now grown so tall
as to almost block Talley's white stone, which was in-
scribed only with his name and the years of his birth
and death. Staring at it, Ingrid felt the familiar loss

rise up in her. The unfairness of his death was a
weight that sometimes struck her like a blow and sent
her mind reeling back to the old times with a sense of
disbelief. How could any happy, energetic child be at
one moment tossing a red rubber ball and at the next
moment dead, destroyed by a machine that didn't
even pause when its clanging metal gears had done
their worst?

"Did you know that boy?" asked a voice.
Startled, Ingrid looked up and saw Thaddeus Temple.
He was sitting astride his beautiful white horse,
watching her from the edge of the woods a few yards
away. He was dressed as he had been earlier in rough
homespun clothes, but on his head he wore a farmer's
floppy brimmed hat. Nudging his bare heels into the
side of the horse, he moved up to the edge of the
stone wall. While the animal pulled and chomped at
the new grass, Thaddeus stared at Ingrid. He made
her feel uncomfortable. She couldn't see his eyes
beneath the shadow of his hat brim and didn't know
how to take his scrutiny.

"He was my brother. Talleyrand Shawn."

"Your family lives on Cooper's Mountain?"

"That's right." She picked up her bonnet from
where she had placed it beneath the dogwood and
tied the long strings under her chin. She felt a little
more confident with her hat on. "This graveyard is
full of Shawns. And Hildebrands, too . . . my
mother's people."

Thaddeus swung down off the horse and, leaping
easily over the wall, came to stand near her. Although
he was a preacher, Ingrid was still uncomfortable
being alone with him in the isolated graveyard. But
he was smiling at her boyishly, distracting her fear
with the sight of his wondrously even white teeth and
bright blue eyes.

"I've learned a lot of history from the graveyards of New England," he told her, apparently oblivious to her discomfort. "I would be pleased to hear what you know of the ghosts that dwell on Cooper's Mountain."

"You believe in ghosts!" Ingrid was shocked.

He laughed and shrugged. "Do you?" he asked, taking off his hat and setting it on the wall.

"Of course not!" Ingrid was a clear-minded Yankee. And a schoolteacher, after all.

Her vehemence amused him. "Very well then, Miss Shawn. It is Miss Shawn, isn't it?"

She nodded. "Ingrid Shawn."

He smiled. "Very well then, Miss Ingrid Shawn. There are no ghosts and you would gladly sleep at night on this hallowed ground." He pointed at one of the oldest gravestones. "Who is that one?"

Ingrid pushed the weeds away and read the name. "Loyal Shawn."

"That's one of yours." He moved closer and together they tried to decipher the date that had been worn to soft obscurity by years of snow and rain and wind. Ingrid did not look at Thaddeus Temple. In contrast to the morbid cemetery, he exuded such a sense of life and vigor that Ingrid felt her own small space disturbed. She had come to visit Talley and spend a few moments in meditation and nostalgic sorrow, but with Thaddeus at her side, she wasn't thinking about her brother.

"Who was Loyal Shawn?" he asked.

"I'm not sure. I only recall my papa saying that he came here a long time ago and kept a little trading post on the river."

Thaddeus looked at the stones nearby. "I find two sons of Loyal here, but no sign of a wife."

"I don't know why."

"Maybe she was an Indian. They were never

buried in family plots like this. The squaws were good enough to keep the house and cook and raise the babies, but no one wanted them to share eternity." Thaddeus laughed shortly. When he saw Ingrid's expression, he explained. "There's almost always Indian blood in the oldest Yankee families. Illegitimate, of course, but as rich and red as ours anytime."

Ingrid didn't know what to say. As it happened, she knew several old family tales of Indian women, but she never had considered them seriously. She was much too young to recall the time when there had been Indians camped in the Amoset River valley. Though men and women, whole families of them, were fighting Indians in the western wilderness, savages had already become rare in Massachusetts in 1843. An Indian? In her family?

"They were brave, these men with names like Loyal and Thrift who came out here away from the cities. There were more bears and wolves in the mountains back then, and the Indians that didn't run from the white man stayed around to kill him. It was a hard life. No wonder they took what warmth and comfort they could get from Indian women." He saw Ingrid's blush and changed the subject abruptly. "How did your brother die?"

"In the mill. He fell into the works of a loom. His neck was broken." She bit her lip and stared at the ground.

"But you must not grieve! He's part of this beautiful mountain now. Let that give you pleasure, Ingrid."

She felt a touch of anger. How could this stranger presume to understand what brought her either joy or grief? And his words had come too quickly, which made her doubt his sincerity, but only for a moment.

"If you miss him now, and I'm sure you do, think on it this way. He was with you for a little time and brought joy into your life and left memories that will never get old like the rest of us. In the minds of those who loved him, your Talleyrand has a kind of immortality, Ingrid. He will be a boy forever."

It was in Ingrid's mind to say something sharp and cutting to silence the young preacher. She understood that his intention was to bring her solace, but she resented the attempt to dull the edge of her grief. She found it wasn't possible to stay angry with Thaddeus, though. His smile was too winsomely candid, his voice too melodious. As he continued to speak of Talley, she was comforted in spite of herself. She smiled.

"That's what I like to see!" Thaddeus cried. "And Talleyrand, too, would prefer smiles to gloomy faces, I'd wager."

From its place beside the wall, the horse nickered.

"That's a beautiful animal," admired Ingrid, glad to change the subject. She went over to the wall and reached up timidly to stroke the white mane. "Does he have a name?"

"What would you like to call him?" Thaddeus followed her and sat on the wall, brushing off a place for her. After a moment's hesitation, she jumped up beside him. "Well?" he asked again. "What shall we name him?"

Her brow wrinkled. "But he must have a name already."

"That doesn't matter. We'll give him another."

Again Ingrid's sense of how things should be was

affronted. "An animal only has the name you give it.
If you change his name. . . ."

"There's only one name a horse cares about and
that's what God calls it. Since we can't know that, we
may call this horse whatever we please and change it
from day to day if it suits our whim." He stroked the
horse's nose. "I call him Silk."

Ingrid looked at Thaddeus strangely. "You think
God cares about horses? They don't have souls!"

Her certainty made Thaddeus laugh. "Don't let
Silk hear you say that! Of course he has a soul and so
do dogs and cats and even that old milk cow of mine.
In every living thing that God created, he placed a
precious soul."

Ingrid shook her head. "For a preacher, you say
the strangest things. Dogs and cats and horses with
souls . . . and all that talk about love and beauty.
Reverend Strickland wouldn't approve of you, I
think." Ingrid pursed her lips, thinking she shouldn't
either.

Again Thaddeus laughed. "You have it wrong,
Ingrid. *I* do not approve of Reverend Strickland. I
dislike his angry God and icy heaven. I would sooner
have nothing than a deity like your Amoset preachers
speak of. I swear that if they had their way the world
would be so grim a place I couldn't bear to live in it."

She didn't say so, but when Thaddeus spoke it
out loud, for the first time Ingrid recognized her own
opinion. Too often, Reverend Strickland's sermons de-
teriorated into lengthy scolds and admonishments to
suffer and be glad for the opportunity. At such times
it did seem that the Christianity taught in Amoset
was cold and unloving.

Silk nickered and tossed his head impatiently.

"He wants a run," Ingrid commented.

"His back is strong. Will you ride with us?"

Thaddeus jumped down from the wall and held out his hand to her.

Ingrid hesitated. She was blushing. Looking up at the sun, she saw it was nearing the rim of the mountain. "I should go home," she said. "It will be dark soon."

"We'll go in the direction of Amoset then." Thaddeus stooped a little and peered into her face, his eyes encouraging her to agree. When he touched her arm lightly, she felt a current course through her body. "Silk canters like the wind. Come, Ingrid, it'll be like flying."

And so it was. Silk's broad back stayed steady while his hooves flew along the trail, their touch to earth so light, so fleeting, that when Ingrid closed her eyes she could imagine they were on a mythical horse. Indeed, they were flying, sailing somewhere miles above the earth in a region of alabaster cloud palaces and sunlight distilled from gold. Their headlong canter became a gallop, and the speed of trees and bushes and boulders darting past took Ingrid's breath away. She clutched Thaddeus' back and implored him to stop.

When they dismounted beside a waterfall at the base of Cooper's Mountain and not far from Amoset, Ingrid's legs were trembling so that she couldn't stand. She fell in a heap on the soft grass beside the little cataract and lay back, breathless.

"It was wonderful," she gasped, clutching her breast as if she had run the whole distance herself. "I never felt so free!"

Thaddeus lay beside her in the grass. In the glade there was scarcely a sound but for Ingrid's sighs.

Thaddeus lay half on his side, his elbow bent, his

head resting on his hand while he watched her. Ingrid never had experienced anything like the intensity of his look. It filled her with conflict, the urge to run, to laugh, to cry, to fly. "Will you ride with me again? I'll be back near Amoset next Sunday."

Without thinking Ingrid replied, "Oh, I should love that. Only may we go farther next time? I know a wonderful trail around the mountain. . . ." Hearing herself, she was mortified. For a woman to be so forthright was unacceptable by any standards Ingrid had heard of. She knew she had demeaned herself by her brazen speech. "I have to go." She stood up, brushing her skirt clean.

Thaddeus scrambled to his feet beside her. Before she could move away, he put his hands on her shoulders. "What's the matter, Ingrid?"

Her face was hot with shame, and the touch of Thaddeus' large hands on her shoulders only worsened her discomposure. "Forgive me for speaking . . . as I did."

"I cannot forgive where there is no wrongdoing. I asked you to ride with me and you accepted my invitation. You haven't changed your mind so quickly, have you?" His voice was as deep and urgent as the throbbing pipe organ in Reverend Strickland's church. The woods roundabout seemed to resonate with the strong, gentle sound. "Say you will ride with me, Ingrid. And promise you will take me along the trail you spoke of."

She wouldn't look at him. "Will it be all right?" she whispered, not sure to whom she spoke.

"I am asking you to share some of God's beauty with me. A fine horse, a beautiful mountain. How can that be wrong?" Thaddeus spoke with such unshakable conviction that Ingrid's uneasiness faded. It didn't go away entirely, but became only part of the back-

ground of her mind and easy to ignore, like the un-
wanted voice of conscience.

"Next Sunday?"

"Come to the prayer meeting, but stay afterward."

She dared to lift her eyes to his for the fraction
of a moment before, once again, she was overcome by
blushes and tremors.

"I have to go," she cried.

"Sunday next," he called after her as she darted
down the hill. "Sunday next." It was much later that
she realized he had not been asking a question. "Sunday next" was a statement made as if he knew she
could not bear to stay away.

On her way back to Mrs. Quinn's, she ran over in
her memory all that Thaddeus had said, and with
each repetition found his philosophy increasingly too
easy for her Yankee intelligence to accept. What of
evil? What of machines without souls that destroyed
boys in their brightest days? She wondered why she
hadn't asked these questions of Thaddeus when they
were together and realized with chagrin that his voice
had somewhat mesmerized her. Under its spell, she
had forgotten every doubt and had been willing to ignore the cautions her mind threw up before her like
hurdles on a bridle path. Now, alone and almost running to make it back to Mrs. Quinn's in time for supper, she remembered that Thaddeus was the man
who had kissed Jerusha under the stars. And then forgot her name.

Chapter 22

Ingrid said nothing about her meeting with Thaddeus or the thrilling ride on Silk. Though at first she feared the news might burst from her, she knew it would hurt Jerusha, and Ingrid was too sensitive of others' feelings to allow that.

"Thaddeus." She said his name aloud whenever she was alone. At school, while the children copied their lessons, she wrote it again and again on her own lap slate. Sometimes she even tried her own and his together in her most flowing cursive script. Ingrid Temple. The name had a fine Yankee ring to it. "Ingrid Temple." When she spoke the syllables aloud, her body quivered with excitement.

The week dragged by.

Early Wednesday morning, Suzannah Paine called a meeting of the employees in the mill yard. The sun had just risen and the sky was streaked with pink and blue. The moist, cool edge already had left the morning. Ingrid was not a mill employee in the sense that Meredith and Jerusha were, but she was curious to hear the substance of Suzannah's announcement. She brought her students with her. Standing straight and silent, they made a neat pair of rows near the iron fence of the mill yard. The operatives and other mill workers gathered in groups of two or three in the yard, and when they spoke it was in whispers. Ingrid could see from their strained expressions that everyone was worried. A meeting of the entire mill staff was practically unheard of. To everyone's mind, it meant trouble.

Suzannah stood on a large packing crate to address the crowd of several hundred. She was dressed in her customary working clothes, a serviceable, drab smock over an unadorned afternoon dress with a high neckline and long sleeves. Her dark hair was pulled severely back and smothered by a snood. Suzannah was a familiar figure to all the workers. Since coming to the mill almost eight years earlier when Martin Hopewell had disappeared, Suzannah had involved herself closely with every aspect of the business. She even had gone so far as to spend an afternoon at the looms herself to better understand the operatives' complaints. Because of these things, she had earned a reputation for caring that was unmatched by any other mill owner and unusual enough to spread her fame to as far away as Boston.

"I will make my announcement this morning as brief as possible, ladies and gentlemen. As you know, New England continues to suffer through an economic crisis that has caused the closing of some mills and factories. Luckily, however, those here in Amoset have fared better, for the most part. The market in piece goods is particularly depressed. To give you an example," Suzannah held up a large swatch of cotton cloth so the crowd could see it, "this is Waltham heavy sheeting. You are all familiar with it. When my father began this business, Waltham sold for just under thirty cents a yard. Today it goes for slightly more than five cents a yard. Frankly," she let the fabric drop, "if Hopewell Mills made sheeting like this, we would all be out of business right now. As it is, even the coarse immigrant cloth that has made this factory famous throughout the Northeast has dropped from almost twenty cents a yard to under ten. I am sure you can understand that to continue operating at a profit some adjustment has to be made."

"Why a profit?" an angry male voice yelled from the crowd.

"An excellent question. Hopewell Mills has to continue to make more than it spends or we will not be able to buy the new materials and machinery required for us to maintain our position in the industry. We must constantly be retooling, refurnishing, and repairing or we will be left behind. Then we'll all be out of work."

The grumbling in the crowd, which had begun softly while Suzannah was speaking, rose now as she waited for the meaning of her words to sink in. Here and there about her, Ingrid heard the word "Irish."

Someone near the front of the group yelled to Suzannah, "You telling us you're hiring Irish?"

"No," she answered quickly. Her hands went up, palms outward, to settle the restless crowd. "I am not hiring Irish." There was a smattering of applause and one or two cheers. "But not because I think they're inferior workers. Believe me, they're not. This past winter it was the Irish from the Gully who kept Amoset clear of snow and ice. Without them we would have been forced to close most of the mills in town until the thaw. Make no mistake, the Irish are good workers and I know it, but I am not about to fire trusted employees so that unskilled Irish may be hired for less. I value each and every one of you too much for that. You are loyal and proficient employees, some of the best in the business, I think." There was another flurry of applause.

"But I have to do something," Suzannah cried over the noise. "Expenses must be cut. I have waited until the spring to tell you all this because I know the winter was bad enough without your having less money. Now I have to tell you that as of next week, I am lowering the price per piece of work. Most of you are earning between two and four dollars a week now and you will be able to maintain your wages at that level if you increase your speed. Those of you who are able may take on more machines."

A woman's voice yelled, "And when are we supposed to do this? We already work seventy-five hours a week!"

"What happens if we won't work?" another woman shouted before Suzannah could answer the first. Soon the air was noisy with yelled questions. This time when Suzannah raised her hands for quiet, the workers were slow to be silent.

"In the first place, I know this is a hardship for all of you. I have only come to my decision after much thought. I hope that when these hard times pass, I will be able to raise the price per piece to its former level."

Several men not far from Ingrid guffawed loudly at this and one, cupping his hand to his mouth, cried, "Who are you kidding, missus! Once they go down, wages never go back up."

Over the angry crowd, Suzannah's voice rang clear. "If you feel you cannot remain here with us on these terms, I want you to know that I will not penalize any man, woman or child who chooses to go. If your employment record is clear, I will see to it that you have an outstanding recommendation. But before you think seriously of leaving, I remind you that many mills are hiring Irish now. Because of that, wages in most places are from fifteen to twenty percent lower than what I offer."

"In other words we have no choice," someone said. Many voices agreed.

"If you have any further comments, make them to Mr. Blake, the overseer. In the meantime. . . ." Whatever Suzannah had planned to say was drowned by the commotion of the crowd. Now that she had spoken the worst, the men and women ignored her, turning to one another with complaints and angry comments. Suzannah waited a moment, but then, seeing that nothing she could say would make any difference, she stepped down from the crate that had been her podium and went back inside the mill. A moment later the bells rang, calling the workers to their positions.

But Suzannah couldn't work that day. By ten in the morning, she realized that her depressed spirits were affecting her work. She sat at her desk, her stylus poised over a column of figures she had added once, twice and then a third time, always arriving at a different sum. When she tried the addition a fourth time and came up with yet another amount, she angrily pushed the papers away and stood up. The school was directly below her office and for a moment she considered going down to visit the children.

Suzannah did not in the least regret her decision to open the mill school and gradually assume greater and greater responsibility for it. Faced with rising costs, she had been advised that closing the school was one way she might economize. But she had only laughed and tried to explain that she was proud of the work the school was doing.

It had been Valentine's suggestion. "Send those boys and girls back into the mill, and Ingrid Shawn, too," he had said. Ever since Suzannah had put Valentine to work hiring and overseeing the Irish work gangs, he had become increasingly vocal about the affairs of Hopewell Mills. It was true that she often found his suggestions short of clear thinking and humanitarian values, but she was pleased for Val's sake that his life had taken a more responsible turn.

But there had been an argument between them the night before. She had just kissed Patrick good night and sent him upstairs with his nurse when, without knocking, Valentine had shoved open the door to her home office. She looked up from her papers with some annoyance.

"I have a lot to do, Val. Will it wait until tomorrow?"

"You're going to announce the cut in the morning?"

"That's what I've decided." She tapped her carefully manicured nails on her desk and glanced at the tall corner clock. Before her lay a pile of bills and requisitions that needed her attention that evening. "I'm awfully busy, Val."

Glancing down at her papers, she didn't see her brother's expression tighten. Over the years it had become habitual for her to deal with him in a perfunctory manner, giving no thought to his reactions. Until very recently, he had shown little interest in the daily affairs of the mill, preferring the pleasures of the Gully over all else. For that reason, she had gradually ceased thinking of him as a legitimate heir to Hopewell Mills and this attitude was communicated clearly by her manner.

"I want to talk to you about the Irish." Valentine sat down in one of the delicate Shaker chairs and slung his leg over the arm.

"Be careful, will you, Valentine?" Suzannah heard the petulance in her voice, and though it disturbed her to think she was becoming the sort of woman who values chairs over human comfort, she didn't bother to conceal her irritation. "I haven't got time to talk about the Irish problem right now, anyway." She gestured at the work in front of her. "I'm afraid you have no idea. . . ."

"Money short?" he asked sarcastically.

"Damnit, Val, what kind of question is that? You know how it is. Even your persuasive brother can't force the Georgia planters to sell their cotton to us if the price isn't right. France and England are clamoring for Southern cotton and paying good money. Besides which, the mortgage our father had to take out on the mill to pay for the reconstruction ten years ago is still a burden. Then, there's the railroad. Eben has borrowed from the mill to get it under way and we won't see a return on it for a while. I'm making a go of things, but believe me, it's not easy sometimes."

"You pay your operatives too much."

She looked up and sighed. "I know what you want. You want me to hire Irish."

"Well, why not? What have you got against them?"

"Nothing, Val, nothing. You know I feel like we must have had this conversation at least a dozen times. I repeat, I have nothing against the Irish, but I will not put skilled, long-term employees out of work so I can hire immigrants for less. You're asking me to cheat two groups of people in order to cut costs. Well, I refuse to do business that way."

"Our father would." Valentine picked at his cuticle. "He wouldn't think twice."

"I am not Martin Hopewell. I have to run this business according to my own conscience." Placing her elbows on the desk, she rested her chin in her hands.

"If the work is so trying, why don't you give it up?"

Suzannah stared at him, smiling slightly. "You would like me to quit, wouldn't you? You think you could step in then and run things your way. But let me tell you something, Valentine. I've been doing this for almost eight years now and it never gets easy. If you were to take over for me now ..."

"You really like believing you're indispensable, don't you, Suzannah?"

"I'm not saying I'm indispensable. I only mean that, like it or not, I know the business better now than even our father. You believe you could do what I do and better, but you couldn't. It would take years. ..."

Valentine swung his leg back to the floor and stood up. He stared at Suzannah with a slight sneer. "If we go under, don't say I didn't warn you, little sister. There're hundreds of strong Irish women in the Gully who will work for eighty hours a week for half what your proud Yankees demand. And they'll bring their children and work them just as hard as themselves if it means more money to live on."

Suzannah shook her head. "You know, Valentine, it's a pity you weren't in Amoset when Foster McMahon was our chief overseer. You and he would have made a remarkable pair!"

"I know Foster McMahon," Valentine said as he went to the door. "There's no call to insult me, Suzannah."

Now, restless after her speech to the mill workers, Suzannah was still pondering Valentine's remark. He claimed to know Foster McMahon and yet, as far as she knew, the former overseer hadn't been in Amoset for many years. Was he living in the Gully? Suddenly she remembered the day of Patrick's birthday party and the boys from the Gully who had thrown rocks at the sitting room window. She remembered one of them, small-eyed and mean, who had seemed less afraid than his comrades. It was Alexander Duffy who had identified him as Simon McMahon. Though there was no logical reason why she should fear McMahon, let alone his young son, she couldn't help feeling uneasy with the notion of their nearness.

Chapter 23

The warm season had gentled the Gully, blunting the edges of poverty and concealing its despair behind the vivid greenery of chestnut, oak and maple. The residents emerged from their shacks like ground hogs, ready to dash back if the wind blew too cold or the sun disappeared for too long a time. Since the coming of warmth, the Gully streets had rung with the shouts of children running after each other, their bodies belly-white and ravenous for sunshine.

Spring was more than warmth and color, however. It was a spirit, an urge, a pulse in almost everyone. It drove tired men to dig their gardens early and women to whisper prayers, and even sing a little, as they planted the seeds they'd hoarded like gold from the previous year. Though the mood of spring is always joyous, it was especially so that year. At St. Anne's the choir was full for the first time and as the warm clear days succeeded one another, even Father Snee felt a rebirth of his faith. For everyone there was a sense of having survived an ordeal and being awarded a second chance. Those who had lost a loved one to the winter had their souls refreshed by lengthening days under blazing blue skies and a generous sun that melted the ice in their hearts.

Feargus Muldoon, proprietor of the Lavender and Lily, ordered his wife's soup kitchen disbanded.

While the tavern was being scrubbed and white-washed, he made a trip to Boston and came back with a wagonload of furnishings to make the place "presentable," as he was fond of saying. He and his sons built a new bar and shellacked the oak timbers to a sheen Muldoon thought equal of any west of Boston. However much the interior of the Lavender and Lily was altered by these ministrations, the clientele remained much the same. There were the regulars, of course, as well as new immigrants who were arriving daily from Boston, New York and even Montreal, where the immigration officials were quick to inform them that there were factories and jobs in Amoset.

By early summer of 1843, several thousand Irish were living in the Gully. Although a few of them found regular work in the mills that hired immigrants, the majority were employed only occasionally. The women who were fortunate enough to be operatives earned twenty percent less than the Yankees working beside them. Many worked in the boarding houses and in the mansions of the manufacturers as maids and cooks and laundresses. Irish children ran errands for shopkeepers who would never trust an Irish immigrant to work at selling or handling merchandise. Intent on making successful American lives for themselves, the Irish worked at any job they could find and for their diligence they were derided.

The Lavender and Lily was almost always busy from the time it opened in the morning until Muldoon barred the door around midnight. Men and boys without work somehow found the few coins needed for a day of drinking. Although Muldoon despaired to see the effects of drink on strong but idle men, he aimed to be rich one day and so he was pragmatic, took their money and listened to their tales of woe.

Mickey Quick was often at the bar. Sometimes he confided his dreams of being a famous magician to Muldoon, but more often he merely stared at the whorled wood of the bar, tracing his misery in its curves and turns.

On the same day that Suzannah made her announcement to her workers, the gambler Jamie Teig, no longer able to count on Valentine Hopewell as an easy mark, tried to woo Mickey into a game of chance. But the young man wasn't tempted. Better it was for him to sip and dream and sink into a stew where even failure didn't matter anymore.

"Here's Simon McMahon," Teig called out, thumping Mickey on the back. "He'll wager a bit with us, won't you, lad?"

Simon ignored the question. "I want to talk to you," he said to Mickey softly, turning his back on Teig.

"So? Talk." Quick didn't bother to look up from his brew.

Simon leaned close. "Want to come with us tonight? Me and Dirk and Gilly and the rest are going after them boys at Cartwright's."

Still Mickey didn't look at him. "I've told you before, Si. I don't do that stuff no more."

"Yeah, I know. But we need you. There's seven or eight of them."

"I don't care." Mickey stared at the gritty sediment left in the bottom of his tankard of ale. Gypsies read tea leaves. Could anyone tell his future by reading the grit at the end of a drink?

"Whatsa matter, Quick? You gettin' soft? You afraid of them Yankee boys?" When Simon sneered, his eyes narrowed and it was easy to see his father in him. Like Foster, Simon had a greedy mouth that looked ready to snap down on something without warning at any moment. His lips were very red and had a greasy wetness that made him look as if he had just finished a rich meal. "You coming with us or not?" he insisted.

Mickey shoved his tankard toward Muldoon.

"Or do you still think you're Lord Muck just because you got to stand in Suzannah Paine's drawing room?" Simon crowed; he could tell he'd hit a tender nerve. "You dumb Paddy! You may be five years older than me, but you're stupid as any bog fly. Don't you know those Yankees'll never let you do your tricks again? You're finished in Amoset. You were washed up the minute that colleen, that Annabella, said you might have been the man what tried to do it to her. You're branded, Mickey, me old pal. They think you're the Amoset murderer, and that finishes you with the Yankees. She might as well have said that you were the one for sure!"

Simon snorted in the disparaging way he found effective with his gang. He had seven orphan boys he could count on now. They took their cues from him and were strictly obedient so as not to risk his derision. Simon had a mean tongue. When he spoke, his mouth seemed even smaller and more twisted than it really was.

When Simon said "me old pal," Mickey wanted to beat him until he bled, but drink had made him listless.

The two boys had known each other since the time when Simon and his mother were abandoned by McMahon and left to fend for themselves in the Gully. After several years in the somewhat rarefied atmosphere of St. Andrew's boarding school, it had been difficult for Simon to adjust to Gully life. Mickey had taken him under his protection though, and had taught him the way of things in a world that rejected

them. For a while Mickey had loved Simon like the
brother he never had. When he had lost some of his
dependency, however, the boy had begun to change.
Or, as Mickey later thought, Simon had revealed himself.

This all went back a few years to the time when
Mickey had been the one who was leading gangs of
Irish boys into Amoset. Back then, Mickey had been
shrewder and much rougher than he was now. Nevertheless, the changing, emerging Simon had been
someone even Mickey couldn't like or trust, let alone
love as a brother. Trying not to be unkind, he began
to place a distance between himself and Simon. Simon had become the leader of his own band of
ne'er-do-wells while Mickey had tried to give up vio-
lence for magic.

Simon went away disgusted and Mickey had
several more drinks. Jamie Teig bought one of them
and Muldoon let him sign for the rest, albeit reluctantly. That is to say, Mickey put an X beside the
place where Muldoon had written his name. Teig
chattered on, but Mickey paid no attention. In his
head, he was turning off. One by one, lines of communication were being shut down with the outside
world and he knew that soon he would forget even
his magic. After a time, Teig got sick of Mickey's
silence and found some gullible new fellows who
were willing to risk a game of cards. Mickey didn't
even notice when he left.

But when he heard the hoofbeats in the road a
few minutes later, his head shot up and his eyes
opened wide. Noisy. Many riders coming fast could
only mean that the Yankees were paying a visit to the
Gully.

Muldoon was over the bar in a moment. "What
the hell . . . ?" A rock shattered the new window

glass, narrowly missing him. It was followed by another from the opposite side. And another. Before
Muldoon could open the door and go roaring through,
it swung open. Muldoon stepped back quickly. Selectman Stoat was standing on the step. He had a rifle in
his hand and behind him were half a dozen men, also
armed.

"Where's Mickey Quick?"

An instant of silence. Then, "Who wants to
know?"

Stoat stalked the voice across the room to the bar
and stopped only inches from Mickey. "You Mickey
Quick?"

"I asked who wants to know."

Feargus Muldoon leaned close and whispered,
"Cooperate, lad. There's laws in America to protect
you. But only if you cooperate."

"Who're you?" Stoat's heavy eyebrows bobbed up
and down several times. The mannerism made Muldoon nervous. "Speak up, Paddy," growled Stoat,
pressing the butt of his weapon against Muldoon's
chest.

"Begging your pardon, sir. I'm Feargus Muldoon.
The Lavender and Lily is my place. It would be a
pleasure to offer you a pint. . . ." Stoat shoved hard
and Muldoon, his hands slipping on the polished surface of the bar, toppled over backward. Stoat's men
laughed and shouted rude remarks.

"Is this Mickey Quick?" Stoat asked. When Muldoon did not answer immediately, Stoat gave a nod of
his head and two men came forward. The first one
walked directly to the bar, ducked under and, coming
up with his knife unsheathed, he gouged and dug
away at the splendid oak bar until Muldoon begged
him to stop. "Is this Mickey Quick?" Stoat asked
again.

"It's me all right," Mickey broke in, feeling some loyalty to Muldoon. "And I still want to know . . . who's asking?" Mickey stared at the selectman woozily, his eyes crossed.

Stoat smiled nastily. "I'll tell you what my name is. It's Justice. It's Revenge."

All at once the tavern erupted. The Yankee who had ruined the bar swung around and let a bottle fly into the mirror. Light exploded in all directions and Jamie Teig and his pals barricaded themselves behind a table.

Peggy Muldoon burst into the room from the back. "What in the name of Sweet Jesus . . . ?" She ran to her prostrate husband, but Stoat dragged her away, his fat little hand clamped to her breast. As he pushed her through the door, he told her, "Stay out of here if you love your virtue, missus. I don't like to hurt women, but I won't vouch for my men."

The room was in confusion. Muldoon watched in horror as Stoat's men determinedly set upon the task of demolishing the bar he had so proudly installed. Mickey also watched the destruction and, gradually, the circuits of his mind that had turned off came on again. He saw what was happening and dimly understood.

"Leave the place alone!" he yelled, lunging off balance toward Stoat. "You can't. . . ."

Stoat grabbed him and held his neck in the crook of his elbow. "I can't murder you outright," he hissed in Mickey's ear, "but I can do anything else I please. I can call my men and they can hold you down while I cut open the front of your pants. . . ." Stoat tightened his grip and Mickey cried out from the pain. "I could do almost anything and no one would blame me, not for a moment. No one has tears for a rapist. You're the kind that deserves to die." Stoat laughed. "Come here, Billy," he called to one of his men.

While Mickey struggled, kicking out at Billy, who was tugging on his pants legs to pull them down around his knees, Muldoon and the others looked on in impotent horror. Each plainly saw that the Yankees could not be stopped, that if they didn't get their way now, they would be back again and again until they did. Muldoon closed his eyes when Stoat dropped his gun and pulled out a knife. He held it up before Mickey's eyes.

"Know what I'm gonna do, Paddy? Eh? I'm gonna cut your pecker off and feed it to the pigs. If they'll have it."

Mickey jerked swiftly to free himself. He lunged for the door, but his legs tangled in his trousers and he fell in a heap. He tried to crawl.

Stoat was laughing as he kicked him in the side. Mickey rolled onto his back, knees up, clutching himself. Two men caught his legs and stretched them out. Screaming incoherently now, the boy tried to scuttle away on his backside, but another kick from Stoat left him paralyzed with pain. When he tried to move again, he was kicked in the side of the head. Blood gushed from his ear and he lost consciousness for a moment.

Stoat's voice awakened him. The selectman was kneeling beside him, the long blade of the knife glinting just above Mickey. "Now you'll get it. Rapist. Murderer. You won't go after our girls again." The knife edge touched him. Mickey screamed and the knife slipped and made a deep gash in his thigh. The boy's eyes opened wide. Stoat was grinning.

"They say there's not enough evidence to prove you did it. I've got my own ideas, but I'm a law-abiding man." Wiping his knife on Mickey's jacket, Stoat looked around the Lavender and Lily. He spoke loudly enough for everyone to hear. "Next time I'll do what I said. And more. My men and I will burn the Gully to the ground if this bastard goes after our women again."

Chapter 24

"Sunday next" finally arrived for Ingrid. Not surprisingly, Jerusha claimed she wasn't interested in Thaddeus Temple's outdoor prayer meeting. Meredith wasn't anxious to go, either. She said she couldn't be bothered with church twice in one day. Ingrid, after hesitating for only a moment, decided to go alone. She would listen to Thaddeus preach, maybe talk with him briefly, but then she planned to visit her mother.

As Ingrid came up the hollow and stood on the lip of the grassy bowl, a pretty view lay before her— the silvery birches, the brook, Thaddeus' brightly painted wagon, a vaporous blue sky. Silk was hitched to the wagon. While he munched on grass, he sometimes lifted his ears and gazed about disdainfully at the gathering of the faithful. Ingrid noted that there were more operatives in the congregation than the previous Sunday and fewer mountain folk. Word of Thaddeus Temple's charismatic preaching had spread during the week. There was a nervous crackle in the operatives' murmured conversations today that struck Ingrid as somehow wrong. After seven days of gossip, the bowl scene had lost its innocence for her. There was something almost jaded in the way the eager girls in their bright frocks and scooter bonnets had come expecting spiritual excitement. Ingrid felt an impulse

to leave that was as swift and sharp as a thorn, but
she ignored it.

As she was settling down on the slope, preparing
to listen, Ingrid noted one person who stood apart
from all the others. He wore a short white coat and
long, loose trousers, an outfit unlike anything ever
worn by either mountain folk or town folk. His head
was wrapped in a plain white turban.

The India Man! thought Ingrid.

Like everyone who worked at the mill, she had
heard of Martin Hopewell's caretaker. Few people
had seen him, however, for he stayed in the mansion
and rarely was far from the side of his patient. From
time to time she glanced back at him during Thaddeus' sermon. The India Man never changed his expression. He might have been painted in oils.

Thaddeus' talk was a variation on the one of the
previous week. On this occasion, Ingrid felt no hesitation, no instant of doubt or uncertainty, before she
succumbed to the music of his voice. She closed her
eyes and the words washed over her like waves pro-
pelled by Thaddeus' own breath. She could feel it
against her skin like the promise of a summer storm.

"God," he proclaimed, "is here with us this afternoon." Thaddeus spread his arms wide in a gesture
that included hill and sky and everyone gathered on
the slope. His boots were planted firmly a stride
apart, and when Ingrid opened her eyes and looked
at him, she thought of an oak rooted for all time in
one place, immovable and certain beyond any specu-
lation. When Thaddeus repeated his words, "God is
here with us this afternoon," Ingrid couldn't doubt
that he was right.

"He is everywhere, in all we do. Those of you
who labor in the mills of Amoset, God is there beside
you. It is His power that drives the water against the

wheel that drives the machinery. It is His power that lights the sun, that causes the rain to fall and refresh the earth. He is everywhere. He is in you as He is in me. You and I are part of God. God is love and we are God and God is everywhere."

On Cooper's Mountain on this glowing day in early June, Thaddeus' words were undoubtedly the truth. When a breeze surprised the quiet it seemed to be a message, an affirmation from God that what Thaddeus said was indeed His Word. Of all the congregation, perhaps only the India Man was unmoved by Thaddeus. As he listened, his expression did not change. His eyes did not waver from their focus on the clearing, the wagon and the preacher. But no one noticed his implacability, so caught up were they in the spirit of the moment. At the end, when the congregation burst into spontaneous, joyful hymn singing, the India Man slipped out of the bowl and away without being noticed by anyone except Ingrid. And even she didn't pay him much attention, for she too was under the enchantment of Thaddeus Temple's unique vision of God. His words had filled her with gladness, with a lightness of heart that was noteworthy even to one as normally merry as Ingrid.

The mountain families and groups of operatives began making their way home, but slowly, and Ingrid felt conspicuous sitting on the slope. Finally, the crowd disappeared and the bowl became silent. She could hear the rush of the stream. Silk nickered. A dog barked.

"I'm glad you came back," said Thaddeus, stretching out on the grass beside her. "I thought of you all week."

"I have to go visit my mother. She lives up there." Ingrid gestured toward the distant peak of Cooper's Mountain.

"You promised me a special trail. And Silk has been worried all week, thinking you might forget." Thaddeus pouted like a spoiled child, but Ingrid saw only his merry eyes. "May I come along on the visit, perhaps?"

Ingrid thought of her last meeting with her mother. It had been on the day that Ingrid had left for Amoset. Helen had been cold, had treated her daughter almost as a stranger. How would she then react to Ingrid's arrival, without notice and accompanied by Thaddeus Temple?

He was staring at her. "Well? May I come with you?" She didn't answer. "Tell me why you're reluctant, Ingrid. Are you ashamed of me?"

"Of course not!" How could she explain her fears without speaking ill of her mother? How could she tell Thaddeus that the children in Amoset had begun to ridicule Helen Shawn, who never left her remote farm, who bitterly hated Amoset and manufacturing and who hurled insults at anyone from town who violated the privacy of her high meadows? "I don't know how to say it. . . . You mustn't think me bad or that I dishonor my mother. . . ." She pulled out a few blades of the sweet grass and chewed on them.

"I can never think badly of you, Ingrid. You are beautiful just as you are."

This seemed so patently untrue that Ingrid could not help but protest. "I am plain," she said simply.

Thaddeus shook his head.

"But I am. I know it and you know it. Please," Ingrid's eyes filled with tears, "flattery does no good to anyone."

"You're weeping! Sweet Ingrid, forgive me. You must think I'm flattering you like some city nob."

"You are, aren't you?" Ingrid's bonnet had slipped back so she reached back, trying to set it firmly on her head, but Thaddeus stopped her. She stared at him.

"You are beautiful, Ingrid. Who has told you otherwise?"

"I have excellent vision, Mr. Temple. I see for myself that my face is neat and symmetrical, my eyes are a pleasant blue, my nose not too large nor my mouth too small. But altogether, the effect is . . . plain." She stood up. Speaking her mind honestly had done Ingrid some good and she felt more confident than she had at any time since being alone with Thaddeus. If there was one thing Ingrid prided herself upon it was having a reasonable grasp of reality, free of illusions and wishful thinking. Though naive in many ways, she didn't include her personal appearance as an area in which she had any doubts or uncertainties. For a moment, when Thaddeus first told her she was beautiful, it had crossed her mind as fleetingly as a deer crossing the meadow with a huntsman in pursuit that maybe she was wrong to disbelieve him. But this renegade idea disappeared almost before she had recognized it.

You are plain, she told herself. Always have been. Always will be. Plain.

She set off up the slope toward the road that ran past the little graveyard and on up to the mountain to the Shawn farm. Thaddeus took a moment to close his wagon and unhitch Silk. Then he followed quickly after. By the time she had reached the road, he was beside her.

"You promised me a ride along some special trail," he reminded her when she didn't immediately speak to him. "But first we will visit your mother."

Ingrid spoke without thinking. Having once begun, the explanation came easier than she would have supposed. "My mother is a strange woman. In town,

the children call her Old Helen because she prefers
the company of the mountain to city crowds. She
hasn't been able to forgive the mills, you see. First
they took my sister Lucy, and then my father. And, finally, they killed our little Talley. Now she lives
alone in the house and keeps the farm while my father is in Boston. She sees no one for weeks at a time
except the animals and the taunting children she has
to drive away with a shotgun."

"Children?"

"They come up from town on Saturdays and tor-
ment her with words." It was humiliating to have to
confess such a story to Thaddeus when Ingrid would
have liked to impress him. But the more she talked,
the easier it became and the more sure she was that it
would be a mistake to visit Helen and bring a guest.

Thaddeus felt differently. "I can hardly blame
your mother for despair. She's suffered more than
most, I think. Let's gather wildflowers for her. No one
can resist God's own flowers."

Reluctantly, Ingrid agreed. Certain as she was
that the visit was a mistake, she couldn't think how to
tell this to Thaddeus without driving him away forever. And despite the increasing confusion she felt
within her, Ingrid knew she could not bear to have
that happen. Walking with Thaddeus beside her and
Silk a few steps behind, she felt happier than ever in
her life. It was a giddy, glorious good humor that
veered close enough to lack of control to be defined
as something more dangerous than happiness.

In a high meadow not far from the house, they
stopped to gather the flowers. Thaddeus knew the
names of all of them and took a boyish joy in finding
and gathering them into a bouquet.

"They'll wilt," Ingrid insisted. "By the time we're
there, they'll all be dead."

Thaddeus looked cross. "Your scant faith appalls me, Ingrid Shawn. We are gathering these for your mother. How can they wilt before she gets them?"

"But they will."

"They'll stay fresh, Ingrid. Trust me." He smiled with unshakable confidence. Despite all her misgivings, Ingrid found herself believing.

What was it about Thaddeus Temple that he could change her mind on anything? At seventeen, Ingrid was still confused by much of what she encountered. After years of illness and isolation, this was not so strange. Thaddeus, on the other hand, was without doubts on any subject that mattered to him. Never had she felt more secure than now, walking beside him. Cooper's Mountain was her home, just as if she'd never left it for Harpers Ferry or Amoset. She was in harmony with it, part of it.

They gathered filarees and coneflowers, blue Jacob's ladders and lady's-slippers and carried them in Ingrid's bonnet, each holding a tie and swinging it between them. On the edge of the woods, Thaddeus stopped suddenly and dropped to his knees.

"See here? This is self-heal." He broke a bit from a low, square-stemmed herb and held it up to her. "Does your mother make her own medicines?"

Ingrid nodded. Long before, when Crazy Edythe was still alive, the old woman had taught her mother all she knew of healing and potions.

Thaddeus gathered a large handful of self-heal and put it in Ingrid's bonnet. "Self-heal can be used for headaches, skin ulcers, stomachaches. It makes a fine tonic, too."

"How do you know these things?" Ingrid was rather in awe of him.

He shrugged, smiling and laughing as he so often did. "I've been traveling around New England ever since I was a boy, Ingrid Shawn. I know the mountains, the animals, the plants and the people as if they were all creatures and characteristics of the little farm where I was born." As they walked, Silk clip-clopping behind them, Thaddeus told Ingrid about his life before becoming a wanderer when he was orphaned. "I lived on a farm like yours, I suppose. I did the chores and worked the land like any farmer's son. But I got my calling early and it changed all that. A preacher came into our remote part of Maine and I heard him speak about some of the things I've told you, about the love of God and the naturalness of all things. This preacher's name was Cameron and he came from England or Wales or Scotland, someplace like that. No one in our part of the world had ever heard such a message. He alarmed some folks and a deputation went around to visit him. They told him not to come to our valley again. That was all right. I had heard enough."

Thaddeus told her about living alone, high on the mountainsides and beside roaring cataracts and in the black stillness of the deep woods. "And it came to me," he said, stopping to gaze fervently at Ingrid, "that God is everywhere and in all things."

Ingrid shook her head. "You said in the mills. Well, what about Talley?"

"In the mills, Ingrid."

"But Talley is dead! How can God have anything to do with the death of children?"

Thaddeus gave a bit of the self-heal to Ingrid. "It's like this plant. It's true that God has put pain in the world, but He has likewise provided the cure for it."

She shook her head. "No. Wait until you meet my mother. Then you'll know. God has brought no cure to her. It seems that with the passing of the years, she only suffers more."

"But the cure exists. It is always God's way. Look at the self-heal, Ingrid. A small and insignificant weed that grows wild on the wayside can cure a dozen agonies."

"But what good is it when it's hidden up here on the mountain?"

"It must be found and put to use, of course. But the point is, it exists. No matter what the suffering, Ingrid, God always provides a cure. Somewhere."

Chapter 25

Thaddeus and Ingrid were just entering the wide clearing where the Shawn homestead stood when they heard a shrill voice, more jay than human. All at once Helen appeared halfway between them and the house. She was running in a slantwise direction, up into the dense brambles that grew around much of the border of the clearing. She began to beat the thorned bushes with the flat of her broom, all the while screaming words neither Ingrid nor Thaddeus could make out. After a moment, her harangue was joined by the shrieks of a child who was obviously in some pain. As Ingrid ran toward her mother, she saw a small boy with sandy hair. He dove out from the far side of the brambles, his shirt torn, a smattering of blood across his back.

"That's Patrick Paine," Ingrid cried as he disappeared into the woods.

Helen slowly lowered her broom and turned to stare at her daughter. "Suzannah's boy?" she asked.

"We met him at the party on New Year's Day." Ingrid approached Helen a little cautiously. Her mother's recent fury had shaken her. "How are you, Mama?"

Helen leaned on her broom. "What was he doing nosing around the barn where I was working?"

Thaddeus was near enough by now to hear the

question. "Perhaps he only wanted to be friends," he suggested.

Helen eyed him suspiciously, as if noticing him for the first time. "What do you know about it?"

Thaddeus grinned and a little light switched on in Helen's eyes.

"Mama," Ingrid cleared her throat, "this is Mr. Temple. He's a preacher."

"What do you preach?" Helen didn't wait for an answer, though. She turned and strode toward the house, digging the handle of her broom into the ground like a mountaineer's staff. "Which brand of hypocrite are you, Mr. Temple?" She threw the question out over her shoulder.

"Mama!"

"It's all right, Ingrid. I don't mind your mother's questions." They had come to the porch steps. Thaddeus moved quickly and positioned himself a step or two higher than Helen. "Won't you let me answer your question, Mrs. Shawn? I hold to no creed that bears a name. Unless it's love." He handed her Ingrid's bonnet, full of flowers and self-heal. The blossoms were still fresh.

"Thaddeus, Mama doesn't. . . ."

Helen whirled on her. "Why have you come home bringing this vision with you? Do you hate it so much up here that you have to bring someone for camouflage?"

"He's a friend, Mama. And he's like us. His family had a farm up beyond Portland. They were hardy, like Hildebrands and Shawns."

"And still hardy, Mrs. Shawn. I thought I might help with a few of the heavier chores that need doing about the place while you and your daughter have a talk. If I'm intruding on your privacy, only tell me to go and I will. But since I'm here, and I can see right off those barn timbers need repairing, why not let me work awhile? To tell the truth, I'd like the exercise."

Hearing the music in his voice, Ingrid smiled. Even the edges of Helen's mouth were quivering slightly. How could she fail to be won by him?

She and her mother sat in the kitchen, a room that figured in Ingrid's earliest memories. Then it had served as kitchen and dining room, and Talley's room as well. Helen took a steaming kettle of hot water from the hearth and made a pot of tea.

"I suppose you want me to feed you?" Helen stared at Ingrid as if she were no more to her than a passer-by.

Ingrid bit her lip to keep the tears from her eyes. She had learned to do this when she lived with the Davis family. Back in those days, she had wept only when she was alone. Mama, Mama, she would cry. It seemed impossible that this cold and weather-beaten old woman was the mama of her dreams, the mama who smelled of lavender and strong soap. It was impossible to think of her as a comforter.

"There's a ham in the smokehouse. You can slice that up. And I might have a few beans. The potatoes are good, too."

"Are you so angry with me, Mama? Won't you ever forgive me?" Ingrid let the tears come. She cared too much to hold them back simply for the sake of pride. "Don't be mad at me for going to Amoset. Everything is fine there. Really it is. And I'm careful, Mama. I don't take any risks. I remember your good advice and I try to behave like a lady. Like you taught me. Please, Mama, say you forgive me." Tears splashed on her hands.

Helen stared at her. Ingrid seemed to be at a very great distance from her, and not really Ingrid at all, but a clever imitation. Helen was conscious of watching and hearing the sobs, but she felt no emotional response whatsoever.

Instead she looked down at her hands, turning them over and over until she had noted every line in their red, cracked surface. I am a real person, she thought. These horrible hands prove it. Then why? Why couldn't she feel something, some fragile reminder of motherhood, toward her own flesh and blood? The girl is suffering, Helen thought. But how does the mother feel? Neutral? No, she knew it was something even more removed than neutrality. As she looked at the top of Ingrid's head and listened to her plaintive sobbing, it came to Helen suddenly. She felt as she imagined a spirit might, one who no longer even inhabited the real world, but spent its time staring down on the foolish goings on of humans trapped in the log jams of emotion.

She is suffering, Helen thought again.

"It's all right, Ingrid. I forgive you."

She could at least be kind, even if she no longer cared.

After their meal, Ingrid and Thaddeus rode Silk up the high trail to the lookout. They slipped off his back and stood side by side near the edge of the mountain, where the dizzying drop was five hundred feet of rock. It was late in the afternoon and the western mountains were turning purple.

"Thank you," Thaddeus said when they had stood quietly for a long time. "Thank you for bringing me up here. This was Talley's place, wasn't it?"

"How did you know?"

"Only a guess. I know that when I was a boy. . . ."

Ingrid laughed. "You're still a boy, aren't you?"

His look was strange. Shaking his head, he

turned to help her onto Silk. "No," he said. "I'm not a boy. I'm a man."

She looked intently at him, wondering why his voice was suddenly strange. But his expression gave no clue.

They rode for a while in silence. Silk was content to walk at a steady, slow pace where the grade was steep, and the gentle bounce of his walk made Ingrid sleepy after her hearty meal. Without thinking, she rested her head against Thaddeus' back and closed her eyes.

He caught her when she almost slipped off. Then he dismounted and helped her down.

"Are you all right?" His voice was full of concern.

Feeling foolish, Ingrid reddened and brushed her hair back from her face. "I fell asleep. It was stupid of me." Again without thinking, she yawned noisily.

Thaddeus laughed. "You need a nap, my girl. I'll find the perfect place."

"No," she disagreed quickly, glancing over her shoulder at the sun, "better not. It's too late."

Thaddeus was unconcerned. "I won't let you be late. With Silk to get us back to Amoset in a flash, it seems wasteful to ignore the sun. It shines for us, you know."

She smiled. "Oh, Thaddeus."

When had she begun to call him by his Christian name? And when had she begun to feel so easy with him that the thought of sleeping while he kept watch was one she could accept unhesitatingly? She climbed back up on Silk and Thaddeus led them farther down the hill and then off on a side path that also sloped down toward Amoset. The forest here was dark and in its first growth, with some trees many arms' length in circumference. Eventually the trail led them to a small bright clearing where there was a stream and a grove.

Thaddeus helped her down. "I wish I had a blanket for you," he said. "Will you be warm enough?" He touched her upper arm.

Ingrid yawned and sat down. The grass was long and deep and sweet-smelling. "I'm fine," she murmured drowsily, lying back. "It's lovely here, Thaddeus." A bee buzzed close by.

All at once she opened her eyes. "Is it time?" she asked, rising up on one elbow. "Did I sleep?"

"Like an angel," he said softly.

Ingrid was confused. "Were you . . . here? Beside me?" She glanced about the clearing to assure herself they were alone. But seeing only the empty forest, she still was not calmed. The lovely, quiet woods were painted now with long sable shadows and she shivered with sudden foreboding.

"It's only been a moment, Ingrid. I didn't mean to lie beside you, but as I watched you doze off, you looked so pure and sweet and defenseless that I couldn't ignore my desire to be near you. If you want me to go, you have only to say so, Ingrid." Thaddeus' voice rose a little when he said this and the melody began. All the subtle harmonies were wreathed about his words like birdsong. "You are so beautiful, Ingrid. You don't know it, but you are perfect. Perfect. When God created woman, He had in mind the girl of seventeen, I think. You are so sweet, so fresh and new, like the season." He took her hand in his and kissed the fingertips and palm lingeringly. "I am enchanted by you, Ingrid. What can I do?" He raised his eyes to hers. They seemed to melt. "You must help me. I need you."

"I?" she breathed, her heart beginning to pound in alarm. Her body that a moment before had been

about to sleep was now a battlefield of passions.
Nothing in her life had prepared her for what she
felt.

"Let me love you, Ingrid," he whispered, pulling
her close and touching his lips to her ear as he held
her hands hostage between them. His mouth grazed
the lobe and his tongue feathered on the shell.

"You mustn't," sighed Ingrid, pulling away. "Let
me go, please. You mustn't." She sat up.

"But I must, Ingrid. We must," he murmured,
pushing her back into the grass and lying on top of
her. "I want you so much, little Ingrid."

"This isn't right. We mustn't. Thaddeus, please!"

He put his hand on her breast and she moaned a
little as she tried to squirm away from under him. But
he was pressing down hard against her, and though
she was frightened, she was mildly excited, too. When
he stroked down her hip and across her stomach and
pressed the skirt between her legs, her body inadvertently moved and rose against his. She shrank back in
terror of what she'd done.

He was grinning down at her. Though nothing
had changed in his face, the expression seemed different now. He seemed to be gloating. For the first time,
her fear had an edge to it.

"I must go!" she cried and pushed hard against
him.

Thaddeus was strong and broad-chested. She
could neither move him nor could she stop him when
he pulled her skirts up above her hips and dragged
down on the drawstring of her pantaloons, tugging at
the thin cotton until it tore. She tried to scream, but
her throat was dry.

"Lovely Ingrid. Sweet confection." With one
hand across her throat he held her still while he slid

down and probed her, first with his free hand and then with his mouth.

"God, help me!" she cried. Thaddeus raised his head. He was grinning again. With one hand he opened his trousers. He looked huge and obscene to Ingrid, and she understood the worst all at once.

She was betrayed, cheated by her trusting heart. "Help me!" she cried again as he penetrated her. Realizing the extent of Thaddeus Temple's perfidy, she began to scream. He had to clamp his hand down over her mouth to silence her. He leaned close and whispered, "There's no use asking God to help you now, Ingrid. He's left you in my charge. But I won't hurt you. I swear I will be kind."

Afterward, he washed her in the stream and helped her dress. She lay without moving and accepted his assistance as if he were a maiden aunt called in to help at a difficult time.

"I'll tell someone," she muttered as he tied the drawstring on her pantaloons.

"No you won't, Ingrid. No one would believe you. Besides, would Senator Shawn want all that bad talk going about? His daughter and a preacher! The schoolteacher might not be fit to teach anymore after such an experience. You won't tell anyone, Ingrid. I know you won't." He pulled down her skirt and helped her stand up. "Besides, I would hate for you to spoil my pleasant memory with nasty talk."

"Your . . . what . . . ?" She felt cold all over and began to tremble.

"I told you that you were beautiful, Ingrid." He grinned. "You so inflamed me that I couldn't help myself."

Chapter 26

Patrick Paine staggered onto the east-west road that led from Cooper's Mountain to the Hopewell estate. The estate actually stood on the lower slopes of the mountain, but because the road cut it off from the wilderness, the house and land seemed more like part of the city. Absorbed in this thought and lulled by the even trot of her mare, Margaret Duffy, on her way home from a visit with Suzannah, was startled to see her nephew, Patrick, charge out of the woods and into the middle of the road in front of her.

"Patrick!" Margaret slipped from the sidesaddle and hurried to clasp the exhausted boy. His shirt was torn and he was bloody. "How did this happen? You must tell me this minute!"

Patrick grew red about the eyes and nostrils as he always did when he was about to weep. "I got caught in brambles up the hill!"

"What kind of foolish boy lets bushes do this to him?" She examined his back and then fixed him sternly. "I just do not believe you got yourself in this . . . this condition alone." She lifted him onto her mare and, taking the reins, turned back to his mother's home. As Margaret walked she scolded him. "I'll be late getting home, Pat, because of this, and your Uncle Bigelow will be worried. I'll have to explain to him how I had to turn back and sneak you into your nursery so that your Uncle Valentine wouldn't see you in this state." She stopped and turned back to the child. "Your Uncle Valentine is in a fearful temper these days, Pat. You'd best stay out of his way." After she had made sure her words had registered, they went on, Patrick slumped over the sidesaddle in total six-year-old weariness. "And when I've got you all cleaned up and in your bed, I want to hear what you were doing on that mountain. Don't you know how dangerous Cooper's Mountain can be? People have died up there!" Margaret shivered. "But the Lord knows it doesn't help to think about that."

An hour or so later, Margaret peeked her head in the door of Suzannah's study. "Can you spare a moment?" she asked.

Suzannah took off her spectacles and rubbed her eyes. "I thought you left an hour ago, Margaret."

"I know." She closed the door behind her and hurried across the room to the table where Suzannah was working. "I have to talk to you about Patrick, dear. Can you put away the books for a while?" Margaret was referring to the financial books that were open on the desk in front of Suzannah. "You need to rest, dear. Your health will suffer."

Suzannah sighed. "I know, I know." She rubbed her eyes until she saw stars, then twisted her neck from side to side, stretching the taut muscles. "I've been over and over these figures and I can't make them work, no matter what I do. I've lowered the wage I'm paying for piece work; I've lengthened the workday by fifteen minutes. I hated having to do those things. You know I try to treat my workers fairly and this . . . this is unfair. I know it. They know it. It shames me."

"But Suzannah, you must survive. In better times you can raise wages and shorten the day."

"That's what I would have said a few years ago. But I've been managing the mill for a long time now and I know nothing ever goes back to the way it was." Suzannah laughed sadly. "I mark my entry into adulthood from the day I realized that. Ever since then I have felt old."

"Don't be silly. You're only twenty-eight. You need a vacation. I think you should go down to Savannah and stay with Eben and Amanda. They've invited you often enough and it would do you so much good. Besides which, your son needs you as much as the mill." Margaret sat down, carefully smoothing the folds of her burgundy velvet skirt across her knees.

"Is that what you came back to tell me?"

"What you need is a husband, of course. A strong man who will take some of this fearful responsibility off your hands and let you have the time you need to be a mother to your boy."

"Is there something wrong with Patrick, Margaret?"

"It's nothing physical, dear," Margaret hurried to assure her. "But the child is growing up wild. At six he thinks nothing of climbing the mountain to the Shawn farm." Margaret began laughing and didn't notice Suzannah's face, which for a moment had turned quite pale. "He told me such a story when I found him with his shirt torn and bramble scratches all over his back. How he went up to the Shawns to make friends with Helen. Can you imagine such a thing? That boy is truly a pet, Suzannah. With the dearest, softest heart. He told me that when he met Helen Shawn on New Year's Day she had sad eyes and he promised himself he would be her friend."

Suzannah shook her head in disbelief.

"He can't do it, of course, Suzannah. It simply

isn't safe for a tyke and besides, I'm rather certain that poor old Helen is no fit companion for a child."

Suzannah was not at all certain of this. She remembered the years when she had lived with the Shawn family and how she had grown to love Helen Shawn. Now that she was older and a mother herself, Suzannah could recognize in her memories of Helen a rare quality, a kind of essential motherliness. But that had been twenty years ago.

"I hear the woman's gone quite mad. You must forbid him to visit her."

For his physical safety, he had to be stopped from climbing the mountain alone; that much Suzannah could agree with. But she felt sorry for Helen. She lived alone, shunning society, a woman without purpose. Was it fair to keep away a little boy who might give her what she most needed? A child to love?

But she would see him and recognize James in a dozen different ways.

"Are you all right, Suzannah?" Margaret leaned forward and touched her sister-in-law's forehead. "You don't seem to have a fever, but one never knows. . . ."

"About Patrick, Margaret." Suzannah stood up and began to move about her study, touching, smoothing the warm-hued Shaker furniture as she spoke. "It is, of course, dangerous for him to be hiking alone. I will tell him that. As to the other, this business of wildness, I ask you to remember that Patrick lives in a most . . . strange home. I don't like to give him too many rules to follow for fear of ending what little enjoyment he is able to get from life."

"You mustn't spoil him though, Suzannah. If you do, you will pay for it the rest of your life." Margaret bit her nail. "I confess to you that I sometimes wish my brother Travis had died," she went on with some anger. "I know it seems sinful to say such a thing, but what a sin it is for you to live here like a widow when you are young and full of life and your son needs a good, firm father to keep him in line. Truly, Suzannah, the raising of sons is best left to the father."

"I know you feel that way, Margaret, but I don't want. . . ."

"Of course you want to get married, dear. Doesn't every woman?"

Suzannah laughed. "At any rate, I'm already a married woman and likely to stay that way."

"How can you say that? Do you ever wonder if, perhaps, in some far-off town on the edge of nowhere, an accident or illness. . . ."

"I'll know if Travis dies, Margaret."

"How?"

"I'll know, that's all. I'll know."

There was a knock at the door and a plump-faced servant looked in.

"What is it, Libby?"

"Mrs. Hopewell would like to see you, Mrs. Paine. Upstairs, in her bedroom."

"I'll just be off, Suzannah. Don't bother to show me out. After all these years!" Margaret Duffy laughed aloud at the idea and bustled out of the room in a hurry. Glancing at the tall clock as she did so, she cried out to no one in particular, "Oh, good Lord! Biggv will be beside himself."

Suzannah also looked at the clock. By rights she should remain at her desk for several more hours to do the job justice. But after Margaret's interruption and now this unusual call from Sarah, she had lost the mood for work. Closing up her study for the day, checking the windows and laying the ledgers away in the cabinet beside the bookcases, she thought how nice a long, soaking bath would be. Sometime in the last hour, her head had begun to ache and her neck was stiff from bending over her books.

As Suzannah passed her father's study, she thought for a moment of the man inside and involuntarily shuddered as a wave of nausea passed through her. She had seen Martin Hopewell earlier in the day, just after the midday meal. As always, she had talked to him of the mill and its affairs. He appeared to listen, but sometimes interrupted with completely irrelevant comments that made her wonder if he heard anything she said to him. During the winter Martin's doctor had insisted that his study be heated, but now that it was early summer the grates were clear again and the room felt as clammy and cold as February.

On her way up to her mother's room, Suzannah stopped at the foot of the stairs and looked back at her father's door. With the mill in trouble, what would he have done? she asked herself. The answer came without pause: hire Irish. He would not have stopped a moment to consider the Yankees who had come to the mill in the dream years and had remained faithful employees even in these hard times. Martin Hopewell would not have considered them, nor, if someone had pressed the unfairness on his mind, would he have cared. For as long as Suzannah could remember, Martin Hopewell had cared only for making money.

Must I put money before people as he did? Must I become as he is?

"Mama?" Patrick was waiting for her at the top of the stairs, wearing a pinstriped nightshirt that trailed about his ankles. Margaret had apparently decided he ought to go to bed early. His face was scratched but scrubbed shiny clean. He looked as if he ached all over.

Suzannah sat on the top step and pulled the boy onto her lap. For a long time they held each other silently. Then Patrick began to squirm.

"I hurt my back all over. Did Aunty Margaret tell you about that?" He looked more proud than apprehensive.

Suzannah knew that expression and grinned. "You think you're very brave, don't you, Patrick Paine? And you know how I admire courage. But you are not going to have your way with me this time, young man. You are forbidden to go up Cooper's Mountain to the Shawn farm. It's not safe." Suzannah heard the word *forbidden* come from her lips and recognized it as the same word her father had uttered to her almost twenty years earlier. She wanted to withdraw the order, but knew she couldn't. For Patrick's safety, he must be kept close to home. Furthermore, the Hopewells, their mill and their town, had interfered enough in Helen Shawn's life. Suzannah told herself she owed it to the woman to honor her wish for solitude.

"But I think she's a nice lady, Mama. And she works up there all alone. I watched her cutting wood and making shingles and all that stuff a man is supposed to do. Doesn't she have a husband, Mama?"

"I introduced you to him, Patrick. Senator Shawn is Helen's husband. And you know the schoolteacher at the mill? Ingrid? She's Helen's daughter."

"They ought to be helping her, Mama. She has to work real hard and all by herself."

"I know, son. I think she wants it that way." Suzannah's head had begun a slow rhythmic expansion and contraction. Her skull had become like a rubber globe from which the air was being sucked out and forced in repeatedly.

"I'm having my supper in my room tonight.

Early. Aunty Margaret said so. Will you kiss me good
night before I go to sleep?"

"What?"

"Will you. . . ."

"Of course, Patrick." She hugged him tightly and
lifted him onto his feet. "I have to visit a moment
with Grandmama and Uncle Val. Then I'll come." She
patted his bottom through the oversized nightshirt.
"Go on in now."

He was at his bedroom door when he turned and
said in a soft, strangely adult voice, "Aunty Margaret
says Uncle Val's in a terrible temper. You should keep
out of his way, Mama."

The warning was issued soberly. For a moment
Patrick was so much like his father! Tears welled up
in Suzannah's eyes.

"Thank you, Patrick. I'll try."

Suzannah hated the way her mother's bedroom
smelled. Beneath the heavy, sticky aroma of her oils
and perfumes and powders, there was always a stale
brandy odor and a whiff of a body rarely bathed.
When she went in, Valentine was standing near a
window, smoking a cigar, and Sarah was across the
room on her pink satin chaise, wrapped in a robe decorated with flamingo feathers.

"I'm glad you've come, Suzannah. Sit near me,
please." Sarah patted a chair beside her chaise. She
hiccupped. "Sit down, sit down!"

"I'd rather stand, Mama. I've been sitting
hunched over my work and I need to stretch my
spine, I think."

"That's man's business, Suzannah." Sarah patted
her pillows and, settling back comfortably, sipped her
brandy. "You should be puttering about the house,
doing things that befit a woman of your breeding. I

mean, Suzannah, it's not as if you are Lucy Shawn off
the mountain who couldn't live without working in
the mill. It isn't your place to be down there. You're a
Hopewell."

"Isn't Father a Hopewell?"

"Don't be argumentative, Suzannah. You know
what I meant."

Suzannah sighed heavily and shifted her weight
from one foot to the other. She would have to try to
be comfortable, for it seemed her mother was determined to give her a lecture. Though she hated such
scenes, Suzannah could see that the situation was not
without its dark humor. Here she was, a woman of almost thirty with a son and, somewhere, a husband,
and she was being reprimanded like a schoolgirl. And
for what? For doing her best. If Suzannah had been
alone and thinking this way, she might have laughed
aloud. As it was, the scene unfolding around her was
likely to be a tired repeat of many other such scenes.
Her head hurt. Patrick was waiting. She wanted to
take her bath.

Valentine spoke up. "Isn't it true, Suzannah, that
the mill is barely making its way at the moment?"

"As you know, Val, we get our cotton from Georgia. This year we had to buy out of New Orleans as
well and that cost us more than the crops we factor
and lift on our own boats. And as you also know,
Eben has borrowed heavily from the mill to help fi-
nance the railroad. There is also the matter of the mill
wheel that had to be repaired after the winter. And
the mortgage."

Sarah and Valentine looked meaningfully at one
another.

"What's this all about, Valentine?" Suzannah
strode to her brother, confident until she saw his face

and knew that this meeting was not to be just another scolding.

"I want the mill," he announced quietly.

"What do you mean?"

"He means you have mishandled the whole business and now it is time to let a man have his say. Valentine is the natural person to manage the mill. For you to do it is positively ... aberrant."

"If you want to learn the business, I heartily welcome you, Valentine. I don't mind admitting that it is a lot of work for one person to do. But I cannot, in the interests of the mill, just hand over everything all at once. Believe me, it is much too difficult an enterprise for that."

"It's a business, Suzannah. There's no good making it sound more complicated than it truly is. I can manage quite well, I assure you."

"You've had no experience, Val. How can you hope ... ?"

"You're a greedy little bitch!" snapped Sarah. Her blue eyes were pricks of light trapped in fleshy folds, her mouth a thin bitter line glossed with brandy. "You've always wanted your own way. Your own way! That was all that ever counted with you."

Suzannah ignored her. "You can't do this, Valentine. You're welcome to the business, but take it slowly. Let me help you."

"Don't listen to her, Valentine. She won't help you. She's never liked you, so why should she help you? She has always ganged up against you with that wretched Eben."

"He's your son, too, Mama!"

Sarah laughed. She tried to pour another drink from the decanter beside her, but her hand shook so violently it looked as if she might drop it. "I never wanted him in the first place. Never wanted your father, either."

Suzannah stared at her mother. She was insane, just as Martin Hopewell was insane. And Valentine?

"You'll ruin us all if you let Mama guide you, Val." In a last hope, she stretched out her hand to her brother. He brushed her away. "Very well," said Suzannah, walking to the door. "But I give you fair warning that I will not let this happen without making trouble. I will call our lawyers and have them shut down the mill if necessary to keep you from destroying what Father and I have. . . ."

At the mention of his father's name, something flared in Valentine. He wouldn't let Suzannah out of the room. Grabbing her wrist, he squeezed it tightly and snarled. "Don't tell me what you and our father have done together. I don't want to hear that. I know he thought you were his little plaything. And what was I? I was just a boy. How could I compete with a live doll?"

Suzannah was frightened now, but she still hoped to make her brother understand. "Mama kept you away from Father because she wanted you all to herself. She wanted you and she got you. And she's ruined you, Val. Or nearly so. Believe me, Val, she only wants you to run the mill so she will have the power over Father. Don't let her do it to you. For God's sake, be a man!"

With that, Suzannah turned and fled from the room. She heard Valentine shouting at her, but she ignored him. There was nothing he could say that would make any difference. She would not leave the mill in his hands. She would fight him. She would hire the best lawyers in the state.

She went to her room and hurried to the dormer window. Many years before, she had discovered a secret panel that opened to reveal a little chamber just large enough to hold a jewelry box. Eventually, she had made good use of it. Now she touched the wood lightly and the panel rose. The box was still there! She snatched it up and opened the lid. Only then, seeing the huge diamond in all its splendor for the first time in years, did Suzannah dare to believe in its reality. She lifted the stone from its velvet bed and held it in the palm of her hand. After years in darkness, the intricately faceted gem caught the flickering candle flame and leapt into radiance.

The diamond had been a gift from Suzannah's Aunt Bronwyn many years earlier. Bronwyn had given it, she said, because she believed that a woman never should be wholly dependent on the whims of a man. Bronwyn, who had told Suzannah about the ways of love and then had encouraged her niece's love affair with Roberto Monteleone, had bequeathed the diamond secretly. For all the years since, it had lain hidden, known only to Suzannah.

"What's that?"

She whirled. Valentine was standing in the doorway.

"Give it to me."

"Get away from me, Val! This is mine."

He lurched toward her, sneering, knowing that in any fight between them he was bound to win. When he grabbed for her arm, she jerked back suddenly and darted to the door he'd left standing open. Patrick was there, staring in.

"Go to your room, Patrick," Suzannah cried, grabbing his shoulders and propelling him along the corridor a foot or so. Valentine was right behind her, his face livid, sweat pouring from his forehead. "Stay away from me, Valentine."

"Give it to me before I hurt you." She screamed

when he grabbed her wrist and with the other hand began to pry her fingers open.

Patrick was crying, "Mama, Mama," and tugging at his uncle's pants legs. Valentine turned on him and shoved the boy to the edge of the landing. The youth grazed his head on the banister and looked around, puzzled.

One by one, Valentine pulled back on Suzannah's fingers. Catching a glimpse of the diamond's fires, he gasped. "Mother!" he shouted over his shoulder. "Have you seen this?"

"No, Valentine!" Suzannah screamed and twisted her body wildly, trying to pull away from him. "You can't. . . ." She staggered backward, the diamond still locked in her fist. But Suzannah was light-headed and dizzy and knew she couldn't think fast enough to fight for much longer. She grabbed for the banister and took one step down. Valentine was behind her, reaching for her like a huge, hungry bear. Terrified, she shrank back against the rail just as she saw Patrick pull at his uncle's legs. Valentine turned to kick him away and lost his balance. His arms flailing like a windmill, he screamed as he fell headlong down the long, carpeted flight of stairs to the floor below.

PART V

Chapter 27

Savannah, Georgia

"But I don't want her here!" declared Amanda White Hopewell, as she and Eben were strolling in the garden of their home, located on the river in Savannah. She stamped her prettily shod foot, tossed her yellow curls and repeated for the fourth time, "I don't want her here. I told you I don't want your family to know about the baby until after it's born. Mostly, I don't want her snooping around down on the island."

"You know as well as I do that my sister is not a snoop. Besides, I have no intention of letting you go down to St. Simon's Island to have your baby with just Biddy and Dora."

"You promised!"

"That was when your mother was alive, Amanda. She would have gone with you. But now . . . well, you can't go alone. I respect your wishes where I am concerned. If you don't want me with you, that's your business. But you'll not go alone."

Eben had suggested the walk, expecting it to be a relaxing exercise for the mother-to-be. However, it appeared to be producing quite the opposite effect, for Eben could never remember seeing his young wife as agitated as she was now. As they walked past a bed of brightly colored zinnias, Amanda tore the blossoms from every stalk, beheading the entire row. It was in Eben's mind to stop her, but he withheld his criticism, telling himself that Amanda's peculiar behavior was just another manifestation of her pregnant state. He glanced surreptitiously at her swollen belly. Her impending motherhood seemed to be something of a miracle, and it never ceased to amaze him. Just as he had begun to believe she was infertile, the good news had come. But to what an accompaniment!

The only other pregnancy Eben had observed closely was Marianna's. His mistress' nature had been sweetened by the nine-month wait for Christian. He could remember thinking that she was like a woman in possession of a secret treasure, biding her time until it could be revealed. By contrast, Amanda never had been more snappish, less civil or less companionable. From the moment she had begun to show, she had hidden her body from him by elaborate means, wearing only the fullest, most sacklike garments to cover her swelling. Once, when he had asked her to let him feel the baby move, she had jumped away as if he had requested permission to strike her.

When Eben thought about the child who would be born in three months, this child who would bear his name, he felt nothing. They might as well have been preparing to take a stranger's child into their home. From time to time, Eben felt guilty about this seeming absence of paternal feeling toward Amanda's child. He loved Christian intensely and longed to feel the same about this coming child. Instead, there was nothing. No feeling. The child hardly seemed real to Eben.

In one corner of the large garden was a massive old magnolia tree around which a bench had been built. When they reached this point in their walk, Eben asked Amanda if she would like to rest a moment. Most days she said yes, but today she shook her head and continued down the path toward the water. Eben followed behind. From the rear, she was still as slim as the girl he had married before she was sixteen. It hardly seemed possible that they had been man and wife for six years. Eben would have been the first to admit that, though they shared a house and sometimes a bed, he scarcely knew Amanda. Her desire to be alone for the baby's delivery was particularly confusing, for Amanda was childlike and dependent in all aspects of her life. All but this one, that is, in which she was exhibiting an unreasonable degree of independence and determination to go against the custom that provided for female companionship at such a time. Since her mother's untimely death from typhoid fever two months earlier, Amanda had been insistent that only Biddy and Dora, her beloved companion slaves, and their mother, Elizabeth, be with her during her labor and delivery.

"Have you forgotten that you liked Suzannah very much when you met her years ago? I believe you told me at the time that she would be like the sister you always wanted. What has changed your mind, Amanda?"

She didn't turn as she answered. "I do like her. I just don't want her with me."

"But, in God's name, why? She can only be helpful."

"Elizabeth is an experienced midwife. And Biddy and Dora will do whatever she tells them. I don't need anyone else!" She whirled around, her arms akimbo, her small round face crimson with the heat. "Why must you always be telling me what to do? You nag me so, Eben Hopewell. I wish I never had this baby!" She turned again, whirling her skirts in a girl-

ish punctuation, and hurried too rapidly down the
stone steps to the water's edge.

"Be careful, Amanda!" Eben cried, running to
catch her. He caught her by the elbow, but she jerked
away. As she did so, her foot slipped on the last step
and she fell with an alarming thump onto the damp
path. Eben was beside her in an instant, full of
chagrin. "Are you all right?" He reached out to touch
her abdomen as if to reassure himself, but she
squirmed away and got to her feet quite easily.

"See what you made me do?" she spat at him.

"Amanda. . . ."

"You're vicious and you're mean and you hate
me! I wish you'd go away and leave me alone. You
and your nasty sister." Aghast at the sound of her
own words, Amanda raised her hand between them
and moved it back and forth as if by doing so she
could erase her message before it reached his ears. "I
didn't mean that, Eben. Truly. Don't be angry.
Please?"

He spoke coldly. "My sister is going to St. Simon's Island with you, Amanda. And when she and
Patrick get here, I expect you to be gracious and loving to them both."

She opened her mouth, but no words came out.
He left her standing at the edge of the still summer
river, her hands clenched in fists at her side. She
chewed at the inside of her lip to keep back the tears.
But her self-pity could not be contained. As a tear
slipped down her cheek, Amanda sat on the last stone
step and began to cry noisily.

"Why did you have to go away and leave me
now, Mama?" she cried out between sobs. "I can't do
this, Mama. You shouldn't have gone away and left
me to do it alone. I know I can't. I know it!" Out on
the river, a fish jumped lazily. The flash of its scales

in the evening light distracted Amanda and for a moment she was transfixed by the widening circles it had made on the flat surface of the water. Then it crossed her mind that it would be easy enough to join her mother if she wished to. She must simply take a few steps into the river and then, by pushing away from the shallows to where the water was over her head, the river would have its way. She couldn't swim. Even paddling was beyond her. The river would know this, she thought, and take her quickly. She would be with her mama again and it would no longer matter that life was very difficult and so perplexingly complicated.

Her marriage never had been successful. Though Amanda had always known that Eben was the handsomest and most successful man in Savannah, a prize for any young woman, she never had been at ease with him. Her mother had assured her that this was not at all strange. Men and women were so basically and unchangeably different in their bodies and minds, she had said, that there could be no thought of companionship between them. She had advised her daughter to resign herself to this and to set about making her life comfortable at Jasmine Gate, Eben's Savannah home.

"That way," Felicity had told Amanda, "your husband will have nothing to complain of. That's the most important thing in marriage."

Because Amanda had never doubted her mother's wisdom, she took these words to heart and did the best she could to order their life at Jasmine Gate. She soon found the task beyond her, but before Eben could complain that the meals were ill-planned or the servants lazy, Felicity White convinced her own husband, Gregory, that their baby girl needed the assistance of the Whites' housekeeper. Belle was a stern-natured and efficient woman whose eyes seemed to see through doors of solid mahogany to where the house slaves were gossiping. Her ears were just as keen. She never missed a word of scandal, even if it was whispered late at night in quarters far removed from her own. In no time at all, life at Jasmine Gate was running smoothly. Amanda could spend as much time as she liked playing with Dora and Biddy, and in the sultry afternoons Belle drew the shades in the bedroom so Amanda and her companions could nap in the still, hot room that was full of brown shadows.

Belle enjoyed her power, for it was greater than any she had known at the Whites. She arranged all the menus. When a party was planned, she helped her mistress make out the guest list and arrange seating at the long dining table. She offered emphatic advice on clothing and etiquette, and as long as she was nearby, Amanda was more confident within her limited social orbit.

But Amanda was not insensitive. She knew that when they entertained the other first families of Savannah, the women and older girls behaved unnaturally toward her as if, though married and mistress of the house, she was still a child in ribbons. To protect herself from their condescension, Amanda made sure that Felicity and Gregory were included in most gatherings.

Amanda and Eben did not argue. Sometimes, however, he assumed a tone with her that she found infuriating because it reminded her of the women in town who treated her like a slow-witted child. But her desire to please him and make him happy was such that she could ignore this and listen eagerly to his advice, hoping to improve herself and, somehow, satisfy him. During the first years of their marriage,

Amanda had been content and gradually she even began to warm in the minor reflected glory of being Eben Hopewell's wife. She knew that other women, women prettier and smarter than she, were envious of her marriage and whispered about it in secret. She could imagine how they raised their eyebrows and muttered words like "business" and "arrangement" back and forth to one another.

Amanda convinced herself that none of this mattered. She knew her marriage was the result of her father's close association with Eben and his late grandfather, Theron, but there was no shame in this. Most matches were made because properties abutted or mergers were planned. Love, Felicity had told her, was a poet's concoction and not at all related to the real world of planting and factoring and banking. In public places, Amanda learned to cling to Eben's arm when her nervousness was acute. She perfected a small smile, alert raised eyebrows, and often nodded her head quickly as she pretended that everything she saw and heard was interesting.

In those early days, it had been Amanda's fondest wish that she should become pregnant. A baby, she thought, would be a doll to play with, and it would be a very long time before that doll grew up and learned to criticize its mother. She had daydreams by the hour in which she dressed and fed and cuddled a baby girl with fair hair like her own. Or would a boy child make Eben happier? Though she was sure a boy infant would be less enchanting than a girl, Amanda constructed an elaborate fantasy around an infant she named Hiram Gregory after her brother and father. Sometimes she would enlist Dora and Biddy in her game. They were told dozens of times over what their duties would be to the "young master," how they must dress him and feed him and protect his fair skin from the sun. But when years had gone by and no young master appeared, Amanda's daydreams lost their substance and their ability to satisfy.

Before her marriage, her knowledge of the origin of babies had been somewhat fuzzy. Felicity had told her that it had to do with that "thing" men did to women. "It's their nature. Men are more like beasts than we are." Sexual pleasure was a concept that Felicity White had not spoken of. This worked to Amanda's advantage, however, for the girl arrived in marriage at sixteen with few misconceptions, dependent upon her young husband for an education. Eben was a tender and careful lover to her, and out of her innocence, she responded to his caresses with a hungry, childlike sensuality. She knew it was forbidden to speak of such matters, but she wished that she might tell Eben how much she enjoyed his visits to her bed, how she wished they were more frequent. Not only did Amanda want him because she wanted his child, but it was her deepest secret that she thought all the touching and pressing and pushing were fun. Eben's hands could make her body tingle all over, and it was like being caught by a great wind that carried her very high and far away, giving her sweet and dreamless sleep. As Eben's attitude toward Amanda became more aloof, his lovemaking was less frequent. Months would go by during which, though he treated her always with kindness and solicitude, he never approached the door of her bedroom suite. He was often out of town in New Orleans or Boston or Charleston on business. She longed for him and tried to sleep with her fingers hidden between her legs, but it was never the same as when Eben touched her there. Her disposition changed through these years of benevolent neglect so that by the time the terrible note arrived, she had become a sulky young woman with a child's petulant, cruel ways.

The note was delivered to the upstairs sitting room where Amanda and her mother were having their afternoon tea. It was raining as it had been for almost two days. The shutters and drapes were drawn over the windows, but the storm was driven by a strong wind from the southeast and the sound of it beat through the thick stone walls of Jasmine Gate.

Amanda was staring sullenly at the fire when Biddy entered the room to give her the note. It came in a plain cream-colored vellum envelope of excellent quality. Quite naturally, Felicity assumed it was an invitation.

"Well, open it, Amanda. Georgina Prince owes you an invitation. That looks a bit like her paper."

Amanda didn't say anything as she stared at the square envelope. For some reason, she felt as if her insides suddenly had lost their place and were floating, trembling, in her stomach, about to rise through her throat and choke her.

"Open it, dear child!" Felicity peered over her pince-nez at Amanda, shaking her head a little from side to side with consternation, confusion and a form of mild despair that she called suffering. "Shall I do it for you?"

Amanda shook her head, gathering her senses back to the moment. It was silly of her to be so upset. Felicity was correct. Almost certainly the envelope contained another formally worded invitation.

She opened it carefully. It was not an invitation. It was a note written in a plain, bold hand that neither Amanda nor Felicity could identify. There were only a few sentences, but they were enough to tell Amanda all she ever would want to know about Marianna St. Clair, Eben Hopewell and a boy called Christian.

Uttering a little scream, Amanda dropped the paper. She stood up, swayed, sat down again and buried her face in the folds of her skirt. Her face burned with mortification, but anger made her pound the settee with her fists. She hated Eben, she wailed. She wished that he and his black harlot both were dead and the wretched, yellow boy buried with them. Felicity tried to comfort her, but it was useless. Finally she could only sit in silence, waiting for the storm to pass. When Amanda was calmer, her mother patted her face dry with a napkin from the tea table and, putting her arms around her daughter, rocked slowly, rhythmically, from side to side.

"I've known for a long time," Felicity said finally, her manner and expression indicating that this was the time for a serious discussion. "I don't know who sent you that note, but maybe even such a cruel act is for the best sometimes. A woman should know when her husband is. . . ."

"But a nigger, Mama! That whore Marianna St. Clair! How could Eben do this to me?" The question began a fresh squall so raging that Felicity had to shake her daughter roughly.

"Have you no sense, child? Do you want the slaves talking about this? You know how they love white folks' gossip and if they know about. . . ."

"They probably already do. I'm the only one who's been in ignorance. He's made a fool of me. No wonder they laugh behind their hands when I come into the room. No wonder I'm not invited to the women's circles. If I were there they couldn't talk about me!" Amanda stood up and began to pace the room. "Anyway, it's not fair. I've been a good wife to Eben. I keep a nice house and my table is the best in

Savannah. Everyone knows that! He has no business going off with that slut. And to have a child by her! A child when I'm barren! I can never forgive him. I wish I were dead!" She flung herself down on the settee and wept anew.

This time Felicity did not trouble to comfort her. Instead she rose and paced the room as her daughter had. She spoke so softly that eventually Amanda had to stop her crying in order to hear what her mother was saying.

"It's the child who holds him to her, of course. Imagine naming a bastard Christian! I wonder lightning hasn't struck them all down. But it doesn't matter. It's all right. We'll make the best of it. You simply must have your own child as quickly as possible, and then Eben will have no reason to devote himself to her. He will have an heir right here at home, a child of his own lawful marriage. One he can be proud of." She stopped pacing and stood in front of Amanda. "Now I know you may not like this, child, but you are going to have to submit to your husband if you wish to become pregnant. It's an unfortunate truth of life that none of us can become mothers without a man involved."

"But I have submitted, Mama. I have, but nothing happens. I'm barren like those women in the Bible." Amanda touched her stomach unconsciously while she spoke.

"What nonsense!" Felicity declared, slapping her hand away. "Women in our family are never barren. You haven't tried hard enough."

"But I have, Mama. I have."

Felicity resumed her pacing, more silent and thoughtful this time.

"Your father must speak to him," she decided after a while.

"No!" shrieked Amanda. "I couldn't bear it. The humiliation would be too dreadful. Besides, it would only make Eben angry." When Eben was angry he became morose and locked himself in his grandfather's old study for hours and hours, missing meals and bedtime. In such black moods he frightened Amanda and the slaves scurried out of his way for fear of his bitter humor.

"Maybe you're right. Anyway, I don't know if your papa knows about this St. Clair woman. Just on the chance that he doesn't, I'd as soon keep it from him. He's got a temper too, you know." Felicity stood before the fireplace, staring into the coals. "No, there must be another way."

Amanda stuck out her lower lip. "I'd rather move back home and forget all about being Mrs. Hopewell."

Felicity turned on her in alarm. "Don't ever let me hear you say such a thing! You will not come home. Not under any circumstances. Is that clear?"

"But think of him with her, Mama! How can I stay here after this?"

"You will and that's all there is to it. No matter what he has done, it is not worth the scandal it would cause if you came home and left him here without you. If you did that, you would be finished in Savannah society and probably all over the South, at the rate Eben's fame and fortune are spreading. And if you think you can't endure what he's done to you, let me just remind you, Amanda, though I dislike talk of such matters, that you are not the first woman whose husband has taken a colored mistress. It's high time you realized a man will have his way. And you'll come to be grateful, let me tell you. It's a blessing to be free of their brutish desires."

"But, I like. . . ."

"Amanda! I don't want to hear what you have to

say. I am your mother and for all that you are a married woman, you are still my daughter. Just heed my words and spare me your intimacies. Swallow your pride, hold your head high and if anyone ever dares to mention Marianna St. Clair or that bastard to you, you must simply smile and say 'indeed' and have nothing to do with that person ever afterward. And be a little patient. Mama will take care of things. If you are unable to have a child, we'll think of some other way to get that man of yours back home where he belongs."

Only later, when the rain had ended and she was riding home in her open carriage, did Felicity White acknowledge just how difficult a task this might be. She sank back against the well-stuffed leather seats of the pretty phaeton. It was small and delicate in appearance, the very essence of what Felicity called "ladylike." So absorbed was she that she did not notice when her friend Mrs. Shepherd waved a hanky from another carriage. Passing down the quiet, shaded streets of Savannah, the moist air sweet with the heavy smell of magnolia blossoms, Felicity White's concentration was entirely devoted to what recently had transpired in Amanda's sitting room.

She had known about Marianna St. Clair for several years. Only a will of iron, coupled with her rigid code of propriety, had stopped her from speaking out to her Yankee son-in-law. Yes, she now thought of him as a Yankee, though at one time she had called him as "fine a man as any Southern gentleman."

It might be true that colored mistresses were nothing new in the South, but that did not in any way excuse what Eben had done to Amanda. As far as Felicity was concerned, he had proved himself to be scum, no better than the slime that formed on the river in summertime. Only in the beginning, when the news was still so fresh it stung her daily, did she consider telling her husband and demanding that he force Eben to change his ways. She sensed that Gregory might already know and, in the way of men, approve of his son-in-law's liaison with the dressmaker. In recent years Gregory had become more critical of Amanda and had on more than one occasion said he thought there might be something "not quite right" about her. One such scene had taken place several years earlier on a spring day in the Whites' rose garden.

"What can you possibly mean by that remark?" Felicity had demanded to know, immediately flushed with protective outrage.

Gregory White was particularly fond of several rosebushes that he had been cultivating for twenty years or more. He pretended to be examining the leaves for aphids and did not answer right away. When he finally spoke, it was without looking at his wife. "I wish she were not so . . . childlike. And her affection for Biddy and Dora seems somehow wrong to me. Amanda is a grown woman, but she cavorts about her house and grounds like a schoolgirl. It doesn't seem right to me."

Felicity had stopped fanning herself long enough to slap the ivory and silk fan against her hand in what was, for her, a show of anger. "She's a lovely, feminine girl. And of course her spirits are playful, for heaven's sake! Haven't we done all we could to protect her from all that is harsh and ugly and trying to a woman's soul? What would you prefer?"

Gregory walked on, scrutinizing the next bush before he said, "It isn't that I don't love her. I do.

She's as pretty as a rosebud. But there is no . . . intelligence in her."

"Since when does a man care to have an intelligent wife, may I ask?"

"I think Eben would prefer a wife he could talk with."

"That's nonsense, Gregory White! He has you and Hiram to talk to." She hurried around in front of her husband and looked hard into his face. "Well? Isn't that true?"

Gregory said nothing. After a bit, the silence became rather embarrassing to Felicity, so she went into the house and ordered a slave to bring her a tall glass of fruit punch which she drank alone in the solarium that faced away from the rose garden. She didn't want to look at her husband that day and, furthermore, his affection for those blasted roses infuriated her. She drank quickly, but it didn't refresh her.

Now, as her phaeton left Savannah and headed out the river road toward home, she could still recall the dreadful headache she had gotten that day and how it had lasted half the week, forcing her into bed despite a dozen social temptations.

Where the cobbles ended, the road became muddy and slow. For a moment Felicity thought of St. Simon's Island where she had gone to live as a bride. She recalled the soft sea breezes that made even summertime pleasant there. She and Elizabeth, her favorite slave and closest companion, the mother of Biddy and Dora, had walked along the beach at low tide when the damp sand flats stretched out to sea for hundreds of yards. With no one else in sight, Felicity had enjoyed lifting her skirts to let the breeze ruffle the lace of her petticoats as if they were sails.

Suddenly Felicity remembered something else.

Some months earlier, during her last visit there, Elizabeth had told her a scandalous story about the overseer on Chevron Middleton's plantation around the other side of the island. The overseer had ten daughters and one of them had gotten herself pregnant by, it was said, a young preacher who came to visit for a while with the idea of opening a church for the white population of St. Simon's. The scandal was that the girl's father had thrown the baby in the sea the moment it was born for fear of what would be said. Of course, this had resulted in more talk than had they simply kissed the babe and brought it up as one of the family, as was normally done in such cases. Felicity sat up straighter in her carriage, oblivious now of the dust. As if Elizabeth sat beside her, she recalled the black woman's laughing words.

"And if that ain't bad enough, Miss Felicity. That poor man's got him nine more girls and the oldest only twenty. You mark my words, that ain't the only baby what's going to have to learn how to swim mighty early."

Just two days after her disturbing tea time with Amanda, Felicity had traveled down to St. Simon's Island, claiming that Savannah was airless and was giving her migraines. She was gone only a week, however, and upon her return Gregory White noted that his wife seemed in brighter spirits than he'd seen her in for some time. But she had no time for her husband and set off to visit Jasmine Gate almost before her traveling boxes were unpacked.

As soon as they had exchanged greetings, Felicity hurried Amanda up the stairs to the sitting room and made sure the door was locked behind them. Then she heaved a heavy sigh and began to speak.

"I've found a way for you to have a baby,

Amanda." Her daughter was about to interrupt, but Felicity spoke right over her protests. "I don't want to hear any contradictions. And don't try to tell me this won't work. I've figured it all out with Elizabeth."

"Elizabeth?" Amanda flopped down on the settee and pouted. "What's that old darkie got to do with . . . ?" Her blue, slightly bulbous eyes were red from crying and sleeplessness, for the foul mood that had descended on her when she had learned about her husband and Marianna St. Clair had not lifted. Instead it seemed to grow heavier and more burdensome with each day in which she must keep silent and try to behave civilly to Eben.

"Just hush and listen to me! Now . . . there's a family down on the island by the name of Sondergaard. He's overseer to Chevron Middleton and it so happens he's got ten daughters and no wife to keep her eye on them. Those girls run wild most of the time and last winter, the eldest got herself with child and the poor little thing was destroyed."

"How do you know all this?"

"I told you. Elizabeth. She's privy to everything that happens on the island. You know that! So, anyway, here's what we plan for you. Sure as the dickens, Mr. Sondergaard's daughters are going to find their way into more trouble sooner or later. Maybe you'll have to wait a while, but most likely it won't be long. I'm told the girls are buxom, comely. . . ."

"Mama!"

"And when it happens that one of them slips up and spoils herself, my Elizabeth's going to make an arrangement."

"Arrangement?"

"Dear child, are you so slow? You will have the next baby!"

Amanda began to sob. "I don't want some white

trash baby. And do you think Eben will care anything
for it?"

"He will if he thinks it's his."

Amanda stopped crying as abruptly as she had
begun. She blinked several times in disbelief.

"Listen here, Amanda. Men don't know anything
about babies. You can put a pillow under your dress
and as far as Eben Hopewell knows, there's twins inside you."

"No!"

"Yes, miss. You just don't let him come near you
in the marriage way and you'll be perfectly fine.
Then, when the girl's time is near, you and I will just
go on down to the island. We'll say it's so Elizabeth
can deliver the baby, that you don't want any dirty-
handed doctor touching you. Next thing Eben knows,
he's got a son or daughter. He'll never know the difference, believe me!"

"I can't do it, Mama."

"Of course you can! I remind you, Amanda, that
unless you can produce some sort of offspring, Eben
is going to tie himself more and more closely to that
St. Clair woman and litter the county with yellow-
skinned bastards. Is that what you want?"

Amanda wasn't listening. She was shaking her
head from side to side, her pretty little mouth hanging open and flaccid. At that moment, it occurred to
Felicity that perhaps Gregory was right. Perhaps their
daughter was a trifle stupid. She grabbed Amanda's
shoulders and pinched her hard to get her attention.

"I know what I'm talking about! There's nothing
can go wrong. I'll be here. I'll help you."

All these things had happened months before.
Now, Amanda stared at the waters of the Savannah

River and thought bitterly that her mother had betrayed her by dying before the baby was born.

"I can't do it, Mama," she insisted for the hundredth time, as if her mother's spirit was hovering nearby. Since Felicity's death, it had become Amanda's habit to talk to her aloud this way. For a while, it had comforted her and she had felt less lonely and betrayed. But as she neared the time when she would have to go to the island to "give birth," she found the one-sided communication with her mother less and less satisfying. She was terrified that the plan Felicity and Elizabeth had so carefully contrived would in some way fail and that Eben would discover the trick. So little did she know her husband, she could not be sure whether he would be angry, hurt or simply wildly amused. Somehow, the last possibility troubled her most. She could not bear the thought that he might go to Marianna St. Clair and with her laugh at his wife's ridiculous hoax.

"I can't do it, Mama," she said again, her eyes luminous with tears. "You shouldn't have gone away and left me. It isn't fair!"

Chapter 28

Suzannah and Patrick arrived by packet from New York just two days before the opening of the Cherokee and West Georgia railway line connecting Augusta and central Georgia. Though there had been several successive depression years in Georgia and a great many enterprises had failed, including banks like the one in which Eben and his father-in-law had a partnership, Eben and those connected to him had continued to prosper. The line between profit and loss, however, was not always as wide and secure as they might have wished.

Eben had been warned against going ahead with the railroad at such a time, but he was convinced that if he waited, the opportunity would be lost, sacrificed to another more daring entrepreneur. Now, after years spent securing the right of way and laying the miles and miles of track, the Cherokee and West Georgia Railroad was prepared to make its innaugural run. No sooner had Patrick and Suzannah set foot on solid ground in Savannah than they were told they must go by carriage north to Augusta where Eben awaited them eagerly.

"But you might need me, Amanda." Suzannah was reluctant to leave her sister-in-law, who looked as if she was suffering in her pregnancy. "I should stay." Suzannah would not have said so for the world, but she was worried about Amanda. Her complexion was a greyed and pasty white and there was an unhealthy puffiness about her face that looked suspiciously as if she had been crying. Within their pockets of flesh, her eyes darted rapidly back and forth like those of a small, wild animal, cornered and at the edge of panic. No doubt the girl missed her mother. Suzannah, her sympathetic heart immediately touched, realized that it must be extremely difficult for Amanda to cope with the loss of her mother when she was with child. She felt maternally protective of the girl, who had always seemed not quite competent to meet life's challenges. "Let me send word to Eben that I won't be coming. I know a railroad opening is exciting, but believe me, I can live without it." She pulled off her gloves and threw them down.

"No, no," insisted Amanda, grabbing Suzannah's hands and squeezing so tightly that she winced, "you have to go. Eben would be just furious with me if I kept you here."

Suzannah looked doubtful. "Surely not. My brother wants your comfort and happiness, I know. Let me stay, Amanda. I know I can be of help."

But the girl was adamant. She stormed about the sitting room, picking up objects and setting them down ringingly, muttering all the while that Suzannah must, *simply must,* go to Augusta. Finally Suzannah gave up trying to convince her.

But all through the long ride that followed, Suzannah thought about Amanda. The coach and four horses sped down dusty, red dirt roads, first along the Savannah River and then through pine woods baking beneath a fiery sun and cotton fields that stretched to the horizon, straight lines broken only by the bent forms of slaves in neckerchiefs of red and yellow and bright blue. Suzannah saw it all, but still she couldn't

erase the picture of her agitated sister-in-law, swathed
in a voluminous gown that disguised her pregnancy
and made her seem merely ugly and awkward, waving a damp hanky, chewing her lip and looking from
side to side to side in what Suzannah could only
describe as terror.

Just outside a pretty village on the river, the carriage drew up at a livery stable beside an inn. While
the hands changed the horses, Suzannah and Patrick
were shown into a little dining room and served a
meal. Patrick ate voraciously, stuffing himself with
biscuits and gravy and red beans stewed with pork,
but Suzannah nibbled without enthusiasm. She was
distracted by her thoughts and by the scene taking
place just beyond the window before which their
table had been laid.

The village was the site of an important cotton
landing, and on the shore of the river, a scene of considerable noise and confusion was taking place. A flat-
boat half-laden with cotton bales was tied to the bank
and a dozen deep-chested Negro men were in the
process of rolling more cotton aboard while others
loaded wood for the little steam engine that moved
the boat. The laborers were being supervised by a
planter, an elegant man in a white straw hat who was
standing beside a tall, nervous, elaborately saddled
stallion. A pair of overseers conveyed his orders and
saw to it that they were carried out. They paced back
and forth along the bank, beating the butt ends of
their whips impatiently against their trouser legs and
bellowing commands from time to time. Here and
there on the grassy bank, black women in colorful
turbans and neckerchiefs, their half-naked children
clinging to them, observed the scene. There was also
a carriage full of young women, perhaps the planter's
daughters, who watched, their pastel parasols raised

like blossoms to the sun. The girls reminded Suzannah of Amanda. She squeezed a bit of lemon into her tea and tried to imagine why the girl was so upset.

Was it possible that Eben had done something to frighten his young wife? Though Suzannah loved her brother and was intensely loyal to him, she was well aware of his fearsome dark moods. In the past, she herself had sometimes been frightened by them, so it wasn't difficult to imagine their effect on the simple, childlike Amanda. For years Suzannah had thought of her brother as a haunted man, a man cursed and weighed down beneath the immense weight of something ugly and secret and black as the grave. But she knew him also as a man who fought the darkness valiantly. During his more recent visits to Amoset, she had seen some indication that he eventually might be victorious over whatever tormented him. He had learned to laugh more readily and also had revealed a tenderness, a gift for empathy, in which he was like his grandfather, Theron Hopewell. Now, however, having discovered Amanda in such an extreme state of agitation and apparent ill health, Suzannah wondered if Eben's black melancholia might have resurged or if he might have regressed somehow to those days when he emulated his father in all things.

The closed carriage had been left in the full sun so that when Suzannah and Patrick returned to their seats after the meal, the interior was as hot as an oven. Immediately, Suzannah's head began to throb. When they were on their way once more, she seemed to feel the drumming of each hoof beat against the membranes of her brain.

I hate it here, she thought. I despise Georgia, its climate, its way of life. I want to go home. I want to go home.

But as long as Valentine remained adamantly

against her, and more particularly against young Patrick, Suzannah would have to make her life in Georgia. She told herself she could do it. She would do it because, for Patrick's sake, she must. The boy's heritage, she reminded herself, was as much Georgian as Yankee. He was heir to a great fortune. The Hopewells had been in Savannah since long before the Revolution and Jasmine Gate was one of the city's noblest homes. If need be, she would raise Patrick in Savannah and he would grow to manhood with a proud sense of his heritage. When her will became weak, when she recalled, as she knew she would and with a vividness that was cruel and quick, the face and form of James Shawn, she would school herself to feel nothing. If she had to, she would search out and make an alliance with the blackness in which Eben had lost himself. For Patrick's sake, she would do anything necessary to accept her fate. For Patrick.

Yet even as Suzannah swore this to herself, clenching her fists in such determination that her nails marked deep ovals in her palms, her lips moved and, possessed by her heart and not her will, her voice whispered, "I want to go home."

Across the carriage, Patrick looked up. "What about home, Mama?" If he missed Amoset and his Duffy cousins, if he thought at all of what had occasioned their hasty departure, he hadn't seen fit to tell his mother. He was jumpy and excited about seeing a locomotive up close and maybe riding in the cab as his Uncle Eben had once said he might. His lively curiosity was tickled by everything he saw because it was so different from Amoset. "Do you want to go home?"

Suzannah smiled, shook her head and patted his knee. For many nights after his Uncle Valentine had fallen down the stairs, Patrick's sleep had been racked by screaming, sobbing nightmares that drove him to his mother's bed, sweating and delirious with terror. He was better now, or seemed to be. He never spoke of Valentine or the accident. When Patrick seemed reassured that his mother was all right, he again became distracted by the view from the carriage window. Suzannah lay back against the cushions and closed her eyes, although she knew to sleep would be impossible. Even if Patrick had forgotten, his mother hadn't. The memories were clear, too clear, always too clear.

When Patrick had pulled Valentine off balance, he had done it to protect his mother. She knew this, but awake or asleep, she continually relived the whole scene. She could see Valentine chasing her, struggling with her, the terrified Patrick pulling at him, Valentine shoving Patrick away and lunging at her and, finally, Valentine falling, falling, falling. Probably because he was full of liquor at the time, Valentine's long fall had been graceful and easy, relaxed as an infant's might be. By the time he had reached the bottom of the staircase, she had run halfway down herself. She rushed to kneel beside him, expecting the worst. But he had only groaned and lifted himself up on his elbows.

"Get out of here, Suzannah," he roared at her, "or I will tell the world that brat of yours tried to kill me!" His face was ashen except for his lips, which were blood red and dripping where his teeth had gashed them during the fall.

At the top of the stairs Sarah, drawn from her room for the first time in years by the commotion, saw the blood and began to scream wildly. Beside Suzannah, clinging to her skirts, Patrick wept and repeated over and over that he hadn't meant to hurt his Uncle Val.

"Get him away from me," screamed Valentine. "Get him away before I kill him!"

It would have been useless to reason with him and, besides, Sarah's shrieks pierced Suzannah's head as if they had been knives. Grabbing her boy, she ran back up the stairs. As she passed Sarah, the old woman beat at her with her fists, tried to pull her hair and screamed more stridently, using foul words and insults so poisonous that Suzannah covered Patrick's ears to block their sound. First in her own room and then in Patrick's, she hastily packed a traveling box. Ignoring the curious servants who hovered about her, wide-eyed and muttering in Gaelic, she grabbed her son with one hand, the box with the other and fled the house by the backstairs.

Only when the family carriage had taken them past the distant side of Amoset, where the boarding houses gave way suddenly to dense forest, had Suzannah relaxed enough to remember the diamond. She touched the bodice of her dress and felt the stone there where she had thrust it as Valentine fell. It seemed to burn her flesh with its cold fire, a reassuring sensation. Aunt Bronwyn had been right. A woman must never be entirely dependent upon a man. Not brother, not husband, not father. She felt her confidence returning.

Beside her, Patrick had fallen into a whimpering sleep. She gathered him tightly into her arms and murmured soothing sounds against his damp brow.

He stirred and looked up at her anxiously.

"Is it going to be all right, Mama? I didn't mean to hurt Uncle. I told you that Aunty Margaret said we should stay out of his way. I only meant. . . ." She would never forget the look on his face, so earnest and frightened, but stubborn, too. He was grappling with the unholy memories of an uncle intent on doing anything in order to get his own way. "Are we in trouble, Mama?"

Now, riding in yet another carriage, this one far from Valentine and Amoset and the precarious affairs of the mill, Suzannah remembered her son's question. She still could not answer it. They had gone first to Margaret Duffy in Marivale. From there they had traveled to Boston where the diamond had been placed in a bank vault, as Suzannah acknowledged it probably should have been in the first place. While in Boston, she had wanted to see James. She felt he would want to know what had happened. Then she chided herself, recalling that despite his talk of friendship months before at the Strickland party, he had made no effort to see or contact her. Though several times she had been on the verge of writing him, she had always thought better of it. This time was no exception.

In the carriage going south on the pike to New York, she had turned back for a final look at Boston, her eyes swimming with tears. She was afraid that she never would be able to return to New England as long as Valentine claimed Patrick had tried to kill him. For the first time since Talley's death and Travis' abrupt departure, for the first time since she and James Shawn had said good-bye on Cooper's Mountain, Suzannah felt painfully and irrevocably cut off from love. In that moment, as Boston became a hazy conglomeration, a pile of children's blocks against a smoky, twilight horizon, Suzannah felt herself lose what little had remained to her of youth. She became a woman without dreams, a woman bereft of hope. She held her son against her and pressed her cheek on soft, silken hair. He was all she had.

Augusta was a small city that had been generously

laid out in wide boulevards and pleasant, hilly streets.
Its handsome Georgian style residences with their Co-
rinthian columns were landscaped in a way that was
only possible in a mild climate where labor was
plentiful and leisure a primary value. On their arrival,
Suzannah and Patrick were met by Hiram White,
Amanda's older brother. He took them to the city's
finest hotel and instructed the management to make
sure that every need of Mr. Eben Hopewell's family
was gratified.

Suzannah liked Hiram, but she didn't trust him.
He had a face so open and expressive that she immediately suspected him of concealing something,
though she could hardly guess what. No sooner had
she entertained these suspicious thoughts than she
chided herself for doing so. She might dislike Georgia
and the Southern way of life, but she had to guard
against being unreasonably critical. When Hiram told
her they would have to hurry in order to be on time
for the official opening of the rail line, she smiled her
most radiant smile and promised that she and Patrick
would make haste.

Several blocks away, Eben was pacing the street
and not paying much attention to the assurances of
his father-in-law and partner, Gregory White.

"What's got into you, Eben, my boy?" the older
man asked, placing his hand on Eben's shoulder affectionately. "I've seen to every detail. In an hour or so,
the first load of settlers will be headed into Cherokee
country," Gregory laughed, slapping Eben's back,
"from which the redskins are conveniently absent!"

While Gregory snorted and guffawed at his own
amusing turn of phrase, Eben nodded absent-mindedly and laughed too. It suited his purposes to have
White believe it was the railroad that troubled his
mind, though, in fact, he was perfectly confident that

this new enterprise would go smoothly. It was
Amanda who concerned him. He couldn't exactly say
why, but he wished he hadn't insisted that Suzannah
and Patrick join him in Augusta. He regretted leaving
his nervous young wife alone, but when he asked
himself why this was so, he couldn't answer. He knew
that she was well looked after by the house slaves
and that, should anything happen and the baby come
early, Biddy and Dora would see to it that the doctor
and the midwife were called in. It wasn't in Eben's
nature to worry overmuch about those things he
couldn't affect or which gave every indication of
being harmonious, nevertheless he couldn't shake his
anxiety all that day.

Eben was a strikingly handsome man. In his
early thirties, he was vigorous and healthy, a man
who had become more attractive with the passing of
years. With his dark hair worn long and tied behind
the neck, his straight nose and intelligent eyes, there
was something of the early patriot about his appearance. On that day in Augusta, county belles cast longing glances at him, surreptitiously of course, and some
even whispered to each other that it was a great pity
Mr. Eben Hopewell was a married man.

More than a thousand people, slaves and free, on
foot and in carriages and wagons and carts, had
gathered in the square where the railway loading
dock was erected. The children squealed with excitement, the women gossiped, the gentlemen puffed on
stogies and discussed the future of Georgia senten-
tiously. The railway platform was laden with boxes
and crates and bits of tired furniture, the simple
goods of pioneers on their way to the fertile lands of
the West. On the track, gleaming blue-black in the afternoon sun, stood the iron locomotive. Brown wood
smoke poured from its stack, making a stinking cloud

that would hang low over Augusta all that windless day and half the next.

On the edge of the crowd, near a scrawny pine tree, Eben caught sight of someone, a beautifully dressed dark woman with a handsome child beside her. For an instant he thought it was Marianna. She had wanted to be in Augusta for the important day and Eben had agreed to it. He was proud of the railroad and wanted Christian to experience the exhilaration of the noisy locomotive, the cheers, the hats and bonnets thrown high in jubilation. But at the last moment, Marianna had decided to remain in her villa on the sparsely populated coast road south of Savannah. Though she hadn't told him so, he knew the reason. Marianna was suffering intensely now and with every visit to her, he became more conscious of it, as if Dr. Wilkinson in Boston had lifted blinders from his eyes and sensitized him to feeling what she felt. And Bess, the old slave woman who stayed with her, had whispered to him secretly that in the night Marianna wept from the pain and sometimes drank from the brandy bottle, without even a glass, to help her sleep.

Gregory White was talking loudly about the great plans they had for the years to come when their railway line would expand to include passenger cars with upholstered seats and covered wagons in which fragile crops could be protected from the capricious climate. Eben nodded appropriately and even contributed an idea or two, but his mind was still distracted by Marianna, Amanda and even Lucy far away in Boston. It was odd the way the women in his life had become sirens with the power to call his mind away and set him wondering and wishing and, lately, even worrying. He sometimes thought he wanted done with them but, as if to prove the impossibility of the mere idea, he suddenly found himself wishing that Lucy could be with him on this important day. And then he wondered whether it would be possible, if Suzannah were to make her home in the South as now seemed likely, for Lucy to visit her. The two women had once been friends; might they not be so again?

Absurdly, despite the crowds, despite the smoke and noise and handshakes all around, Eben began to imagine ways in which a secret rendezvous with Lucy might be arranged. He would take her riding, show her the beautiful south coast, the clumps of sharp grass growing in the dunes like pincushions, the line of breakers stretching into the blue haze of the horizon. They would walk together, their bare feet washed by the warm, gritty wavelets. . . .

"What's got into you, Eben? You aren't worried about Amanda, are you?" Gregory gave his arm a firm shake and looked at him closely. "Don't be silly, my boy. She's still got some time to go before the young one comes. The little girl will be all right. And anyway, women have been having babies since time began and there's no amount of worrying and wondering can affect that. Men just have to wait and be patient at these times, believe me." Gregory chuckled. From his expression, it was clear that he was convinced that he had at last hit upon an explanation for Eben's peculiar mood. "You heed my words, son. Don't forget I fathered that little girl of yours. Not to mention Hiram. I know whereof I speak."

Eben tried to smile. "You're right, of course. I know it's foolish, but I wish I hadn't left her behind."

"Great Scott, man! You couldn't bring her to a public occasion like this! Not a decent woman like Amanda."

"Perhaps I should have stayed. Or Suzannah."

But Gregory would hear none of it. Adamantly, he shook his head and clapped his son-in-law on the back. "Nonsense, lad, nonsense. Mark my words: business can't stop for babies."

Chapter 29

Patrick shrieked when the firecrackers went off, fat, noisy things followed by pinwheels of light. And then—his delight was boundless—around the corner from the town hall came a band dressed in sparkling blue. There were flags and drums and a pair of buglers and then an open wagon festooned in Georgia's red, white and blue. Standing up in the wagon were four grownups and one of them he immediately recognized as Uncle Eben.

Patrick's face was hot with excitement. He looked around to see what his mother was doing. She was waving her handkerchief at Eben and smiling the nice way, the special way she did when she wasn't tired or worried or any of the things she had been during the past weeks. Patrick hoped she might be feeling better. The smile was very like her old familiar one. Instantly Patrick loved his uncle because he returned his mother's smile with a flash of sparkling white teeth. Best of all, his smile included Patrick and made him feel welcome.

The settlers, fifty couples and their children who had been invited to travel free on the train's inaugural run, were crowded around their goods and boxes on the loading platform. The children were near hysterical with excitement and kept jumping on and off the platform, yelling and screaming. Big boys frightened

Patrick and he reached for his mother's hand. Somehow, by a magic he took for granted, her hand was
always there.

After the arrival of Uncle Eben and the parade,
the scene quieted down and Patrick felt a bit less nervous. The band had stopped playing. All at once he
realized how hot it was in the full Georgia sun. He
was wearing a small straw hat his Aunt Amanda had
shoved on his head before he and his mother had left
Savannah. It made Patrick feel like a girl and,
besides, his head was sweaty. He tore it off and then
swung it guiltily against his leg, waiting for his
mother to notice.

Suzannah didn't notice at all. Her attention was
fixed on Eben as he addressed the large crowd.
Unconsciously, she stood straighter. She was so
proud of him that she hoped everyone in the crowd
knew she was his sister. Slaves, masters, free and
bound children, animals, babes on shoulders waving
little flags of red and blue—all stood in the midsum-
mer sun, listening with good-humored attention. The
belles held ruffled parasols that kept their faces in
perpetual twilight, most of the men wore hats and the
slave women wore bandannas. Suzannah stared at one
of the dark-skinned women, frankly curious. She was
struck by the same impression she had felt while visiting Georgia years ago, not long before her marriage
to Travis. The slave's strong, sensual face remained
perfectly placid as she listened to the white masters
talking about their railroad.

How can that be? Suzannah asked herself. The
woman appears to accept her lot with equanimity.
She doesn't scream or groan or complain that she is a
human being and sick to death of doing white
peoples' work so they can play with railroads. The

more Suzannah considered this apparent lack of resentment, the less likely it seemed. She knew the woman must be seething inside, seething and waiting. She recalled what she had read about the growing number of abolitionist groups in the North. Thomas Kilmaine had written several impassioned articles on the subject, and there were some in Amoset who declared that sooner or later, it would come down to a matter of North versus South, free versus slave.

I don't want to live here, she thought, and touching Patrick's shoulder lightly, drew him back against her.

Eben came to stand beside Patrick and, in a moment, hoisted up the boy on his shoulders so that he could see the gleaming iron locomotive get up steam. Men in their shirt sleeves were loading wood onto a flatcar behind the engine. A man standing on the flatcar, a dark brown man with the biggest arms Patrick had ever seen, threw the logs into the engine. Clouds of tobacco-colored smoke made a filthy column straight up in the still air. A whistle blew from somewhere, louder than a dragon's roar. Patrick held on tightly to his Uncle Eben and got an affectionate pat on the knee in response.

"It's going! It's going!" Patrick screamed, bouncing up and down and swinging his legs back and forth, giving Eben quite a beating. The whistle sounded again and everybody cheered, including Patrick, who wasn't exactly sure what was happening. "It's going! It's going!" He thought he'd burst from excitement. The crowd was waving and the band had recommenced its wonderful tinny playing. There were flags and bright colors and, best of all, wonder of wonders, that big iron monster was moving and pulling, not just four or five men and women, but fifty families and all their goods to last them forever. It was more than Patrick could bear.

He vomited all over his Uncle Eben.

Suzannah and Patrick traveled back to Savannah with Eben three days after the inaugural run. As their carriage moved through the early morning fog that came from the river, the incident still had the power to make Suzannah laugh. Glancing up, half-asleep, Eben glowered at her.

"I know what you're thinking about."

She blushed. "It was funny, Eben. Horrible, but funny."

"Poor little colt." Eben gently ruffled Patrick's hair. The boy was deeply asleep, curved like an S on the long seat. "I don't think I ever saw anyone so completely humiliated as this small person."

Eben spoke with such tenderness that Suzannah suddenly felt overcome with love for him. Impulsively, she leaned across the seat and kissed him.

"Thank you for taking me in."

He was quiet for a long time. Now that he was on his way home he seemed to sag, as if he were Job resuming his burden. Finally he asked, "How long will Valentine last?"

"I see no reason to be optimistic, Eben."

"Nor I, nor I." Reaching into a small leather pouch, he took out his pipe. He pressed the tobacco in carefully, sculpting the soft leaves to the bowl with his fingertip. "You gave me everything you could for the railroad. I shouldn't have asked you. . . ."

"If I could have retained control, I could have managed, Eben. Neither of us could have reckoned on Valentine's behaving this way. Mother encouraged him, I think. And I believe he has a woman, one of the Irish down in the Gully. For all I know, he may have children. That cannot help but have made a difference in him. But it's Mother who's chiefly to blame. Nothing would gladden her heart more than to imagine that she has gained power over Father."

Eben didn't respond. They would be home in a few hours and he must face the fact that the diversion the railroad had offered was gone. He could no longer use it to occupy his mind. He felt a terrible letdown, a hollow in his stomach that food could never fill.

Amanda. Marianna. Lucy. They never went away. They only faded for a moment or two, just long enough to admit a fleeting impression of enjoyment. For several days Suzannah had been the tonic his spirits craved, but now even her smile and her spirit had lost their power to cheer him. Amanda. Marianna. Lucy. Eben didn't know whether to laugh, as he had after Patrick's horrible accident, to weep or, and this was most awful, to just give up. There were days, hours, minutes when he thought he'd like to get the finest rifle made, a bowie knife and the best kind of horse with a comfortable saddle and simply leave town and head west. West. The escape land, the place where no one would find him unless he wanted to be found.

But in his heart he knew he couldn't leave. He didn't even want to, not really. He was a man of business and he craved the challenge of the marketplace the way outdoorsmen yearned for open spaces, tall mountains and uncharted rivers. And wherever he went, Eben knew he always would carry the faces of those three women in his mind. His yellow-haired wife with her wisps of pale eyelashes and little-girl coyness. In his memory he would always see those slightly protruding blue eyes, so wide they were almost perfect circles, filling up with tears. Marianna, the dark flower, her skin the color of browned butter, dark and golden at the same time. Eben groaned, remembering the way her ribs showed beneath breasts that had begun to hang on her chest like an old woman's. Something was killing her, and much as he longed to protect her, there was nothing he could do.

And Lucy.

He shifted his weight.

"Are you all right, Eben?" Suzannah touched his knee. "You seem ... distressed. Is it Amanda?"

He seized upon this truth, thankful to Suzannah for the buoy. "Did you notice anything strange about her? I know you weren't together long, but did you see anything about Amanda that seemed, well, not right to you?" Eben spoke in rushes, needing to talk, not think, for a time.

"At first, I thought it was her mother's death that troubled her," he went on. "It was a terrible thing for Amanda to lose Felicity that way, without any warning. They were closer than most mothers and daughters are, I think."

"Pray do not let my case set the example," put in Suzannah dryly.

"Allowing that, they were still unusually close. It had to do with Amanda's ... youthfulness. Childishness is more the truth, I suppose." He tamped his pipe and sighed. "I always thought she would outgrow it, you see. When I met her she was the same way, but Grandfather told me she would outgrow it and I believed him. But now ... I don't even know what she thinks about having a baby. Since Felicity died, Amanda won't speak of the baby for more than a moment. I would expect a girl of her sort to be frightened, but she's not. She seems to have this outrageous confidence—Felicity gave it to her—in an old slave woman called Elizabeth. Dora and Biddy's mother. She insists upon going down there, to St. Simon's Island, to have the baby. And when I told her you would be in Savannah and might wish to accompany her to the island, Amanda became almost hysterical. I can't understand her, Suzannah. I've tried. I'll be frank with you, I don't love her. But I have been considerate, I have spent time with her and squired her about the county as she wished me to. I have, in my own way, been a good husband to Amanda." He stared at his knees, wondering if he had said more than Suzannah cared to hear.

"Eben, neither of us has had our way where love is concerned."

He was instantly apologetic. "I've been tactless, Suzannah. You didn't come down here to drown in my problems."

"I'll do all I can, Eben."

"You won't be welcomed on the island. She seems to think she needs no one but. . . ."

"I think she'll change her mind when the time comes. She'll be frightened. We all are. Giving birth is like coming face to face with God."

He nodded, distracted again.

"There's more than Amanda on your mind, isn't there? Why not tell me, Eben? I want to help if I can. Is it the business?"

Eben laughed bitterly. "I have the family gift for making a profit, Suzannah. Despite Valentine and the Irish and whatever, Hopewell and Company will continue to grow rich."

"If it's not finances that trouble you, then what is it?"

The carriage slowed at a crossroad where two boys, one black and the other white, both with fishing poles over their shoulders, bare feet scuffling in the dust, were squatted in the shade of a big sassafras tree. Eben stared at the lads for a long moment until the carriage resumed speed. Watching him intently, Suzannah thought that she had never seen her brother's face so ravaged by anxiety. Though Eben was a grown man, of course, it was a shock to realize that he was no longer a boy, different to feel it as acutely as she now did. She saw a man, his handsome face gaunt with worry and depression. He was suffering. Her heart swelled with love for her brother, as it had a moment before when he touched Patrick with affection. She realized in that moment to what extent they were all of them alone in a world neither kindly nor accommodating, not even to the wishes of the powerful Hopewell family. When they were growing up in Amoset, they had been set against one another by the jealous rivalries encouraged by Martin and Sarah Hopewell. They had, she now thought, wasted years and years of their lives when love and trust should have been growing between them.

Perhaps Eben also thought these things, for he seemed to have come to some conclusion in his sober thoughts. He looked at Suzannah and began to speak quickly, his eyes never leaving her face. He spoke of Marianna and how he had found her in Aimee's brothel that long ago night when he was a virgin boy with an ideal of womanhood that could not permit beauty and innocence to be corrupted.

"It's not precisely love I feel for her. Not love as we think of it when we are young and romantic, at any rate. I admire her because she is so strong and unafraid, despite all the fearful suffering she has undergone. And she needs me. Without my care and help, she would still be at the mercy of Aimee or someone like her." As he went on to tell of Marianna's illness, Eben felt a great sense of relief. He had carried the fear for her within him for so many months without speaking of it to anyone that now, expressed at last, it was as if the fear were being lanced, the poison drained off, the pressure and pain relieved for a little while.

Suzannah reached for him, but he pushed her away gently. "Before you think too sympathetically of your brother, let me finish. Now that I've begun this maudlin confession, I may as well be done with it entirely. Then you will know me as I truly am. If you wish to despise me, I will understand."

"Eben, I could never. . . ." Throughout his story, Suzannah kept her expression neutral. A calm and earnest face disguised the surprise and, she must admit, faint disgust she felt at the idea of her brother and his mistress. One might favor Abolition while still disapproving of . . . consorting. She was shocked by his story, but did not want him to know. Above all else, she wanted him to continue his revelations until she saw the light return to his eyes and the marks of pain disappear from the face she loved fiercely, protectively. It was almost as if he were, like Patrick, her son and her responsibility.

Eben talked about Christián, making sure Suzannah understood that he loved the lad and acknowledged his paternity almost eagerly. "I'll see that he has the best education and all the advantages. No matter what this baby of Amanda's is like, it will never supplant Christian in my heart. No matter how many children I have, Christian will always be my first-born." He glanced at Patrick, who was stirring restlessly in his sleep. "My boy's just four years old. You know how innocent that is, Suzannah. He doesn't know yet how hard his life will be in this part of the world. I have to get him out of the South. He can't stay here."

Suzannah only nodded, not trusting her voice or

the words she might say. She had thought she had a
worldly point of view, but she was shocked. She had
a nephew, a black child whom Eben intended to treat
as legitimate! How would this change Patrick's leg-
acy?

Something in her thoughts must have shown on
her face because Eben laughed wryly and said, "I
have surprised you, eh, little sister? You asked for
confidences and got perhaps more than you reckoned
on." He laughed again, a sound without humor. "If
you only knew. If you only knew."

"More, Eben?" Try as she might, she could not
keep her mouth from dropping open. Aghast.

Eben laughed so gustily that Patrick stirred and
even opened his eyes to look about the carriage before he drifted back to sleep.

"I won't burden you further, Suzannah. My in-
trigues are not particularly tasteful. I'll give you that."

She thought of her Aunt Bronwyn and knew she
would not have been critical or condemning of Eben.
Bronwyn's spirit had been warm and accepting, without rancor or prejudice. As if her late aunt's spirit had
invaded the carriage, Suzannah felt her presence and
was ashamed.

"Let me make a confession," she blurted quickly,
eager to melt the chill in Eben's face and manner. "I
too have not behaved as I should, perhaps."

So it was that Suzannah told her brother about
Sicily and Roberto Monteleone, about her love affair
with James Shawn and the birth of Patrick Paine.
Like Eben she spoke candidly and, once she had begun, gladly.

Though neither Suzannah nor Eben was aware of
it, their talk had drifted in a strange zone where contact between them was no longer bounded by conven-
tion. For the space of just a few hours, a slice of time

and no more, they were to speak quite honestly with one another. Perhaps it was the swaying and lurching, the drum of eight pairs of hooves, the compartment warming in the sun as the carriage raced along a narrow track through the gritty pine woods. Perhaps it was that they had been through a lot together, Eben and his independent and willful sister. But through all the hating and misunderstanding and amidst the collision of their two enormous wills, a passionate affection had grown up. In those moments of intimacy, each was to the other a sweet harbor, where for a time they could unburden themselves and be refreshed.

They arrived in Savannah just before supper time. It was cooler near the ocean, and despite Eben's conviction that Amanda wouldn't welcome Suzannah's company on her trip to St. Simon's Island, Suzannah was still looking forward to it. It would be fine being at the seashore. She was sure of that.

"How is Mrs. Hopewell, Zeke?" Eben demanded.

The old black footman just shook his head and said he didn't know, but Eben wasn't fooled for a moment.

"There's something the matter. Belle!" he called, storming through the inner courtyard. "Belle!"

Belle was a big woman and she had the firmest jaw Suzannah ever had seen. She frankly was scared of Eben's formidable black housekeeper, another excellent reason for visiting St. Simon's Island. The more she considered the idea, the more enthusiastic she became. She and Patrick would enjoy themselves. They could pretend they were visiting on an island in the Caribbean and go for beach walks every day and. . . .

"Gone!" cried Eben. "Gone where?"

"To the island, Mr. Hopewell."

"Has the baby started so soon?"

"I don't believe so, Mr. Hopewell. They didn't confide in me," she added. What had Eben said about Belle on the long ride home? Oh yes, that she held the house in the grip of necessity. Belle and he both knew Jasmine Gate would collapse without her, so she could be as arrogant as she wished. "Mrs. Hopewell did leave a message for you, sir. She said to tell you Mrs. Paine shouldn't come to the island. Said to say it wasn't safe for Yankees what don't know it. Specially little ones like Master Patrick there."

Eben looked at his sister. "That's a threat. You heard it. My wife just threatened you and Patrick."

"She's sick, Eben. I have to go."

"I don't understand this." He paced the courtyard, digging his heels into the flagstones angrily. "What primitive celebration is going to take place on that island that no one is permitted to attend my wife at her delivery but a crowd of superstitious old women? Will someone for God's sake tell me the truth?"

"I'll go to her tomorrow, Eben. Let me go upstairs and arrange my things." Suzannah took Patrick's hand and started toward the house.

"What about the child, Miz Paine?" asked Belle.

Eben spoke up firmly. "He'll have to stay here with us, Suzannah."

"But, Eben, you'll be gone. You're off to Charleston in two days' time." Suzannah looked at Patrick. All at once, from across the field of her memory, came a vivid image. She was on the lawn, the ellipse in front of the Hopewell mansion in Amoset. In the background was the monstrous stone residence her father had built to declare his empire. In the foreground, darting in and out among the folds and

ruffles of her full-skirted dress, a floral cotton impor-
ted from the English mills of her grandfather
Gladwyn Jones, a dozen Irish setter pups not more
than eight or ten weeks old were gamboling and
growling and engaging in mock battles. They were
spirited and brave, she thought, with their bright
little eyes and their tumbling bodies full of confidence. She remembered the dog handler saying to her
father, "They'll be strong one day, Mr. Hopewell.
They're just in training now."

Wasn't that true of children as well? Should Patrick stay? He'd suffered a lot in recent weeks, not to
mention the endless traveling from place to place.
Besides, Eben would give him plenty of attention
when he was home. And wasn't it part of life's training for a strong and independent nature that he be
left alone from time to time? Wasn't now a better
time than any for that most frightening first time?

Then Belle said, "I'll take the best care of him,
Miz Paine."

"No, thank you, Belle," she replied without thinking. "The boy and I will go to the island together."

PART VI

Chapter 30

St. Simon's is a large sea island located off the coast of Georgia at about its midpoint and at the mouth of the Altamaha River. Suzannah and Patrick were approaching the island in a boat like no other Suzannah had seen. It was more like an exotic immigrant wagon, really, with its ragtag collection of miscellaneous necessities for the families living on the island. There were medical supplies and plows, beds and ancient armoires, chickens in crates, ducks, raucous geese, even a miserable, bleating goat as well as a half-dozen passengers like Patrick and Suzannah. The oarsmen were slaves, hired out to the man who owned the boat by a plantation owner on the mainland.

Near its terminus, the mighty Altamaha River becomes fan-shaped and then unravels its waters into the Atlantic. The boat crossed a narrow channel and moved down a swampy coastline for about five miles. Rounding a sandy point of land, they came into a shallow harbor, hardly more than an indentation. On a little rise overlooking this point, in a stand of huge evergreen oaks draped in moss, was the plantation house of the late Jonas White, Amanda's grandfather and a contemporary of Theron Hopewell.

The house was run-down and almost pathetic, a two-story structure with one-story additions that

sprawled across the knoll overlooking the water. But
as Suzannah's eyes became accustomed to the sloven-
liness of shutters hanging on a single hinge, of crumbling chimneys and rotting shingles, she perceived a
kind of beauty that almost compensated for the decay
and neglect. The vegetation was a jungle of luxuriant
growth, teeming with insects and crying birds, flashes
of blue and red whose screams were announcing the
boat's arrival.

Hiram was at the pier to greet Suzannah.

"Welcome to Wild Rose, Mrs. Paine," he said.
"You had a pleasant trip?"

"I didn't know you were coming here, Mr.
White." Suzannah was so taken aback by Hiram's
presence that she forgot to answer his question. "Did
you tell me you were coming here when I saw you in
Augusta?"

"I don't believe so."

There was an awkward, quiet moment, then
Suzannah recovered herself. "How is my sister-in-law?
Is everything all right?"

Hiram became jovial as they walked up the path
to the house. Patrick, unnoticed, trailed a little behind, helping an old black man carry the traveling
boxes.

"Amanda is doing splendidly. Being at Wild Rose
has revived her spirits as our mother knew it would.
Really, Suzannah, though of course I am delighted to
have you here, there was no reason for you to leave
Eben when I know how eagerly he has anticipated
your visit."

Suzannah stopped a moment to fan away the
minuscule black flies that swarmed before her eyes
and about her ears. "I'm worried about Amanda, Mr.
White. When she left Jasmine Gate, she left a
message that seemed almost threatening. Both Eben

and I thought this might be an indication that her mind was troubled."

Hiram guffawed. He beamed at her. "Amanda's mind is just fine, Suzannah."

Suzannah ignored Hiram's use of her first name and continued to talk as they approached the house. "It's not at all uncommon for women to become unlike themselves during and immediately after pregnancy, Mr. White. And in Amanda's case, this might be expected particularly, her mother having died so recently."

Hiram was still laughing. "You may be right, of course. Being a bachelor, I don't know very much about these things. You see, my mother, before she died, asked me to be here with Mandy and she specifically asked that I not speak of it to anyone else in the family. My mother knew we've always been close, my little sister and I." His brow wrinkled. He thought a moment and sighed. "But you may be right about Amanda's mental state. She says and does strange things sometimes."

They smiled at each other and Suzannah said, "Thank you for not calling me an interfering sister-in-law. I certainly don't want to be that. But you have no idea how agitated Eben is about the birth of his child and Amanda's well-being. I think knowing that I'm here reassures him."

Before Suzannah could go on, they were surrounded by a crowd of slaves, mostly women and children. They were dressed quite fancifully in colored neckerchiefs and mismatched headscarves and their skirts and jerkins were covered with patches. They were all barefoot and an inordinately large number of them were old and visibly ailing. A few children had taken a great fancy to Patrick, with his hair shining sometimes silver and sometimes gold in the waning sunlight. They danced about him, singing out what seemed to be questions in a tongue Suzannah couldn't understand. She thought Patrick would be frightened and almost stepped in to rescue him, but she was surprised to discover that he wasn't alarmed. She could tell by the expression on his face that he was calm but completely alert. She was thankful for that.

Suzannah had been a little afraid to bring Patrick to the island with her, and only the thought of the formidable Belle as nursemaid had prompted her to change her mind. The island was, after all, notorious for its infestation of rattlesnakes. Furthermore, Suzannah would never forget Amanda's implied threat. Every time she went over it in her mind, it sounded more ominous. Despite that, she felt somewhat at ease now. Patrick's equanimity in the unfamiliar situation and the knowledge that Hiram was at Wild Rose had helped considerably.

As they crossed the wide verandah, Hiram turned to her and, smiling broadly, said, "Whatever it is that has brought you to Wild Rose, I consider it my great good fortune. I didn't expect such a pleasant diversion."

For Suzannah, life on the island wasn't exactly pleasant, but it wasn't exactly uncomfortable or distressing either. She found much to occupy her mind and set about several tasks with enthusiasm. Amanda was only six and a half months pregnant, after all, so the island sojourn might be a long one. She got Hiram's permission to raid the attics and cupboards of the old mansion. In the process, she unearthed box after box of fine china, as well as boxes of linens that had been chewed up by nesting rodents. The stink was terrible, but she persevered and discovered several real treasures. Hiram appeared appreciative, but a little embarrassed, too. She wondered why.

A long time before, in the days when cotton from St. Simon's demanded the highest price and the planters and their families lived lives of opulence, Wild Rose had been the gemstone of the island. The house had been built with grand entertainments in mind. Suzannah had counted twenty bedrooms and then had given up and gone on to dining rooms. She discovered four of these, with two more for the house slaves. Furnishings in many of these rooms had either gone to ruin or had been hauled away to other White family houses on the mainland. There were termites in the rafters and the windows were wide open to the air. The overseer and his family managed Wild Rose from their house and offices which were half a mile away.

As Suzannah got to know the house and grounds, she realized that Hiram White was probably the richest man she had ever known, apart from her own father, of course. Then why had the house been permitted to run down? Why had wild jasmine and roses been permitted to overtake whole sections of the roof, thus rendering the rooms beneath uninhabitable? The family now lived in eight somewhat sparsely decorated rooms under siege, Suzannah imagined, by forces of nature. Why? She would have loved to know the answer, but thought she must wait until after the baby was born and then ask Eben. She wouldn't dream of asking such a thing of Hiram White.

He was attracted to her, and she became increasingly aware of this as the weeks passed. Slowly, it seemed. At Wild Rose, meals were taken at nine a.m., two p.m. and six. Often Patrick and Suzannah saw no one at breakfast and, just as frequently, they dined alone at two. But the evening meal brought them all together: Suzannah, Patrick, Hiram and, quite often, Amanda. Suzannah found the food scarcely palatable. There was an overabundance of beans and pork and highly seasoned greasy concoctions that turned her stomach slightly. Despite the primitive conditions, the family dined in elegance, their table laden with priceless china and polished silver.

At dinner Suzannah and Hiram often discussed what each of them had done throughout the day. He was using the time of his sister's confinement to oversee the huge plantation property. Several times Suzannah rode out with him on a beautiful dark mare named Tea. Suzannah found the rides invigorating and the island countryside more beautiful at every turn. Moreover, she discovered much to her surprise that she enjoyed Hiram White's attentions. Though not the sort of man she had found attractive in her youth, his burly handsomeness was appealing now, symbolizing as it did strength and security. On other days she either rode to the beach and walked on the sand with Patrick or occupied herself with tasks like cleaning cupboards that made Hiram laugh and call her a Yankee.

Her understanding of that word had grown considerably by the time she and Patrick had been on the island for a while. Among other things, she discovered that her dislike for slavery was no mere affectation lent to her by James Shawn. It was rooted in her soul and, with each passing day, Suzannah despised the institution more. It made her feel ashamed of her race. But her Yankee nature extended beyond the issue of Abolition. She couldn't tolerate the idleness that seemed to be expected of her at Wild Rose. Whenever Suzannah suggested a bit of work she would like to do, Hiram tried to discourage her from it. Why else did he own slaves?

"If you want it done, have one of the women do it. You needn't trouble yourself."

Soon she had told him, "But I *want* to do it" so many times that the phrase had become a joke between them.

After she had been on the island for about two months, Suzannah's insistence on activity made her part of a situation that was to permanently fix the colors and shadows and lights of St. Simon's Island forever in her mind. She had decided that on her way back from an excursion to the ocean, she would stop at a remote and rarely visited slave settlement to deliver sundry supplies, including rolls of bandages which she had rolled herself. She told Patrick where she was going and reminded him to be cautious and watch for snakes, but apart from these final words, no fuss was made about their separation.

Since their arrival on the island, Patrick had demonstrated an admirable degree of independence. Every day, he would charge off to play with his black friends, the crowd of children who hung about the big house. They had little to do, though on call they would fetch an armload of wood for the cook or chase the birds out of the kitchen garden or scare a snake out of the poultry yard. Suzannah had warned Patrick against having anything to do with reptiles, but otherwise she approved of the way he mixed his fun and his labor.

Patrick had picked up the local patois quickly and one day even said to her, when she was speaking crossly, "You vex-ed with me, Mama?"

"Try to speak like a white man when you're with me, Patrick," she said, trying not to laugh. How proud she felt that her son was adapting to new and perhaps even hostile surroundings! James would be proud, too, she reflected, and the mere thought of his name stung her heart as if it were a nettle.

Waving to Patrick, Suzannah set off on Tea for the ocean. She had been anticipating her excursion eagerly, for it was uncomfortably hot at Wild Rose. Though the house was on a knoll, the knoll was tucked away within the folds of land and vegetation, and the air around the house was almost completely still for day after endless day. She could almost feel the refreshing sea breeze the moment she rode away from the house.

Suzannah had made up her mind to disregard her fear of snakes and travel by the beautiful woodland paths. Inland, as she crossed the corner of the island, she rode through a forest of evergreen oaks overgrown with wild jasmine, the tiny yellow trumpets draped like a beaded shawl from the lower branches of the trees. To protect her face from the millions of tiny flies that inhabited the bush, Suzannah had designed herself a bonnet made half of mosquito netting. While it was somewhat eccentric in appearance and provided Hiram with a source of great merriment, it worked very well. Unfortunately, custom demanded that she wear a full riding habit fit for an English lady of leisure, and besides looking somewhat ridiculous in her ludicrous hat and snugly tailored habit, yards of heavy cotton skirt and yards and yards more of cotton petticoats, she was dreadfully warm. But at the point when she thought the heat had become unbearable, the dense growth gave way to a lovely, aromatic pine that grew in airy clusters, its needles the color of old bronze. Soon the land opened out and she was on the edge of the Atlantic.

It was all she had dreamed it would be and more. The sky was the palest blue and the blue sea beneath it extended on and on until it seemed to meet and become part of the sky itself. She was all but surrounded by light and space and water in a way that made her feel both immense and infinitesimal.

She spotted a bleached log and used it as a backrest as she ate her lunch, facing her eyes eastward toward . . . England? Sicily and Roberto Monteleone? Suzannah closed her eyes and wondered what had become of her first lover. From time to time his name appeared in fashionable or scholarly journals. He had become a noted sculptor. But what, she wondered dreamily, was he like now? How did he live? Was there a fat Italian wife and children at home and a mistress in Rome? The very idea was so preposterous that she laughed aloud, frightening two seagulls that had come to examine what was left of her lunch.

After she had dozed a bit, Suzannah walked along the shore swinging a cloth sack and picking up stones and bits of wood she thought would look attractive in the garden or on her dressing table. The sea air cooled her thoughts as well as her body. She realized that she had been rather foolishly overreacting to Amanda's peculiarities when she'd feared her mind might be going. These last weeks she had seen a lot of her sister-in-law. Apart from being quiet and childlike, there was nothing out of the ordinary about Amanda's behavior. In the morning and afternoon she was always with Biddy and Dora and Elizabeth, but at dinner and afterward she was frequently in a happy party mood. The piano in the drawing room had been badly neglected, but Suzannah could still force a tune from its moldy interior and Amanda liked nothing better than to sing along with whatever she was playing. She was also eager for dominoes or charades or even word games, for which she had no talent whatsoever. As far as Suzannah could see, Amanda's mood was mostly jolly.

Once, however, Suzannah came upon the young woman when she was alone in a corner of the kitchen, playing jacks. Amanda, a fully grown woman, looked sad the way only a child can look sad. Her whole body, from her glistening lower lip to her bent back, spelled grief and misery. Tears came to Suzannah's eyes and she would have liked to approach her at that moment and simply hold out her arms as she would to Patrick. But something kept her from it. She knew that Amanda didn't want her, would resent her, would probably hate her for catching her off guard. Suzannah turned away and left the room quietly, and Amanda never knew.

Reclining again on the sand, her head propped up on the white driftwood, Suzannah thought back on what Eben had confessed to her that day in the carriage. Now, knowing Amanda, she understood far better the need that had driven him to women other than his wife. Marianna. Lucy Shawn.

When they were children, Lucy and Suzannah used to dream of going to the seashore for a visit, of riding horseback through the waves, splashing water everywhere. "Now she and my brother are lovers." It sounded more believable when she spoke the words aloud. "Eben is in love with Lucy." Surprisingly, the news hadn't shocked her. There was something right about the match that Suzannah recognized immediately. And anyway, who was Suzannah Paine that she should be critical of love affairs? How Eben lived was his own concern.

She wondered what Hiram would think if he knew about his brother-in-law. She did not have to consider the matter long before she came up with the answer. No doubt Hiram would be outraged and think only of defending his baby sister.

He was truly sweet with Amanda. Kindly and helpful and never condescending. He handled her as one would handle a delicate object, a treasure of china or crystal. Indeed, now that she thought about it, Suzannah had to admit that Hiram was a very special man. So special that she had, the night before, broken a cardinal rule. She had let him kiss her in the hall outside her room as they parted for the evening. She'd had a glass of brandy with him a little earlier and it had relaxed her. When he leaned toward her, his tongue just touching his lips to moisten them, she didn't move away and say good night as she knew was wise and proper. Instead, she closed her eyes just enough to blur Hiram's face and parted her lips a bit for his kiss. As he kissed her, her resistance ebbed. It had always been this way for Suzannah. When would she learn? He pulled her toward him and, swaying sensuously, her hips just touching his, she let him circle her back with his thick arms and rub his hands up and down while their mouths were still pressed together. Suzannah blushed, remembering her response. But she knew there was no use in pretending to be a coy maid. The heritage from her mother's side of the family was deep and hot-blooded in her, as it had been in all the other Jones women she had heard about.

After a long afternoon of relaxing on the beach, Suzannah headed inland again, but by a different path this time, to deliver the supplies she was carrying in her saddlebags.

The slave community was called St. Louis, for some reason, and contained about a dozen wretched hovels. Each hovel was made up of four sides and a flat roof and had a dirt floor. Cooking was done centrally over an open fire pit.

When some slave women saw Suzannah, they dropped their ladles and sticks and hurried to her. St. Louis settlement was located in a remote, low area of the Wild Rose plantation and the slaves who worked the fields surrounding it rarely saw any white person other than the overseer or his representative. A white woman, therefore, in full English riding attire and an absurd hat, was the stuff of tales and stories and memories that age had dimmed.

Molly, for instance, had forgotten almost everything. Though the old slave woman knew there was a master, and presumably a mistress, in the world beyond her fields, she had no clear idea of what that meant until she saw Suzannah.

Molly was the last of the women to join the crowd around Suzannah that afternoon because she had been lying down in her shack on the straw mat she'd made for herself once upon a time. It wasn't much comfort anymore, but she was too stiff in her bones to scour up fresh hay. And, anyway, it was the dark and familiar corner she had claimed for herself that gave her what little comfort she thought about, and not so much the mat. When Molly saw Suzannah, suddenly her mind flooded with memories of a time more than twenty years earlier, when she had slept in a real bed in the big house. Those were the days when cotton from St. Simon's was some of the finest in the world. Looking at Suzannah, she saw instead the girl she remembered clearly for the first time since age had begun to seal her memories over. Felicity White, the bride of Master Gregory, had come to Wild Rose. She too had visited the slave quarters and had gone to the slave settlement on horseback, bringing sweet things and sacking and rolls of white bandages shaped like sausages.

Molly suffered from a variety of ailments, as did most of the slaves Suzannah had met at Wild Rose. Eben's slaves were healthy, well dressed and well spoken, but like all of Hiram White's property, his slaves seemed uniformly ailing and complaining. No sooner had Suzannah dismounted in St. Louis than she was surrounded by eight excited women who babbled in a patois different even from that spoken by the blacks closer to the big house. Unable to understand more than a few words of their questions and comments and pleading, Suzannah smiled nervously as they touched her lightly on the shoulder or hand or skirt. Then through the crowd she saw Molly as the old woman emerged from her shack, moving in the slow, jerky way she had adopted to compensate for the pain in her rheumatic joints.

Molly had borne fifteen children, eleven of whom had died from this and that. Sometimes, thinking hard over the names—Sophie, Addie, Felix—she lost them one by one and ended up unable to remember any of them. Where were they? Or were they at all?

Like the rest of the women who had borne children and had been made to return to the fields after three weeks, Molly blamed her aches and bleeding on the work she did. Her back was permanently bent from leaning over and picking while a baby in a sling dragged on her breast. About a year after she had come out to the St. Louis settlement, she had been carrying a load balanced on her head when she had tripped on a root and fallen on her shoulder. The pain had never quite gone away from that fall and she moved more by miracle than from any strength.

Suzannah could see this determination, this amazing endurance of pain. Molly's astonishing frailty, her bright brown eyes, her skin lined all over like the stitching on a quilt and her bold curiosity had a striking effect on Suzannah. For a moment she felt as if she had been transported to the wilds of Africa. The tribe of slave women, most particularly Molly, frightened her.

But she had come to St. Louis to deliver bandages and conduct a routine health check of the women. She was determined to fulfill her mission. After all, she was a Yankee.

Someone brought her a stool. Suzannah sat perched on it and they sat cross-legged on the dirt in front of her while she asked questions and listened carefully, trying to understand. Gradually, her fear ebbed as she became absorbed in what they were telling her. They spoke of bleeding, tumors, abesses, miscarriages. And more than half were suffering from suppurating ulcers on the ankles and wrists. Suzannah's distress became so acute that she thought she might weep and then her distress turned to horror. She stood up. She had heard enough. Sufficient it was to know that Hiram White and his family allowed their slaves to live in pain and disease and still drove them to work every day, as if they were animals. It was enough to know that human beings could be so wretchedly mistreated and yet still retain their humanity and, sometimes, even a sense of humor.

She turned, finally, to Molly, whose eyes flashed with amusement despite her pain. She chattered like a three-year-old who had just discovered a world of questions, and so rapidly that Suzannah understood almost nothing. Something about Felicity and babies and flannel.

Another old woman, her name Sophie, tugged on Suzannah's sleeve. "Dat Old Molly from the big house. She think you be wife to Master Gregory." Sophie touched her forehead and rolled her eyes expressively.

"What can I give her? Does she need something?" Even as she spoke, Suzannah thought how ridiculous, even condescending, her questions were.

"She say she need flannel."

Suzannah rummaged in one of the saddlebags and came up with the last of several lengths of piece goods she had brought to the settlement. Molly's gratitude was effusive and made Suzannah feel even worse than she had felt earlier. Horror gradually became a mix of shame and rage that overcame her by stages.

"Molly say her back hurt, missus. Say she got sores."

Suzannah helped the old woman up and gently lifted the thin cotton shirt to inspect her back. She saw the sores first. "Molly needs a fresh bed, Sophie. These are bites. And these. . . ." Above the bites was a wide band of smooth skin, a swath of scar tissue in which Suzannah could just make out the ridges that marked the edge of a whip.

"Who did this?" she asked Molly, but the old woman had no idea what she meant. "Sophie, who did this?"

Sophie swung her hips from side to side and looked at the sky and the dirt. "That a long time past now, missus. Molly forget all about that."

Suzannah's voice rose. "I said, who did it?"

"Overseer. Someone. Long time past, missus."

"Why was it done?" She spoke through clenched teeth.

Sophie, sensitive to Suzannah's mood and not understanding it, stared at her dusty toes and shrugged.

Lottie, another woman, answered for her. "Molly all the time sleepy when she got little ones. Man caught her sleepin' one time too many."

Suzannah stared at Lottie for so long that the old woman began to giggle nervously. But after a moment, she stopped and stared at the white woman as did all the other slaves. Men had begun to come in from the fields and they too stood on the outer edge of the women's gathering, watching Suzannah with the same fascination. Her face had suddenly gone bright red and there were tears—imagine tears!—slipping down her cheeks, but no sounds were coming out of her mouth. And she was staring at Molly now. One or two of the women didn't like the look in Suzannah's eyes and moved away nervously.

She spoke finally, wiping the tears away, ashamed of parading her useless emotions. "I wish I could do more for you all. I will speak to Mr. White and try to make arrangements for more sacking and a new iron pot. Molly," she dared not look at the old woman, "you must have a new bed. Fresh straw and. . . ." All at once, Suzannah's voice gave out. She wanted to talk, but she knew that if she opened her mouth, she would say things that Molly and Lottie and Sophie and the rest would not understand. Or she might scream at God for what she saw around her. And the slaves, born into a life that was devoid of options, would not understand her rage. It would only frighten them.

Controlled again, she fixed her mind on the conversation she would have with Hiram White when she saw him that evening. She mounted Tea and arranged her skirts. Taking up the reins, she called, "Lottie, Sophie, you must make Molly a new bed. And use a broom to brush away the vermin. She's been badly bitten." She turned her horse and quickly left St. Louis.

Chapter 31

"You mean you believed them?" Hiram asked. He was handing his sister a glass of wine after dinner, but his hand stopped in midair as he turned to look at Suzannah. "You believed whatever they told you?"

"You should have seen them, Hiram. You should have. I have never seen such neglect, such miserable animal poverty. As Christians in a great democracy, we cannot permit. . . ."

"You believed that old woman?"

"I saw the scar tissue, Hiram. Her back was shiny with it."

Amanda sipped her port and watched her brother and sister-in-law intently.

"She was beaten brutally," Suzannah continued heatedly. "And why? Because she was tired. Well, I ask you, if the overseer who did that to her had borne fifteen children and worked in the fields all his life, he would have gone to sleep under a bush somewhere, too." Suzannah was sitting down, but the strength of her emotions made relaxation impossible. "She was beaten like an animal, Mr. White. How can you countenance that?"

"My dear Suzannah, your plea is most eloquent, but I assure you that it is uncalled for. You have come to us from the North where life is very different. You view life here on the island with the eyes of a Yankee. In time, all this will seem less strange to you."

"Are you saying you *do* tolerate brutal beatings?"

"You said the woman's name was Molly?" Hiram laughed and scratched his temple. "Well, there are so damn many Mollys at Wild Rose, but it seems to me that one of them, years back, tried to hide in a boat somewhere with some foolish notion of escaping." Hiram grinned. "Now, like I say, every other female of them is called Molly, so I can't hardly say for sure it was the same one. But my point is this, Suzannah . . . if your Molly was beaten, it means she disobeyed, forgot her place." He shrugged, hoping to dismiss the subject. "Anyway, that's Overseer Blake's department. We have an arrangement that I stay out of running Wild Rose and he doesn't bother me with details. He produces cotton and that's all I care about. And as it is, Wild Rose just barely breaks even on the ledgers. The great cotton growing days are over on this island. To tell you the truth, Suzannah, those slaves are likely to be sold off in another couple years or so."

"Sold? For what? Who would want them when they're half-dead with exhaustion and pain?" She felt sure that if she could just make him understand that the blacks had feelings the same as other humans, Hiram would instantly, like a prayer meeting convert, see the error of his ways.

No more the innocent country boy, Hiram leaned forward confidentially, his eyes narrow and self-righteous. "Don't you know all niggers are lazy, Suzannah? Don't you know they all lie?"

"And anyway," Amanda cut in, smirking a little behind her wineglass, "whoever asked you to come and play Lady Bountiful at Wild Rose? We get along just fine without Yankees. Didn't I tell you not to come? Didn't I say you wouldn't like it? Must you always tag along where you aren't wanted?"

"Stop it, Amanda." Hiram tried to touch Suzannah's shoulder, but she moved it away and put down her glass.

"I'm here because my brother wishes it, Amanda. You might remember him?"

"Why should I?"

"Amanda, he cares for you deeply and he's been hurt by your rejection of him now, at this important time in your lives."

Amanda's face became livid. "You're as bad as he is. You can't open your mouth without speaking one lie or another. I'll wager I know where precious Eben is right now! He's with that . . ."

"That's enough, Amanda." Hiram put his arm around his sister's shoulders.

She whirled on him. "Why is it enough? Why can't I ever in my life say what I really mean?"

Suzannah got up and started for the door.

"Go away from Wild Rose," Amanda shouted at her back. "Go away and never come back. Why should I want you here? Or him? The rich and powerful Eben Hopewell! I hate him and I hate you just as much. I never want to see your Yankee faces again."

Suzannah turned and lifted her chin. "I doubt that Eben would wish me to remain after this. So you shall have your wish, Amanda. A boat will be leaving at the end of the week and Patrick and I shall be on it." She raised her dark brows and, after looking at both Hiram and Amanda directly, her green eyes unwavering, she nodded her head just once. It was as graceful a show of disdain as Suzannah ever had managed. With that single arrogant gesture, she told Hiram and his sister that she despised them.

Patrick Paine did not see the raised eyebrows, the elegantly curled lip. He was on the other side of the door, standing in the hall with his ear pressed to the wood panel. He had heard all the insults and angry words clearly, however, and had trembled for his mother, wishing himself a man the size of Uncle Eben. Then he'd show that mean Mr. White. Patrick did not like Hiram White, but until that evening he had felt rather guilty about it, especially since his mother had seemed to regard the man as a friend. Sometimes Patrick even had thought that she liked him more than as just a friend and that had always made him angry. When he felt that way, he would go in search of his mother so he could hold her hand and tell her things, just in case she might forget him and ride away again with Mr. White. Now, however, it was pleasant to hate him and Patrick imagined himself a knight of old, willing and prepared to protect his damsel against the force of evil.

When the nurse assigned to care for him came calling his name, Patrick hid in the big armoire in the hall where no one would think to look for him. If Lilly found him, she would make him go to bed in the silly ruffled nightshirt she thought was proper for a white boy his age, although he knew it made him look like an old woman. He hated that nightshirt and in no sense could it be made to harmonize with the gallant fantasies in which he imagined his mother tossing fitfully in her big canopied bed and himself, her guard, watchful in the next room.

When Lilly's soft Southern voice had faded into the far corner of their living quarters, the boy opened the armoire and scurried along the shadowed passageway to his bedroom, which adjoined his mother's. He undressed quickly, kicked his clothing under the bed and, clad in only his drawers, snuggled under the covers. When Lilly came in a few minutes later, Patrick successfully feigned sleep. She left and after a short time, Suzannah came to his bedside.

"You can't fool me," she said and gently blew on his eyes. She smelled nice, and he hugged her. "We're going back to Savannah, Patrick. The boat will come for us at the end of the week."

"I know. I was listening."

He saw her repress a smile before saying quite severely, "That was a naughty thing to do. I think you wander about much too freely here, Patrick. Lilly does no kind of job at all with you." Suzannah's gentle lecture was interrupted by the sound of someone running in the hall and whispers too soft to understand. Her brow lined with worry. "It isn't really safe, you know."

"It's okay. It is. It's safe around here." Patrick made a tough face. "For me it is."

"You're quite a hero, aren't you?" Patrick could feel her love touch him like waves.

"Don't cry, Mama. I'll take care of you."

St. Simon's Island, and particularly the Wild Rose plantation, was a wilderness full of dangerous surprises. It reminded Patrick of Cooper's Mountain. He was unafraid and confident in both places because he sensed that no harm would come to him if he kept his wits alert and his eyes and ears attuned to every sound, from a shifting wind in the high trees to a rustle in the grass beside his feet. At Wild Rose he felt no malevolence at all directed toward him. Despite what he had heard about his Aunt Amanda's warning that he shouldn't come to Wild Rose, Patrick felt perfectly safe. Except for his mother, the household ignored him as much as it could without absolutely neglecting him. But his senses, unblunted by age and experience, told him that something was wrong. There were secrets in the old house that he felt keenly, though he didn't understand their nature.

That night, to keep himself awake, Patrick sat up in bed and thought about home and the mountain he loved. In his mind he found the path, the secret one to the caves where Crazy Edythe had kept his grandfather prisoner long ago. And he also found the long way up to Old Helen Shawn's place. He thought that was the best path on the mountain. He had taken it a dozen times to spy on the old woman while he tried to stir up his courage to speak to her. To make friends with Helen Shawn was his goal and although his mother had forbidden him to visit her, she had done so in an uncommitted fashion that made him think she would forgive him if he broke her rule.

Resisting the urge to lie back and close his eyes, he thought of ways to make friends with Helen and help her on the farm. And when he tired of this, he recalled the other mountain paths he loved and had dawdled along, all of them. There was the circle around the pond, the way past the stables to Uncle Eben's old tree house and. . . . From a distant corner of the apartments, Patrick heard a clock strike the hour, but he lost count before the end and couldn't tell the time. The house was quiet, but from time to time he heard a door slam or a voice raised. Secrets he had only sensed by daylight took on wraithlike forms that flitted through the walls and doors of his imagination. Something was afoot and he, the protector, was ready for whatever it might be.

He thought about the paths he had discovered on St. Simon's Island. There was a way to a fishing hole and an old grove of orange trees with their roots half in the water, and he knew where there was a boat because one of the black children had taken him out in it. He remembered the rattlesnake he'd seen a few days earlier. He could still hear the noise it had made to warn him away. The memory of that sound and a loud whisper right outside his door awakened Patrick just as he began to doze.

"That baby child have come, Master Hiram. A little boy." Patrick slipped out of bed and tiptoed over to the door. Spying at a crack in the timbers, he saw the green dirndl skirt marked with mud at the hem and the bitten down fingernails and, hearing the flat, rather stupid voice, knew the speaker was Elizabeth. "Master Sondergaard, he say hurry up come now and get the young'n 'fore he throw him out."

Hiram White hissed, "You stay with Miss Mandy. And see you mind yourself and keep that girl of mine in line. I'll be back before midnight strikes."

They talked a little more about matters that made no sense to Patrick, and then there was quiet in the hall. Patrick sat down on the floor to think about what he had heard. Why had Uncle Hiram just galloped off in the middle of the night when the baby was coming, had come already? Already? And the baby was a boy? Patrick scrambled to his feet and crept to the door of his mother's room, intending to tell her the exciting news. But just at the last moment, as his hand was on the knob, he stopped himself, not sure why he did so, but knowing that it wasn't yet time to alert his mother.

Back in his room, he closed the door softly and sat down on the floor. It was harder to stay awake now. The paths and secrets of Cooper's Mountain too easily became a dream where he was chasing butterflies or eluding the servants who always were being sent to look for him. Patrick wished he could make them all understand that the wild places were safer than what went on in drawing rooms and passageways late at night. He'd heard a thousand arguments in his short life and the sounds of anger had taught him to be wary. But he scarcely understood what it was he longed to explain. What was clear to him as he strove manfully to remain awake on sentry duty was that his family was full of hurting and mean secrets and that these translated into danger signals even a boy as young as he could not ignore.

He was still awake, eyes burning, when Hiram returned. Patrick had opened the hall door a fraction of an inch so he could see clearly. In his arms Hiram carried a bundle wrapped in a pink blanket the color of strawberry birthday sherbet. Elizabeth hurried to him and peeked at whatever was wrapped in the blanket. As she did so, Hiram shoved it at her. A baby began to fuss and whimper.

"Shut him up or the poor bastard'll never live to inherit the Hopewell fortune!"

Now what did that mean? And why was the baby making funny little coughing noises? Patrick was fully awake again and puzzled in a way that made his palms sweat and itch. Suddenly he had to go to the bathroom. After that it would be time to tell his mother that the baby was coming. Or had it come already?

His mother made him tell his story three times over until he felt mad enough to hit something. She explained to him that it wasn't that she distrusted him.

"You've had a peculiar dream, my darling. I know it seems real to you, but. . . ."

They were talking on Suzannah's bed. Patrick was half under the covers, trying not to cry or fall asleep before he could convince his mother and make her believe that something strange was going on.

"That baby," he said finally, "you go and see if I'm right. He had a pink blanket. Remember my birthday party, Mama? Remember the ices? The blanket was pink like that, Mama."

So saying, the poor lad gave up his tug of war with sleep and sank into the goose down pillows. His breathing was immediately regular and deep, and for a time Suzannah was thoughtful, watching the rhythmic rise and fall of his chest. Because she knew her son well, she couldn't easily dismiss his story. On the face of it, though, it was quite fantastic. Hiram had gone out and come back with a baby in a pink blanket. How was Elizabeth involved and who was Mr. Sondergaard? In the hall outside her room, the clock chimed midnight. Listening hard, she heard nothing. The house seemed asleep.

Smiling to herself, Suzannah lifted Patrick from her bed and returned him to his own, thinking as she did that the freedom he had enjoyed on the island had stimulated his imagination. It would be good for him to get back to Savannah and a more orderly life. She was back in her own room, just removing her silk wrapper, when she thought she heard a sound—a cry?—from the direction of Amanda's room. She waited, standing very still at her bedside, and presently the cry was repeated. It was piercing, yet somehow hoarse and broken at the same time.

She hurried quickly to her door and opened it softly. The hall, lit by tapers in wall sconces, flickered in shadows. She heard the cry again and recognized it instantly as the sound of a baby. Silently, in bare feet, Suzannah ran down the hall to Amanda's room. Not stopping a moment to ask herself if what she did was right or wrong, she put her ear to the door and heard quite clearly now the sound of a baby crying and coughing. Unhesitatingly, she knocked.

Hiram opened the door. His burly frame blocked the doorway.

"I heard the baby, Hiram. Is it all right? The coughing. . . ." She looked around Hiram and saw Amanda standing over a cradle. Biddy and Dora were nearby and so was their mother, Elizabeth. The pink blanket was exactly the color Patrick had described. Suzannah caught her breath as she began to guess at what had happened. Amanda's slim silhouette was clear to see in the light gown she wore. For the moment it was all the proof Suzannah needed.

"Where did that baby come from?" she demanded to know, ducking past Hiram into the room. He tried to stop her with a hand clamped on her arm, but she pulled away. "Who is Sondergaard, Hiram?"

"I don't have to answer your questions, Mrs. Paine. You have no right to walk in here and begin an interrogation."

The coughing and crying stopped abruptly. Suzannah looked at Amanda. "What's the matter?"

Amanda didn't answer. She was staring into the cradle and her expression riveted Suzannah's attention. Her mouth hung slightly open, her eyes were wide.

Hiram grabbed Suzannah by both shoulders and gently began to push her toward the hall door. "The baby is fine, Amanda is fine and we will notify Eben immediately that he has a son."

But Suzannah was shaking her head. "You can't do that. Look at Amanda! She hasn't given birth! This is all some sort of . . . of . . . hoax to make my brother think he has an heir. But I won't let you get away with it. I won't."

Suzannah looked at Amanda, whose expression had knotted up in fury. The eyes narrowed, the brows pinched together. Her mouth was distorted, twisted, opening and closing soundlessly. Suzannah tried to go to her, but Hiram held her back.

"What's the matter with you?" Amanda screamed. "Close your eyes if you're asleep. Don't just look at me!"

The bedroom was breathlessly still.

"You beastly thing. Close your eyes, close your eyes, close your eyes!" Amanda leaned into the cradle and shook the infant hard.

Hiram's hands dropped from Suzannah, but she couldn't move. A sense of horror was rising in her, threatening to choke her.

Amanda lifted the infant and the pink blanket slipped to the floor. She brought his face close to hers and stared into it. Suzannah could see the eyes, open and without life.

"Oh, my God!"

"What's the matter, you wretched little maggot?" Amanda began to shake the tiny infant roughly and its large head lolled grotesquely from side to side. Suzannah could see its purpled face, the bulging eyes. "Ugly, nasty, stinky thing! Nasty, nasty, nasty!" cried Amanda and, with a snarl of rage, she flung the tiny creature back in his cradle.

PART VII

Chapter 32

In the grey autumn morning, May McMahon was awakened by a rough hand shaking her shoulder. A deep male voice disturbed her dreams and she opened her eyes all at once, terrified. She knew it was her husband.

"Get you and the lad up," he growled at her. "You're coming with me."

Still half-asleep, she stared at him, not moving.

"Get!" he insisted and this time he accompanied his command with a sharp blow that made May cry out and stumble off her mat in a panic. She knew the back of Foster McMahon's hand too well to hesitate a moment longer.

No need to wake up Simon. The boy crouched on his bedding and asked, eager and excited, "Where we goin', Da? New York, like you promised?"

McMahon ignored him. He paced the tiny hut impatiently, muttering softly to himself in a way that alarmed May. He hadn't been drinking, at least she couldn't smell spirits on his breath, and yet he was acting in a way that reminded her of his wild drunks when he behaved with a violent disregard for all but his own momentary whims. She wanted to ask the same question as Simon, but her forehead still hurt where he'd hit her and she knew she could expect more of the same if she so much as opened her mouth. Her husband had something on his mind. He seemed to be planning something and she guessed from his expression that it both excited and frightened him.

"Where we goin', Da?"

"Shut up." McMahon glanced around the hut at the primitive furnishings, at the grime of poverty that lay over everything. He spat on the sod floor. "We'll be done with this 'afore long." He shoved May roughly. "Waste no time, woman. 'Twill be light soon. I don't want to be seen in the Gully." He shoved open the rude plank door and looked about cautiously. "I'll be on the ridge," he said as he ducked out.

Simon grabbed his boots and dragged them on, then reached for his only jacket and the woolen cap he wore low over his eyes.

"Where you goin' to?" cried May. She was standing in the middle of the hut, looking around her for something, anything, that she might take as a memento from this place where she had spent so many years. There was nothing she cared about, though. Nothing mattered to her at all.

"To the ridge with Da." Simon hurried out the door without a backward glance.

It had rained hard in the night and the Gully streets were boggy with a sticky black mud that clung to Simon's boots and made for slow going. The fog that sank into the Gully most nights was mixed with the smoke of fires starting up in the shacks and huts by which he passed. He heard voices from inside and the whines of sleepy children. Simon ignored them and trudged on.

During his first few years in the Gully, when he had come home to Amoset from St. Andrew's Academy to find his father gone and his mother deep in a life of poverty and shame, Simon had been a peeper. He had entertained himself by looking in boarding house windows when the operatives were dressing, eavesdropping on family battles in the Gully and listening at the door while his mother entertained men for the money they needed to survive.

But Simon sensed that those days were over for good. His father had come back to the Gully with a plan that would restore the family to its former status. Not the slightest doubt existed in the boy's mind that this was the case. Simon grinned to himself as he thought of what he'd do when there was money in his pocket and his father to back him up no matter what.

McMahon was waiting in a grove of trees on the ridge of land that separated Amoset from the Gully.

"Where's your ma?"

"Comin', Da. I hurried to get here first. Where are we goin' to? What's your plan?"

McMahon regarded his son, chewing his lower lip thoughtfully.

"You can tell me, Da. I won't say nothin' to Ma. You can trust me." He was scrawny and eager as a young hound and McMahon looked as if he was about to satisfy the boy's voracious curiosity, but something stopped him.

Roughly, playfully, he chucked the boy's chin with his fist. "Mind your own business, lad, and do as I say."

"But, Da...."

"It won't be long. Then you and me can go away like I promised. Just us two, eh? Won't we have a time of it?" McMahon looked over his shoulder at Amoset in the distance and his eyes became misty with thought. "Not much longer," he muttered. "Not much longer."

Chapter 33

"Heaven preserve the man!" Thomas Kilmaine dropped the letter he had been reading and stared at Lucy in horror. It was breakfast time and they were seated opposite one another at the table.

"What is it?" Lucy knew that Thomas had been reading a letter from Eben. She had recognized the handwriting. Now it took all her control to keep her voice neutral when her heart was pounding in terror that something had happened to her lover.

"His wife. She's dead."

Lucy was instantly lightheaded with relief. "In childbirth?"

Thomas looked at the letter, scanning its contents once again. He was perplexed. "I don't believe so. I would guess by reading this that she . . . took her own life." He looked up at Lucy, perplexed. "Now why would a young woman with everything to live for do such a monstrous thing? She seems to have drowned herself in the sea!"

Lucy stood up, pressing her hands white against the oak table.

"My dear! I've upset you with this shocking news."

"Of course it's a shock, but I am perfectly well." Was it possible? Her world was whirling like a windmill before a rising storm and yet her voice was calm. Firm.

"But your cheeks are scarlet, Lucy." Thomas made a move toward her, as if to feel her brow, but she stepped away quickly. Her voice had a sharp, almost shrewish edge to it. She heard the tone and hated herself for what it sometimes seemed she was becoming but was, nevertheless, helpless to stop.

"You know this weather doesn't agree with me, Thomas. Why must you always be pampering me like some prize piece of livestock?"

Thomas looked hurt, but just beneath this outward appearance, Lucy sensed dislike as well as a shadow of anger. She realized how little she knew Thomas after so many years of marriage. She could predict his day-to-day behavior and she understood his taste in food and clothing. But, at the heart, she knew next to nothing about Thomas Kilmaine. Early in their marriage he had confided in her, haltingly, as if to test her trust. But that had stopped when it had become clear that their marriage would not be a happy one.

Now we are like distant cousins sharing a residence, she realized. He in his room, I in mine.

He smiled thinly, tearing a roll and spreading it with peach preserves. "I will endeavor not to treat you like an animal, if that is what disturbs you."

"You know that's not what I mean, Thomas."

He raised his eyebrows. "Indeed? What is it then exactly that you object to, my dear?"

Lucy started to speak, but changed her mind and returned his smile with one equally watered. "I will write to Eben today."

"As you wish, Lucy." Thomas nodded and turned away, apparently no longer concerned with what his wife said or felt. She left him staring out the window and hurried to her sitting room at the back of the house.

Thomas stared out the window at Mrs. Flynn, who was down on her hands and knees scrubbing the stoop. Once she had been a widow woman. And Flynn's first wife had died young and left him with a peck of little ones. Then there was Eben, a married man with a child on the way, and now, suddenly, he was free. The thought of all these widows and widowers fascinated Kilmaine.

Thomas hated himself for it, but he was actually envious of his friend. He repeated over and over that he in no way wished his wife dead. Yet, undeniably, there was something of that bitter thought in his mind. If Lucy were dead, Thomas would be free to go West and open his rural newspaper. If Lucy were dead, he would not have to face her over breakfast every morning of his life and know he didn't love her and that she, in turn, cared nothing for him. Once he had cared for her deeply, but his memories of that time had lost their vitality and every passing moment further drained them. It wouldn't be long before Thomas would ask himself, why did I ever marry Lucy Shawn?

Later that morning Lucy and Delphia went for a walk down Moon Street to the busy square where Lucy purchased a few necessities. It was one of those rare Indian summer days when everyone shoves aside the thought of the coming winter. Though Lucy had told Thomas that the weather didn't agree with her, she felt wonderful. Dressed in a light cotton frock with a ruffled pelisse, her fair hair uncovered, Lucy carried a yellow parasol that matched her daughter's and several people commented that they made a pretty pair. Lucy thought what a wonder it was that, while the world was oblivious, inside her a pinwheel was spinning out of control. And in her ears there was a singing scream like the noise of field insects on a summer midday. She heard the words distinctly (he's mine! he's mine!), but the world heard only the racket of the wooden-wheeled pushcarts on cobbled streets, the vendors calling, the packs of noisy children running wild.

He's mine! He's mine!

But, of course, he wasn't.

She bought a bag of butterscotch from the confectioner at the corner of Moon Street, then she and Delphia crossed to the little park. It was only a tiny stamp of green bordered by a spiked iron fence and some rather dismal bushes, but Delphia liked to play there and Lucy found it pleasant to sit and quietly observe the busy street. As she sat, she sucked on the candy and watched her daughter learn to roll a hoop. Gradually, Lucy's giddy spirits disappeared and she became depressed.

Eben never would belong to Lucy. If, in fact, it were possible for people to belong to one another, *still* Eben would not be hers. She belonged to Thomas Kilmaine. She was his wife and ever would be. An old woman, toothless and worn to a wraith by despair, her body still would belong to Thomas. But for as long a time again, her heart would belong to Eben.

His wife was dead! Now he was free to visit Boston as often as he liked. He might even choose to live in Amoset again. Lucy thought how she could visit her mother on Cooper's Mountain and meet Eben at the little meadow on the lookout. No matter that she was married for eternity, Eben was now free to be near her as often as he wished.

But, what if . . . ?

No! She refused to doubt the love for which she

had broken the laws of man and God. Eben loved her, of that she was certain.

But, what if you're wrong? Lucy couldn't silence the persistent voice of doubt. Think of Foster McMahon, it prodded her. Remember how you vowed never to trust another man.

Lucy looked around her for distraction. A handsome new dark blue phaeton was just passing. Its eight hooves and four wheels made a tremendous noise, but the society couple inside it appeared utterly untroubled. For an instant, Lucy forgot Eben. It made her angry the way the Boston Yankees—they called themselves the Brahmins—put themselves above most people. But Boston was a city of business where fortunes were made every day and the richest of the rich lived like European nobility. When Delphia rushed up to her mother, clutching her hoop and looking utterly forlorn, Lucy further distracted herself by teaching her how to roll it, letting her fingertips just graze the wood as it circled.

"May we visit Grandpa?" Delphia asked when she had tired of her sport. "You said we might."

"But I had forgotten that he has gone home to Cooper's Mountain." Lucy took the hoop from her daughter. "It's Grandmama's birthday. Remember you drew a picture for her?" She held Delphia's hand as they stood at the corner, awaiting a safe time to cross. "I have one or two errands to run and then we'll go home and I'll read you a. . . ." Lucy's voice trailed off and, inadvertently, she took a step backward. Her hip hit one of the iron spikes, hurting her and making a tiny right-angle tear. "Damn!" she muttered.

"Mama, what's wrong?"

"I don't know, Delphie. I thought I. . . ." What had she thought? She'd seen a face in the crowd and it was someone she knew, but the face was gone in an instant, taking its name with it.

"You thought what, Mama?" Delphia sounded exasperated. She was hot and tired of waiting and waiting. "What, Mama?"

"I thought I saw someone from Amoset and the old days. But I was mistaken."

Once, in a hired carriage going along Whittier Street in the evening, Lucy had actually seen her old friend from the mill, Marie Leveroux. She was with a man, a seaman by the look of him, and they were laughing boisterously as if they had been drinking. Lucy didn't mention it to Thomas. She still harbored bitterness toward Marie and she certainly didn't wish to know her again. But still, seeing her had resolved something in Lucy's mind. She was glad to be able to form a picture of Marie laughing and was content with that. Seeing her had closed yet another window on her memories of the mill. If only she could forget McMahon. . . .

"McMahon."

"Who, Mama?"

"It was McMahon."

"*Who* was McMahon?"

The question stopped Lucy. She stood still in the street outside the poultry shop, her face as grey and drawn as an old woman's. She looked awful suddenly and Delphia began to cry. The morning had grown oppressively hot, but Lucy picked up the little girl and carried her, walking quickly back toward home. Once or twice she stopped to scan the crowded street. A sheen of sweat covered her neck and face as she hurried on, pressing the weeping child to her.

"McMahon, McMahon, McMahon." She said his name again and again, almost ritualistically, as if by so doing she could weaken the power of his memory.

Just after she rounded the corner of Moon Street and passed a little alleyway, an arm reached out and grabbed her from behind. An elbow crooked about her throat and a knife point nipped her waist.

"Drop the girl."

Lucy thought her neck would break as she bent a little and gently dropped Delphia to her feet.

"Now go home and tell them someone nabbed your darling mama." Delphia stopped crying. She was staring at McMahon, taking in the small, burning black eyes, closely set, the sallow, fat face and snaky mouth.

"Get," McMahon hissed and kicked the girl. She fell and began crying again.

Lucy struggled against his strangle hold and he let her speak. "Do as he says, Delphia. You must go home. You know the way." The alleyway was only a block or so from their house.

The child's uncertainty was agonizingly apparent. She walked toward her mother, begging, "Mama, Mama," then tried to run, half-backwards. McMahon made sure Lucy could feel the tip of the knife again. "If she doesn't get out, I'll use this on her." He smelled of drink and sweat and rotting teeth. Delphia had stopped again, but her mother, sobbing now herself, cried, "Go home, Delphie! You must go home!" She would have fallen to her knees if McMahon hadn't held her. "Go home, Delphia, before the man hurts you!"

Delphia turned. She stumbled, but she ran. Lucy could hear the sound of her wailing all the way up Moon Street.

Chapter 34

Waking up early in the morning in the Hopewell mansion, Victorine always felt a sense of blissful unreality. She had spent so many years of her life serving in grand houses that to lie abed and listen to other servant girls padding up the thickly carpeted stairs, laying the fires and preparing breakfast filled her with a gloriously sensual lassitude, incomparable to any other feeling she had known. She could stay in bed all day if she chose. She could have her meals sent up on a tray and make as many outrageous demands as occurred to her and no one would dare say a word against her. She heard a servant in the next room opening the drapes and she smiled to herself. How many millions of times had she done just that herself and envied her mistress who was still asleep?

Victorine stretched and rolled against Valentine, pressing her pelvis into his hip. He made no responding move, for his morning sleep was often thick and binding. When he had spent the night drinking and playing cards with his friends, he awoke only by slow and painful stages.

Sometimes the games were held in town or in an upstairs room at the Riverway Hotel and, occasionally, Valentine found Jamie Teig at the Lavender and Lily and spent half the night with his old cronies. Last night's game, however, had been played in the

Hopewell dining room. By now, Victorine knew the servants had fed the town gossips all they needed to hear to keep them chattering maliciously for days on end. She smiled, thinking what a merry time the affairs of Valentine Hopewell were providing for the good ladies of Amoset at their tea parties and sewing bees. She could just see Beatrice Strickland shaking her head from side to side, her mouth a little circle of prim horror as she listened to the latest tale of debauchery.

It was bad enough, Victorine could hear them saying, that Valentine Hopewell chose to live in sin openly with his mistress and the deformed boy who was, quite clearly, his son. Was it any wonder that poor Sarah Hopewell (who was never, Beatrice Strickland knew, a robust or healthy woman) never left her room and had (Beatrice saw no reason not to mention this when half the town knew it already) taken to drink in a wretched and excessive way?

Victorine almost laughed aloud. In all her life nothing had ever felt quite as good or given half the satisfaction of throwing dirt in those superior-minded biddies' faces. Valentine had told her he didn't give a damn what people thought of the way he lived. He was a rich and powerful man now and intended to do precisely as he wished.

He loved being the boss. Victorine was shrewd, and living in other people's houses at their beck and call had made her observant and a better than average judge of motive and character. She watched Valentine closely, for though she loved him with a passion that had become obsessive since Hart's birth, she had few illusions about him. For the first time in his life, he had power and it was likely, perhaps even inevitable, that he would abuse it. She knew next to nothing about business herself, but even so she guessed it wouldn't be long before trouble erupted at the mill. Not only had Valentine hired unskilled Irish workers, but he had lowered wages for the second time in three months in order to make the payroll. His losses to Jamie Teig had amounted to several thousand dollars by now and she could only suspect that he owed large amounts elsewhere in the community as well. Sooner or later, she knew there would be trouble for Valentine. He was in no way a businessman and, in his continued care, the entire Hopewell fortune might be lost.

But for now. . . . She rubbed her cheek against the satin comforter and recalled for an instant the daydream of her Irish girlhood when she and her family had lived on a farm on the estate of Lord Carrington. Though His Lordship had preferred the society of London, sometimes he had brought his family over for brief holidays while he inspected his vast holdings. Victorine remembered Larissa, Carrington's daughter. How she had envied the elegance of the girl and her absolute and unquestioning attitude of superiority! Victorine had dreamed of one day becoming a fine lady herself, never really believing it was possible. And yet here she was in a wide, soft bed with a satin comforter, listening to a dozen Irish servants as they scurried to make the house ready for the day.

For now, she would enjoy her life of ease. For now, she wouldn't ask too many questions or permit worry to darken days made bright by luxury.

Even so, she wished there were some way to make Valentine marry her. She had been raised a strict Catholic and, sometimes, she was taken unawares by thoughts of hellfire and damnation. In her family Bible there had been pictures of demons, nasty creatures with razor teeth and hands like claws, and thinking of eternity spent at their mercy made her sweat and moan as if they had already begun to torture her for her godless life. But even more than her own soul, she ached with concern for Hart, who was not even baptized. The thought of those loathsome harpies of hell tearing at his poor disfigured body was always intolerably vivid.

Much as she relished her life of ease, Victorine knew she would trade it gladly for marriage to Valentine and a quiet life somewhere. She was, after all, a farm girl who would have found contentment in the homey chores that had formed her early life. Working beside Valentine, she thought she wouldn't mind so much the early hours, the exhaustion, the disappointments of life on the land. It would all be worth it if she and Valentine were man and wife and Hart their legal son.

It worried her that Valentine had no affection for his boy. She couldn't understand it, for she had long ago stopped seeing his deformities, focusing her love and attention instead on his face, that beautiful and melancholy Hopewell face. But as she thought about it, she realized that Valentine's chilly manner toward Hart was just what she should have expected. Had he ever known affection from his own parents? Victorine doubted it. She most certainly didn't count Sarah's cloying, sick devotion as normal, and she knew that Martin Hopewell had never loved his sons. She shuddered at the thought of him down there in his chilly room, a bloated fish of a man with a mind wandering in and out of darkness. A monster! No wonder Valentine was cold-hearted. But Victorine, whose own childhood had been spent in a crowded, loving family, believed she could teach Valentine to love his son in time. After all, in the beginning, after he had overcome his initial shock, hadn't he shown a flicker of compassion for Hart? If they could work side by side, a bond would be forged between the man and boy. When Valentine was spending time with them in the Gully, organizing the Irish laborers, he had been warming up to Hart. For that to happen again she must discover some way to make Valentine marry her. Locked in marriage, he would see life differently.

But for now there were satin comforters and pillows of goose down in slips of fine embroidered cotton and, overhead, a tucked and quilted satin canopy the color of the sky.

There was a soft and very discreet knock at the bedroom door. Victorine slipped out of bed without disturbing Valentine and pulled on a silk robe, just one of dozens Valentine had bought for her when he had brought her to live in the Hopewell mansion.

The maid's name was Maudie and she was trembling with nervousness, for there was a house rule that Valentine and Victorine were not to be disturbed before breakfast.

"Well?"

"Ma'am, there's a woman to see you." Maudie was breathless from running up the stairs. "She says it be urgent."

"A woman? At this hour?"

"She comes from the Gully, ma'am."

Victorine's face crimsoned. "Have you awakened me for . . . ?"

"P-p-please, ma'am. She says it be urgent and I thought. . . ."

"Does this woman have a name?" Victorine yawned without covering her mouth.

"May McMahon, ma'am?"

Victorine forgot her irritation at having been roused from bed before her time. May wouldn't say she came on urgent matters unless it was absolutely true. "Where is she?"

"At the kitchen door, ma'am. She looked so tired out that Cook gave her a cup o' tea and a bit of bread and jam."

"Yes, yes. Make her comfortable. Tea, food, whatever she needs. Tell her I'll be down as soon as I'm dressed."

May was at the kitchen table when Victorine entered the room a short while later. She had dressed quickly in a filmy morning dress. It was beaded and fur-trimmed and showed a remarkable lack of good taste. When May saw her, she burst into tears.

"Now don't do that, May. Nothing can be all that grim." She embraced her friend and led her into the dining room where the servants had laid two places. "You'll feel better when you've had a decent meal, love. Food always makes the world seem right again."

But May was not to be comforted. Her crying—great belching, gagging sobs accompanied by a rain of tears—went on and on until Victorine became quite out of sorts.

"If this be urgent, May, you must control yourself and say what's on your mind. Surely it ain't so very terrible. . . ."

"Oh, but it is! 'Tis worse than terrible. 'Tis sin and shame and. . . ."

"Well then, in the name of the saints, you must tell me."

"It's Foster. For the last week he's had me locked in hiding, me and me boy Simon. Now, just last night, he's returned and brought with him. . . ." The tears began again and only by an act of visible will was May able to overcome them. "He's got Lucy Shawn Kilmaine with him and he says unless Mr. Hopewell gives him what he wants, he's going to kill her! And if you bring in the constables, he swears he'll do it sure. Like he did the other ones."

"Other ones?"

"All those poor colleens, those blonde-haired operatives, the murders and . . . all what they blamed on Mickey Quick."

Victorine's teacup clattered and tipped, spilling its contents on the fine lace tablecloth. "Jesus, Mary and Joseph! Your man hurt those poor girls?"

May nodded her head and squeezed her eyes tightly shut. "And he'll hurt her, Mrs. Kilmaine, if he says he will. He wants ten thousand dollars."

"But I'm sure Valentine doesn't have that kind of money. You know he lowered wages, May, because he couldn't make the payroll. Ten thousand dollars!" Victorine crossed herself and fell back into her chair. The spilled tea had begun to drip off the table and onto her dress, but she didn't notice. "You'll have to tell your man it can't be done."

"He says he never should have lost his overseer's job. He says the Hopewells have ruined his life and sacrificed our boy, Simon."

"It's impossible, May. No matter, even if his cause was fair, I just don't believe the money exists."

May looked about the elegantly appointed dining room at the Chippendale chairs, the delft fireplace and damask hangings. Across the sideboard was laid more silver than she had ever seen. And behind it, reflecting not only the precious tea service and chafing dishes but her own incredulous face as well, was a gilt-framed mirror six feet wide, reaching to the lofty paneled ceiling.

Victorine could almost read her mind. "This would have to be sold and I don't think Valentine would do that, May. Not for Lucy Kilmaine, not for anyone."

"But he must! Foster'll murder that poor young woman, for sure he will, unless he gets his way. Go to the old man. He'll find the money some way."

"You don't understand, May. Valentine and his father are the same in this. They won't pay your man a penny."

"Oh, God preserve us all!" wailed May, beginning to cry again. "He'll beat me sure if I tell him no. He'll say I didn't try hard enough to make you understand. Please, Victorine, you're my friend. You were always so good to me. You have to convince Mr. Valentine!" May clutched at Victorine's arm. "You have a son. Think of him and then of my poor Simon. Think of the shame he would suffer if his father. . . . You've got to find the money somewhere. It's the only chance that boy will ever have."

Victorine wasn't listening. Her mind was racing in all directions, seeking some way out of this impossible situation. Lucy Shawn Kilmaine. Of course! Her father was the legislator. Their family had land on Cooper's Mountain. Maybe they could raise the ten thousand themselves. They would have to.

"How long do we have to find the money?"

"Twenty-four hours. A day."

"Sweet God in heaven! The man is mad!"

"I have to go back to him with your answer. What shall I tell him?"

"Tell him. . . ." She stared at the floor, shaking her head slowly. Her mind was empty and she couldn't think of anything to tell McMahon. "I'll speak to Valentine immediately," Victorine promised at last.

"It won't satisfy him, Victorine. For the love of God, I must have a message. Yea or nay?"

"Then you must tell him . . . tell him we'll find the money . . . somehow." But even as she said it,

Victorine knew that her words were a lie. Lucy Shawn Kilmaine was going to die, just as surely as Victorine's sweet life of luxury would die. Already, she could feel the glow slipping from around her. As she dragged herself upstairs to awaken Valentine, she thought she could smell the stink of the Gully, carried to her on the wind by the harpies of hell to remind her of her destiny.

Chapter 35

James Shawn slammed his fist into the palm of his hand; Valentine winced, but maintained his position of authority behind the desk in his office at the mill. It was an unpretentious room, with an uncarpeted hardwood floor, a few indiscriminate pieces of furniture and plenty of shelving of one sort or another. Suzannah had arranged it to her own practical taste and though Valentine's preferences were more self-indulgent, he was far too preoccupied with his gambling and drinking to care much about his office.

"You cannot get away with threatening me, Shawn. I remind you who I am and what this mill stands for."

"You're a coward, Valentine. You were a gutless kid and you're a gutless man. Since Mrs. Paine left, the mill has come to stand for exploitation and second-rate goods."

"How dare you!" Valentine stood straighter, let his square, bony chin jut out and hoped that he looked as imposing as his father would in such a situation.

"I dare damn well! From the beginning, this mill has brought naught but misery to me and mine. First Talley, then Ingrid fired from her job because you're too cheap to keep a miserable excuse for a school, and now this." James caught his breath, feeling the disgust turn in his insides like a sickness he knew he'd never get rid of.

"I didn't kidnap your girl, Shawn. And I don't see why I should be expected to hand over ten thousand dollars to a criminal extortionist solely because both of them used to work here. And as I recall, you were the one who suggested McMahon be terminated, back in the days when you acted as negotiator for the operatives. If anyone should pay, it's you, Shawn." Valentine almost smiled. He felt he had made an excellent argument and his expression challenged James to come up with one better.

"I'll wager you haven't got the money. Tell me, Valentine, have you squandered everything Suzannah's worked so hard for? Have you gambled or drunk or whored it away?"

"You think you could bully Suzannah into giving up the money, but that won't work with me. This is business, Shawn. And there's no room for sentiment in business." He was winning! He was winning! Valentine was sure of it now. It was like when he gambled and could taste the victories as they came to him. There was no way Shawn could force him to give up the money and both of them knew it.

"If my daughter dies. . . ." James didn't finish his threat. The rage in him was too great and he knew that if he didn't leave the mill office soon, he would do something violent. Not that James objected to the idea of hurting Valentine Hopewell, but it would have to come later. Lucy was in danger and there was no time to waste. He looked at Valentine, at the pale blue eyes and fair hair, the sallow, unhealthy look of his skin and the way his shoulders bowed forward, as if by years of leaning over card tables and bars the shape of his bones had been altered. James' blue-black eyes had a piercing intensity

that could unnerve all but the most upright of men.
Valentine squirmed and shifted his stance. His arms
crossed, uncrossed.

"Perhaps we should call in the law. I wouldn't
object to that, Shawn. I know McMahon said not to,
but the law. . . ."

James laughed. Grabbing his soft buckskin hat
from where he had placed it on the desk, he turned
toward the door. He looked back at Valentine, cutting
him again with his pointed gaze. "As of now, I am the
law."

He made his exit through the counting room,
passing desks of petty accountants and clerks, all of
whom stared after him with a kind of awe. By now
an abbreviated version of Lucy's abduction and
McMahon's threat had spread throughout the mill
and by day's end, the whole town would know. Only
a flimsy wall separated the counting room from Valentine's office, so the sound of the men's argument
had come through clearly. And though none of the
employees had been subjected to James Shawn's intense stare, the mood of it was like an atmosphere
that surrounded him and affected everyone who saw
him storming out of the mill that day.

Jerusha, working on the second floor, watched
him pass. She signaled to a factory mite, a doffer
named Rosie, and whispered something to her
quickly. The little one was off like a streak, bounding
up the outside stairs two at a time, the ribbons of her
scooter bonnet flying, hurtling herself against the
swinging door into the weaving room. She found
Ingrid at a loom near the windows and tugged on the
older girl's skirt for attention.

In appearance, Ingrid Shawn was unchanged.
Like the other mill girls, she was plainly and neatly
dressed and her hair was pulled back tightly in a

knot. When the mite tugged at her skirt, she looked irritated, however; and this alone was a visible mark of the difference in her since her teaching days, before Thaddeus.

Months had passed, but her memories of the day with Thaddeus were still painfully vivid. She couldn't help recalling his words: *you so inflamed me that I could not help myself.* Rather than accuse Thaddeus, she wondered over and over how she had inflamed him unknowingly. He was, after all, a man of God, and one had only to see his smile and hear his voice to know his good and pure heart. The more she examined her behavior, the more apparent her guilt became. Too late, she saw that it had been wrong to take that first ride on Silk. Even more, it had been wrong to take Thaddeus to the lookout, the place that had been so special for her and Talley. Most wrong of all was falling asleep in the glade beside Thaddeus as if he were not a stranger, but a brother, same as Talley. The mere thought of it made her face flush! It soon had become all too clear to Ingrid that the responsibility for the attack was her own, for she had behaved in a careless and ill-bred manner.

Shame had descended on her like a black fog. When Suzannah had left Amoset and Valentine had closed the mill school, Ingrid took it as just punishment. She knew she wasn't fit to teach the young. But she didn't go home, for she knew Helen Shawn would see right into her corruption and condemn her. That would have been more punishment than Ingrid could bear, so she had stayed on at the mill and had gone to work in the weaving room. This was hard physical work and her health was suffering, but she was convinced she deserved no better.

The mite dragged again on Ingrid's skirt and begged to tell her story. The details were vague, but it was enough to know that someone named McMahon had kidnapped Lucy and was threatening to hurt her unless Hopewell Mills came up with the money for her ransom.

Ingrid called across to another operative, "Watch my work for me!" The girl looked up sharply and nodded, but her manner was brusque. Like all the operatives, she was already tending as many of the looms as she could manage.

Ingrid found the supervisor instructing a spare hand on the proper threading of a shuttle.

"Go back to your work, Miss Shawn," the supervisor ordered in a harsh voice. Once she had been an operative herself, but since gaining her elevated position she had lost her empathy for the workers with whom she had shared bed and board and hours of labor.

"It's my sister. There's some trouble and my father is here and I have to go to him and. . . ." Ingrid was taken by a fit of coughing and could not continue.

The supervisor stopped what she was doing and stared hard at Ingrid. "If you don't want your position, Miss Shawn, there's a goodly number who do. If you walk out of here today, you need not return to us. Do I make myself clear?"

Ingrid felt something like the sinking of a great weight down in the pit of her stomach. Like everyone else in the mill, she needed her work, despite the wretched conditions and measly pay. The threat of termination was something against which she had no defense. It was not work, she realized, but servitude.

"And I don't like that hack. If you aren't well, perhaps you're not suited to mill work. I told Mr. Hopewell when he sent you up here that you looked frail to me." The supervisor had narrow, dark eyes,

flattened beneath heavy lids. Jerusha called them
crafty eyes and Ingrid knew what she meant. It was
as if she was always on the lookout for a way to make
the girls uncomfortable. Most operatives stayed away
from her in all but emergencies. Ingrid's expression
quickly became neutral. She straightened herself and
said politely, "I am well, ma'am."

"Then go back to your work before the pieces are
ruined." As Ingrid turned, something in her posture
must have pricked the supervisor's heart in a rare, un-
guarded place. The older woman touched her shoulder and said, "I've heard about your sister, Shawn. If
there is further news, I'll let you know."

James Shawn strode out of the mill, jumped on
his horse and rode into the Gully at a full gallop. He
pulled his horse up sharply, stopping in a cloud of dust
in front of the Lavender and Lily. Muldoon was out
there, sweeping the stoop. Despite the circumstances,
he was pleased to see James, whose reputation for
honesty and impartiality had made him many friends
in the growing Irish community. He leaned the broom
against the wall and, after wiping his hands on his
long white apron, grasped James' hand firmly.

"I've heard the news, Senator Shawn. And it's terrible. Terrible."

"Thanks, Muldoon."

"But I hope you won't be blamin' the Irish for the
goings on. That Foster McMahon is a good-for-noth-
ing and always has been."

"I need your help, Muldoon. I must find Mickey
Quick. I have to talk to him right away." James'
horse, a grey named Shadow, pawed the dust and
nickered, as if he shared his master's impatience.

"You're in luck, Senator. Mickey's inside and only
half into his cups." Muldoon made a face. "If there's

something you can do to halt the ruination of that boy, 'tis a good deed you'll be doin'." He pushed open the tavern door and yelled into the dark interior. "Get out here, Quick. It's Senator Shawn to see you."

A moment later a somewhat bleary-eyed Mickey Quick appeared in the doorway. His clothes were dirty and he smelled bad. For a moment James couldn't believe that this was the same lad who, just months before, had told him proudly that he'd been called to entertain at the Hopewell mansion. He had transformed himself into a derelict. James wondered whether there was any magic that could restore what Mickey had lost.

He couldn't conceal his disgust. "You're a wreck, boy. Why have you let this happen?"

When Mickey was reluctant to answer, Muldoon replied for him, "It's that Selectman Stoat and his cronies. They've got it in their minds that Mickey did those foul murders, and they won't let up on him. 'Tis a wonder the lad has any life at all in him."

James didn't tell Muldoon what May had said, that McMahon had confessed to the murders in Amoset. The Gully and town knew enough already. If men like Stoat were to get wind of it, half the town would rise up, and there was no telling what a mob like that might do and who might be hurt in the process.

"Walk with me, Mickey," Shawn directed, taking the young man's arm and pulling him along beside him. Mickey went reluctantly, thinking perhaps of the grog he had left half-drunk on the bar.

When they were well out of earshot of Muldoon or anyone else, James held him by the shoulders and faced him squarely. "Look at me, Mickey. And listen. Listen hard. I know you didn't hurt those poor young women."

Mickey laughed bitterly and spat into the dusty road. "Tell that to Stoat, then, Senator Shawn. If it wouldn't be too much trouble."

"I know you're bitter, and you have cause to be. I don't deny it. But now I'm offering you a chance to clear your name once and for all. It'll be a second chance, Mickey."

"My hands are too slow. They shake now." He held them out before him. As if to prove the point, they trembled violently.

James felt a mix of emotions. On the one hand, he had great pity for the boy. Mickey had been unjustly accused at the very moment when his life and ambitions were coming together successfully. But he disliked the ease with which he had fallen into decadence, the almost eager way he had embraced the alternatives of sloth and drink. As James had noted many times before, a current of darkness ran through the Irish, a current in which they seemed too willing to drown themselves.

"A month off the drink will steady your hands, Mickey. You're young. Your life's ahead of you."

"If Stoat has his way, it's all behind me."

"But he won't. By God, Mickey, after I tell the town you're innocent no one will even remember Stoat! I know you didn't hurt those girls because *I know who did*. And if you'll help me, the whole blasted Gully and Amoset will know it, too." James shook him. "Will you help me, Mickey?"

He nodded, but his eyes were still wary.

"Good. Now, I'll tell you this and swear you to secrecy for the time being. 'Twas McMahon did the murders. And Foster McMahon is now holding my Lucy prisoner somewhere."

At James' disclosure, Mickey's eyes grew very

bright. As if to wipe the taste of grog from his mouth, he rubbed his hand hard across his lips.

"McMahon will murder my girl." James' voice did not break as he spoke. He was a Yankee, raised to hold his emotions close. But the pain was written on his face, for it was too great to conceal. "He wants ten thousand dollars from Valentine Hopewell as compensation for some imagined grievance or another, dating back to the time when he was overseer for the old man. But Mr. Hopewell is not willing. . . ."

"More than likely he don't have the money, sir. He's a gambler and I know for God's truth he owes Jamie Teig better'n five hundred dollars."

"I imagined as much."

"But what can I do, sir? I'm not a rich man, you know." Mickey Quick laughed mockingly.

"You have friends throughout the Gully and Amoset. I want you to talk to them all. You have to find out where McMahon's hiding out."

"McMahon was not well liked. Apart from Simon, his son, there's not a man in Massachusetts with a good word to say for him."

"That's right. And if someone saw him recently, they'd be willing to talk. He can't have disappeared entirely." Mickey looked distracted, as if his thoughts were wandering. "See here, Mickey, I'm offering you a way to clear your name and become something of a hero. You must cooperate."

"I know, I know, sir. And I'll do what I can. Already my mind's out rovin' the town. I know a fellow or two. Not wholesome lads but . . . knowledgeable, if you take my meaning, sir."

"Good." James hurried the young man back to the Lavender and Lily. "This is my horse Shadow. Do you ride?"

Mickey looked uncomfortable. "No, sir. Not since I was a wee one."

James thrust the reins into his hands. "Well, today's the day you learn again. Shadow's a decent animal. He'll take you where you need to go faster than your feet. You can leave messages for me at the Riverway Hotel. And if you find my girl, I'll give the horse to you, saddle and all. A gentleman needs a horse!"

It took James half an hour to walk back into Amoset. He thought the walk might do him good, help to cool his temper, but the effect was exactly the opposite. By the time he reached Front Street his rage had mounted like a bonfire, fed by fear and frustration. There was so little that could be done! He had sent Mickey off to ask questions and he supposed he must do the same himself, though he hardly knew where to begin. Mickey had friends and acquaintances in the seamy districts of Amoset, and it was there that the truth about McMahon was most likely to be uncovered. For James, the prospect of success seemed dismal. He could ask at hotels and taverns. The bargemen along the river might know something. And then there were the caves. It was possible that McMahon had discovered them just as Crazy Edythe had, long ago. Beyond that. . . .

Was there any way he could raise the money? The question had scarcely formed in his mind before he knew the answer. It was impossible. True, serving in the General Court had put him in contact with many wealthy individuals, but he couldn't number them among his friends. And even if he could, there was no time to make the ride to Boston that such a financial transaction would require.

Never had James Shawn felt so helpless as during

that walk between the Gully and Amoset. It was the helplessness, coupled with fear for his child, that had combined to create in him an anger such as he had never known. It was almost as if some monster had taken up residence in his stomach and begun to eat him alive and he was helpless against it. Helpless! Damn Valentine Hopewell! If Suzannah were in Amoset, the situation would be entirely different and Lucy's life would not be in jeopardy. Shawn knew that Suzannah wouldn't have hesitated to pay McMahon the ransom and then support whatever it took to bring him to justice. But Suzannah was gone. She'd left no word for him and Shawn could only imagine that her brother had driven her off, perhaps forever.

Before he knew what he was doing, James was striding up the steep, flagged pathway between Hopewell Mills and the mansion on the Knoll. He was at the ellipse of lawn before his mind had settled on any firm plan, and his fist was on the door before the plan had crystallized.

A maid with a terrified expression opened the door a crack. James kicked it open the rest of the way. Taking two long steps, he stood in the middle of the foyer and bellowed for Valentine.

In the dining room, Valentine's fork clattered to his plate and he jumped up from his midday meal. He hurried toward the foyer, a big linen napkin still tied around his neck.

"What in the name of God are you doing here? Who gave you. . . ?" Crimson-faced, Valentine stepped back, glancing at Victorine who stood behind him in the dining room doorway, covering her mouth with her hands.

James seemed to have grown with his anger. His physical presence dominated the foyer, dwarfing everything else. The maid cowered in a corner and, like her, Valentine had begun to tremble.

"Get out," he spluttered. "Get out!"

Though he was burning with anger, James Shawn's voice was like ice. "Hopewell, there's something I've wanted to do for a long time. I want to do it because you made your sister's life miserable and because you're willing to see my daughter murdered before you'll part with your treasure."

"See here, Shawn, you have no right. . . ."

"First I want to say that you're a worthless, no good son of a bitch and I hope you rot in hell."

"You can't insult me in my own home! Get away from me, Shawn!" Valentine croaked for help a time or two. No one came forward, but at the end of the hall and over the banister rail the servants were crowded, their faces bright and eager.

"I am a man of law and you may be glad of it, else I would put a bullet through your head and be blessed for it." James shoved Valentine against the wall and, tearing aside the napkin, grabbed him by the lapels of his coat. Grinning, feeling halfway good for the first time that day, Shawn drew back his arm and then slammed his fist into the middle of Valentine's face. He heard the sound of crushing bone. Blood spurted everywhere as the injured man began to cry. Disgusted, James watched him slip to the floor. "There," he said to Victorine as he wiped his hands on his handkerchief. "You can have the bastard."

Then he turned and left the house.

Chapter 36

James went to the Riverway Hotel and waited for some word from Mickey. He sent messages of reassurance to Ingrid in the mill and her mother on the mountain. He had sent a message to Thomas Kilmaine earlier in the day, but it would be hours before it reached him in Boston. Reassurances were hard for James to write. The optimistic words, the soothing platitudes were like blatant lies, for as the day passed and no word came from Mickey, the situation looked increasingly bleak. A red October sun beat down on Amoset, but inside James' heart it was already winter, a season that would never end.

Ingrid came to the hotel after the mill closed. He held her, feeling her special warmth and wondering if she would be his only child by the time the next day dawned.

After a while, he sent her away. "There's nothing for you here, Ingrid. Be with your friends and take their comfort. When your sister is safe. . . ."

"Nothing will happen to her, Dada?"

He avoided the question. "I'll come to Quinn's. No matter what time, I'll come to you when I know."

"Let me stay, Dada."

But he was adamant, and at last she went away.

The hours crept by. James sat at the little writing table in the hotel room, looking into the darkness. After a long while, a pale moon rose. Exhausted, he laid his head on his arms, but he couldn't have slept even if he had wanted to.

Suddenly, he heard the clatter of hooves. He leapt to his feet and tore out of the room. Someone was banging on the door. James rushed down the stairs and flung open the door before the grumbling innkeeper could reach it. Mickey was standing there in the cold midnight air. He looked exhausted, but exhilarated, too. After hours of questioning and cajoling, he had discovered the whereabouts of McMahon.

"An old man told me, name of Ephraim Grace. He used to work at Hopewell Mills, but they blacklisted him years ago. His wife and family are gone now and he lives in a shack east of town, near the river. He knew McMahon, it was long ago, but he remembers him well. He was glad for the chance to talk."

Mickey had brought James a pair of worn, homespun breeches and a yeoman's shirt of coarse immigrant cloth. The two men set off down Front Street in the wagon James had hired and kept ready for the purpose. It was a nondescript, mule-drawn vehicle of the sort owned by mountain farmers. As they passed the rows and rows of adjoining boarding houses on one side and the broad, fast river on the other, Mickey told James all he knew and they made their plans.

"You don't have to come, Mickey. It may be dangerous, most likely will be, and I'm prepared to do this thing alone. You've done all I asked. Shadow is yours, and by this time tomorrow the whole area will know you have been unjustly accused. I can let you off right here."

But Mickey felt a personal involvement. Though he didn't know Lucy Kilmaine, Mickey felt his name never would be completely cleared unless he took part in McMahon's capture. Reluctantly, James accepted his help. As they neared their destination, he realized that he was glad to have the young man along. There was no telling what they might encounter at McGill's Tavern.

A short distance from McGill's, James stopped the wagon. Reaching under a bit of old sacking in the bed of the wagon, he withdrew a long-barreled flint-lock pistol and a small bag of powder. By the light of the moon he primed and loaded it.

"Have you ever used one of these?" he asked Mickey.

"No, sir."

"Well, God willing, you won't have to. Let me show you how the thing is cocked." He pulled back the big hammer and held the weapon straight before him, the index fingers of both hands touching the trigger lightly. Then he eased the firing mechanism back into the safety position and handed the gun to Mickey. "Since you're intent on coming inside with me, I want you to carry the pistol. That way, no matter what happens between me and McMahon, you're likely to come out safe." He reached under his loose shirt and patted a six-inch knife sheath holstered at his waist. "If there's any fighting to be done, leave it to me, Mickey."

"But, sir. . . ."

"No, I mean it. I brought you into this to save your life, not to have you bleed to death in a seedy tavern. Lucy is my daughter."

"But, sir, you're a . . . city man! You can't fight."

James laughed a little. More and more, he liked Mickey Quick. "You didn't know me years ago, Mickey. Back when I was a mountain boy and as out of place in a city as any man you'll ever know, I learned to use this knife. Someday," he flipped the reins lightly and the team moved forward slowly, "if we live through this, I'll tell you about the time I met a bear on Cooper's Mountain."

When they walked into McGill's, they looked like two poor men, down off the mountain and on their way to Marivale, hoping for work as woodcutters. The barmaid, a buxom, toothless redhead with a lined face and eyes that had long before given up looking for anything but trouble, served them tankards of cheap, bitter grog without a word.

"You got rooms?" James asked her.

"You want to stay the night?"

"How much?"

"There's a big room at the head of the stairs. It's empty tonight, so you and your friend can each have a bed. Twenty-five cents apiece."

James looked at Mickey, who shook his head.

"Too much," he said, his voice disappointed. "Ain't there nothin' else?"

"There's a room at the back, but it's taken by a family."

From behind the bar, a thickset, evil-looking man said, "If you use one bed in the big room, it's forty cents for the two of you."

Again James looked at Mickey. This time he nodded.

"Pay up first," the barkeep ordered, sticking out his palm. James crossed the room and handed him several coins. As he did, the man looked him over carefully.

"Don't I know you? Ain't I seen your face 'afore?"

"I'm off the mountain."

The man guffawed. "That's plain enough. But

seems to me I know you from somewheres. Take off
your hat."

James' mind was working fast. If he were identified, it would be all over. There would be a commotion and McMahon, up there in his back room, would
be alerted.

"Whatcha waitin' fer? Who are you, anyways?"

James smiled. "No one, friend. No one." He took
off his hat and waited.

"Humph." The barkeep gestured toward the
stairs. "The room's at the top of the stairs."

The room in which McMahon, his wife and son,
and Lucy Shawn Kilmaine were hiding was a simple
rectangle big enough for a couple of swaybacked
double beds and an old dresser from which two
drawers were missing. Three slatted chairs were the
only seating. May lay on one of the beds, her skinny
body in a fetal curl and covered by a blanket. Lucy
was on the floor, sitting up, with her hands tied to the
bedpost and a filthy gag in her mouth. The dress she
had been wearing when McMahon snatched her was
filthy now, and her hair was a mass of tangles.

During the harrowing time since her abduction,
she'd given up thinking of Eben. McMahon and his
threat filled every corner of her mind, obliterating
memory and hope with a shroud of terror. Near her,
Simon tilted his chair on its two back legs, his head
against the wall, one foot resting on the same post to
which she was tied. McMahon was pacing. Like a cat,
he'd been moving back and forth across the room for
the last hour.

"You'll go next," he told Simon. "I don't care
what time it is, you'll go right up to Valentine
Hopewell's and bang the knocker until someone
comes. Make sure Hopewell knows if I don't get that
money by dawn, if he don't meet you by the old

bridge like May told him, the lady here is going to get it."

May moaned.

"Shut your mouth, woman."

"I told you, he won't make a deal. There won't be any money, no matter how much you threaten or how many times you ask. I told you what Victorine said."

"I don't care what one whore tells another."

"Simon, hear what he calls me? Your own mother? Do you hear him? How can you let him . . . ?"

McMahon laughed. "The boy and me are mates. Right, Simon?"

Simon nodded. For added emphasis, he sneered at his mother. "You want me to go now, Da?"

"No. We'll wait a bit. There's folks in the bar below. I heard a wagon a bit ago. We'll wait until they've left or gone to sleep. I don't want you recognized."

McMahon's manner was arrogant, assured. But that was on the surface. Inside, he felt increasingly uncertain. It had been a gamble to bring Lucy to McGill's and use her as a hostage. And he was just beginning to allow as how it might possibly have been a mistake to carry on the plan when he had found out that Valentine Hopewell was in charge of the mill now, and not Suzannah Paine. He had known without question that Suzannah would pay the price, but this Valentine was a man he didn't know and couldn't predict. Maybe, just maybe, he should take the girl and leave McGill's. They could go into hiding, maybe in the network of caves on Cooper's Mountain. May could bring them supplies. They would just wait out the time until Suzannah or Eben or James Shawn came up with the money. Maybe he had made a tactical mistake in setting too short a time limit. He was biting his nails now and pacing more rapidly.

Foster McMahon was so preoccupied with his worries that he didn't hear the muffled footsteps in the hall. May was rocking herself gently on the bed and struggling to push down her terror. Simon wasn't there; he was far away in his dreams, in a fine house with his da, servants at their beck and call. But Lucy heard. She heard random sounds, a door closing softly, a footfall, but they meant nothing to her. She had lost hope.

Suddenly the door flew open and James Shawn and Mickey Quick were standing on the threshold. Mickey had a pistol.

May screamed. Simon's chair slipped and clattered to the floor, taking him with it. McMahon, after one frozen moment, leapt for the window, his heart pounding.

James grabbed the back of his jacket, but McMahon jerked free and spun around, a long knife in his hand. He slashed wildly at James, cutting through the immigrant cloth and into his left arm. Ignoring the pain and the blood, James whipped out his own knife. The men faced each other, bent slightly forward from the waist, their knives extended, the handles gripped in their slightly upturned palms.

James yelled to Mickey. "If Simon makes one move, shoot his legs off!" The men began to circle one another slowly, each taking measure of the other. James' eyes never left McMahon's. The small black orbs buried in folds of skin reminded him of that bear he had faced long ago when he was a boy. Back then James had worked with a knife almost daily because it was a sign of manhood to be adept and fearless with a blade. Now, after years on the farm and then in the legislature, he feared—though he would not

have told Mickey this for anything—he feared he
might have lost his skill. At first the slow, stalking circling felt uncomfortable to him, and the knife that
must be balanced so precisely in his palm seemed
heavy and awkward.

No one spoke. The close little room was silent
save for the sound of rapid breathing and boots shuf-
fling on the wooden floor. The moments stretched.
Who would move first and how? In what direction?

James saw his opening and swiftly thrust forward
and then back in a skillful feint. McMahon jumped
back and his arm went up. He was unprotected, but
the distance between them was too great and James
didn't move to follow through.

McMahon grinned and showed his yellow teeth.
"Been awhile, eh, Senator Shawn? And I'll bet you
never killed a man neither. Eh?" He laughed a little,
deep in his throat. James remembered the bear, the
way it had growled as it faced him in the clearing,
taking his measure. "That gives me the advantage,
don't it? I guess I ought to tell you I've killed half a
dozen men in my time. I don't mind doin' it anymore."

McMahon jerked forward, slashing James' arm
again. This time the cut was deeper. Pain raced up
James' arm and into his head. For an instant, the
space of a breath, there was lurid red before his eyes.
Blood was flowing from the arm freely. Somehow he
had to stop it.

"Mickey, her blanket!" The boy moved without
taking his eyes off Simon and wrenched the blanket
from May's trembling body. James grabbed it away
from him and, with a swinging motion, wrapped it
four or five times around his wounded forearm. He
held it out before him like a shield.

All at once McMahon lunged, thrusting his knife

hand straight out and then to the side. James side-stepped and kicked, hitting him in the knee. McMahon pitched forward onto the floor and then rolled, coming up in a crouch before James could get to him. McMahon rose to his feet and the slow circling began once more.

I should have got him then, James thought. That was my chance. He remembered his father telling him that in a knife fight a man never gets a second chance. Well, he simply would have to prove his father wrong. There was Lucy to think of. If something happened to him, Mickey could never handle McMahon. He had to be ready for the next opening and make it count.

McMahon sliced upward. James' left arm, shielded by the blanket, went out to meet the knife blade. There was the sound of tearing fabric as James moved in low under McMahon's arm and plunged forward. His knife found home, sinking deep into the soft belly at the base of the ribs. McMahon's knife clattered to the floor as he fell to his knees, clutching his middle. His mouth was open. He seemed to be trying to scream, but the only sound he made was a strangled, gurgling noise. He held out his hands and saw the blood, then looked at James Shawn. Neither fear nor rage nor even pain was on his face. Instead, his expression was one of total mystification. Even now, in the final moments of his life, McMahon could not believe that he had lost. As he died, as his black eyes glazed and greyed, they seemed to ask what and why and how.

Chapter 37

Margaret Duffy examined the bandages on James Shawn's arm. "The cut must have been very deep," she murmured, touching him gently. "Is there much pain?"

James, awkward under her solicitous care, just shook his head and wished she'd quit treating him like an invalid. It was two days after the fight and James had come to Marivale to ask Margaret's advice. He didn't want sympathy. All that mattered was that the miserable affair be over, finished once and for all. He handed her an envelope. "I took your advice, Mrs. Duffy. In this letter to Suzannah and Eben, I've told them all I know about Valentine, about the mill and about Lucy, too, of course."

She took the envelope, placed it beside her and poured him a cup of tea. "I know how you dislike the thought of intruding in family matters, Senator. But believe me, they will want to know all of this. And they will believe whatever you write. You have great credibility."

"Thank you, ma'am." He sugared his tea, hoping Margaret would not launch into another litany of praise. He had done what had to be done and now it was over.

"I know you're anxious to put all this behind you,

Senator, but tell me, how is Lucy now? And young Mickey Quick?"

"Lucy and her husband are with my wife at the farm. She's been badly shaken, but on the whole she's in remarkably good spirits, I think. Mickey has been exonerated, of course. There was a long piece about him in the newspaper yesterday. And Selectman Stoat has agreed to pay for all the damages he caused at Muldoon's Lavender and Lily when he was harassing poor Mickey." James smiled over the fragile teacup. "Not without some pressure, I might add. He's fond of his position and wants to be re-elected."

"And Simon McMahon?"

"He's with his mother for the time being, but the boy's burning up with bitterness and anger. I don't know what will become of him."

Margaret tucked the caddy more tightly about the teapot, considered a moment and then said, "Bigelow and I have discussed the matter of Simon McMahon. We have decided that we would like to help him. It seems to us that the lad has never had a fair chance. My son Alexander tells me that when Simon was a student at St. Andrew's, he did well. So he's bright enough, just badly misled by his father's dreadful example."

A little current of alarm went through James. He tried to discourage Margaret, but the woman was convinced.

"We all deserve a second chance, Senator. We'd like to help him get the training he needs."

"But May. . . ."

"His mother is welcome to join our household. As it happens, the bishop—God bless him—has increased Bigelow's remuneration this year and we can afford to keep another servant."

"I wish you wouldn't do this, Mrs. Duffy. Simon is no ordinary child. I'm afraid. . . ."

But she would not be dissuaded. Her eyes, as blue as bits of china, and her round face glowed with the fervor of her desire to do good, to rescue a soul she knew to be lost otherwise. James thought of the kindness this woman had repeatedly shown Suzannah, and he forgot the dozen ways in which he found her irritating. For a moment he saw her only in her goodness and charitable spirits, and he couldn't help but respect and admire her.

"I must go, Mrs. Duffy," he said a bit later. James tried to put on his heavy coat, but found the maneuver impossible with his injured arm.

"Will you be able to ride?" she asked, helping him.

"Oh, yes. Mickey Quick is staying at the farm and he loaned me his horse, a fine grey named Shadow!" James laughed to himself, remembering with what a grandiose show of Irish generosity Mickey had offered him the use of Shadow when James told him he was off to Marivale.

"The horse and I are well acquainted," James had said wryly, accepting the offer.

Margaret accompanied him to the door and out onto the terrace. At the edge of the flagstones, where the steps descended to the stable, she stopped and touched his arm gently. Her expression surprised him.

"Are you unwell, Mrs. Duffy?"

She shook her head. "No. I'm in excellent health. It's only. . . ." She looked away over the edge of the terrace, across the fields to where the Amoset River was just visible in the distance: a long silvery snake glimpsed among tall grasses. "I have decided to tell you something, and having made that decision, I find it not quite as simple to say as I thought it would be."

He was about to interrupt, but she held up her hand. "Please. Let me stammer through it. I want you to understand something, James Shawn, and if what I'm about to say seems wrong in the eyes of man, I am nonetheless certain that God in his wisdom will understand. I know Suzannah loves you. I have known it for many years."

James stared at her.

"And I know that Patrick is your son. I nursed her through her long confinement and in her delirium she called your name again and again. Even then, the knowledge didn't come as a great surprise. Somehow, I think I've known it from the beginning."

"Mrs. Duffy," James grasped her hand, "despite what we have felt and do still feel for one another, Suzannah and I. . . ."

"You have behaved as the good gentlefolk you are. Believe me, I have no accusations to make, no guilt to name. Suzannah loves you and, frankly, I don't blame her. My brother was a cold and unkind man and I have known that since I was a child. You see, I watched our father make him that way. And when Suzannah married him, though I hoped in the beginning that she might effect some wonderful change in him, I soon saw that it was impossible. And I saw him begin to do to her what my father did to my mother. I pitied her then, but there was nothing I could do."

"Why do you tell me this now?"

She shrugged, as if to make light of her revelation. "When I say her name, I see in your face that you love her. And though you are married and the father of grown children. . . ."

Like a maudlin fool, James' eyes filled with tears. The compassion that radiated from Margaret Duffy was like warmth from the sun. "As you said, Mrs. Duffy, you believe in second chances."

She smiled and stood on tiptoe to kiss his cheek. "Second and third and even more. As many as are necessary to bring you the happiness you deserve, James Shawn."

FIRST IN THE HOPEWELL SAGA

Broken Promises

by
Drusilla Campbell

Suzannah Hopewell is a young woman of eighteen in *Broken Promises*, the first in the HOPEWELL SAGA. In this powerful and moving story of her life in Amoset, her first love for Travis Paine and her friendship for Lucy Shawn, all the elements of nineteenth-century New England life are woven into a dream of a young woman's pride and passion. But it is far from the Hopewell Mills—in a villa on the shores of Sicily—where Suzannah learns the true character of her family history and faces her own troubled destiny. And when her brother Eben witnesses a cruel and tragic struggle for family power, Suzannah too must bear the scars of her brother's suffering. . . .